Praise for the novels of JoAnn Ross

"A wonderfully uplifting story full of JoAnn Ross's signature warmth and charm."

—Jill Shalvis, *New York Times* bestselling author,
on *Snowfall on Lighthouse Lane*

"The connection between a deeply conflicted man slowly coming to terms with loss and a woman who understands him adds strength and intensity to a perceptive story that is more than the average friends-into-lovers romance... Verdict: An excellent start to a promising community series with a stunning Olympic Coast setting."

—*Library Journal* on *Herons Landing*

"*Snowfall on Lighthouse Lane* is another deftly crafted gem of a romance novel by an author who is an impressively consistent master of the genre."

—*Midwest Book Review*

"Perennial favorite Ross delivers the emotionally intense first book in her small town contemporary romance series, Honeymoon Harbor... Ross has always been known for her ability to create truly memorable characters whose stories resonate sharply. This amazing book is touched by pain and grief, but also love and hope. A wonderful novel!"

—*RT Book Reviews* on *Herons Landing*

"A widower gets a second chance at love with his wife's best friend in this... sweet first book in Ross's Honeymoon Harbor series... Fans of cozy small-town romances will be willing to read further in the series."

—*Publishers Weekly* on *Herons Landing*

"It's a cause for celebration when a favorite author gifts us with a new series... Seth and Brianna are a delicious couple."

—*All About Romance* on *Herons Landing*

Also by JoAnn Ross

Honeymoon Harbor

SUMMER AT MIRROR LAKE
SNOWFALL ON LIGHTHOUSE LANE
HERONS LANDING

For a complete list of books by JoAnn Ross,
visit her website, www.joannross.com.

JOANN ROSS

The Inheritance

HQN

Recycling programs
for this product may
not exist in your area.

ISBN-13: 978-1-335-41856-2

The Inheritance

Copyright © 2021 by JoAnn Ross

This edition published by arrangement with Harlequin Books S.A.

For questions and comments about the quality of this book, please contact us
at CustomerService@Harlequin.com.

HQN
22 Adelaide St. West, 40th Floor
Toronto, Ontario M5H 4E3, Canada
www.Harlequin.com

Printed in U.S.A.

As always, to Jay,
who went above and beyond living up to the "in sickness and in health"
part of those vows we exchanged so many years ago. I love you.

The
Inheritance

Prologue

Aberdeen, Oregon

Conflict photographer Jackson Swann had traveled to dark and deadly places in the world most people would never see. Nor want to. Along with dodging bullets and mortars, he'd survived a helicopter crash in Afghanistan, gotten shot mere inches from his heart in Niger and been stung by a death-stalker scorpion while embedded with the French Foreign Legion in Mali.

Some of those who'd worked with him over the decades had called him reckless. Rash. Dangerous. Over late-night beers or whatever else passed as liquor in whatever country they'd all swarmed to, other photographers and foreign journalists would argue about whether that bastard Jackson Swann had a death wish or merely considered himself invincible.

He did, after all, rush into high-octane situations no sane person would ever consider, and even when the shit hit the fan, somehow, he'd come out alive and be on the move again. Chasing the next war or crisis like a drug addict chased a high. The truth was that Jack had never believed himself to be immortal. Still, as he looked out over the peaceful view of rolling hills, the cherry trees wearing their spring profusion of pink blossoms, and acres of vineyards, he found it ironic that after having evaded the Grim Reaper so many times over so many decades, it was an aggressive and rapidly spreading lung cancer that was going to kill him.

Which was why he was here, sitting on the terraced patio of Chateau de Madeleine, the towering gray stone house that his father, Robert Swann, had built for his beloved war bride, Madeleine, to ease her homesickness. Oregon's Willamette Valley was a beautiful place. But it was not Madeleine's childhood home in France's Burgundy region where much of her family still lived.

Family. Jack understood that to many, the American dream featured a cookie-cutter suburban house, a green lawn you had to mow every weekend, a white picket fence, happy, well-fed kids and a mutt who'd greet him with unrestrained canine glee whenever he returned home from work. It wasn't a bad dream. But it wasn't, and never would be, his dream.

How could it be with the survivor's guilt that shadowed him like a tribe of moaning ghosts? Although he'd never been all that introspective, Jack realized that the moral dilemma he'd experienced every time he'd had to force himself to remain emotionally removed from the bloody scenes of chaos and death he was viewing through the lens of his camera had left him too broken to feel, or even behave like a normal human being.

Ten years ago, after his strong, robust father died of a sudden heart attack while fly-fishing, Jack had inherited the winery with his mother, who'd professed no interest in the day-to-day running of the family business. After signing over control of the winery to him, and declaring the rambling house too large for one woman, Madeleine Swann had moved into the guesthouse next to the garden she'd begun her first year in Oregon. A garden that supplied the vegetables and herbs she used for cooking many of the French meals she'd grown up with.

His father's death had left Jack in charge of two hundred and sixty acres of vineyards and twenty acres of orchards. Not wanting, nor able, to give up his wanderlust ways to settle down and become a farmer of grapes and cherries, Jack had hired Gideon Byrne, a recent widower with a five-year-old daughter, away from a Napa winery to serve as both manager and vintner.

"Are you sure you don't want me to call them?" Gideon, walking toward him, carrying a bottle of wine and two glasses, asked not for the first time over the past weeks.

"The only reason that Tess would want to see me would be to wave me off to hell." In the same way he'd never softened the impact of his photos, Jack never minced words nor romanticized his life. There would be no dramatic scenes with his three daughters—all now grown women with lives of their own—hovering over his deathbed.

"Have you considered that she might want to have an opportunity to talk with you? If for no other reason to ask—"

"Why I deserted her before her second birthday and never looked back? I'm sure her mother's told her own version of the story, and the truth is that the answers are too damn complicated and the time too long past for that discussion." It was also too late for redemption.

Jack doubted his eldest daughter would give a damn even if he could've tried to explain. She'd have no way of knowing that he'd kept track of her all these years, blaming himself when she'd spiraled out of control so publicly during her late teens and early twenties. Perhaps, if she'd had a father who came home every night for dinner, she would have had a more normal, stable life than the Hollywood hurricane her mother had thrown her into before her third birthday.

Bygones, he reminded himself. Anything he might say to his firstborn would be too little, too late. Tess had no reason to travel to Oregon for his sake, but hopefully, once he was gone, curiosity would get the better of her. His girls should know each other. It was long past time.

"Charlotte, then," Gideon pressed. "You and Blanche are still technically married."

"*Technically* being the operative word." The decades-long separation from his Southern socialite wife had always suited them both just fine. According to their prenuptial agreement, Blanche would continue to live her privileged life in Charleston, without being saddled with a full-time live-in husband, who'd seldom be around at any rate. Divorce, she'd informed him, was not an option. And if she had discreet affairs from time to time, who would blame her? Certainly not him.

"That's no reason not to give Charlotte an opportunity to say goodbye. How many times have you seen her since she went to college? Maybe twice a year?"

"You're pushing again," Jack shot back. Hell, you'd think a guy would be allowed to die in peace without Jiminy Cricket sitting on his shoulder. "Though of the three of them, Charlotte will probably be the most hurt," he allowed.

His middle daughter had always been a sweet girl, running into his arms, hair flying behind her like a bright gold flag to give her daddy some "sugar"—big wet kisses on those rare occasions he'd wind his way back to Charleston. Or drop by Savannah to take her out to dinner while she'd been attending The Savannah School of Art and Design.

"The girl doesn't possess Blanche's steel magnolia strength." Having grown up with a mother who could find fault in the smallest of things, Charlotte was a people pleaser, and that part of her personality would kick into high gear whenever he rolled into the city. "And, call me a coward, but I'd just as soon not be around when her pretty, delusional world comes crashing down around her." He suspected there were those in his daughter's rarified social circle who knew the secret that the Charleston PI he'd kept on retainer hadn't had any trouble uncovering.

"How about Natalie?" Gideon continued to press. "She doesn't have any reason to be pissed at you. But I'll bet she will be if you die without a word of warning. Especially after losing her mother last year."

"Which is exactly why I don't want to put her through this."

He'd met Josette Seurat, the ebony-haired, dark-eyed French Jamaican mother of his youngest daughter, when she'd been singing in a club in the spirited Oberkampf district of Paris's eleventh arrondissement. He'd fallen instantly, and by the next morning Jack knew that not only was the woman he'd spent the night having hot sex with his first true love, she was also the only woman he'd *ever* love. Although they'd never married, they'd become a couple, while still allowing space for each other to maintain their own individual lives, for twenty-six years. And for all those years, despite temptation from beautiful women all over the globe, Jack had remained faithful. He'd never had a single doubt that Josette had, as well.

With Josette having been so full of life, her sudden death from a brain embolism had hit hard. Although Jack had immediately flown to Paris from Syria to attend the funeral at a church built during the reign of Napoleon III, he'd been too deep in his own grief, and suffering fatigue—which, rather than jet lag, as he'd assumed, had turned out to be cancer—to provide the emotional support and comfort his third daughter had deserved.

"Josette's death is the main reason I'm not going to drag Natalie here to watch me die. And you might as well quit playing all the guilt cards because I'm as sure of my decision as I was yesterday. And the day before that. And every other time over the past weeks you've brought it up. Bad enough you coerced me into making those damn videos. Like I'm some documentary maker."

To Jack's mind, documentary filmmakers were storytellers who hadn't bothered to learn to edit. How hard was it to spend anywhere from two to ten hours telling a story he could capture in one single, perfectly timed photograph?

"The total length of all three of them is only twenty minutes," Gideon said equably.

There were times when Jack considered that the man had the patience of a saint. Which was probably necessary when you'd chosen to spend your life watching grapes grow, then waiting years before the wine you'd made from those grapes was ready to drink. Without Gideon Byrne to run this place, Jack probably would have sold it off to one of the neighboring vineyards years ago, with the caveat that his mother would be free to keep the guesthouse, along with the larger, showier one that carried her name. Had he done that he would have ended up regretting not having a thriving legacy to pass on to his daughters.

"The total time works out to less than ten minutes a daughter. Which doesn't exactly come close to a Ken Burns series," Gideon pointed out.

"I liked Burns's baseball one," Jack admitted reluctantly. "And the one on country music. But hell, it should've been good, given that he took eight years to make it."

Jack's first Pulitzer had admittedly been a stroke of luck, being in the right place at the right time. More care had gone into achieving the perfect photos for other awards, but while he admired Burns's work, he'd never have the patience to spend that much time on a project. His French mother had claimed he'd been born a *pierre roulante*—rolling stone—always needing to be on the move. Which wasn't conducive to family life, which is why both his first and second marriages had failed. Because he could never be the husband either of his very different wives had expected.

"Do you believe in life after death?" he asked.

Gideon took his time to answer, looking out over the vineyards. "I like to think so. Having lost Becky too soon, it'd be nice to believe we'll connect again, somewhere, somehow." He shrugged. "On the other hand, there are days that I think this might be our only shot."

"Josette came again last night."

"You must have enjoyed that."

"I always do."

Although Jack suspected Gideon believed he was suffering end-of-life hallucinations, he was seeing his true love more and more. And not just in his sleep when she'd appear to calm the night horrors that had plagued him for years, but occasionally in the middle of the day. Or he'd wake in the morning to see her perched on the edge of his bed, soothing his forehead with her gentle hand. When death came, would Josette take his hand and lead him to wherever he was going next, the same way she'd led him into her bed that first night? The night when, beneath a full moon shining its silvery light through the window, he'd discovered the difference between having sex and making love.

They sat there for a time, drinking the 2006 Pinot Noir Gideon had brought along. They didn't talk. Jack damned the fatigue that was claiming him more and more every day. Worse than that, it was stealing his sense of self. He no longer felt like the man who'd embedded with the troops at the front of the spear in the race to Bagdad during Shock and Awe. Or who'd captured the photos of Fallujah that had won him another Pulitzer.

He'd always insisted that age was just another number and he could run rings around any of the younger photojournalists, many of whom were, to his mind, too risk-averse to be in the crisis business. But over the past months age had caught up with him. Followed by his old nemesis, death, who was coming up behind, about to finally catch him.

"This is damn fine wine." Jack held up the bottle. A shimmering ray of sun from a Pacific Northwest rain shower penetrated the dark green glass, making the wine gleam like liquid rubies. "One of my best decisions, in a lifetime of fucked-up ones, was hiring you."

"One of my best decisions was letting you talk me into leaving Napa for Oregon," Gideon said. "The fact that you'd actually built a house for Aubrey and me before coming down to recruit me demonstrated you were serious. And in it for the long haul."

"I did my research and people said you were the best in the business, having not only gained knowledge working those two years in Burgundy, but also that you had a magic touch."

"People exaggerate."

"I considered that possibility, but decided that if your ability with grapes was even half what others claimed, you were still at the top of a very elite pyramid. So I hired you for your skillset. Both in the vineyard and management." Jack's speech was labored, his breathing painful. "I had every intention of keeping hands off the business."

"Which you have."

"I'm smart enough to know what I don't know. And all I knew about wine back then was drinking it. But over the past ten years, you've become the closest thing I have to a friend. Even, perhaps, the son I never had."

Feeling as if he was drowning, Jack coughed again, trying to shake things loose in lungs scarred by years of oil field smoke, dust and cigarettes. "I probably should've told you that a long time ago."

"It would've complicated things."

"Probably. And while you might have avoided that, depending on how things shake out with the girls, you could be facing your greatest complication yet."

"It'll work out," Gideon assured him.

"I've got faith in you." It had to work out. Because if his plan didn't work, what generations of Swanns had built would be lost.

He pushed himself to his feet, patted Gideon on the shoulder and feeling as if he was climbing Mount Hood, managed to walk the few yards to the guesthouse to see his mother for the last time. One of his many regrets, when it came to relationships, was how he'd stayed away from the vineyard for so much of his adult life.

Rose White, who, along with having grown up on the property, had spent twenty years as an army nurse before retiring to serve as Maison de Madeleine's housekeeper, opened the door and greeted Jack with a smile. "Your mother's taking a short nap, but I was about to wake her so she'll sleep the night. She spent most of the morning, right before it started raining, outside with a sketch pad, plotting out changes she wants to make in her herb garden. I certainly hope I have her energy when I'm ninety-six."

"She's always insisted that daily wine is the secret of a long, well-lived life."

"I'm not going to argue with that," Rose said. "Especially when the wine comes from this vineyard."

Jack opened the door quietly, not wanting to jar his mother awake. Watercolor paintings of the vineyard in all the seasons hung on jeweled purple walls that echoed the hue of the grapes that she'd lived her life surrounded by. Tabletops and a wooden dresser made from trees harvested on the property to make room for the original orchards were crowded with photographs of the family, including two different wedding photos, one taken in an old stone church in France, the second beneath a greenery-covered arbor here on Swann property.

Her eyes were closed when Jack quietly pulled up a chair next to the bed.

"I wasn't sleeping," she insisted the moment he sat down. "I was merely resting my eyes. If I'd been asleep, how would I know you'd come in?"

He took her age-spotted hand, trying not to notice, despite being able to spend an hour outside, walking the garden rows, planning this summer's yield, how much frailer she'd become since the last time he'd been home. As the heart that many had accused him of not possessing ached, Jack covered the hand wearing the same simple gold wedding band his father had put on her finger so many decades ago.

"I was dreaming of your father."

"Good dreams, I hope."

"We were back in France, during the time he was hiding in our cellar. When I knew for certain that I loved him."

"Your father's generation was labeled the Greatest Generation for having saved the world."

"It wasn't just Dad risking his life."

His mother had been a true war hero, joining the *Maquis*— the guerrilla bands of French Resistance fighters—and had been awarded the French *Médaille de la Résistance*, the British George Cross, the highest award given to a civilian, and equal to the Armed Forces Victoria Cross, and the US Medal of Honor.

"I only did what I had to do," she insisted, as she always did when the topic would come up. "But the point I was about to make was that in your own way, you are every bit a hero as your papa."

Because he didn't want their last words to be an argument, Jack merely shrugged.

"You are," she insisted, her gaze showing the determination that had kept her family, her father and so many others alive. A strength of will that had helped save her country.

"Those photographs you take make the world aware of the evil that still exists," she insisted. "In your own way, you've spent your adult years risking your life to save the world. I am so very proud of you, *mon fils*."

"Thanks, Mom." He had to choke the words past the lump in his throat.

"It isn't fair," she complained. "A parent shouldn't outlive their child." She blew out a breath as her eyes brightened with tears. Tears she firmly resisted letting fall. "But of course, as your father so often reminds me, life isn't always fair."

Her use of the present tense had Jack wondering if his father appeared to her, the way Josette did to him. He smoothed a few strands of silver hair that had once been a burnished auburn from her forehead. "I've got to go."

"I know." She took hold of his hand, touching it to her lips. *"Aller avec dieu, mon fils." Go with God, my son.* After all these years in Oregon, her English, which still carried a bit of France in its accent, had become that of a natural-born American, but when excited, tired or under stress, she'd slip back into her native language.

As he left the room, Jack's own eyes were swimming.

"How was it?" Gideon, who was waiting in the main house's great room, asked.

"Better than I'd hoped. She talked about Dad. If he hadn't died, they'd have been married over seventy years. I wonder how the hell they pulled it off." The idea seemed as impossible to Jack as achieving peace on earth.

Jack coughed, a long, painful honk that made him feel as if he were hacking up a lung. Despite being surrounded by death, he'd never given much thought to his own. But when he'd received his cancer diagnosis, he'd immediately made the decision to come home. Yet, rather than die in this sprawling house he'd grown up in—he didn't want his daughters' thoughts of it to be those of death and suffering, but hopefully a place where they could discover their Swann family roots he'd never taken time to explore—he'd chosen a local hospice for when his body told him it was time.

"Take me to Passages," he said as they walked out the door. The rain had stopped as he looked beyond the vineyards to where Mount Hood's icy peak had risen majestically above its self-made clouds. "It's time."

Gideon called Rose from the hospice, telling her that he'd be spending the night. A night, the nurse had told him, that would probably be his employer and friend's last. Although everyone at Maison de Madeleine had known it was coming, he could hear the crack in the sixtysomething woman's voice when she assured him that she'd clean her employer's room.

"You'll also need to prepare three rooms in the guest wing," he said. "We may be getting company."

"The girls," she guessed.

"We'll see."

"I should start making food for the funeral luncheon."

"Jack said he didn't want a fuss."

"Jack won't be here to complain. His girls might be of a different mind," she said. "One's a famous actress and writer, the other a Southern socialite and the third is French. They're fancy over there." Not that Rose had ever been to France that Gideon knew of. "And you know a lot of people in this valley will want to show up to celebrate Mr. Jack's life."

Gideon strongly doubted the oldest, most neglected of the three daughters would be in any mood to celebrate their absent father's life. If she did make an appearance. "Why don't we decide on all that if they come," he said, rubbing his chest where his heart was aching.

Jackson's passing had not taken long. Unsurprisingly, despite his firm instructions that his mother was not to be brought to the hospice, Madeleine had insisted on being with her only son at the end.

For a man who'd lived so many years surrounded by violence, Jack had gone peacefully, slipping into that void where, despite claiming to have become an atheist during his years of documenting the world's horrors, he'd come to believe, at the end, that Josette would be waiting for him. Having lost his own wife too young, who was Gideon to argue with that?

So much was up in the damn air, he thought as he returned to the vineyard and the house that would have looked more at home in France's Burgundy region than Oregon's rural Willamette Valley. Although they didn't know it yet, two women he'd never met, and a third who'd visited every summer, would soon be holding his and his fifteen-year-old daughter's futures in their hands.

1

Sedona, Arizona

Tess Swann sat out on her wraparound deck overlooking the tree-lined burbling crystal waters of Oak Creek while Rowdy, her rescued Irish setter, lay at her feet, basking in the sunshine. The bright, endless blue sky overhead vividly contrasted with stunning, luminous crimson buttes and towering monoliths.

A light spring rain had fallen early this morning, washing the high desert air clean and leaving it scented of piñon pine, juniper and perfume from the carpets of eye-dazzling scarlet, gold, blue and pink spring wildflowers. The view that inspired reverent feelings in so many visitors usually filled Tess with a sense of peace. Her home was a haven she'd created in order to unplug from her hectic life and connect to what was really important.

The brochures handed out at the visitors' center claimed that the town was a cathedral without walls. In actuality, it had no cathedrals. The only ancient, established holy sites were those considered sacred by local Native American tribes. It had no major airport. Most of the small town's three million annual visitors flew into Phoenix's Sky Harbor International Airport, then took the two-hour drive, rising three thousand feet from the cactus-studded Sonoran Desert, ending with a spectacular view along the Red Rock Scenic Byway.

The former sleepy little farming town had become the New Age capital of the country in the 1980s, when a psychic claimed that the same type of powerful energy vortexes that existed at the Great Pyramid in Egypt, Machu Picchu in Peru, Bali, Stonehenge and Ayers Rock in Australia, could also be found in Sedona. Since Arizona was easier for Americans to visit than the other locations, tourism boomed, driven in large part by those who believed the claim that by simply visiting a vortex and closing your eyes, you could tap into the frequencies of the universe, and thus change your life.

Tess, who'd drastically changed her own life, didn't believe the vortex hype, but to the despair of those original longtime residents, what *had* changed was the personality of the town. New Age stores popped up like weeds, offering crystals, aura readings and spiritual tours of the vortexes. Chain stores, fast food, hotels, resorts and outlet malls followed.

There were times when she found the relentless barrage of wellness, purification and enlightenment a bit too over-the-top. *E.T.* meets *Close Encounters of the Third Kind*. Even her real-estate agent had insisted on doing a sage cleaning of the house before turning over the keys. While she remained a skeptic, even after eight years of living here, she couldn't deny that the dramatic scenery of red mesas and buttes and the endless, almost blindingly blue sky, was emotionally uplifting.

But not today.

"I don't understand the problem," Phyllis Newhouse, her agent, said yet again. They'd been having the same conversation for the past month even before she'd turned in what she'd planned to be the final book of her latest contract. "The series is doing great. Each book hits the top of the *Times*, sells more copies in all formats than the previous ones, and not only does the TV series always show up on the weekly ratings lists, it continues to climb with each season. There's a huge audience. Why would you want to write anything else?"

Tess decided that admitting to her agent that she'd been hit with her first serious case of writer's block might be oversharing. "I need a change."

That was true. After eight years spent writing a wildly popular series of novels set in a fictional mid-American high school, Tess was beginning to feel stuck in a rut.

Most of her own school years had been a small room carved out of a vast television sound stage, where between the ages of eight and sixteen, she'd played a pair of crime-solving twins—one a nerd always needing to chase down facts, the other preferring to rely on her intuition. Even more unrealistically, they managed to pull off these feats without their parents—one a principal, the other a classics teacher at a ritzy boarding school—having a clue. Literally.

In real life she'd spent the few months of the show's off-season attending Beverly Hills High. While admittedly, the student body at BHHS didn't mirror the middle-American one where she'd set her fictional high school novels, her characters shared the same universal trials and tribulations of teens anywhere. Her storylines dealt with peer pressure, navigating cliques, first loves, heartbreak, self-image, bullying, substance abuse, eating disorders and gender identification. The latter subjects had never been addressed in her perky detective series, and were only lightly brushed over in the afterschool movies she'd also been cast in.

Although she'd been out of high school for over a decade, Tess wrote from internal, personal truths and was self-aware enough to realize that she'd been working out her own neuroses on those pages.

Having moved past the recovery stage of her life, Tess was ready for the next chapter. The only problem was that she hadn't come up with any idea what that chapter would be. Meanwhile, she did know that it was time for her fictional teens, who'd entered high school from various and often very different middle schools—"Diversity!" her agent and editors had proclaimed happily over dinner in a restaurant where the entrée prices could feed a family of four for a week—to graduate and move on with their lives.

"I had lunch with Danielle yesterday," Phyllis revealed. Danielle Williams was the new publisher who'd been promoted from the Australian branch of the company to "bring new eyes and fresh energy" to the list. "Sales and marketing were there, as well, and we believe we've come up with a dynamite idea that will make everyone happy."

"What's that?"

"We follow your suggestion and graduate the kids out of Pleasant Meadows High."

Finally!

"And have them move on to college."

"*That's* your dynamite idea?"

Tess could feel the nails being hammered into the coffin of her career. Phyllis had taken her on as a client when many in the publishing world had been reluctant to give her a try after she'd so spectacularly blown up her music career with a public meltdown while on a European tour. And for that, Tess would always be grateful.

She'd been happy at her publishing house for over a decade. During that time she'd had supportive editors who could often see the entire forest, whenever she'd find herself stuck writing down in the trees, and had made her books better. The art department continued to give her covers that practically leaped off bookstore shelves into readers' hands, and sales and marketing had played a huge part in getting her to where she was today. But if there was one thing she'd learned, first in the television business, then in music, and now publishing, was that the powers that be could often be resistant to change. If nothing was broken, why fix it?

"Your audience has a strong connection with the characters. Both in the books and the TV series. But even I'll admit they've been in high school a very long time. So," Phyllis suggested, "you'll simply explore those challenges as they enter their new adult age. Which, while allowing more conflict and more mature content, also gives you the opportunity to bring in additional characters to expand your world."

"But it's still the same world. The same characters. They'd only be older." If she'd wanted to do that, she'd have already made the move. She didn't want to simply move on from Young Adult to New Adult. She was done with them. Done. Done. Done.

"Just give it some thought," Phyllis urged. "Sleep on it. I'll bet you'll see a new world of possibilities."

"I'll do that," Tess agreed, only to end the call.

"Great, great. I'll pass the news on."

"Tell them that I'm thinking about it," she clarified. "I don't want anyone talking about a new contract yet."

She needed to reinvent herself. To take a much-needed break until she'd found the right story. One she could be excited about. Which, in turn, would hopefully translate to not only new readers, but also current ones who might not have realized that they were ready for something new, too.

When Rowdy roused and uncharacteristically growled low in his throat, she glanced over and saw red dust being kicked up by a car headed up her hill. Fortunately, she wasn't on a so-called vortex, but that didn't stop the occasional tourist from ignoring the private-property signs posted at the turn-off to her road.

"Someone's coming," she said. "I've got to run. We'll talk soon." She pressed End before Phyllis could throw out another argument. Having an idea who her trespasser might be, Tess leaned back in the chair, folded her arms and waited.

Her first clue that her visitor wasn't a local was the Hertz sticker on the Range Rover. As he got out of the SUV and walked toward her, his dark suit—definitely overdressed for Sedona—was yet more proof that he wasn't from around here. She also had a very good idea who he was. The man she'd been doing her best to ignore for the past twenty-four hours.

"I told you that I wasn't interested in anything you have to say." After hanging up on the Oregon attorney three times yesterday, Tess had blocked Donovan Brees's number.

"True," he agreed easily. "But when a client hires me to do a job, I get it done. And, as I said during our abbreviated call, your father—"

"The correct term would be *sperm donor*." As a writer, Tess was very particular about word choice.

"Jackson Swann," he continued, switching on a dime while not backing down from the conversation, "hired me to handle all his business."

"Meaning he paid for that Armani suit." Okay, she was being rude, but the man was trespassing on her land.

"It's Tom Ford, actually. I believe in buying American. And if you're trying to insult me, you're going to have to do better than that," he said easily. He held out a hand to Rowdy, who, having apparently decided the stranger didn't represent a threat, bounded over to him. "We attorneys develop thick hides pretty fast. Mine's like Kevlar... And getting back to my reason for having come all this way, I also handled Jackson's estate."

Even annoyed that her traitor dog was not only licking the man's hand, but also wagging his fringed red tail, Tess caught the past tense immediately. And, dammit, felt something shift inside her. Something sharp and painful she thought she'd put behind her years ago. "Are you implying that you've come all this way to tell me that he's dead?"

"I'm afraid so. And the reason I'm here is that he insisted you be told in person."

"Yet, you kept calling."

"Only to make an appointment to save us both time and inconvenience in the event you weren't currently in Arizona. But you hung up on me as soon as I mentioned his name. Three times. Then blocked both my numbers."

"Most people would have taken the hint that I didn't want to talk about Jackson Swann."

"Well, since I'm here now—"

"After trespassing."

"Point taken. You can call the police, sheriff or marshal, or whoever represents the law around here if you want. Meanwhile, I'll make this short. You're one of his heirs."

"Whatever he's left me, I don't want it. I've done well enough on my own."

"So he told me."

That caught Tess's unwilling attention. "And what, exactly, did he tell you about me?"

"Nothing personal," he assured her. "Just about your television show, which my sisters couldn't get enough of, by the way. Your movies, and a bit about your pop-star years—"

"Which I'd rather not revisit."

"Understood. But you went on to establish a remarkably

successful career. *New York Times* bestselling author plus a popular television series made from your work—"

"*Adapted* from my books. I certainly don't write the scripts." No way would she ever claim another writer's work. Even when those writers veered away from her storyline to, as it had been explained to her, "up the drama and build more sexual tension." Meaning a lot of steamy scenes that weren't in her books. Scenes that undoubtedly would have to be written into the stories if her characters moved on to college.

Nope. Not happening.

"Those scripts wouldn't exist if you hadn't provided three-dimensional characters and the framework for an addictive storyline."

"You know what they say about flattery getting you any-where?"

"I've heard it."

"Well, FYI, it doesn't work on me."

"I'll keep that in mind. And *FYI*, it wasn't flattery. I know all about every book you've written." He held up a hand to cut off her planned remark that stooping to lying would be even less effective than flattery. "My twelve-year-old niece and all her friends are addicted to your Pleasant Meadows High series.

"Whenever Jamie visits, that's my niece's name, she fills me in on all the details. At the moment she's desperately waiting for the next book to find out if Madison ends up with Ethan or bad-boy Brock." He paused. "I don't suppose you'd be will-ing to share and help me gain major uncle points."

"Sorry." Tess suspected with his good looks and much easier-going attitude than she'd expect for a city lawyer wear-ing a designer suit, the man had probably already scored major points with his preteen niece. "It's top secret."

He shrugged broad shoulders that narrowed down to a long, rangy torso that had Tess picturing him as a cowboy as she mentally switched out the suit to Wranglers and a snap-front shirt. A fawn Stetson on his dark head, well-scuffed boots— would spurs be overdoing it?—in place of those Italian shoes.

"I figured you'd say that," he said. As admittedly good-looking as he was as a lawyer, he would make a hot cowboy. Perhaps she should try her hand at a Western romance. "But a guy can always try. And speaking of trying—"

"No." Tess shook her head as the too-sexy-for-his-Stetson cowboy faded away, leaving her arguing with the deceptively easy-talking, but annoyingly stubborn attorney. "If my sperm donor left me anything, you have my permission to donate it to charity. Just write up any paper in the legalese you people converse in, and I'll sign it."

"That would be difficult."

"You're the attorney. Figure it out."

"As I said, it's complicated."

"And you're not going to tell me what, precisely, it is, are you?"

"Sorry," he said. "Attorney-client privilege applies to the actual details of any inheritance until the will is officially read."

"Which will be when?" Not that she was the least bit interested. *Liar.* Damn the man. He'd piqued her curiosity.

"As soon as I can get his daughters together. Jack warned me that you wouldn't be all that cooperative. But as I said, he instructed me to deliver word of his death in person. I'd already decided to go in order. From the eldest, who would be you, to the middle, to the youngest."

"Youngest?" Lawyer man had just garnered her attention again. "I have one half sister who lives in Charleston."

"Charlotte," he agreed. "She's next on my list."

Tess knew all about Charlotte. She'd even based a ditzy blonde, Southern belle transfer student three books ago on the half sister she'd only learned about when she'd read an article in the *L.A. Times* about Jackson Swann winning his second Pulitzer Prize. A sister she'd never had any interest in meeting. But had, admittedly, Googled. Merely out of curiosity. "Were her mother and father still married?"

"Yes."

"Then why aren't you notifying her mother?"

"I'm sorry." His chocolate-brown eyes revealed what seemed to be sincerity. "But again, it's client privilege."

"And you're saying that Jackson Swann had a third child?"

He nodded. "That would be Natalie."

"The man had many failings, Mr. Brees, most of which, for some unknown reason, he was never held accountable for. Yet, even he couldn't get away with bigamy."

"He and Josette Seurat were together for twenty-six years, but never married. They had one child. Natalie, whose story is hers to tell."

Although Tess had convinced herself that she didn't give a damn about her father's desertion, that he'd been long dead to her, that little newsflash stung. "Jackson Swann managed to spend twenty-six years with the same woman?" And a daughter. The one of the three of them he'd apparently decided to keep.

"They were together until Josette died suddenly last year, though they didn't have what most people would consider a traditional relationship. Your father—Jackson," he corrected at her sharp look, "never gave up racing around to conflict hotspots. I have my own ideas about why he was so unrelentingly driven, but I'm not a psychologist, so it's just a guess from having known him all my life."

"You started representing him at birth?"

He laughed at that. A deep, rich baritone that undoubtedly appealed to both women clients and jurors. The lingering cowboy image faded as she envisioned him as a high-profile divorce lawyer, helping a steady clientele of abandoned wives achieve, if not revenge, then a substantial settlement. He'd be a great white shark ripping apart errant husbands, while at the same time providing empathy and reassurance to his clients. Like a golden retriever comfort dog.

"My father handled Jackson's business while I was growing up," he said. "Whenever Jack came to Oregon, he'd stop by Portland and have dinner with my family. When I was young, he was like a favorite uncle, always showing up with cool gifts. By the time I reached my teens, he had me fantasizing about a life of death-defying adventure."

"And when you grew up?"

"I decided that risking my life every day works well in novels and movies, but would be overrated in real life. Jackson was a friend. He could also be a challenge."

Tess wanted to ask why the man she did not want to talk about, to think about, kept going to Oregon, but since she'd already insisted that she had no interest in him, managed to hold her tongue.

"Josette was a free spirit herself, which I always thought was why they meshed so well. Neither put expectations on the other."

"How lovely," Tess said, her tone as dry as the Arizona high desert air.

"I'm sorry. I was merely attempting to give you some family background for when you meet Natalie."

"That's unnecessary. Because I've no intention of meeting her."

"You're sisters."

"Half. And total strangers."

"Aren't you a little curious?"

"No. Not even a little bit."

"May I ask a question?"

It was her turn to shrug. "I suppose."

"Is it all lawyers you dislike? Any lawyer handling Jackson Swann's legal affairs? Or is it just me?"

"It's not you," she said. "I'll admit you'd begun to win me over with that story about your niece and my books."

"You liked hearing she and her friends read them?"

"No. Well, that, too. But mostly because you sat through her recitation of the stories. And even knew the characters. I haven't met many—perhaps any—men who'd do that."

"Sounds as if you've met the wrong men," he said mildly. "And believe me, it's a lot easier than when she used to paint my nails. One time I got an emergency call from a client who'd just been arrested for bank robbery. It turned out to be a case of mistaken identity, but I'll admit it was a bit humiliating showing up at the police station with my *I'm Feeling Sashy* purple fingernails."

"You didn't take it off first?"

"My sister was out of polish remover. And my client was having an anxiety attack, so I didn't want to take the time to stop at a drugstore."

"That's impressive." And showed a great deal of self-confidence. He had to have gotten ragged by the cops.

"Thank you."

"But I think you mean *sassy*."

"No, it was part of a Miss Universe collection, thus the *sashy* reference. My niece loves sparkly nails and collects tiaras. Along with your Pleasant Meadows High series, she's also a fan of any books or movies featuring princesses. But as frivolous as that may make her sound, she's also in STEM."

"Sounds as if your niece is a girl of eclectic tastes and talents."

"I realize most proud uncles say this, but Jamie is brilliant. At the moment she's torn between becoming a NASA engineer and heading up an all-woman team to establish a permanent colony on the moon to use as a base to explore other planets. Or becoming president. More recently, after seeing you on the *Today* show, she's considering writing. She's already on the school newspaper and has had two short stories chosen for a class anthology."

"Good for her."

"We were all very proud. Though the stories are pretty dark and grim."

"It's the age. Adolescence is when kids begin to think about life and death." She smiled, really smiled, for the first time since his arrival. "When I was that age, I filled my journal with doom and gloom poems that always ended tragically."

"But you changed."

"My life changed," she said. And wasn't that an understatement? "I began to view situations with more nuance. Most of my characters are good, but flawed people. Even Maureen, queen of the mean girls, has a tragic home life with her mother dying of cancer. But that's still a secret."

"My lips are sealed." Dual dimples flashed when he put a finger to his lips.

With his thickly lashed brown eyes, curly medium-brown hair and those dimples, he could have played any lawyer on TV.

He continued, "Now that we seem to be getting along so well—"

"You're going to drag me back to the unwelcome topic of my sperm donor's funeral."

"At the moment there's no funeral planned. Jack didn't want a fuss. But if the three of you want to plan something—"

"I don't know about the other two. But I have no interest in pretending I'm unhappy about his death."

Damn. As soon as she heard her words spoken out loud, Tess

realized she truly wasn't unhappy. But she was angry. How *dare* the bastard die before she could confront him and show him how successful she'd become? That he'd made a mistake deserting his family? When she'd been younger, before her life had blown up in a spectacular public scandal, she'd dreamed of him one day showing up on the set, marveling at what a brilliant actress she was. And, because she'd been a normal adolescent girl, she'd wanted to hear from her father that she was pretty. Smart. Talented. Wanted.

He reached into his briefcase and pulled out a manila envelope. "Here are the details, and the location of my office in Aberdeen, Oregon. That's about thirty miles southwest of Portland. I've also included some flight options you might want to consider."

"Not going," she insisted.

"Look, I understand your feelings," he said. "I honestly do. But you really do need to come check out your inheritance. Because there are some serious decisions to be made."

"I've made my decision. I'm not going. I don't want anything from Jackson Swann."

"I get that. My problem is that there are contingencies that all three of you are going to have to sign off on. And although I'm going beyond my charge, we're talking about property that requires your presence."

"There you go again. Trying to pique my curiosity." But she did finally take the folder he was still holding. "How much property?"

"The Swanns were early settlers in wine country, although back then wine wasn't a viable crop. So your ancestor grew cherries."

"You're saying I inherited a cherry orchard?" She liked cherries. Especially in pie. But that didn't mean that she had any intention of becoming a farmer.

"These days a small part of the property is cherries. The main business is wine. There's also a house and other items. My job, in any inheritance situation, is to help the parties develop a strategy on dividing property. Real and otherwise."

"Once again, I don't want anything."

"Understood. But you're not the only person involved here."

"So what you're saying is that it's not all about me."

"I'm saying, yet again, that there are decisions that need to be made, and as your father's attorney, I'd hate to see any of you have regrets. Believe me, this isn't the way I advised Jackson to handle it. It's hard for heirs who haven't been told up front about inheriting a business. Especially when they're not given any indication what the deceased would want done."

"Let me put it this way. I care about what Jackson Swann wanted for the future of whatever property he left behind as much as he cared about me. Which would be zilch."

"That's too bad. So since you don't care, it shouldn't take that long to check things out and sign off to the other two heirs. But the terms of the will state that it must be done in person. At the site. And if one of the heirs refuses to take part, the entire business would probably be sold off and the proceeds given to charity."

"Sounds good to me. And you're being pushy again. Playing on my sympathies toward two women I've never met."

"I'm merely doing my job the way my client laid it out."

"Lucky you," she muttered. "He must have been one of your more challenging clients." She *was* curious, dammit. Just as Jackson Swann had planned.

"He was that. But at the same time, he was the most interesting. Which is why I'm not surprised to discover that at least one of his heirs didn't fall far from the cherry tree."

"I'm nothing like him." She'd spent her life trying to be the exact opposite of her father.

"You both chose creative careers. And your own paths, especially when you left music and turned to writing."

"That wasn't exactly my choice." It no longer stung. Like her characters who'd had disaster rain down upon them, she'd persevered and moved on.

"Perhaps it seemed that way at the time. The music business is filled with comeback stories. Yet, when you finally reached a stage in your life where you could make your own decisions about your life, you chose a different path. One that appears to suit you well."

"There you go with that flattery again."

"Not flattery. Truth. You also appear to have inherited your father's strength. And tenacity."

"Some have called it stubbornness." Her mother, for starters. And, more recently, Phyllis. "And you're no slouch, either. I keep turning you down, yet, you keep pitching."

"Just doing my job." He glanced around, taking in the scenery. "This is stunning country, but Oregon is just as spectacular. And green."

"I've been to Oregon."

"Oh?" He arched a brow "What part?"

Damn. He had her there. "PDX," she admitted. "But we flew past Mount Hood, which looked as if I could reach out and touch it. And I had a cup of what was billed as world-famous clam chowder while waiting for my flight out."

"I don't know if it's world famous, but Mo's is certainly well-known for its chowder. The recipe and original restaurant have been around since right after World War II, and Hollywood stars like Paul Newman, Joann Woodward and Henry Fonda ate there." Those dimples flashed again. "And now they can add your name to the roster of stars."

"I'm no star."

Though she had been, once. The TV gig had been fun.

She'd enjoyed the challenge of playing dual personalities, and while the show could admittedly get a little saccharine, the writers had written in enough family conflict—all which would be resolved by the end of sixty minutes, minus time for commercials. *Double Trouble* had been a feel-good show, suitable for all ages, which had made it a national meeting place on Wednesday nights, leading off the network's prime-time lineup.

Tess had literally grown up on that show, but after what had happened, she hadn't been able to watch reruns for years. Until late one night, while channel surfing, she'd found it available for streaming, and after spending nearly a week binge-watching every episode, she finally realized why all the media back then had claimed that she was a natural actress, like young Jodie Foster decades before. What no one had realized was that except for the mystery-solving part, it had never felt like acting. Because the cast had all come to feel like family. Certainly more than her own.

Although much of the storyline had centered on the twins using their talents to solve light crime, no one was ever murdered, vehicles were never carjacked and children were still safe from predators. The overriding theme of *Double Trouble* celebrated the American family, and if there were times that critics suggested that the loving, purposefully exemplary family—written and produced by William Moore, who played Tess's screen father—was too perfect, the audience had continued to keep the show in the top ten of the ratings for each of its nine seasons.

Her real-life mother had gotten divorced twice during those years. While her TV mother had given birth to twin girls and still managed to be a school principal who baked cookies for class events and was always there to offer her daughters—Ella and Emma—her motherly wisdom.

Realizing that he was patiently waiting for her to return to the conversation, Tess shook her head and raked her fingers through her long mahogany curls. "I'm sorry. One of the annoying things about writers is our minds can drift off. And getting back to our topic, one of the best things about being a writer is that most of the time, except for the very occasional book tour, I'm pretty much anonymous."

"And you prefer it that way."

"After my flameout, which you're surely old enough to have witnessed along with most of the rest of the world, the answer is yes. I absolutely prefer to keep my life private." Bad enough that she would undoubtedly show up in Jackson Swann's obituary.

"Which is why you rarely do book tours and choose instead to hide away here in Arizona's red rock country?"

"I'm not hiding. A lot of residents know who I am. But they're used to 'famous'—" she put the word in air quotes "—people filming movies or buying vacation homes here, so I'm no big deal."

He rocked back on his heels. Put both hands in his pockets. "So you never made it to Oregon's wine country?"

She shook her head. "No. I would've liked to. But back when I was getting established, my publisher put me on a tight tour schedule that had me in Seattle one day, Portland the next, then down the coast to San Francisco, Los Angeles and on to San Diego that same week. I *have* been to Napa." *Double Trouble* had filmed an episode there when she was twelve.

"Oregon's a lot more downhome than Napa. Unlike the traffic jams of tourists' rental cars and tour buses, the Willamette Valley still has empty roads, smaller wineries with crowd-free tasting rooms and lawns set aside for picnics. And, as an added incentive, and since Jackson left it up to me to handle the disposition of his wealth, I might as well tell you that the Swann family vineyard is not only one of the best just in Oregon, but the whole country. And if awards count for anything, which in the wine business they do, then also the world. Perhaps you've heard of Chateau de Madeleine Vineyard?"

That got Tess's attention. "Get out. You're telling me that Jackson Swann owned that winery?"

"It was established by your grandfather, Robert. He converted part of the family's cherry orchard to vineyards after he returned from World War II. Though the wine business didn't really take off until the boom of the 1980s."

"Damn. You've just hit on one thing that makes the trip tempting. I buy their Pinot Noir. It's fabulous." Which still didn't change her mind about wanting any part of the man's estate. All she knew about wine was drinking it. She had no desire to get into the grape-growing business.

"You won't get any argument from me about that." He glanced down at his watch. "I'd better get going. I've got a flight out of Phoenix this afternoon. Give it some thought," he said. "If you decide to come, just call and I'll meet you at PDX and drive you to Aberdeen."

"If I do go, I'll probably drive so I can take my dog. Rowdy's a rescue. I've only had him a few months and it wouldn't be fair to board him again so soon after him having been in the shelter."

"While Portland traffic isn't anything like Los Angeles, it can be a confusing drive for a newcomer anytime, but especially during morning rush hour. Also, the bridges can make drivers nervous."

"I grew up driving on LA's infamous four-level stack," she said. "I doubt any of your bridges would be a problem."

"Point taken. But if you're driving, you won't be able to enjoy the river view as much as you would as a passenger. It's just a suggestion, but it's less than a two-and-a-half-hour flight. You could bring Rowdy with you. I'll meet you at the airport and you can rent a car in Aberdeen. You'll be staying at the house, where Rowdy would be welcome. That way you could save travel time, but still take a few days off and explore wine country. And the coast."

Tess wondered if he practiced litigation. Not only was he good at reading people—knowing she'd resist being pressured—he'd also proven to be persuasive. She could easily imagine him winning over a jury. As, damn it, he was winning her over.

"He's flown before. From the rescue group in Amarillo." And had arrived at Phoenix's Sky Harbor International Airport with his tail wagging. "And, luckily, I still have his crate."

"Whatever you choose to do, the estate will cover all expenses, both traveling and while you're in Oregon. For each of his heirs."

"It sounds as if Jackson was a great deal more responsible with his money than he was his children."

"He was a complicated, complex man. As you'll undoubtedly learn when you come to Aberdeen."

"*If* I come."

"If," he agreed. And although he had his neutral attorney face on again, she could see the glint of satisfaction in those brown eyes.

Tess stood on the deck, watching as he strolled back to the Range Rover. And over the birdsong, she heard a new sound. He was whistling.

2

"Damn," Tess muttered as he drove away in another cloud of red dust. "That's all I need. More complications in my life." And what the hell was she supposed to say to her half sisters? It would be like playing a part, she decided. More improv than script, but she was always good at that.

William used to like to try to throw her off by saying lines that hadn't been there during their morning read-through. But she'd not only become used to the dialogue he'd toss in from left field, she'd actually enjoyed it, too. It made them seem like a real family. Until that memorable day when William Moore, beloved by all for being America's "perfect" father and husband—not only to his TV children, but also to his own five kids and wife of twenty years—had been caught in a torrid affair with the show's makeup artist. Sponsors who'd staked their reputation on the all-American family began pulling out as soon as tabloid headlines exploded onto grocery checkout stands all over the country. It had taken all of three weeks for the show to be canceled, putting Tess out of work at the ripe old age of sixteen.

Shaking off that bad memory of those days, Tess now called

her mother, who had apparently finally found true love with husband number four, a Greek shipping magnate who owned his own private island.

"I suppose it's not surprising," Amy Curtis-Swann-Kendall-Mathis-Christopoulus said when Tess told her of Jackson's death. "Quite honestly, with the risks he took, I'm surprised he lasted as long as he did. One of the reasons I divorced him was because I didn't want to be a widow in my twenties."

"He died of lung cancer."

"Again, not surprising, since he smoked like a chimney. And not just tobacco. But I am truly sorry. He might have been a miserable husband and father, but I finally realized that was because he was so driven. And wounded. Not just physically, but emotionally."

Her mother had told her that before, reassuring her that his leaving them was not Tess's fault. Tess hadn't believed that excuse about his being emotionally wounded when she was young and now, while she accepted that might be possible, given the nature of his work, she didn't care. The fact remained he'd deserted his family and never looked back.

"He had two other daughters. With two different women."

"You told me about finding out about the second on Google a few years ago. But I had no idea there was a third."

"Why would I make that up?"

"No, of course you wouldn't. So he married three times?"

"No. The daughter I told you about, Charlotte, is from wife number two in Charleston. They never divorced. The other is from a woman in Paris he lived with off and on for twenty-six years."

There was a long pause, making Tess think one of their phones might have dropped the call. "Mom?"

"I'm sorry. I was thinking. About how many times Nikos

and I have been to Paris. Wouldn't that have been weird if we'd run into him?"

"Paris is a big city, Mom. It would've been pretty unlikely."

"True. But I could have been sitting next to his mistress in a restaurant. Or shopping in the same boutique and never would have known it."

"Would you have cared?"

Another long pause. "Let's just say no woman ever forgets her first love," her mother said finally.

Surprised, Tess didn't know how to respond to that. She'd been in her twenties when she realized that the reason for her mother's multiple marriages was that Amy Curtis was one of those women in love with the idea of being in love. She'd never know if her mother had found that with her Greek husband or had decided that marrying a man with more money than he could spend in a lifetime was a worthwhile compromise.

After another pause, her mother picked up the momentarily dropped conversation. "So this lawyer, Donald—"

"Donovan Brees. Apparently, his father was my sperm donor's attorney for several years."

Even with the somewhat scratchy connection, Tess could hear her mother's long sigh. "I do wish you wouldn't call Jackson that."

"What would you have me call him? Daddy? Maybe if he'd stuck around, that would fit. I'm a writer. I choose my words to fit a situation. And since I have no memory of him, as far as I'm concerned his only contribution to my life was all those fertile tadpoles swimming in his semen."

"Must you be so crude?"

When Tess didn't immediately respond, her mother went off on a different track, reminding Tess that she'd never said anything negative about her first husband. When asked about their marriage, she'd simply stated that they were young and had made a mistake not getting to know each other well enough to realize that their desired lifestyles were incompatible.

"He sent monthly child support for years. Until you found out about the checks when you were eleven and insisted I stop accepting them, even though they were going into an education fund for you."

"I was earning enough for us." They'd moved into a house in Beverly Hills by then, just north of Sunset Drive's iconic palm trees. "I didn't need his money."

"Perhaps he needed to send it."

"Why? To ease his conscience? Try telling that to someone who cares."

Another sigh. "Let's not argue," Amy said. "So getting back to my question, why did his attorney go see you?"

"Apparently, I inherited something."

"What?"

"You're not going to believe this. A winery. He says I need to go to Oregon for the reading of the will."

"Your father was living in Oregon?"

"Apparently so. At least at the end. In some town called Aberdeen."

"He never said a word."

"Well, although the lawyer was annoyingly vague, I may now be part owner of a vineyard. Chateau de Madeleine is a big deal, Mom."

"Hmm. I've never heard of it, but that doesn't mean anything," she answered. "I was never much of a wine drinker, and since marrying Nikos, when I do, it's either Greek or French. Which has nothing to do with your situation and not that you asked me, but I think you should go."

"I don't want whatever damn inheritance he left me to soothe his guilty conscience. And I definitely have no desire to meet my two half sisters." She'd have to Google Natalie Seurat. Or perhaps he'd given her his last name. Making her one of the Swann sisters. And didn't that sound like a country music trio?

"I wasn't suggesting you accept it. Or reject it. That's up to you. But going to his funeral might provide closure."

"I don't need closure." What she needed was a damn story idea.

After promising her mother she'd think about it, solely in order to end a less than satisfying conversation for the second time today, she opened her laptop, which, instead of pages of words taking up the screen, was currently open to a game of Candy Crush.

Maybe getting away and a change of scenery would clear her mind. Something had better help solve her problem soon. Or she'd end up spending the next ten years writing her characters through college. Then what? Marriages, careers and babies. And, if she wanted to make them even a bit realistic, affairs and divorces. Hell, if she wasn't careful, she could spend the rest of her life writing them into old age.

Why didn't she write thrillers? she fumed silently. At least then she could kill her characters off at a prom. Like Stephen King's *Carrie*, but with a lot less blood.

The thought of writing romantic triangles among the group who'd aged into their eighties, living together in senior housing, was enough for Tess to go online and book her flight to Portland.

3

Charleston, South Carolina

Butterflies were fluttering their wings in Charlotte Aldredge's stomach. The conference room was already beginning to fill up with interior design students from colleges all over the country who'd come to hear her speak about using design to evoke human emotion by stimulating the senses—the soothing sound of a fountain, the eyes following a curve of a wall, the tactile sensation of varying fabrics beneath your fingertips.

Being invited to speak at the American Society of Interior Designers' annual National Student Summit was a high point in her career and took the edge off her dissatisfaction with how, over time, little by little, she'd felt not just her work, but also her identity being diminished. Being here today provided a much-needed boost to her confidence.

Her workshop, which she'd worked on for weeks, was titled *Function Meets Form Meets Feeling*, and her goal was to teach the attendees how architectural form and decorative arts could empower well-being and affect the quality of lives.

She stood at the front of the room, setting up her laptop

she'd preloaded with a video and several still shots, when she heard a murmur, like a building hum of bumble bees behind her. At the same time the student volunteer who was going to introduce her came over and cleared her throat.

"Um, Mrs. Aldredge, I think you forgot something."

Charlotte looked over at her handouts, the tidily stacked notecards for her speech, and the video paused on the screen waiting for her to press Play. The conference coordinators had also provided a bottle of water.

"No," she said. "Everything seems to be fine."

"But…" The young woman was wringing her hands. Then she leaned forward and whispered, "I'm sorry. But you're not wearing any clothes."

Charlotte jerked awake from a restless sleep. The dream had seemed so real, she had to look around the room to make sure she was still at home in her own bed.

She'd been having the nightmares for weeks. Along with varying versions of this one, another was having not studied for her Environmental Psychology for Interior Design final needed for her MFA. Others, more physically terrifying, of her being chased down one of the city's cobblestone streets late at night by a shadowy stranger, or drowning in a hurricane's tidal wave.

Once her heart stopped its wild pounding, since the sun had begun shining through the plantation shutters, she managed to drag herself into the over-the-top master bathroom that was large enough to practically house a wing of its own. The walls and floors were marble, the steam shower could have fit a basketball team, and a massive chandelier hung over the freestanding soaking tub, which always had Charlotte worrying that one of these days it might fall into the water and electrocute her. Which was why, as much as she loved bubble baths, more often than not, she stuck with the safer steam shower.

There was a large padded white ottoman separating the long marble his-and-hers counters, and the domed ceiling had been painted blue to represent the sky. She brushed her teeth and washed her hands in one of two hand-beveled crystal vessel sinks, which, like the rest of the room, felt excessive even for this private, gated enclave of Charleston homes.

As she'd done every morning for nearly a year, she peed into a plastic cup, which she took to the counter where her digital ovulation test kit was waiting. She dipped the strip into the cup, then, because she couldn't bear to watch, sat down on the ottoman—it had turned out to have a use, after all—and waited. Until she and Mason had started trying to get pregnant, Charlotte had never realized how long five minutes could be. When the display finally flashed a solid smiley face, she felt a surge of anticipation.

Perhaps this was the universe telling her that the time was finally right. Mason had been scheduled to come home from his three-day business trip to Las Vegas last night, but had called and told her he was stuck in meetings and wouldn't be able to make his evening flight back to Charleston. The morning after he'd left, and for the next three days, the face had been blinking, signaling high fertility, and though it wasn't as optimal as the smiley face peak fertility sign, she'd been looking forward to welcoming him home last night and hopefully making a baby. But a peak was perfect. Which meant she had plans to make.

She'd prepare his favorite dinner, the same one she'd made the first time she'd ever cooked for him. He'd often told her that that was when he'd decided to marry her. They always laughed about it, because she'd taken it as the joke it was meant to be. Still, they'd had world-spinning sex that night, so hopefully memories of that seduction dinner would add some fire to their sex life, which had admittedly been sliding downhill.

Their lovemaking had turned decidedly routine, which all the books had assured her wasn't unexpected. But if sex by calendar was what it took to have a baby, then that was what she'd do. There were times, and this was one of them, that she was annoyed that he'd been acting as if getting pregnant was a chore when he'd been the one who'd begun talking about starting a family six months after they'd returned from their honeymoon.

When she'd suggested waiting a couple years in order to let them enjoy the early days of their marriage, and, honestly, to keep the momentum going on her design career, he'd dropped the bombshell that he was planning a run for the Senate, and a candidate with an attractive family always polled better. It wasn't as if he was insisting that she quit work, he'd assured her. They would, after all, have a nanny and housekeeper. She needn't worry about losing her identity or turning into one of those insufferable new mothers who had nothing to talk about but their child.

"There could actually be an upside," he'd said. "By continuing to grow your high-end client base, which has generations of old money to donate, you could open up more avenues of campaign funding."

Which was when she'd belatedly realized how far ahead he'd been thinking about a political career. Wasn't that something you'd discuss with your fiancée before marriage? And if he had, what would she have said? As a senator, he'd be spending his weekdays in Washington, DC. The same night he'd pressed for a child, he'd assured her that he had no intention of disrupting her life, taking her from friends, family and her work, so he'd get an apartment in the capital. Her life wouldn't have to change all that much, he'd promised.

But Charlotte knew it would. Having grown up with an absentee father, the idea of Mason being a weekend parent was less than appealing. And, although she didn't want to be selfish, how would they be able to carve out personal husband and wife time during those short weekends he'd be back in Charleston? Where he'd be having to meet with constituents?

"You're borrowing trouble," she muttered to herself. She showered, put hot rollers in her hair, made up her face and chose a white silk shift dress with a row of red-and-yellow tulips around the hem from her closet. It was still months before he'd have to declare. And maybe, just perhaps, he'd change his mind about moving from law to politics. It could happen.

She'd already bought the Frenched organic lamb chops yesterday, intending to make them last night after assuring the dubious housekeeper that had come with her husband and the house, that she was perfectly capable of making dinner.

Although Mason had effusively complimented her on her culinary talents that first night, it was basically a simple meal. All she had to do was rub an herb mix of thyme, oregano and crushed rosemary over each chop, let them sit in the fridge for thirty minutes and cook them in the cast-iron skillet she'd received as a wedding present from her mother. It was the same skillet Blanche Lillington Swann had inherited from Charlotte's grandmother, Matilda, but since her mother had a live-in cook, and never so much as boiled an egg, before the old skillet had been passed on to Charlotte, it had sat unused for decades.

For sides, she'd serve roasted asparagus sprinkled with grated parmesan and, since Mason was a meat-and-potatoes man, she'd roast red, white and purple fingerling potatoes to add more color to the dish. The wine would be an Oregon Pinot Noir. Mason, who considered himself a connoisseur, had explained that the wine was aged longer that many others in high-quality French barrels, giving it more body.

She'd also have to go shopping for some new ravish-me-now lingerie. The past two months, although he'd been the one pushing to get started on a family, Mason had become increasingly reluctant to follow the Sperm Meets Egg plan that had proven helpful for many of the women on her infertility Facebook group. The detailed plan involved having sex every other day after she'd ended her period, then once she'd hit peak fertility—which was today!—they were supposed to have sex three days in a row, take one day off, then repeat.

There had been times, especially the past three months, when Mason had come home late and exhausted from work, that they hadn't stuck completely to the plan, so Charlotte wasn't hopeful. But as she had during their entire two years of marriage, she wanted to please her husband. Although things, in fact, might be strained right now, she was certain that once she got pregnant, fulfilling the bargain she hadn't realized she'd been making as they'd exchanged vows, he'd go back to being the dashing, romantic man who'd swept her off her feet.

From day one she'd done everything her mother had advised for a solid marriage. She kept fit with a sadistic private trainer, kept her hair Southern glossy, her nails done with weekly manicures and pedicures, never left the house without lip gloss and spent so much time smiling that she understood why so many of her friends had become addicted to Botox. Smiling, it turned out, caused lines.

Despite his promise that her life wouldn't change, she'd allowed herself to be pressured to cut back on the career she'd spent five years studying for at SCAD and had worked hard for the six years after graduation to get off the ground in order to accompany him on various business-focused social events. By the time she and Mason had met, two of her homes had appeared in *Southern Living* magazine, another in *Coastal Living*, she'd become a fixture on Houzz and Pinterest and was steadily growing followers on her blog and Instagram account.

Back then she'd begun to acquire some small commercial accounts—a teahouse, a bakery, an architect's office—and had high hopes for obtaining more. As a newer sideline she hadn't anticipated, both the teahouse owner and baker had wanted a grand opening, and three of her wealthiest clients had asked her to help plan a party to show off their newly decorated home. That was how she'd fallen into event planning, which, for a secondary career, was beginning to prove surprisingly profitable.

Just blocks from Charleston's protected historic district was a two-story brick Georgian house whose new owner, a local real-estate development company, had had plans to turn into a small but pricey boutique hotel. Her architect client, who'd designed the remodel, had recommended her for the job, and although she'd been up against some stiff, big-named competition, she'd won the commission.

Mason Aldridge had been the handsome attorney who wrote up the contract, and as soon as she'd signed her name on the line flagged with a yellow Post-it, declaring the business part of the meeting over, he'd asked her out to dinner to celebrate her winning the deal. The restaurant, in the historic French Quarter, was one of the most romantic in the city. And so popular, she was surprised that they'd managed to just walk in off the street until she learned that he'd called for a reservation during a brief moment he'd been away from the meeting.

"You were that sure I'd go out with you?" she'd asked, looking at him over the rim of her wineglass.

"Let's just say I was hopeful," he'd responded with a smile meant to charm. Which it had.

Over a dinner of she-crab soup and Carolina crab cakes for her, grilled filet mignon with marinated shrimp for him, she discovered that he was twelve years older than she was, and, like Charlotte, was a descendant of the First Families of Carolina. She learned that his legal specialty was real estate, including, along with her boutique hotel, large international transactions from hotels to shopping centers located all over the world.

Brushing over his own accomplishments, he'd flattered her by telling her how impressed he was with her career. She'd been a bit surprised when he told her that he'd never dated a woman who had her own business, but under the spell of his charm, the rich food and wine, she'd basked in his admiration. By the time she'd been talked into a chocolate martini for dessert, as she drowned in eyes as blue as a summer sky, she'd fallen. Hard.

He'd swept her off her feet emotionally that first night as they'd strolled hand in hand through the Quarter, and literally when, after their third date in as many days, he'd carried her to bed.

He'd proposed at sunset, in front of Sullivan Island's light-house, two months after their first date. Although her mother had complained that it would take at least a year to plan a proper wedding, six months later Charlotte and Mason had ex-changed vows in a beautiful, formal ceremony beneath a moss-draped tree on the lawn of the Creek Club on I'On. Cocktails were served to their wedding guests on the wraparound porch, which offered panoramic views of the surrounding gardens and water. And after the sun had set, everyone moved inside for the sit-down dinner and dancing. Although she and her mother differed over many things, both had agreed that it had been a perfect Low Country wedding to remember.

Charlotte still had that ovulation test on her mind as she sat through a meeting of the garden club's annual visitation committee. Once a year her neighborhood of fifty stately homes opened their lacy wrought-iron gates to the public as a fundraising event for a local animal shelter. Although Charlotte hadn't been allowed to have a dog or cat, she'd volunteered at the shelter in high school, cleaning out cages, cuddling cats and taking dogs waiting for adoption for walks.

Unfortunately, Mason, like her mother, was not a fan of animals in the house. Dogs shed all over the furniture, he'd said. They were also dirty. Did she have any idea how many germs were in a dog's mouth? And their nails would ruin the wooden floors. As for a cat, there was no way he was going to have his antique furniture and silk draperies clawed to pieces. She'd dropped the idea, even as she'd hoped that once they had a child, he'd change his mind.

Charlotte realized her mind had drifted off when she noticed all the other women sitting around Melanie Lee's cherry dining table—capable of sitting eighteen at a formal dinner—looking at her expectantly.

"I'm sorry." She shook her head. "My mind was wandering. Mason's coming home tonight from Las Vegas and I was planning his welcome-home dinner." She did not mention that she intended to be dessert.

"We're making a list of what each of us will be serving to guests." Melanie tapped the tip of her pen on a personalized Crane & Co. notepad. Charles Lee had dropped over a thousand dollars on the lacquered, dark blue platinum-adorned limited-edition Montblanc pen to celebrate his trophy wife's being elected president of the garden group, a fact Charlotte knew because Melanie had shown it off at their first meeting.

With the exception of Melanie, Charlotte liked these women, many of whom she'd grown up with. Yet, it had occurred to her from time to time that they could have been clones. Or bought in bulk from Costco. Today, although the calendar might not yet have declared it to be spring, the season had definitely turned south of the Mason-Dixon Line. While not everyone had chosen a floral print Lily Pulitzer shift like hers, all the dresses were as bright as those flowering in the gardens an army of landscapers had created into a showplace.

That thought led to another that had been keeping her awake. If Mason ran for office and got elected, she'd undoubtedly be expected to attend political functions. What did women wear in Washington, DC? Although she'd subscribed to *Town and Country* magazine for years, she'd never paid all that much attention to anything other than the interiors of the featured couples' homes.

"I asked, what are you planning to serve?" There was a definite edge to Melanie's tone. They'd been frenemies ever since Duncan Landsdale had invited Charlotte to the Azalea Ball their senior year at Magnolia Preparatory Academy. She'd accepted, having no idea that Melanie had harbored a secret crush on Duncan.

She said the first thing that came to mind, the one item no Southern party would be without. "Cheese straws?"

"Sally already volunteered for those." Melanie impatiently tapped the page on her notepad. "She makes the best of anyone."

Sally should, since she'd stolen the idea of adding Rice Krispies to the mix from her, Charlotte thought. She really should've been paying more attention so she could have jumped in to claim those. "Pimento cheese finger sandwiches."

"I'm making those." This from Shelby Carlson, who, upon her marriage, had obtained two teenage stepsons who didn't take up much of her time or energy since they spent the major part of the year away at boarding school.

Damn. Charlotte knew deviled eggs, another party staple, would have been snapped up while her mind had been drifting. Along with mint sweet iced tea. And, she quickly found out, red velvet cupcakes had also been claimed.

"Fine. I'll serve tea cakes and peach tea."

"Carol Ann is already doing tea cakes." Melanie's voice had grown tight with frustration.

"That won't matter. No two bakers make them the same way." Tea cakes were as old-fashioned Southern as church fans, porch rocking chairs and sweet tea. Part cake, part cookie and part biscuit, the best ones, to Charlotte's mind, were flavored with vanilla bean, nutmeg and lemon zest. And they should melt in your mouth.

"People are going to be visiting several different gardens." Carol Ann Talbot tossed her long blond hair, which Charlotte knew to be extensions. "Their culinary experience should be as unique as the garden they're visiting. They might not appreciate being served the same thing at different venues."

It took an effort, but Charlotte managed, just barely, not to roll her eyes. "Surely you wouldn't be suggesting they'd feel cheated if they get offered tea cakes at two of the houses?"

"You put nutmeg and lemon zest in yours."

After this morning's test and wanting everything to be perfect for Mason's homecoming, Charlotte was already on her last nerve. And this woman was getting close to cutting that off. Butting heads with a tea cake purist, who considered those ingredients a heresy, hadn't been written in today's square of her sticker-adorned planner.

She folded her arms and lifted her chin. She didn't have time for this foolishness. "That's what makes them so good. Everyone has their own tastes. This way, visitors will be treated to different ones, which has to be preferable to the same-old-same-old you find served at every tea or party south of the Mason Dixon Line."

A united gasp suggested that she'd just crossed an unspoken line. She may as well have professed to dislike SEC Saturday football.

"That's a great idea." Tara Dillard, her best friend since second grade, jumped in brightly before things turned ugly. "Now that we've settled the various menus, I move to adjourn."

"I second," Charlotte said quickly.

"Well, that was a fun way to waste a morning," Tara said as they left the white Greek Revival house the architect had modeled after Twelve Oaks. "Why couldn't we have simply done this by emails? Or Google docs?"

"Because then Melanie wouldn't have been able to show off her newly redone house." The decorator had gone so heavily on gold leaf, Charlotte felt as if Marie Antoinette would've felt right at home. "Has it ever occurred to anyone that it might be easier to have people simply mail in donation checks instead of putting on these elaborate events that take up so much time and money?"

"People, especially when you get into the big spenders, like entertainment with their philanthropy," Tara pointed out. "That's why the theme-decorated Christmas trees and the spring Magnolia Ball bring in the most dollars. The garden party is also high on the list of big contributions because everyone wants to get ideas for their own gardens."

"I know you're right." Charlotte sighed. "But it seems we could be doing something better with our time for the shelter than arguing over tea cakes."

"Are you saying that you'd honestly rather volunteer to clean out cages every week than bake for the garden tour to raise money for the shelter?"

"No. Though I have been thinking of signing up to walk some of the rescues."

"I'd think that would be hard. I'd want to bring every dog home."

"Which would be problematic given that you already own three."

Tara laughed. "I have three kids. That way they don't fight over them. At least that was the plan. Spencer's still a toddler. Sharing isn't part of his skillset yet. Since I have a sitter for another two hours, what would you say to having lunch?"

"I'd planned to do some shopping." As close as they were, Charlotte felt comfortable sharing the next bit. "I just hit maximum fertility today and thought I'd get something so sexy that Mason wouldn't be able to resist ravishing me."

"Sounds like a plan. But he's not getting home until tonight, right?"

"His plane lands at seven."

"It's half-past noon. You've lots of time to find the perfect seduction lingerie to knock his boxer briefs off." She paused, her expression turning into a frown. "Besides, I have something I want to talk to you about."

Charlotte caught the hesitation in her friend's tone and hoped that she wasn't having trouble with her own marriage. Or worse yet—

"Oh, my God. What is it? You don't have some deadly disease, do you?"

"Nothing like that. I'm fine. So are Wyatt and the kids."

"Well, that's a relief. Don't scare me like that. I nearly had a heart attack."

They went to Magnolia's where Charlotte ordered the cucumber salad of baby greens, heirloom tomatoes and black-eyed peas. "Please hold the croutons, and I'd like the apple cider vinaigrette on the side."

After dithering between the crab cake sandwich with Creole rémoulade, and the spicy buffalo fried chicken Cobb salad, Tara went with the salad. "You can never go wrong with bacon," she said on a laugh as the server took their orders to the kitchen.

Charlotte secretly agreed and was a little envious, until she reminded herself that she'd be having lamb for dinner tonight. Not that she'd eat more than a few bites. Mason was very vocal about preferring women to be model sleek and slim. Tara was always telling Charlotte that starving herself was not healthy, physically nor emotionally, but adding to Mason's tastes, she could never quite escape her mother's edict that a woman, especially a Southern woman, could never be too rich or too thin.

While waiting for their salads, they discussed the paint chips and fabric samples for the master bedroom Charlotte had dropped off at her friend's last week, and their upcoming plans for the summer. Charlotte and Mason hadn't had time to discuss when, or even whether or not he'd be able to get away during the busiest of construction months, but Tara, her husband, Wyatt, and their brood were off to Disney World.

"That's brave of you." Charlotte took a sip of the Virgin Mary she'd ordered. She'd stopped drinking alcohol as a precaution in case she got pregnant. Being about to take off on vacation with so many young children might explain why Tara, usually the most zen person she'd ever met, had seemed on edge since they'd left the meeting.

"Mother's coming along. She has a sorority sister living in Orlando, so she'll be able to visit with her when she's not helping out with the kids."

"Sounds like a perfect solution. Though I can't imagine *my* mother taking care of a toddler."

"You were a toddler at one point."

"True. But she had both a full-time housekeeper and a nanny. Being with her was a bit like how the queen appeared to be on *The Crown*. Leaving her children with the nursery staff and scheduling appointments with them after dinner and before bed. Then sending them off to boarding school."

"I remember the year your mother tried that. You kept running away."

"I hated it," Charlotte agreed. "The place was a nest of Queen Bees and I missed my friends. Mostly you."

"We did have ourselves some good times over the years."

Although it may have been due to her own anxiety, Tess seemed to feel tension building during the lunch, increasing after the server had delivered dessert. The warm pecan pie topped with vanilla bean ice cream made on the premises came with two forks for sharing, but even though her mouth was nearly watering, Charlotte resisted.

"You said you had something important to talk with me about," she finally said to her friend.

"I do." Tara put down her fork and took a long drink of the sweet peach tea they'd ordered after lunch. "It's about Mason."

"Oh?" From the way her expression had turned so serious, Charlotte could feel a storm coming, the way the sky would turn that eerie shade of yellow before the arrival of a tornado.

Tara sighed. "I've been struggling for two days to figure out how to finesse this," she said, rubbing her temple.

"Why don't you just say it straight out?"

"Okay." Tara took a deep breath, then reached across the table and covered Charlotte's hand with her own. "Mason wasn't in Las Vegas."

"Of course he was. He called me every night."

"From his cell phone, right?"

Which would have shown his local number on the screen. An inkling of unease skittered beneath Charlotte's skin. "Yes, but why would he make up a story about that?"

"Because he was in Savannah, with another woman."

Charlotte's hand, which she jerked away, turned to ice.

Her heart quickly followed. "That can't be true. Who told you that?"

"No one. I saw them myself. Wyatt and I decided that if we were going to brave Disney World with our boys, we owed ourselves a weekend alone beforehand. Just to remind ourselves that we were more than parents. That we were lovers, too. Which, you'll learn, once you're a mother, is all too easy to forget...

"Anyway, we'd splurged for the Mansion on Forsyth and last night we were waiting for a taxi to take us to dinner when we saw Mason and another woman in the lobby. Fortunately, our taxi arrived before they saw us, so we were all saved an embarrassing moment."

"Perhaps he'd had an unexpected business meeting and made a stop on the way home," Charlotte suggested, wanting desperately to believe it.

"They didn't look as if they'd been conducting business. I'm sorry, Char. I've argued with myself trying to decide whether or not to tell you. But since you and Mason are planning to become parents, I wanted you to know before you ended up pregnant. And possibly a divorced single mom."

"Lillingtons don't get divorced." Wasn't that why her parents were still officially together, despite her father being gone most of the time, and her mother having male "friends" who were always available to take her to charity events? It wasn't the happily-ever-after marriage that Charlotte had always dreamed of for herself, but she couldn't deny that it seemed to work for them. "It must have been business. Mason's a workaholic. He even took work calls on our honeymoon."

"That could be it," Tara said. Her tone was meant to reassure, but Charlotte could see the sympathy in her friend's eyes. "I'm sorry. I probably shouldn't have brought it up. I just thought, if the situation were reversed, I'd want to know."

"I understand. I also sincerely appreciate you caring and I realize this must be a difficult conversation for you." And wasn't that an understatement? "But I'm sure the situation is perfectly explainable."

"I hope you're not angry with me," Tara said.

"Of course I'm not." Though the little niggling doubt that slipped through her belief that her friend must've been wrong had definitely put a pall on her plans for a romantic reunion.

The thing to do, Charlotte decided as they left the restaurant, each headed in a different direction, was to go ahead with her lovemaking plans. She had, after all, already bought the ingredients for dinner. And although she still believed there was an innocent explanation, hitting her husband with an accusation of adultery the minute he walked in the door was no way to welcome him home.

It had to be a mistake. Even so, despite holding tightly to denial, she was no longer in the mood to shop for lingerie.

4

As she arrived home, a distracted Charlotte merely waved at the security guard the homeowners' association employed to screen visitors from his booth at the black wrought-iron gate. From the exterior, Charlotte and Mason's house, while only a decade old, looked as if it had been standing there since the South's antebellum period. Built of red brick, with double doors that gleamed like sunlit snow, it had the towering white columns and front portico that had become the template for mansions and plantation houses of the time. The shutters were a deep forest green while the front porch and second-story gallery boasted gleaming white railings. Like Melanie Lee's home, the stately house had been built to impress. She'd just parked in the four-car garage that would not have been a feature in the pre-Civil War 1800s, when her phone chimed.

"Mrs. Aldredge?" the familiar voice of the guard, a retired cop working part-time to supplement his pension, said.

"Hi, John." It occurred to her that while he always referred to her by her married name, he was just John. To be honest, she wasn't certain she even remembered his last name. But she did know that he had a six-week-old granddaughter, because he'd shown her the photos of the pink-cheeked newborn, wearing a knitted hat to help keep her head warm.

"You have a visitor," he informed her.

"A visitor?"

"He says he's Mr. Swann's attorney. Name of Donovan Brees. The address on his business card has him from Oregon."

That didn't make any sense. Why would her father have an attorney who lived in Oregon? Although she knew he'd grown up in a small Oregon town he'd wanted to escape, she hadn't realized he'd ever returned. Concerned about what trouble he might have had gotten into now—his work took him to dangerous places where he'd once been held prisoner for three months in a country ruled by a brutal despot—she decided this was definitely not turning out to be the day she'd been planning a few hours ago.

"Please send him in, John," she said.

Having had manners drilled into her at Miss Annabelle's Charm School for Young Ladies, she hurried into the house through the interior garage door and took some shortbread and lemon-ginger cookies from the freezer. Given the time crunch, she nuked them in the microwave instead of warming them in the oven. As the house filled with the aroma of baking, she chose some peach cloth napkins from the stack neatly sorted by theme and color in the linen closet, and had just placed the cookies on a plate on a cherry butler's table that sat on a Persian rug between two sofas when the doorbell rang.

Having never been west of the Mississippi, whenever she thought of her father's birth state, visions of cowboys herding cattle over wide-open spaces came to mind. This man was definitely no cowboy. Donovan Brees was wearing a dark Tom Ford suit. Mason had an entire walk-in closet of suits sorted by season and color, allowing her to recognize it immediately.

"Mrs. Aldredge?"

"Yes, I'm Charlotte Aldredge." Something he undoubtedly already knew because, for some reason, he'd come here specifically to see her.

"I'm Donovan Brees. Attorney at law." He held out a crisp card, printed on ivory linen.

"Yes, John at the gate told me." She moved aside, inviting him into the front entry where more columns led to a double curved stairway that soared toward a ceiling where crystals dripped from a huge chandelier. The walls were covered with murals of life in early Charleston and gilt-framed paintings of stern-looking men and women she'd always assumed were Aldredge ancestors. Or perhaps not relations at all, but merely ones Mason's decorator had found scouring antiques stores.

"Would you like tea? Or coffee?"

He appeared surprised by the offer. "Coffee would be great, but you don't have to go to any trouble."

"It's no trouble. I have a machine."

She led him into one of two front parlors on either side of the entry hall. Another possible ancestor, clad in stately robes and a ruffled white cravat at his neck, glowered down at them from another gilt-framed painting, this one towering six feet over the fireplace mantel. When, after moving into the over-decorated house, Charlotte had suggested replacing the portrait with a more cheerful painting, Mason had reacted as if she'd wanted to paint graffiti on the wall. French doors, framed by a pair of tall windows, looked out over a sparkling blue swimming pool surrounded by Grecian-inspired stone statues that she often wanted to take a hammer to. There were times, and this was one of them, that although she had no reason to explain herself to this stranger, she longed to ensure a visitor understood that she'd married into this house. That it was not her personal style. At all.

"You made cookies?" He seemed surprised.

"The housekeeper made them. I merely defrosted them." Afraid of what he might be going to tell her, she was grateful for the excuse to leave the room and slow down her heart, which felt as if it was about to leap out of her chest. "Please, sit down. How do you like your coffee?"

"Really, you needn't—"

"It's no problem." Her voice quavered. The sympathy in his cocker spaniel–brown eyes didn't help.

"Just black," he said more gently than a man merely ordering a cup of coffee.

She went into the kitchen and as the coffee, ground from Ethiopian beans, dripped into a cup, she pressed her hands hard on the counter, steadying herself as she took several deep breaths. With every nerve screeching, she decided the one thing she didn't need was caffeine.

By the time she returned to the parlor, she'd somewhat regained her shaky composure. "Is my father in some sort of trouble?"

"No. At least not the kind you're probably thinking of." He took a breath, dragged his hands through brown hair that had a slight curl. Again, that look of sympathy.

She placed the cup and saucer on the table, then sat on the couch across from him. Southerners were admittedly infamous for not getting straight to the point, but she would have thought Westerners would be more direct.

"I don't want to seem rude, Mr. Brees, but why don't you just tell me straight out what you've come all the way here to say?"

"I'm sorry." Another swipe of his hair. "I'm afraid your father has died."

Her heart, which had momentarily frozen during her conversation with Tara, and pounded like a jackhammer during that seemingly endless time the coffee had dripped through the machine, now felt as if it'd been struck by an arrow and was in danger of shattering.

"Of course he has," she murmured. She'd spent most of her life waiting for that day her father was never coming home again. As a child, once she was old enough to understand what he was doing during all those trips away, she'd worried continually about him dying. More so after seeing him interviewed on television from a hospital bed in some city whose name she couldn't pronounce and could no longer remember.

"I'm sorry," he repeated.

"How did he die?" Saying that word out loud made it horribly, painfully true. And didn't this unwelcome news just cap off a wretchedly troublesome day?

"From lung cancer."

Of all the possibilities that had been tumbling through her mind, that never would have occurred to her. "My father had cancer?" And hadn't told her? Some unseen force was tightening a clamp around her head as she felt the color draining out of her face. "Did my mother know?"

"No. He preferred to keep his illness low-key."

She surprised herself by laughing at that, then realized how inappropriate it must have sounded. "I'm sorry. It's just that if there was one person who was the antithesis of low-key, it was my father. He would've preferred to have died doing his job."

"So he told me. More than once. If it's any consolation, he received very good palliative care and was able to stay at his Oregon home until the end."

"That doesn't make any sense." This news, following what Tara had told her about Mason, made Charlotte feel like Alice, tumbling down the rabbit hole. Or Dorothy, right after her house had landed on a wicked witch. "Charleston is—was—his home. If he'd been sick, he would have come back here."

"Charleston is a lovely city. A beautiful one, from what I've seen driving in from the airport, but in many respects, he'd always seemed to consider where he'd grown up to be home."

"I don't understand. All my father told me about his childhood was that he'd grown up in a town that was too small for his dreams. His ambitions."

He'd also encouraged her to follow her dream. There had been that one time, when he'd made it home for her sixteenth birthday, that her mother had been very vocal about her opinion that Charlotte would never find a husband at an arts college where most of the males were probably gay. Her father had countered that the days of a young woman attending college to achieve her Mrs. degree were long over. And she shouldn't be so bigoted.

Her mother had immediately shot back that she was only thinking of their daughter. And someone had to because he was never around to do so.

Which was when Charlotte had left the room, gone upstairs, put her earbuds in and drowned out the argument with NSYNC while hugging the stuffed pink poodle that was a poor substitute for the real dog her mother refused to allow.

A few minutes later her father came in, gave her a big hug and told her to always stick to her guns and follow her passion, wherever it took her. Although she couldn't imagine anyone's dream being to spend their lives in combat zones, her first semester at SCAD she understood what he'd told her. Her dream was undoubtedly as impossible for him to imagine as his was to her.

"Did my father return to Oregon often?" She wondered if he'd been visiting some woman. Perhaps an old girlfriend from his past. She'd been a freshman in high school when she realized her parents had an open marriage. While not an arrangement she'd ever accept for herself, she knew many supposed pillars of the community who, in their private lives, didn't stick to the often stultifying social norms of the South. She'd even heard of private members-only restaurants that existed solely for men to dine with their mistresses.

"I wouldn't say *often*." The lawyer's voice broke into her thoughts as she worried that just possibly, Mason could be one of those men. "Perhaps once or twice a year. More so the past few years as his mother—your grandmother—got older."

"She's still alive?" Charlotte had never seen any photos of her father's parents. Nor had the couple visited Charleston. Not even for her wedding. Once, when she'd asked about that, her mother had hinted at a Swann family rift and told her that it would be best not to discuss it with her father, given that it was a painful topic.

"Yes. And doing well, considering her age. She's in her nineties."

She wondered if her mother knew that the woman who was technically her mother-in-law was still alive. Which brought up another thought. "I'm surprised my mother didn't tell me that my father had been ill."

"Jack didn't want anyone to know."

"But surely you've told her about his death." Charlotte had kept her phone on all day, in case Mason called to update his arrival time.

"Actually, I haven't. Jack was very firm that his daughters be the first to know."

Charlotte was still digesting the fact that her mother had not yet been notified, when his full statement sank in. "Daughters? But I'm an only child."

"I'm afraid Jackson left it to me to tell you he has two other daughters. From different relationships."

"That's not possible. My father never could've kept a secret like that."

"Tess is the oldest, from his first marriage."

"He was married before he married my mother?"

"To an actress. His daughter, Tess, was also an actress."

Tess Swann. Charlotte recognized the name immediately. She'd always thought it cool that she shared a last name with the star of her favorite program, the girl who was always showing up on *Entertainment Tonight* or the covers of glossy fan magazines. For a time, when she'd been in middle school, she'd even created a fantasy that they were sisters separated at birth by some family drama no one would discuss.

"I used to watch *Double Trouble,*" she said. "And bought her CDs until she quit recording."

"She moved on to writing books for the past decade." He answered the question she was hesitant to ask. "Books for young adults. They're very popular. There's even a TV series based on them."

"That's nice." The only TV Charlotte ever watched these days was design or fashion programs. Was it possible to have sibling rivalry for a sister she'd never known existed? Tess Swann had not only had her own TV show for years, she'd also been a world-famous pop star, and now, apparently, a successful author. While Charlotte, who'd had a promising career only two years ago, was now reduced to blogging and designing master bedroom suites and pool houses for friends when she wasn't reading fertility books and arguing about tea cake ingredients. "What about my other sister?"

"Natalie is the youngest. Her mother was a singer in Paris. She died last year. As you can imagine, it's been a rough time for her. As difficult as it's been to inform you and Tess of your father's death, it's Natalie I'm looking forward to the least."

Unlike that stab of jealousy toward the eldest Swann sister, Charlotte could only feel sympathy toward this third daughter she'd never known existed. "What does she do? Is she a singer, too?"

"No. She's a photographer."

"Like our father." It wasn't lost on Charlotte that each of Jackson Swann's daughters had chosen some sort of artistic career. But it had been the youngest who'd followed most closely in his footsteps.

"Is she a conflict photographer, too?"

"No. But like Jack, she mostly photographs people. Not portraits, but street scenes. She's having her first New York showing this week."

Damn. She felt another twinge of envy toward someone she didn't know. Someone who'd shared her father.

"The reason I've come here today is because Jackson left each of you something in his will."

"What could that be?" Claiming that stuff tied you down, her father had never been one to collect anything but cameras.

"A house. And land. An orchard to be exact, and the Maison de Madeleine winery."

Her very difficult day was turning surrealistic. "That's my husband's favorite wine."

"Your husband has excellent taste. I can't get into specifics of the inheritance now, but there's a provision that the winery ownership might end up shared by his heirs. Depending on what you all three decide. It's rather complicated."

"Heirs." Charlotte had always wanted a sister growing up. Someone to share girlish secrets with. To give her advice about boyfriends. To shop with. To provide a feminine warmth she'd never received from her mother. Now, amazingly, she had two. "Do his other daughters know about me?"

He looked as if he'd rather be anywhere else. Which gave her the answer. "They do, don't they?"

"Tess and Natalie know about you," he allowed. "But Tess didn't know about Natalie, and it appears you didn't know about either of them." Another swipe through his hair revealed his discomfort with this task he'd been given. "Jack was brilliant at his work, but his personal life was a little complicated."

"You think?" Now a flare of anger rose to burn away her shock. She hated having been the only one of them kept in the dark.

Her daily quote in her planner had read: Your Attitude + Your Choices = Your Life. And hadn't she once believed that? Now as it seemed as if much of what she knew about her life was suddenly spiraling out of control, the grandfather clock in the foyer chimed the hour. Mason would be home soon.

"I'm sorry, and I appreciate you coming all the way to tell me this, but all this is a little overwhelming and my husband has been away on a business trip. He's coming home tonight and—"

"No problem," he said immediately. "I understand that all this has come out of the blue and you'll need some time to process it. I have a plane to catch, anyway." He reached into his briefcase and pulled out a manila envelope. "I've made a list of possible itineraries to Oregon. The estate will, of course, cover all your travel expenses. And I'll pick you up in Portland and drive you to Aberdeen."

"That's the name of the town?"

"Yes. It's small but set in a beautiful part of the state. I suppose the word you could use would be *quaint*."

"I could be there by the weekend. Sunday, perhaps," she said, thinking of those fertility days she didn't want to miss.

"That should work. I'll get back to Tess and see, if she decides to come, if the reading on Monday would work for her."

Charlotte wondered why the eldest of the three Swann sisters might not want to go to Oregon, but with the clock ticking away, decided to wait for that story later. After seeing Donovan Brees out, the first thing she did was call her mother.

"Did you know Daddy had another family before ours?" she asked, not bothering to say hello.

"I did," her mother said in a shockingly matter-of-fact way. "He told me when we first met. He met the woman in Vietnam."

"But their daughter isn't half-Vietnamese." Charlotte had always admired Tess Swann's long, deep red curls.

"Amy Curtis was a would-be actress on a USO tour. He was taking photos of the war for *Time* magazine and was assigned to cover her."

"Why didn't you tell me?"

"It never came up."

"Of course it didn't!" For the first time in a very difficult day, Charlotte gave way to her emotions and yelled. "What child asks their parents, 'Oh, by the way, Daddy, do you have another family you failed to mention?'"

"There was no point in mentioning it. Jack wasn't in their lives. He'd moved on."

As betrayed as Charlotte felt, it crossed her mind that her father's apparent desertion of his actress wife and their daughter could be the reason Donovan Brees had implied that Tess Swann may not show up in Oregon. "Did you also know that he had another daughter? In Paris?"

"Yes. But she and her mother didn't have anything to do with either you or me, so there was no point in mentioning them. How did you learn all this?"

"A lawyer showed up at the door. Daddy's dead."

There was a pause on the other end of the line. Then her mother answered. "I suppose that's not surprising. Given his line of work."

"It was lung cancer."

Another pause. "I doubt he took that well. Especially since

I'd always thought he'd prefer to go out in a blaze of glory in some godforsaken hellhole."

How could she not care? Charlotte couldn't imagine what she'd do if Mason died. Even as difficult as things had been lately, she knew she'd be an emotional wreck and certainly not as coolly unmoved as her mother appeared to be.

"He left me an inheritance. Part ownership in a winery in Oregon."

"I knew he'd grown up on some sort of farm, but he never mentioned that. We didn't have that type of relationship."

From what Charlotte had observed over the years, they didn't have any kind of relationship. Which had, as she'd grown older, made her wonder how they'd ever gotten close enough to create her.

"I have to get going," she said, desperate to end this conversation. Like so many other talks they'd had over the years, this simply wasn't working. "Mason's coming home tonight and I need to get started on dinner."

"Enjoy your evening," her mother said. Then simply hung up.

Enjoying the evening had been Charlotte's intention only a few hours ago. Now with the bombshell news of her father's betrayal all these years—how could he keep the secret of two half sisters from her?—and Tara telling her about possibly seeing Mason in Savannah with another woman after he'd claimed to be in Las Vegas, Charlotte wished she could just go upstairs to bed and pull the covers over her head.

5

New York City

Natalie Seurat-Swann loved New York. She reveled in the energy, the pace, the buzz, and tonight she quickly noticed a major difference from Paris. In her home city, although there were no actual fashion rules carved on a stone tablet, there was an agreed-upon uniform of classic pieces, clothing not worn for attention. Every Parisian woman knew that neutrals were your friend and once you developed your look, you followed it, with no need to chase fashion trends.

Here on Manhattan's Upper East Side, fashion seemed to be about individuality, making a statement. Dresses were worn tight and short to show off toned bodies, the dazzling mix of patterns and fabrics, the bright colors, the oversize accessories, seemed to be all about having fun. Many she recognized from this year's spring collections. She'd once dated an up-and-coming designer who'd stated that if it weren't for the Americans, Saudis and Kuwaitis refilling their closets with haute couture every year, the fashion business that so much of Paris thrived on would be in serious trouble.

The gallery had an unobstructed view of the East River, with an outside deck for mingling, and as she sipped a glass of champagne—the only one she'd allow herself all night—she was cornered by a potential buyer, a volunteer docent at the Museum of Modern Art, who, for the past twenty minutes, had been comparing her work to that of Helen Levitt, an American photographer noted for street photography around New York City. Levitt had been referred to as the most celebrated and least known photographer of her time. Her father had given Natalie a book of her photographs when she was twelve.

"Were you influenced by her work?" the matron, wearing an emerald the size of Alaska on the ring finger of her right hand, asked. Unlike the new spring look from Fashion Week in Paris, Milan and New York worn by the majority of the other potential buyers, the seventysomething-year-old woman was wearing a pink Chanel suit trimmed in black, dating back to the 1990s. "While the majority of your scenes portray your own country, the feeling is much the same."

"Levitt's photos are iconic. And it's impossible not to be influenced by others," Natalie responded. "In my country, Monet often painted impressions of people living their everyday life. Although I use a camera, where he used a paintbrush, I enjoy capturing those fleeting glances of life."

Natalie neglected to mention that her strongest influence had been her father. He'd taught her that a single moment captured on camera could reveal more emotions than a thousand words. Although Jackson Swann's work captured the grim and brutal side of life, forcing people outside the bubble of their own comfortable lives to see the violence and suffering of others, having seen firsthand how much he'd suffered, both physically and emotionally for those photos, she'd purposefully chosen more carefree, optimistic moments meant to make viewers smile and hopefully feel joy.

Although she'd been given a hyphenated surname at birth, she preferred to use only her mother's name in her professional life, to prevent having her work compared to her father's. Fortunately, the buyers of her photographs were not usually ones drawn to the dark and deadly events Jackson Swann covered, so only a very few people had ever made the connection.

"Yet, like Levitt, your work so often features children," the woman pressed on. Although Natalie was supposed to mingle with guests, she'd been told that this classically dressed septuagenarian had one of the most extensive private collections in the city. And in this situation, her job here was not just to look pretty and mingle, but to sell her photos. Because the gallery needed to stay open, and she needed to eat.

"Children are freer with their emotions," she explained. "You can catch them in moments of pure joy that most of us have lost over the years. By the time they're in their teens, they're more likely to pose the instant they see a camera."

"The selfie generation," the woman scoffed with a sniff.

"At least they're documenting life."

"An inconsequential life that in most cases does not need documenting."

Natalie was trying to decide how far she could allow this conversation to slide downhill, when she heard a familiar voice calling out her name.

Donovan Brees was wearing a dark suit, subtly striped silk tie and shoes polished to a mirror gloss. While on other men that look could seem terribly stiff and stuffy, for some reason she found it undeniably sexy on him. He turned toward the woman and flashed his sexy dimples. "I apologize for interrupting, but I have an important issue I must discuss with Ms. Seurat. You could even call it a bit of an emergency."

"Oh, dear." The hand with the emerald flew to her breast. "Of course, you two must speak." As she touched Natalie's arm with her other hand, a diamond large enough to sink the Titanic glistened like an iceberg in the moonlight. "I did so enjoy our chat, dear, and hope the next time you're in the city, you'll pay me a visit. I'd love to share my collection with you. And continue our discussion on art and life."

"I'd enjoy that," Natalie said, even as the naughty part of her mind was imagining taking off Donovan's tie. Slowly. Teasingly.

"Grand. Now, I'll leave you two alone to talk, while I go add another work to my collection. I was drawn to that photograph of the children riding the Jardin des Plantes' Dodo Manège carousel. It takes me back to a childhood trip I took with my parents. I'd insisted on riding every carousel in the city, but that was my favorite." Her eyes twinkled with the memory, taking decades off her age. "I rode the Triceratops."

"That's my favorite, too." Built at the turn of the twentieth century, the carousel was dedicated to extinct or endangered animals. "But I also love the Barbary Lion." It was the first Natalie could remember riding as a toddler sitting in front of Jackson, who'd promised to hold her tight. "I felt very brave riding it with my father."

"The moment I walked in, I asked Brenda to put a hold on it until after I spoke with you. I'd already decided to buy it," she assured Natalie, "but I'd wanted to hear what inspired you. That it's personal makes it all the better."

She looked up at Donovan. "I always dreamed of being an artist," she said. "But apparently, my only talent is *recognizing* talent. This young woman's work is truly inspired, and I have no doubt someday, when she's fabulously famous, I'll be telling visitors at MOMA about our evening together."

She gave Natalie two air kisses, then returned to the party

going on inside. The crowd, Natalie noticed, was beginning to thin out.

"You have a fan," Donovan said, sticking his hands in the pockets of his slacks and rocking back on his heels.

"Hopefully, more than one. The butterflies in my stomach turned into giant condors while I was getting dressed tonight."

As his eyes skimmed over her, Natalie wondered what he was seeing. She'd dressed in a black-and-white-striped *la marinière*, which, in the 1800s had been worn by the navy. Now every woman in France had various versions of the shirt in her closet. Though she typically wore it with jeans, tonight she'd paired it with high-waisted black silk toreador pants and a black Cacharel blazer. She'd kept her accessories simple—black ballet flats and a jet beaded Peter Pan collar necklace she'd inherited from her mother.

After her mother's death, she'd impulsively cut off her long copper hair into a short, curly pixie style shaped close at the nape of her neck, accenting her almond-shaped, gold-and-brown hazel eyes. Although she didn't wear a lot of makeup she'd found a bold red matte lipstick that gave her confidence. Which she needed during these necessary showings.

Her *maman* had been a glamorous extrovert, born for the spotlight. While Natalie was quieter, more introverted, Josette had never made her feel less. Not once had she given any indication that she'd wished her daughter were more of a mini-me, than one who tended to view life through a camera lens.

"You look fabulous," he assured her. "I like your sexy new do and your outfit is *très* chic. Though your work speaks for itself. It'd sell if you showed up in jeans, a T-shirt and sneakers."

"You've just described my working outfit." He'd called her sexy! Well, at least her hair. Which was a start. Tamping down another flash fantasy of unbuttoning his starched white shirt, Natalie folded her arms. "So what brings you all the way across the country?"

Her father's birthday was next week. Perhaps his Oregon friends were throwing him a surprise party and Donovan thought it would be nice if she showed up. No, that couldn't be it. All his friends knew that he hated surprise parties and never celebrated his birthdays. "If I remember how old I am, someday I may get too sensible to go rushing into conflict zones," she'd heard him say numerous times when her mother would worry. And yet, ironically, it was *Maman* they'd lost first. Which brought up another thought.

"Oh, God, Donovan, please tell me he's not ill." She couldn't go through that pain again. Not so soon after losing her mother. Her best friend.

The light left his brown eyes. She knew the answer before she heard it. "I'm sorry, sweetheart, he's passed. From lung cancer." He answered what he knew would be her next question and held out his arms. She stepped right into them, but not for the type of embrace she'd wished for whenever she was with this man.

"I suppose I knew this was coming. After *Maman* died, he lost his spark. Despite refusing to acknowledge birthdays, he wasn't a young man, and his work had aged him."

"It had to. Spending his life in such adrenaline-loaded situations was undoubtedly harder on him than we could ever understand."

As she'd grown older and found comfort, and even security, in the distance the camera lens provided, she'd occasionally wonder if her larger-than-life father was, deep down, more like her than he appeared. She'd decided the next time he showed up, she might suggest it to him. Perhaps get a window into that emotional wall he'd spent decades building, brick by brick around himself. Now she'd never know.

"True. Yet, I preferred to live in denial." She pulled away as she felt tears on her cheeks, wiping them away with her fingertips. "I'm going to get your shirt damp."

"It'll dry." He took a white handkerchief, embroidered with his initials, out of his pocket and handed it to her. She'd gotten him a box of them just last year for Christmas, telling him that tissues simply weren't debonair.

"How long will you be in the city?"

"I'm leaving tonight. Although I'd already planned to surprise you by coming to your opening, unfortunately I'm also here for business reasons. Jackson left a will. The reading, if you can make it by then, is tentatively scheduled for Monday."

"Is that also the day of the funeral?"

"There isn't going to be one. He insisted that he didn't want any fuss."

"That sounds so like him. In his attempt to spare people pain, he didn't realize that funerals are more for the living than those who've passed on." She sighed. "But if there's to be no service, surely it's not necessary for me to be there for the reading of the will. I doubt that I'll receive anything all that substantial, since he knows—knew—how well I'm doing."

She felt as if a stiletto had stabbed her heart as she changed to past tense. As dangerous as his work had been, Jackson Swann had been so strong, so energetic, until her mother's death, so much larger than life, always seemed to take up all the oxygen in any room he entered. "It's not as if he was married to *Maman*, which puts me in a different category from the other two."

"You were his daughter. Not having some piece of paper making his and Josette's relationship official doesn't change that. Will never change that." He took hold of her shoulders, his eyes, which had turned uncharacteristically intense, on hers. "Don't ever think otherwise."

She'd never had a reason to, until now. Another thought suddenly occurred to her. There was more to Jackson Swann's estate than money, which he'd never seemed to care about. "What's to become of the winery?"

"That's something to be discussed."

She was tearing up again. Realizing that they'd been out here long enough to have been missed, she saw Brenda, the gallery owner, looking out the glass door for her.

"I love the vineyard and would hate to see it be sold off." And then there was Gideon. And Aubrey. What would become of them? A new owner intending to continue making wine, would, if he or she had any sense, keep him on. But what if a developer wanted to destroy four generations of Swann family work by razing the fertile earth to build a subdivision of American McMansions?

"Jack made provisions for how to handle things between you all," he assured her. "But that's all I can tell you now."

"Have I ever mentioned I hate it when you act like an attorney?" In truth, she found it sexy. He was so different than other men she dated, most of whom were in the art world. Donovan wasn't stuffy, as she might have assumed a lawyer to be. But he was precise and preferred an orderly life. Which, she suspected, had made her father a challenging client.

"You've mentioned it. And, as it happens, I am an attorney," he reminded her. "You already know more than Tess or Charlotte. As least you've been to Maison de Madeleine."

"He never had them visit? Not even Charlotte, whose mother he stayed married to?"

"No. The first time they heard about it was today. And before you ask why that was, it's because he'd made it very clear that my job was to be his attorney, not a counselor or therapist. I never asked, and he didn't tell. But I suspect it was because he'd emotionally distanced himself from his first wife and daughter, Tess, when he left California. And his relationship with Charlotte's mother was less than cordial."

"I suppose so." Her brow furrowed as she considered what she might be walking into. "They're going to hate me, aren't they?"

"That's impossible. Everyone adores you. You're a ray of sunshine wherever you go. And believe me, Oregon can use all the sunshine it can get."

"Flatterer." She went up on her toes and kissed one of his cheeks, then the other.

There'd been a time, the summer of her fourteenth year, when Natalie had developed a wild crush on Donovan. An "older man," about to enter his junior year of college, he'd treated her feelings in a gentle, kind way that hadn't left her embarrassed whenever she'd see him as she'd grown into adulthood. Even then she realized that his kindness and tolerance was proof that he was a good and decent man.

Jackson Swann's judgment had been terrible about many things. His choice of attorneys was not one of them. Unfortunately for her, every year she'd returned to Oregon for those two weeks with her father and grandmother, her feelings had grown more and more powerful, leading her to believe that her initial emotions hadn't been merely a schoolgirl crush, but the real thing. That Donovan Brees was The One.

But even if she was willing to risk losing his friendship by attempting to move their relationship to the next level, he'd never shown an iota of sexual interest. She knew he wasn't gay because during those summers she'd visit the farm, she'd hear gossip about all the different girls he was dating. The fact that none seemed to last very long suggested that he was either a player, which didn't fit his personality, or simply had no interest in a permanent relationship.

She sighed, putting away the dilemma she'd been thinking of more and more often as summer approached, signaling her yearly visit with her father. "I need to get back to work, selling my photos." Which was the part of her career that she disliked. Unfortunately, it wasn't merely her income on the line. Fifty percent went to Brenda, the first gallery in New York willing to take a risk on her.

"And I need to get back to La Guardia. By the way, while all your work is fabulous, I really like that photograph of the snowman sitting on a bench with the Eiffel Tower and the lone skier in the background."

"It was a rare Paris snow day." She smiled at the memory. "Overnight the city had turned into a winter wonderland. I'm especially fond of that one because of the whimsy of the situation."

"It caught my eye the moment I walked in, so I bought it before anyone else could."

"Thank you." She kissed both his cheeks again. "You couldn't have given me a more special gift." She saw Brenda waving her inside while a couple stood in front of a photo of Notre Dame, taken before the devastating fire, gleaming in the dawn light. "Well, I guess it's back to business for both of us. I'll make arrangements and see you Sunday."

"Or I could have my secretary make them, and let you know the time." He glanced around at what had become a crush of people inside. "You're dealing with enough right now."

"Thank you."

He knew her well. Although she'd never admitted it out loud to anyone but her mother, he understood her butterflies. Stage fright, *Maman* had reassured her before her first showing. It was perfectly natural. The difference was that for Josette, it had gone away the moment the spotlight turned on her. Natalie's butterflies would continue to flap their wings in her stomach until she'd escaped to her apartment or hotel room and stood beneath the shower and allowed the hot water to soothe and untangle her nerves.

She was, she'd learned, a situational introvert. With friends and other people she knew, she could be comfortable and chatty. It was situations such as this, when she was thrown into a group of strangers, that created anxiety.

"No problem." He brushed his knuckles down her cheek, a light, casual gesture that warmed her skin.

As they returned to the gallery together, Natalie pasted a smile on her face as she approached the couple who appeared to be waiting to talk with her. She'd learned early on that while some buyers simply wanted to take care of business and leave, many more, like the elderly woman who'd once ridden a wooden elephant-size dinosaur, wanted to hear the story behind a particular photograph they were considering purchasing.

If she'd glanced back, she would have seen Donovan pausing at the door, looking at her the way a man looks at a woman he wants to take to bed.

6

Charlotte couldn't stop her mind from spinning. How could her father have lied to her? Oh, not telling that she had two half sisters out there wasn't precisely a lie. But only because the thought would never have occurred to her. Like she'd told her mother, why would she have ever asked?

Whenever he'd return home, the first thing her father would do, as he'd walked into the house and dropped all his dust-covered belongings on the front marble floor, would be to shout out, "Where's my princess?"

And from wherever she was in the house, whatever she'd be doing, she'd run to the door and fling herself into his arms and bask in the warmth of his love. And he *had* loved her. Charlotte had no doubt about that. One night when he'd come to see her at SCAD, they'd gone out to dinner and he'd gotten a little drunk, and later, back in his hotel room, he'd drunk a little more, opening up enough to give her a window into his life. A horrifying and painful look that had her wanting to put her arms around him. Not to receive comfort. But to give.

"Why do you choose to do such work, when it takes such a terrible toll on you?" she'd asked, taking in the deep purple hollows beneath his eyes and a wan face accented even more by the amount of weight he'd lost since the last time she'd seen him.

He'd taken his time to answer, turning the glass of Scotch from the mini bar around in his hand. "I didn't choose my work," he said finally. "It chose me." Then, as if realizing that he'd brought such a dark and heavy cloud down on a visit that had previously been a joyous occasion, he switched gears and flashed that smile that had always made her understand why her stiff, formal, uptight mother had succumbed to its charm. "Just as creating spaces that not only are functional, but make people comfortable and lift their spirits, is the work you were born to do.

"So…" He'd put the now-empty glass onto the side table, slapped his large, scarred hands onto his knees and said, "Show me what you've been working on."

Grateful for the change in topic, she'd taken out the portfolio she'd created for her MFA project: a home for women and children needing protection from family abuse. A place where women could gain working skills and the confidence to achieve the careers they were working toward, a place where they'd receive counseling to remind them, or often teach them, since so many had grown up in equally damaging homes, of their intrinsic value. Which, in turn, would hopefully help them rid themselves of the gnawing guilt at having put their children in a situation of such physical and emotional abuse. A place where tears were replaced by laughter, and young voices were not always being told to remain quiet so as not to anger their fathers. Or whatever partner their mothers had brought into their young lives.

"I've always known you were talented," he said. "But this displays a brilliance of not only understanding your clients—" she'd told him that she'd visited several women's shelters and homeless crisis centers, and with women whose children were being fostered because they were no longer able to care for them "—but possessing the empathy to see needs that they might not even know they have."

Unlike her mother, who'd asked her why she'd chosen such a dark and depressing topic, his words of praise had had her basking in their glow. It was the last time Charlotte had seen her father.

"I don't care what he wanted," she decided as determination rose, strengthened by the memory of that evening that had lasted until dawn. "His life needs to be celebrated."

And if Tess Swann and Natalie Seurat-Swann had a problem with that, she thought as she wiped away the tears that the memory had triggered, they could just damn well leave things to her.

In the meantime, she had to finish preparing for Mason's arrival. Donovan Brees's bombshell had, for a time, blown away her earlier niggling fear that she'd been trying to deny since her luncheon with Tara. Now she realized that if it was true, she'd have to decide how to deal with her husband having an affair. And even if he was innocent, she still had another problem she had to turn around. She had, while not paying attention, fallen under her husband's control in much the same way as the women whom she'd created her project for.

Oh, she'd never been physically abused. But while working on the design, she'd come to realize that little by little, Mason had begun to control her emotionally. He'd set the marriage rules from the beginning so narrowly, with their joint focus on his "more important" career that her confidence had begun to wane, causing her dreams to narrow in response to her husband's idea of what the ideal wife should be.

It wouldn't do any good to pepper him with questions the moment he walked in the door. He'd only close himself off behind those icy walls he'd put up whenever he was displeased and refuse to engage. She'd have to come up with a plan. One where she'd be able to control the situation. More recently, Mason had developed a habit of walking out of the house whenever they'd argue. After he'd return—minutes, hours later, or once, even the next day—there'd be no words of apology, no kissing and making up. They merely picked up their marriage as if nothing had occurred.

Not this time.

Then again, she reminded herself, she was working solely on conjecture. She needed facts. Wiping away the tears on her cheeks, she called Tara, who cared for her enough to risk their friendship to attempt to save Charlotte pain.

"What did she look like?" she asked without preamble, the moment Tara had answered her phone.

There was a pause. Then, "She was tall. And whip thin. All angles instead of curves."

"What color was her hair?"

"Black. And cut into an inverted bob as sharp as her face. I'm so sorry. I've been sitting here beating myself up for having told you."

"You were trying to protect me. That's what friends do."

"But you're probably right about me being mistaken. She wasn't at all the type of woman he'd be attracted to."

"What do you mean?"

"She looked cold. And not at all mannerly or decorous, like the women he prefers."

Mannerly sounded like the elderly white-haired DAR matrons who had weekly tea at La Pâtisserie. And *decorous* was something pretty, but having little use. Is that how people, even those who knew her best and cared for her most, viewed her?

Charlotte realized while considering the unpalatable thought that the conversation had come to a pause.

"It's hard to explain," Tara tried again. "Let's just say that watching her, if she'd been cast in *Fifty Shades of Grey*, she'd be the one with the whip."

"You're right. That's not Mason's type at all. It had to have been a business meeting. But could you do me a favor?"

"Anything," Tara said quickly, obviously wanting to make amends.

"Call Mason's office." She gave her the number. "And ask for Olivia Wainwright."

"And what if I get connected?"

"I don't know," Charlotte uncharacteristically snapped. Then pressed her fingers against her eyes until she saw swirling rainbows and sighed. "I'm sorry. Just make up a name and say you're looking for a new firm to handle your considerable trust fund and her name had come up."

Despite the seriousness of the situation, Tara laughed. "If only I had a trust. Considerable or otherwise."

"You know that. And I know that. But Olivia Wainwright doesn't."

"And if she makes an appointment?"

"Then don't show up. You're going to give her a false name. I'm sure potential clients occasionally bail on an appointment. Or you can call later and cancel. Afterward, let me know how it went."

"I'll do it as soon as we hang up."

Charlotte was pacing the kitchen floor when the phone trilled. "The receptionist told me that she's out of town. On business."

"In Savannah?"

There was a long pause. "Yes."

Charlotte hated the pity she heard in her friend's voice. "Thanks."

"What are you going to do? It still could be business," Tara suggested with weak conviction. "Perhaps there's a deal they're both working on."

"That could be it." It occurred to Charlotte that this was the first time in all their years of friendship that they'd lied to each other. "Don't worry about telling me," she said again. "I'd rather find out from a friend than be blindsided by stopping by his office to take him out for a surprise lunch and catch them having sex on his desk." Had they? she wondered. "Now I'd better run."

At any other time she would've told Tara about Donovan Brees and the wild tale he'd come all the way from Oregon to tell her. About her father's death. And her sisters. But right now she had to think. And plan what she was going to do when her cheating husband finally came home from his mistress.

After a quick goodbye, she sat at the kitchen counter, wondering if this day was ever going to come to an end. Suddenly, cheese straws and damn tea cakes were the least of her concerns.

Olivia Wainwright was the type of woman Charlotte had always found intimidating. Her hair was black as a raven's wing, styled in the sharp, inverted bob cut close at the back of the neck that Tara had described. Rather than the softer, more feminine look Charlotte, her mother and friends had always worn, both times she'd met Olivia she'd been dressed in a severely cut power suit Charlotte imagined a woman might wear in New York City, Chicago or San Francisco. Her jewelry, rather than the pearls that every Southern woman knew attractively lit up your face, had been metallic signature pieces designed to be noticed. And to show strength. They were, in their own way, much like the armor knights had worn into battle.

Olivia had been born, Charlotte had learned the first time they'd met at a Christmas party when she and Mason were engaged, in the Chicago suburb of Glencoe. Her tone, when tossing off the mention of her toney birthplace, like her sleek body-fitting black dress, was intended to impress. After four years at Sarah Lawrence, followed by Harvard Law, she'd worked in a Manhattan law firm for three years when a head-hunter hired by Mason's firm had convinced her that she could either spend a decade working her way up in the strictly structured environment of her current firm, or she could take the very lucrative offer, which, while not nearly what she'd been earning in New York City, given the lower Charleston living costs, had resulted in a substantial rise in income.

Having been brought up to believe that talking about money was gauche, Charlotte had changed the subject, asking how she was enjoying Charleston. "It's been an extreme culture shock," she'd responded. "I was telling Mason just the other day that there are times when I feel as if I've landed on another planet."

Her brittle smile and crisply spoken words implied a superiority Charlotte had encountered years earlier at the boarding school her mother had sent her to. The smile warmed a few degrees as she smiled up at Charlotte's fiancé. "But I'm beginning to adjust."

"How fortunate." *Bless your heart*, every Southern woman's most deadly putdown, rang in Charlotte's head.

"And what do you do?" Olivia had asked.

"I'm a designer," Charlotte had responded.

"Ah." She'd skimmed a glance over the red, scalloped-hem dress that had felt so fun and festive when Charlotte had put it on that evening. "That's very cute." She'd made it sound like something you'd design for a four-year-old.

"Not clothing. I have an MFA from the Savannah College of Art and Design." Okay, that was name-dropping, but if this woman could drop Harvard Law, she could brag about having graduated from the country's top-ranked school of interior design.

"I've been looking for a good decorator. Maybe you and Mason could come over to my apartment for dinner and you could give me a few ideas."

"I'm a designer. Although many people confuse the two, the professions are very different. A decorator works to furnish a space with fashionable things while working within its functionality, which is what you're looking for. As a designer, I work with builders or owners to create a functional space. The simplest way to explain it is that a decorator knows how to change the layout of the furniture. I create the shape and location of the rooms, walls and floors, and other construction elements. Although, I also do enjoy decorating the finished spaces."

"That sounds a great deal more fun than law. I envy you, getting paid to shop all day."

Charlotte resisted, just barely, grinding her teeth. "It's always a bonus when you love your work. And I'll admit to a warm feeling of joy when I create an environment that's perfect for my client."

Refusing to allow this Midwestern mean girl to get under her skin, Charlotte placed her hand on Mason's arm in an obvious possessive gesture that drew a smirk from Cruella de Law. She'd had her nails done in a bright red that matched her dress. A Christmas tree had been painted on her ring finger where a two-carat marquise-cut diamond ring set in platinum sparkled like ice. When her manicurist had talked her into the tree it had sounded festive and fun. Now, looking at the other woman's French manicure, she felt frivolous.

"I have my own business," she said. "Which is how Mason and I met. He handled the contract for my design work on a downtown boutique hotel."

"That must have felt like quite a coup."

"It was love at first sight," Mason declared loyally, putting his arm around her waist. "The moment Charlotte walked into my office conference room, I knew she was the very woman I'd been looking for."

"Well." The smile on Olivia Wainwright's crimson lips wasn't reflected in her calculating green eyes. "Isn't that sweet." Her tone was saccharine, and, Charlotte had known, meant to demean. "I'll be honest. I always thought love at first sight was one of those tropes thought up by romance writers to get their characters into bed earlier in the book."

A temper Charlotte hadn't realized was lurking inside her began to rise, bringing heat to her cheeks. With Mason's arm still around her, they were hip to hip and, feeling him tense, she decided this was not the time to accuse the firm's new hire of being a literary snob.

She was relieved when Dirk Ashurst, one of the senior partners, appeared to tell Mason that he had someone he wanted him to meet. "Jonathon Pickney-Gibb's mother passed last month. As you know, his father died five years ago." The former state congressman, another member of South Carolina's first families, had lain in state beneath the iconic dome in the capitol's main lobby. "He's twenty-six and has been with Bellinger, Lee and Vareen, only because they'd handled his parents' affairs," Dirk said. "Bellinger had taken over the account but now that Jonathon's inherited the family fortune, he's decided that he'd rather have new representation."

"That firm's an institution, not only in Charleston, but the entire state," Mason had noted. "Hell, probably the country. Leon Bellinger has argued before the Supreme Court three times."

"And lost two of the three cases," Dirk returned. "Bellinger is also way past his prime and should have retired a de-

cade ago. At any rate, Jonathon is building a strong career in
real estate, and wants a younger, hungrier attorney. One on
his way up rather than one who's outlasted his time."

"Well, then, sounds as if we'd be a good match." Mason
turned back to Olivia. "I'll be seeing you after the New Year."

"Count on it," she said with a smile. "I'm already dreading
going home to a Chicago winter." She skimmed another of
those dismissive glances down at Charlotte. The six-inch ice
pick heels of her shoes gave her a decided height advantage.
"It was nice meeting you. Have a wonderful holiday." Her
smile was not nearly as warm as the one she'd given Mason.
In fact, it was as chilly as Charlotte imagined a Chicago winter would be.

As Mason ushered her through the crowd to the potential
client with his hand on her back, Charlotte assured herself
that although the new associate might have her eyes on her
fiancé, *she* was the one wearing the engagement ring. And
besides, there was a firm rule about partners not dating as-
sociates, and she knew her Mason well enough to know that
he'd never risk the opportunity of becoming an equity partner. Especially with an associate with whom sex would probably be as icy as her attitude.

That was what Charlotte had assured herself at the time.
Apparently, she'd been wrong.

How to do it? Charlotte stood in front of the open refrigera-
tor door, looking in at the long-boned Frenched lamb chops.
She hated conflict, but she couldn't see any way to avoid it.
Oh, she had no absolute proof Mason had been sleeping with
that female barracuda. But deep down, thinking back on all
the times she hadn't been able to reach him, when he'd been
out of the office, or his phone would be off, she knew.

Although it was the most difficult thing she'd ever done,

Charlotte decided to play the evening out. She needed to know, but as conflict averse as she was, she opted to take things slowly. Just in case. Because, beneath his smooth Southern Ashley Wilkes charm, she'd discovered on their honeymoon that Mason possessed a quick-fire temper she'd learned not to trigger.

She'd been in the dining room, lighting the candles, when she'd heard the door open. "Hi, honey," he called out. "I'm home!"

Pressing a hand against her clenched stomach, she suddenly thought of the sister she hadn't known she'd had and wished that she had even an iota of Tess Swann's acting skills. Pasting a warm smile on her face, she went to welcome her husband.

As he'd gathered her into his arms and gave her a perfunctory kiss, nothing like the sweep-her-away ones she'd received during their courtship, she immediately caught an all-too-familiar exotic scent that was the perfume equivalent of a power suit.

"You've changed your aftershave," she said in what she'd intended to be a teasing manner, but heard the accusation in her tone and knew he'd heard it, too, when guilt flashed in his eyes. It had come and gone so quickly, if she hadn't been watching for it, she would've missed it.

"I sat next to this woman who'd bathed in the stuff," he said with a grimace. "I don't know why airlines don't ban perfumes on planes. Everyone sitting within ten rows of her had to breathe it in the entire flight. They'll probably have to fumigate the entire first-class cabin before turning the plane back to Vegas." He leaned down and pressed his lips to hers again, causing her to think about where that mouth had been. When that caused an involuntary shiver, he backed away. "Let me go shower to get rid of it," he said. "So the scent won't ruin dinner. Are those rosemary roasted potatoes I smell?"

"They are. We're having lamb chops and chilled asparagus with a lemon Dijon mustard vinaigrette."

"That's the first dinner you ever made me."

"You remembered."

"Of course." His cheating eyes warmed. "I remember everything about that night."

As did she, dammit. As he left the room, Charlotte knew the dinner was already ruined. But determined to maintain some control as they played out this long-overdue scene, she returned to the kitchen and heated up the pan for the lamb.

7

Over the meal, which had always been one of her favorites, but which she vowed to never make again, Charlotte listened to Mason talk about the project he'd been working on in Vegas. There was a time she would have hung on to every word, wanting to prove herself an intelligent, enlightened conversationalist. Even when the conversations tended to revolve around him. Tonight his words about his supreme success in Las Vegas were little more than a buzz in her head.

"So," he said, finally turning the conversation from himself, "what have you been up to?"

"Oh, you know." She shrugged as she pushed the untouched potatoes around her plate. "The usual. I posted to my blog, finished a mood board for Tara's master bedroom makeover—they're doubling the size and adding his and hers closets and a spa bath—and attended a meeting of the garden club tour."

"It's already that time again?"

"It's always in the spring," she reminded him. "I also had lunch with Tara this afternoon."

The telltale sign flashed in his eyes. Quicker than the earlier one, but she'd been watching carefully. It appeared Tara had been wrong about not having been noticed. "Oh? How is she doing?"

"Fine. She and Wyatt are taking the kids to Disney World."

"That's ambitious."

"Her mother's going along to help with the boys. But beforehand, they decided to take a romantic weekend."

"Sounds nice," he said as he speared a piece of spring bright green asparagus. "We should do that one of these days."

"That would be nice," she agreed. "They went to Savannah, which had me thinking how long it's been since we've been there."

"I thought more along the lines of London or Paris."

"But you've been so busy the last few months. And Savannah is so close. They stayed at the Mansion on Forsythe Park."

The fork clinked as he lowered it to his plate. A chilly cloud descended over the table. "Did they?"

"They said it's lovely. With wonderfully personalized service." She paused a beat. "And here's the funny thing. Tara thought they saw you there. Of course I assured her she had to be mistaken—"

"She wasn't." He refilled his wineglass. "I had a call while I was leaving for the airport in Vegas. A slight problem with a contract point on a planned new boutique hotel. A project much like the one that you and I met on. I changed my flight to stop by there on the way home."

"You didn't tell me."

"I wasn't aware that I had to get approval from you to conduct my business affairs."

Affair being the definitive word. "Of course you don't." Although every nerve in her body was screeching, Charlotte managed to remain calm. "Did you get the situation taken care of?"

"Yes. It turned out not to be such a big deal, after all."

"Allowing you to handle it alone?"

He lowered his glass, which had been halfway to his mouth. "So that's where we're going with this?"

"If you're going to tell me that you were with Olivia Wainwright, I suppose we are."

"Christ, you're insecure." He tossed his napkin on the table. "I've been trying to be patient with you, Charlotte, while you've been so obsessed with getting pregnant."

"Which you wanted."

"I had no idea that your fertility levels and inability to conceive would become the centerpiece of our marriage. Or that our sex life would be put on a damn schedule. You've spent months treating me like a stud horse you're using for breeding. Why should you care if I prefer the company of an intelligent, attractive woman who talks about more than procreation? Who doesn't expect sperm on demand?"

Charlotte drew in a sharp, painful breath. "It's not like that. And, again, let me remind you that my taking time off from my career to have a baby in an attempt to attract more potential voters was *your* idea. And, by the way, according to all the books, constant stress can adversely affect fertility."

"So now you're blaming me for your infertility?" His tone was like an ice stiletto to the heart.

"No." This conversation, which she'd hoped to keep calm and civil, was on the verge of getting out of hand. "Of course not."

Still, if he'd only been tested, as she'd done, to ensure that their problem wasn't due to anything wrong with her, which the doctor had assured her it wasn't, at least they'd have something more scientific than the plan she'd been dutifully trying to stick to. Other women on the infertility boards had described, in vivid detail, their experiences with IVF. Not only was it expensive, it was also hellish to go through with all those shots that would have her hormones raging out of control. Charlotte had always disliked her annual flu shot. She couldn't imagine having needles in her stomach.

The fertility plan she'd found that had proven successful with so many other women in her position was, if done according to the rules, admittedly sexually rigid. But it hadn't been a picnic for her, either. And she certainly had never felt any urge to cheat.

"Are you sleeping with her?"

He sighed heavily. Wearily. "Since I appear to have been busted, in a word, yes." He no longer appeared angry. Merely bored with this conversation. "And you, of all people, should understand that my having sex with another woman has nothing to do with us. With our marriage."

"What? How could you believe that? What part of forsaking all others did you not hear when we were exchanging those vows?"

"It wasn't something I planned. It just happened. Considering that you grew up in an open marriage, while I saw no need to mention it, I assumed that if you did find out, you'd be more reasonable."

"Wait." She'd held up a shaky hand, which, dammit, gave away her screeching nerves. "You believed that my parents' marriage arrangement would make me okay with my husband fucking around?"

"Must you be so crude?"

This conversation had her head on the verge of exploding and he dared to be annoyed by her tone? "Apparently so. Excuse me if I find my husband sticking his dick into another woman not all that helpful to our marriage. And for your information, my parents' marriage no longer exists."

That got his attention. "They're getting divorced? After all these years? Fuck. That's all I need, a family scandal."

Charlotte realized that, unsurprisingly, Mason's first thought was for himself. "My mother has always insisted that Lillingtons don't get divorces."

"I know. That was one of the pluses on my prospective marriage ledger."

"You had a marriage ledger?"

He actually colored a bit at that. Not a full face, but the tips of his ears, which was the most emotion he'd shown thus far tonight. "Not an actual written-down one. But you know, a mental idea of what type of woman I might marry when the time came. You ticked all the boxes."

"What a relief I passed your qualification test."

"You don't have to sound so snarky. Everyone has one. You can't tell me you didn't."

"I suppose I did."

"See?" Mistakenly believing the discussion over, he cut a piece of lamb chop. "Everyone does," he repeated.

"Mine was, it seems, a bit shorter than yours."

"Oh?"

"I wanted to marry someone I was in love with. And who'd be in love with me."

"You've been wasting your time wallowing in those romance novels again, haven't you?"

Wallowing? She tossed her head, feeling a white-hot temper rising inside her. "I don't have to defend my choice in reading to anyone. Least of all an adulterous husband. Have you ever considered that perhaps one of the reasons I enjoy romance novels is because our marriage is so lacking in that department?"

Anticipating the accusation that any problems in their relationship were her fault, due to her apparent inability to conceive, she held up a hand to cut off any response. "But getting back to my parents, which apparently were one of your boxes—"

"Only your mother. Her old-line lineage made up for Jackson's less than respectable career choice."

Okay. He'd crossed the line with that one. "My father happens to have three Pulitzers!" A hat trick, he'd told her over a celebratory dinner at Savannah's The Olde Pink House. Although he brushed it off, saying he was just doing his job and had gotten lucky, she could tell he'd been pleased. But more for the fact that it brought more attention to a refugee problem than any acclaim for himself.

Realizing that she'd used the present tense, the cold, hard fact of his death hit again, slashing through her own domestic problems. Charlotte felt her eyes filling up. She resolutely blinked the threatening tears away, rather than let them fall and have Mason think he was the cause.

"Well, you won't have to concern yourself with him being a black mark on your unrelenting climb to the top of your legal and political careers, because he's dead."

"I'm not surprised," he said, mirroring what she herself had first thought about hearing the news from Donovan Brees. But his tone held not an iota of regret. In fact, as she watched him process her statement, she could tell that he felt no sorrow for the loss of a bold, brave life well lived. Not even if that life had been his wife's father.

"How did you find out? I didn't see a newsflash come in on my phone. And while he wasn't exactly a celebrity outside his own world, I would have suspected his death would have been worth noting."

"His attorney is attempting to keep a lid on the story until all the family has been notified." She didn't admit that he was probably correct about Jackson Swann not being a household name. The work he did was of a nature most people didn't want to look at and the only time he appeared on television to do an interview was to stress the need for the world to protect the vulnerable. Once she'd asked him if he'd been disappointed in her career choice, which was a very long way from trying to save the world.

He'd appeared openly surprised by the question. When he'd asked why she'd think such a thing, she'd responded that designing attractive, albeit functional living places seemed insignificant compared to his work. Which was when he'd reached across the table and taken both of her hands in his larger, scarred, life-roughened ones. Two of his long fingers were crookedly bent, the result of some long-ago beating.

Unlike her mother, who'd always rejected physical contact, her father was a toucher. As was Charlotte. Mason was not. At least he'd never been with her. Apparently, Olivia Wainwright was a different story.

"His lawyer told me they wanted to keep the death under wraps until he'd been able to tell all three of my father's daughters."

"He had two other children?"

"Apparently, my mother wasn't his first wife. He has one daughter from that marriage. And another from a mistress."

"So whatever inheritance you'll receive will be divided three ways?"

"I assume so. But I doubt there's much to inherit. Given that my father mostly lived on whatever he could carry." She'd decided, while fixing dinner, not to tell him about the winery. Unlike this house, it would be something in her marriage that was all hers and she didn't want to give him a chance to try to get his greedy hands on it until she heard the details and could get legal advice. "I'm going to Oregon for the reading of the will in the morning." Any plans for sexy times tonight had gone down the drain after he'd so easily admitted to his affair.

"Oregon?"

"It's where he grew up. And chose to die."

Alone, as he'd lived. When she'd been in her teens, she'd asked him if he'd stayed away because of her. A reasonable assumption, given that many of her parents' fights had been their disparate ideas of what her future should be. He'd assured her that wasn't the case. That the only reason he stayed away so long was that there were stories to be told, dark stories filled with pain and death that he didn't want to bring home to her. Into her life.

That hadn't stopped her from constantly searching the internet for his name. And wondering how anyone could possibly live with all those images of what the worst people around the world could do to each other in his head.

"How long will you be gone?" he asked.

"I'm not sure." She somehow managed to keep her emotions—which were swinging back and forth between devastation and fury—tamped down to get through this conversation. "The will is being read Monday. Probably a day or so. I don't suppose you'd want to come with me?"

That was admittedly a test born of the question billowing in her mind since Donovan Brees had left. Should she fight for her marriage? Was it worth saving? Perhaps sleeping with Olivia Wainwright had been just a onetime slip and some time away together would remind him what he'd be throwing away if he continued the affair.

"What would be the point?" he asked, his tone edged with derision. "Your father didn't bother to hide the fact that he never considered me good enough for his princess daughter. And I considered him rough and uncouth. I never figured out why your mother didn't just get an abortion rather than marry a man so far beneath her status."

Charlotte felt the color leaving her face as his cold, uncaring words stunned. "You do realize that if she had, you never would have met me. That we'd never have been married."

"It was merely a hypothetical. And you can't deny that you haven't wondered yourself why they bothered to get married."

"They must have loved each other in the beginning. Or I wouldn't exist."

He actually had the audacity to laugh at that. "Sex and love can be mutually exclusive."

"I know that." And now, dammit, she had to ask. "Do you love her?"

The pause, which Charlotte knew was only a moment, seemed to last forever. She held her breath, waiting for an answer to a question that only this morning she never would have imagined that she'd be asking.

"I don't know," he said finally.

Even as the answer was like a dagger to her heart, Charlotte refused to lower herself and give him the satisfaction of asking her if he still, in some small way, loved her. Or ever had.

"Well, then." She stood up and began carrying her barely touched plate into the kitchen. "My trip to Oregon will give you time to decide the answer to that question. Because, when it comes to marriage, I am *not* my mother." Yet, it was her mother's cool, controlled voice Charlotte heard coming out of her mouth while everything inside her was trembling like a leaf in a hurricane.

She was in the kitchen when she heard the sound of the front door open and close. It was not the first time Mason had simply walked out on an argument.

Damn, how she hated when he did that! Treating her as if any upset between them was her fault. She listened to the sound of the heavy metal garage door lifting. As his car backed out of the garage and headed out to the road, she wondered if all those other times he'd left, he'd been on the way to his mistress's condo.

But he wasn't the only one who could coldly walk away. Leaving the dishes for that housekeeper who'd always behaved as if Charlotte was an interloper in Mason's overly decorated house, she went upstairs and retrieved the suitcase she'd packed earlier. Then, feeling too shaky to risk driving, she called a cab to take her to the airport.

8

Mount Hood was wearing a halo of lenticular clouds as the Delta jet approached PDX. In the distance, Tess could see the rugged peak of Mount Rainier. The last time she'd flown into Portland, on that hectic book tour trip, Rainier had been hiding in its self-made cloud cover.

Donovan Brees was waiting for her at the baggage claim area. He'd ditched the lawyer suit for a pair of jeans and a blue-and-black-plaid flannel shirt over a black Henley and tan hiking boots. He was still hot, but in an easier, more approachable way.

"I need to pick up Rowdy at excess baggage," she told him. "I decided I'm glad you suggested I bring him. This way I'll have someone on my side."

"There aren't going to be sides," he assured her. "Everything's very straightforward."

They'd been walking toward the counter where she'd been told her dog would be waiting when she stopped and looked up at him. "I distinctly remember you saying the reason that I needed to be here was that it was complicated."

"It was. Is. But less so now that all of you have agreed to

come. I'll have to admit that I thought you'd be the holdout. Charlotte and Natalie will be arriving tomorrow."

"That should be fun," she said drily. The idea of meeting her two half sisters was far from the high point of her day. Reminding herself that the reading of the will couldn't take that much time, she decided to focus on the remainder of this trip. Her visit to wine country. She was still hopeful that driving through the vineyards, and even over to the coast, she might come up with a new story idea. Perhaps she should try a thriller. Drown a person in a vat of wine. Put them through a winepress.

She wasn't certain what, exactly, a winepress even looked like, but wouldn't it have to be large to press grapes for a commercial winery? That could be a good way to murder people. Like the wood chipper in the Coen brothers film *Fargo*. Perhaps an easygoing vintner, popular with both townspeople and tourists alike, could, in a dark secret life, be a serial killer. But where would he hide the bodies?

"Do wineries still have caves, like I've seen in movies?" Those movies had been set in France, during World War II, but that might still be a possibility.

"Not all. But Maison de Madeleine is one of two in Oregon that does have natural ones. They're a series of connected lava caves."

"That could work," she mused. Then realized she'd spoken out loud, a habit she'd developed by living and working alone.

"I was just playing with a plot idea," she explained as they reached the window where she handed over the paperwork and was allowed in a room containing lost luggage and a large gray crate with red "live animal" stickers. The moment they entered the room, enthusiastic barking came from the crate.

She crouched down and opened the door. As soon as she'd unhooked the harness clip, Rowdy dashed out and nearly knocked her down, vocalizing with wild canine glee. After duly welcoming Tess with many dog kisses over her face, he noticed Donovan, and recognizing him from Sedona, practically dragged her across the three feet separating them as he bounded over to greet him, his tail wildly wagging.

Since the lawyer was too tall for the dog to stand up and put his paws on his shoulders as he always did with Tess whenever she returned from a trip into town, he headbutted Donovan's crotch, still barking in a way that sounded more like speech than a nuisance bark.

"Hello, gorgeous boy." Tess reluctantly gave Donovan points for appearing not at all disturbed at having a fifty-pound dog's head colliding with his junk. He squatted down so Rowdy could give him the same wet-faced welcome he had Tess. "Does he always talk like this?" he asked as he rubbed the large head and ran his hand down the setter's neck, which had the dog rolling over in a paroxysm of canine joy, offering his stomach to be rubbed.

"Only when he's overly excited or happy," she said. Although Irish setters' personality meters were set at joyfully friendly, she was, yet again, a bit irked by how easily he shared his favors with Donovan Brees. "Setters aren't nuisance barkers."

"I had a cocker spaniel growing up," he said. "She was the same way. A bundle of energy and joy."

"Damn it, you're doing it again."

"What?" He stood up, holding on to the dog's leash to keep him from racing rings around all the luggage carousels. Which, having been penned up for over two hours, he was all too likely to do.

"Being likeable. Even worse, you had a cocker, which is one of the sweetest dogs on the planet."

He laughed, a rich, deep baritone that drew the attention

of more than one woman walking past. "Not all lawyers are sharks."

"Maybe not here in the Pacific Northwest." She wondered if this man was normal for the area, or an anomaly. "But I never ran across one like you in California." She'd certainly met more than her share, especially after having been sued by her record company for not finishing her third worldwide tour in as many years.

"This isn't California." He handed her the leash. "Why don't you take him outside to the pet relief area right out those doors, while I collect your luggage?"

It made the most sense, she decided as she handed him the claim tickets. "It's a medium-size royal blue Titanium bag with an oversize red tag with my last initial on it."

He took the claim tag. "Got it."

Tess led Rowdy out to the small dog area created with some sort of bark mulch. As energetic as the dog was, fortunately, his temperament didn't run to nervous because not only was the location across the busy main terminal roadway from the parking garage, it was also situated beneath an overpass from which the thud of tires and roar of engines echoed.

Donovan—she was now thinking of him by his first name, rather than *lawyer man*—turned out to be as efficient as he was friendly because Tess soon found herself riding along the river, while Rowdy sat up in the back seat, taking in the scenery.

"How was the flight?"

"Uneventful. I mostly read. About..." She paused, deciding that referring to a man who'd done even half of what the articles about him had claimed as merely a *sperm donor* was both juvenile and spiteful. "Jackson."

It was the first time she'd ever said his name aloud. It felt foreign on her tongue. But not as strange as *Dad* would have been. She'd never called any of her stepfathers by anything other than their first names. Except for William Moore, who she'd only called *Daddy* on the series. But he'd also been the only father figure she'd ever known. And look how that had turned out.

"Did you learn anything you didn't know?"

"Quite a bit, actually. If the stories were even halfway true, he lived life to the fullest, that's for sure." She'd also come to realize why her mother had been swept off her feet, and also, why they'd had no choice but to divorce. She certainly couldn't have been married to a man who was never home and deliberately putting himself in danger all the time.

"All I've ever known is that my mother met him on a USO military tour when she was an actress. Shortly afterward, he took a few days off to visit her in California for the preview of a movie she'd been in. Unfortunately, her scene got cut, so he took her to Vegas to cheer her up, where, as the story goes, they got drunk and woke up married. Although she didn't know it yet, she also got pregnant with me. Obviously, the marriage didn't last."

But surprisingly, from her mother's wistful tone when she'd mentioned first loves during their phone call, it sounded as if she'd never entirely stopped loving him. Over the past years, she'd watched all her mother's movies as she moved from extra, to talking extra, to bit player, to lead in a series of low-cost B movies, some of which had gone directly to video, not even attempting a theater release. She'd also appeared in three *Star Trek* episodes because, as the casting director had apparently told her, she was sex on a stick and her long legs were created for those miniskirts women tended to wear on planets the Enterprise's crew would visit in the exploration of space.

Amy Swann had always claimed she was a terrible actress. Which had, unfortunately, been true. But she had a spark that lit up a screen, which during Tess's younger years had gotten her enough work that she didn't have to, in her words, "sleep with a bunch of hairy old farts."

Tess had been nine, and already working on *Double Trouble*, when twelve-year-old Denny Marksem—who'd played the older bad boy her nerdy character had had a secret crush on—had explained what her mother had been talking about. But he'd been more graphic, referring to it as "sucking some producer's dick," which he'd then had to explain. She could still remember the embarrassing color flooding her face, and as much as she'd liked him, she'd been extremely grateful that was the last episode they'd done together. Because she would have had difficulty looking Denny in the eye after that.

Her career had begun serendipitously. When she was two years old, her mother had been auditioning for a soap opera role with a producer she'd worked with before, and, unable to afford a sitter, had brought Tess along.

"And who is this pretty little girl?" he'd asked, tipping her chin up for a closer look.

"I'm Teth," she'd responded with, as the story went, what had been an "adorable" lisp. "Who are you?"

"I'm Benjamin. But you can call me Ben." He shot Amy a look. "You've been holding out on me," he said. "Sweetheart, do you like cookies?"

"Ben." She'd huffed out a breath. "Everybody likes cookies," she'd scoffed with the same don't-fool-with-me-brush-off attitude she'd tried pulling off with Donovan Brees. She didn't remember the occasion that had put her life on a fast track, but her mother loved telling the story at parties, so she'd had it memorized by the time she was three.

"Do you like Giggles cookies?"

"I lurve Giggles cookies!" And without any cue, she began giggling, pretending she was eating one of the cookies with the laughing emoji-type face. Her voice, her mother had claimed, had people coming out of offices to see where the musical, happy giggles were coming from. "They're my bestest cookies, aren't they, Mommy?"

"Yes, of course," Amy had answered, going on to tell listeners that, in truth, she'd never allowed her daughter to eat sweets because she couldn't afford to get cavities filled.

As it had turned out, the cookie's manufacturer had been searching all over for a little girl who could giggle. Which Tess, who'd also inherited her mother's talent for garnering attention, could. In spades.

Six weeks later Tess's infectious giggle was causing people to laugh in front of their TVs all over the country. By the time she was four, she'd appeared in commercials for American Girl dolls, many sugary cereals—another thing she'd been forbidden to eat—LEGOs, and even Toyota had put her in the back seat of a minivan with a Labrador retriever on a supposed vacation road trip with her parents. During that time Amy had married the producer, moving them into a house in the flats of Beverly Hills.

"The most amazing thing," Amy would say with maternal pride, "was that she would always profess that every commercial item she was up for—toys, food, amusement parks—were supposedly her most favorite. And I didn't even train her. She's a natural."

Aberdeen's welcome sign included the usual list of civic groups, and with small-town pride claimed it to be the home of a national spelling bee championship and a country singer whose name Tess recognized, but whose music she'd never heard. In addition, another sign invited tourists to the visitors' bureau to pick up maps to local wineries and tasting rooms.

The main street, lined with trees in tall planter boxes surrounded by a profusion of spring daffodils and tulips, reminded her of the set in *Double Trouble*, and much like the town she'd created for her fictional students to attend school. It could have been used on a tourist bureau postcard for the area, or, she considered, still toying with the idea of writing suspense, the type of town that could harbor simmering, long-held feuds leading to a murder. They passed the high school, home of the Aberdeen Highlanders. The message on the changeable school sign reminded students that tickets for the Creative Media Student Showcase were now on sale.

The storefronts had been painted in colors that appeared to echo various wines, from the deep purple of a cabernet sauvignon to the pale yellow of a Pinot Grigio. There were the expected wine-tasting rooms and for those who wanted to learn to prepare special meals to eat with their wine, a kitchen shop that also had a cooking school on the premises. A rainbow of yarn stacked in baskets brightened the windows of a yarn shop, while the window of Your Next Read bookstore had a display of wine-themed books. Next door was an organic candle shop like those that proliferated in Sedona, and beside it, beneath a vine-green-and-white-striped awning, the front windows of Left Bank Patisserie tempted with a dazzling display of pastries. On the corner was a larger building housing a market with a mural of workers picking grapes painted on the dusty red brick.

"This may not be bustling like Napa," she observed. "But obviously, tourism is high on the income-producing scale."

"It helps pay the bills," he agreed. "Though we are getting more and more tech companies moving up here from Silicon Valley and down from the Seattle area. Like I said, it's a quieter lifestyle, so we attract businesses whose workers mostly telecommute."

"It reminds me a bit of what old-timers tell me Sedona was like. Before it became a New Age mecca."

"We're more fortunate in that most of our land is taken

up with agriculture, so it's harder for the fast food places and chains to move in. Salem has the big-box stores, so people in Aberdeen figure they have the best of both worlds."

After passing through the town, they were back into miles of green vineyards with the coastal mountains in the distance wearing a hood of clouds. Although the scenery, bathed in the glow of a flaming red-and-gold sunset, was beautiful, so far Oregon's Willamette Valley wasn't giving Tess what she needed.

"The red soil reminds me a bit of Sedona," she murmured after they'd left the city behind and were following an empty, curving road westward with the river on one side, gently rolling hills covered with rows and rows of leafy green staked vines on the other. In other ways, it couldn't be more different. In contrast to Arizona's crisp, dry air, a light rain had begun splashing onto the windshield. Donovan had set the SUV for fresh-air intake, which she'd been enjoying, despite the fact that she could practically feel her curly hair tripling in size and turning into springs.

"It's basalt volcanic, which, although I'm definitely no geologist, I'm told makes it ideal for growing grapes. Gideon Byrne, he's the vintner, can explain it a lot better than I can. I'm sorry Jackson had to die too young, but at least you're here at a time when the valley really comes alive. Wait until you see the grapes ripening. It's gorgeous."

"You were right about it being truly lovely," she said. "But I don't intend to be here that long." Tess planned to attend the reading of the will, turn down her share of the property, giving it to the other two half sisters, and buckle down on her search for a story.

"You never know," he said mildly as he turned off the main road onto a gravel-paved lane.

"Yes. I do."

"There's something I need to tell you," he said. "I didn't earlier, because I didn't want to be accused of emotional co-ercion." That got her attention, but before she could ask, he said, "You have a grandmother."

"She's still alive?"

"She is, and quite well, given that she's ninety-six. Though we did have a little excitement this morning when she had some slight heart fibrillations. She insisted she was fine and initially refused to be hospitalized when the doctor told her he was going to admit her for observation. She can be stub-born, which is undoubtedly partly what's kept her alive all these years, but then, Mrs. White—she's the housekeeper—reminded her that she wouldn't be able to meet her grand-daughters if she was dead. That did the trick."

"Oh no! Is she doing all right now?"

"From what I was told while waiting for your flight to land, she's doing fine. The doctor believes the fibrillation was an understandable reaction to the stress of your father's death, along with excitement about finally getting to meet you. Which, erring on the side of caution, has been delayed until tomorrow."

"Are you certain she'll be up for what will undoubtedly be a stressful situation for her?"

"The doctor believes she can handle it. And, quite hon-estly, I think having the three of you there will lift her spir-its. Except for that heart issue, despite her advanced years, she still gardens and likes to cook. Her French dishes beat any I've eaten anywhere. And although we're obviously not Paris, Or-egon has gotten some good press for its food scene. Not just in Portland, but many smaller towns, as well. Several of the wineries have gone beyond the usual tasting dishes and have added restaurants."

"I can cook, but except for Julia Child's recipe for beef

Bourguignon, which I taught myself to make after watching *Julie & Julia* three times and buying the cookbook, French cuisine is beyond my skillset."

"Madeleine is originally from Burgundy and grew up when farm to table, or, as they say here, vine to table, was the everyday way of living."

"Small world," Tess murmured. When Donovan glanced over at her, she clarified. "I did a concert in Dijon." It had been a spur-of-the-moment occasion, after her tour bus had broken down outside the capital city on the way from Bern, Switzerland, to Paris. It was also free and within two hours of the announcement that Tess Donovan was in the city, all six hundred and ninety-one seats were claimed. It had been her smallest venue on the tour, but the audience had been one of her most enthusiastic.

"When did she come here?"

"1946."

"Was she a war bride?"

"One of many. She was also part of the French Resistance. She met—and rescued—your grandfather when his plane crashed in the woods near her family's vineyards."

"Wow. Okay, now I am really annoyed that it's taken me this long to meet her."

"She's very excited about you all coming. Actually thrilled. I think you're going to like her. Everyone does."

A story stirred. Just a whisper of an idea of a heroine French resistor. Not that Tess knew all what those resisting the Germans in France had been doing. But she'd been hoping for some inspiration. And perhaps, just possibly, this could be it.

He drove around a bend, then went through a wrought-iron gate that opened when he pushed a series of numbers into the control on the dashboard. A script letter *M* in a circle was in the center of the gate and five minutes after they'd passed down a tree-lined lane, they came to a calligraphed sign announcing Maison de Madeleine.

She couldn't hold back a gasp as a large house came into view that would have looked at home in seventeenth-century France. Built of gray stone, with a red-tiled roof, it rose elegantly above the vineyards. The entry towered upward, with rows of windows across the front of the house with more on the second story, four with dormers. A riot of creamy camellias, scarlet azaleas and burgundy rhododendrons bloomed around a fountain in the center of a large stone circular driveway while rows of fringed parrot tulips lined the beds in front of the house like red-and-yellow sentries.

"You've got to be kidding me." Tess had not lived a sheltered life. There was little that could surprise or shock her. But the house that she recognized from the label on the bottles of wine, named for a grandmother she'd never met, stunned.

"My father grew up here?" She'd never given his childhood much thought, but if asked, she never would have pictured this.

"Until he was eighteen. Gideon Byrne, who you'll be meeting, has taken care of both the grapes and the business since your grandfather died ten years ago."

What would it have been like if they'd been a normal family who enjoyed holidays together? If, perhaps, she'd spent summers here in this stunningly beautiful place with its vineyards, orchards, gardens and a chateau out of a fairy tale, visiting her grandparents, instead of working on sound stages?

"My mother didn't know anything about it, either."

"Like I said, my dad handled both the winery and Jack's photography business, once he went freelance, which allowed him to choose his own assignments. Although he never shared his feelings about it with me, my guess is that he thought that it'd ruin his tough adventurer's image if people, especially other photographers he worked with, had known he grew up in such a bucolic place in what could be considered a mansion."

"*Could* be?"

"Perhaps Robert got carried away, but the house was literally built from love. Madeleine was homesick, so he attempted to replicate the house she'd grown up in. Her family was descended from royalty and had owned one of the most prestigious vineyards in Burgundy. In later years Jack came back at least once a year, at times more often, to decompress. Having known him all my life, I could tell that all the death, destruction and horrors he'd witnessed for so many years were taking a toll on him."

"So essentially he came back here to die."

"He did. But it was fast."

"Damn him." Tess had told herself that she'd quit having any feelings toward Jackson Swann years ago. But the loss still stung. Not so much grief, but anger that he'd never known her. Or she him. She'd occasionally wondered what might have happened if she'd tracked him down, which given his fame, wouldn't have been all that difficult. Now she'd never know. "So many missed opportunities."

"He was all too aware of that. At least at the end. Which is one of the reasons he wanted his daughters to meet."

"I don't know what he thought he'd be accomplishing. From what you've told me, the only thing the three of us have in common is the fact that we shared a DNA donor."

"That's harsh."

She folded her arms. Turned and looked away at the orchards nestled in the lee of one of the hills, their trees wearing pretty pink flower spring coats. "You can't survive in LA without developing a Kevlar hide."

"I'm sorry." Both his expression and his tone matched his words. "My father always said that Jack didn't believe he deserved to be happy. That he felt guilty about only being a by-stander to evil, not doing anything to help."

Tess sighed. "I saw his photos with the articles." Some of which she'd recognized from newspapers and magazine covers. To call them brutal would have been an understatement and more than a few had caused her to tear up, drawing an occasional sideways glance from her seatmate. "He documented tragedy. He made people look at it. Bringing atrocities into the light must have made some difference." Yet, who'd choose that life? Why? And what would it do to you?

"It undoubtedly did. But it also left deep scars."

"That still doesn't excuse his personal choices."

"No. It doesn't. And I'm not trying to make excuses. Merely explain."

What was she doing here? She'd long gotten over the man's abandonment. She'd proven that she hadn't needed him. Despite having won all those awards, it wasn't as if he was a household name, except among those in the journalism world. While she'd not only had two very successful careers—two out of three wasn't bad—she'd bet she'd earned more. She hadn't needed his damn money. She'd needed *him*.

"I hate this," she said.

"Join the club," he said as he parked in front of the wide entry steps.

9

Tess had no sooner gotten out of the SUV when the front door of the mansion opened and a sixtysomething-year-old woman wearing a burgundy-colored sweatshirt with the Chateau de Madeleine logo on the front, a pair of khaki pants and sensible brown leather shoes came out of the house, heading toward her.

"You'd be Tess," she said. "And aren't you the picture of your grandmother when she was younger? Welcome to Oregon!"

"Thank you." It had been surprise enough that she even *had* a grandmother, let alone a French war bride that she resembled. "I hope you don't mind." Damn, she should have checked to make certain Rowdy would be welcome. "But I brought my dog."

"Of course not. And what a beauty!" The woman looked into the back seat where Rowdy was jumping and straining against the harness Tess had put on for the short road trip. "Boy or girl?"

"Boy. His name is Rowdy, and I'll confess that while he has a habit of living up to his name, he really is quite well behaved. When he hasn't been in a plane for two hours, then a car from PDX."

"Poor baby." She bent down to pat the dog, who'd leaped from the vehicle as soon as he was unfastened from the seat belt harness. Proving that all those obedience classes Tess had gone through with him when he'd first arrived from Texas had kicked in, Rowdy immediately sat on his haunches in front of the woman whose name she still hadn't learned.

"Tess, this is Mrs. White," Donovan said. "She runs the house and private grounds. I guess you could call her our majordomo, like Higgins in *Magnum P.I.*"

"He exaggerates," the woman said, waving the words off. "And despite the look of the house, we're not formal around here. Just call me Rose. Your grandmother and I used to watch your television program all the time. That must have been difficult for a girl of your young age. Playing two such disparate characters."

"It could be a challenge. But a fun one."

"Well, you certainly brought a lot of enjoyment into this house every Wednesday night. We were so sorry when it was suddenly canceled."

"Thank you. We all were sorry, too." They'd been in negotiations for a three-season extension when the scandal had broken.

"But look at you now." Rose White crossed her arms, leaned back and gave Tess a long study. "All grown up and pretty as a picture."

"Thank you, that's very nice of you to say." Apparently now fully recovered from the flight, Rowdy tugged on the leash, ready for their next adventure.

"We'd best get you two settled in. Aubrey, that'd be our vintner's teenage daughter, has been wanting a dog. She's going to be thrilled."

Tess decided against repeating yet again that she'd be leaving, with Rowdy, as soon as the will was read.

"Since Rose will take good care of you, I guess I'll be getting back to the office," Donovan said. "I have an appointment for an adoption finalization in court this afternoon."

"That must be a more pleasant part of your work than dealing with death notifications and will readings," Tess said.

"The adoptive parents already had one surrogate adoption fall through last year," he said. "This time they're adopting an eleven-year-old boy they've been fostering, which, yeah, makes it an even better day to be a lawyer." His smile lit up his eyes.

Donovan Brees was a good man, Tess considered as he drove away. Which made her feel a bit guilty at how rude she'd been to him.

As imposing as the stone house was from the outside, Tess was surprised how comfortably inviting the interior turned out to be. The wide-planked cherry floors had been hand-scraped and the aged depth of the red tone suggested that they were original to the house. The walls, curved at the corners, had been painted a creamy pale gold, with towering arched windows designed to welcome every bit of sun this rainy Oregon valley might experience and offered a breathtaking view of vineyards, rolling hills and the peak of Mount Hood rising above its cloak of dark clouds. The furniture was solid, either purposely distressed or well lived in, and looked as though it had been taken from a Provençal farmhouse. A huge wrought-iron chandelier hung from the open beams in the living room, and a stone fireplace soared nearly to the cathedral ceiling.

"It's spectacular," Tess said. "But comfortable. At first I thought it looked a little out of place, but once you get inside and take in the view of the vineyards, it's like being transported to the French countryside."

"Your grandfather worked with the builder and your grandmother had some of her family's furniture shipped from France." Rose gazed around. "Though, like all older homes, it could definitely use some updating. Perhaps your sister Charlotte might have some ideas."

When she'd Googled Charlotte Aldredge, Tess had learned that Jackson's second daughter had attended a prestigious Southern design school, graduated with an MFA and had established a promising career, working on both residential and commercial properties. She also had a popular design blog focusing on achieving personal style titled *Your Home Your Way*, and was married to an attorney. She had noticed there'd been fewer recent projects. The last property she'd found on Houzz was a master bedroom redo. Tess suspected that the couple's appearance at so many social charity events could have a great deal to do with that. Seeing the focus of the online photos and articles change from Charlotte's work to what she was wearing at such events suggested that she'd surrendered a career she must have worked hard for in order to become a trophy wife.

"Let me show you to your room," the housekeeper said, breaking into Tess's thoughts. "Madeleine found the house too large after her husband, Robert, died a few years ago. She said she felt as if she was rattling around in it, so she moved into the guesthouse. There are five bedrooms, each with its own bath, so each of you girls will have your own private space."

In the spirit of harmony, Tess decided not to mention that she was no longer a girl. A girl who had never been invited to visit her father's family. And having only had a roommate during her short time in Hell House, her name for the boarding school her mother had sent her to, she had no desire to share a room now.

"What was my grandfather like?" she asked as they climbed

the stairs, keeping Rowdy on his leash, planning to take him for a walk as soon as she'd claimed her room.

"He was a quiet man, born right here on what was called the Swann Family Farm back then, and grew up when it was mostly orchard land with some Concord grapes and berries for table wine. That was supposed to have stopped during prohibition, but the Swanns continued to grow the grapes, and stories have a lot of them ending up as wine in Portland mansions and speakeasies."

"My family were bootleggers?" Tess rather liked that idea. It would've made a nice segment on a PBS *Finding Your Roots* episode.

"I wasn't alive back in those old days, so I wouldn't have any firsthand knowledge. But people talk, and while I'm not saying they were, I'm also not saying they weren't. Yet, I suspect not all those grapes and cherries ended up in pies.

"The family went back to making wine after prohibition, but it wasn't until the 1960s that the first Pinot Noir grapes were grown outside Corvallis. One thing led to another, and more and more people got into the business, leading to the valley becoming an important name in wine circles." She paused at the top of the stairs. "Since you arrived ahead of the others, you get first choice of rooms."

Great. Tess suspected that adding room envy to any possible friction among Jackson Swann's daughters would only make an uncomfortable situation even more difficult.

"I'm sure any of them will be fine," she said, putting the choice into the housekeeper's hands.

"They're all lovely," Rose assured her. "But the ones on this side of the house have a view of the mountain." She opened the door and sure enough, the first thing Tess saw was Mount Hood, framed in the window, the mist in the air making it appear to be a watercolor painting backdrop to the rows of vines.

"We have towering red rocks in Sedona, where I live. They're spectacular. But I think they may have met their match." For a fleeting moment Tess imagined waking up to this view every morning, then reminded herself she wouldn't be staying. But she was certainly going to enjoy it for the next few days.

"It's always special when the mountain is out," Rose agreed. "Though I'll admit that we locals probably take it for granted. Living here, as we do, in God's country."

Tess stifled a smile at hearing the familiar term, even as she couldn't deny that this valley was definitely one of nature's more beautiful places. Apparently, Rowdy agreed, because he surprised her by immediately circling three times on a thick rug, then settling down in a slice of sunshine with a satisfied, happy dog moan.

"You were telling me about the winery's history," Tess said.

"I was, and this is my favorite part. After Robert married your grandmother, he planted Pinot Noir and Chardonnay vines, which her family had grown in their vineyards back home. Originally, he tried planting vines that Madeleine's family had given him in gratitude for him having helped save their country. But only one of those adjusted to their new land, so the fledgling wine business stayed local as Robert kept the orchard while buying more vines from California. That was about when my mother, who'd been widowed young, came to work for them. Truth be told, I had a crush on Robert for a while in my teens. He was, after all, a war hero, and sinfully handsome. Your father was the image of him."

When Tess failed to respond to that, the housekeeper continued her monologue. "According to Mother, Madeleine was so homesick he built this house, which resembles the one she'd grown up in, and named it after her. That was when he changed the name of the farm."

"That's why the house looks as if it belongs in France, rather than Oregon, like most of the others we passed driving here from Portland."

"That's why. Since my mother had a house on the property, I grew up here and to me this always felt like being in a castle. Just like a princess in a fairy tale... Well, I'll leave you to your unpacking while I fix you some supper."

"Please, don't go to any bother. I ate on the plane."

"Still, you might be wanting a snack later, after your long day. Are you sweet or savory? More cheese and crackers or cakes and cookies? It's your choice. I want you to feel comfortable."

And wouldn't that take a miracle? "Really, I don't need—"

"A mix," Rose decided. "I'll bring it up shortly."

"That's not necessary," Tess tried again.

"It's no problem. It'll help you settle in before the others arrive tomorrow, and things could get complicated."

As if they weren't already.

"I really need to take Rowdy for a walk." Both women glanced over at the dog, who was now happily snoring from his sunbeam.

"Why don't you do that," Rose agreed easily without mentioning that he seemed perfectly content just where he was. "And I'll have a plate ready for you when you get back. There's certainly enough space for him to run here."

With that, she left the room, leaving Tess to wonder, yet again, what the hell she was doing here.

10

The flight, which had her changing planes in Atlanta, gave Charlotte plenty of time to think about events she'd locked away into one of the compartmentalized boxes in her mind. Like her concerns about her father. And why, whatever she did, she never seemed to be able to please her mother, who, for as long as she could remember, disliked her so.

No. That was an exaggeration. Dislike was, at least, an emotion. Something her ice queen of a mother seemed incapable of. Yet, she must have, at one time, possessed at least some passion, or, as Charlotte had reminded Mason, she'd have never been born. Never married Mason.

Having gotten no hint of his true personality during their courtship, she'd naively expected their honeymoon to be equally as idyllic. But although the St. Croix beaches were as spun-sugar beautiful as they'd been in all the brochures and online videos she'd watched, and the stunning house they'd rented was right on the water, Charlotte had sensed a distancing from her groom.

At first she was concerned that something might have happened at the wedding, or someone, perhaps her politically outspoken father, might have said something to annoy him. Then she assured herself that she was being overly romantic by expecting a honeymoon to be perfect. Even with a wedding planner, there'd been so many decisions to make, so many tastings, so many thank-you cards to write, anyone would be stressed out. She'd certainly been when she'd gotten on the plane the morning after the reception with a bit of a hangover from too many champagne toasts. And he'd drunk far more than she had.

If he snapped at the waiter their second day during a seaside lunch at the resort, for taking too long to deliver the bill, it was only, he'd assured her, because he couldn't wait to get back to the house and make mad, passionate love to her.

When he carelessly dropped his towel on the floor after every shower, she told herself that was merely because he'd grown up with servants. As she had. But she'd always hung up her own towels and wiped out her bathroom sink, even when living at home with her parents. Mason had been on his own for several years now. She hoped he didn't expect her to pick up after him during their marriage, then assured herself she was merely overreacting. Even bubbly, optimistic Tara had suffered postpartum depression after each of her children. Could post-wedding blues be a thing?

Perhaps her lack of bridal bliss was due to suddenly having too much downtime after the frenzied pace of planning a wedding—including what friends had assured her were normal arguments with her mother over logistics—while rushing to finish a nursery with attached bath for a client pregnant with twin girls. The project, on the Isle of Palms, had included an adjoining en suite for the nanny. Having factored in the possibility of a premature birth due to the babies being twins, Charlotte had been ahead of schedule when the stone supplier delivered the same marble for both bathrooms. It was a beauti-

ful white Tuscan Carrara, its light gray veining thin and feath-
ery, making it one of the more popular stones used in homes.

Unfortunately, the expectant mother, wanting something
different from all her friends, had chosen a pure, sparkling
white—and highly impractical for children, Charlotte had
warned—Greek Thassos marble for her twin princesses' bath.

With the timeline in danger of blowing up, and a hormonal
client having a meltdown, Charlotte had gotten on the phone
and found a supplier in Atlanta who'd not only had the Thassos in stock but had also put the slab on a truck that very same
day. Crisis averted and working nearly around the clock, she'd
finished the project two days before her client went into early
labor and a mere three days before her wedding.

After the past months of nonstop activity, it only made sense
that she'd be exhausted. She wasn't clinically depressed, she'd
assured herself. Just suffering a bit of a letdown because she
wasn't having the grand fun that couples on the resort's website always appeared to be enjoying. She just needed to take a
deep breath and allow herself to relax. They'd certainly come
to the right place for that, even if Mason had kept taking calls
from his office. Which now had her wondering if they'd been
from Olivia Wainwright.

As the plane approached Portland, she viewed the city
spread out beneath her, the lights of several bridges crossing
what the interactive flight map on the back of the seat in front
of her revealed to be the Willamette River shining beneath
her. One double-spanned bridge appeared to be putting on a
light show with strikingly changing colors.

She'd called Donovan Brees before leaving Charleston, in-
forming him of her change in plans. As the wheels hit the
runway, she was rethinking what for her had been an unfath-
omably rash decision. It would have been nice to have the
lawyer waiting there to take care of the rest of the trip. Then

she reminded herself that before allowing Mason to chip away at her self-confidence, she'd flown by herself to New York, Paris, Madrid and even India, which had proven a treasure trove for textiles. The rental car would have a GPS, so how hard would it be to find her way from Portland to Aberdeen?

"Just breathe," she murmured as the plane taxied to the terminal. While deplaning, she managed to hold back another of the panic attacks that she'd never experienced before all the pressure to get pregnant. She left the jetway into the terminal brightly lit with high, open-beamed ceilings and trees in big boxes lining the concourses.

She paused to watch a busker wearing a cowboy hat playing a rollicking, honky-tonk rendition of Johnny Cash's "I've Been Everywhere." Three little children, siblings from the look of them, burned off travel energy by dancing to the up-beat music, and she felt the tension that had been tangling her nerves and causing her heart to beat like a snare drum begin to ease. When the song ended, she dropped some bills into his fiddle case, causing him to tip his hat. His Texas-drawled "Thanks, pretty lady" lifted spirits that Mason had crushed only a few hours ago.

The young woman at the Hertz counter proved equally friendly, taking time to explain the directions to Aberdeen, even drawing the route on the old-fashioned paper map that came with the claim ticket. She also put an Oregon State tourism guide in the bag. Not that Charlotte intended to stay long enough to see all the wonders allegedly included within the glossy pages, but it was a nice bonus.

By the time she'd found her car and left the terminal, following the signs that would lead her to her father's home, she'd decided that she hadn't made a mistake coming alone. It was giving her more time to calm down. To think. And hopefully decide what her next move would be. When and if Mason contacted her.

A light shower, more mist than rain, added a glossy sheen to the street in the glow of the headlights. And while it wasn't a yellow brick road, having just had her life turned upside down by an emotional tornado, Charlotte felt a bit like Dorothy, headed off into the unknown on an adventure.

11

After a surprisingly good night's sleep, Tess was sitting at a table in what she'd been told was the breakfast room, looking out over the vineyard. Although she usually just settled for yogurt and a muffin before starting writing, she was indulging in light-as-air lemon-ricotta-blueberry pancakes topped with brown sugar and butter. The berries, Rose had informed her, had been grown on the premises. The crisp, thick-cut bacon had been sourced from a local organic farm and the coffee she was drinking was from organic, fair-trade, light-roasted beans grown in the mountains of Colombia.

From the enthusiasm with which the housekeeper imparted all these details, Tess got the impression that Donovan had been serious about Oregon, at least this part of it, being a foodie scene. Which had her idly wondering why, when she Googled the winery last night, she noticed that not only was any connection to Jackson Swann not mentioned, it didn't offer a tasting menu either, as many neighboring vineyards did.

Not that it was any of her business, but still, it seemed whoever ran the place was missing a good profit opportunity. It was just as well that she wasn't intending to stay, she decided, mentally calculating the calorie value of just a single pancake as she cut into her second one.

No. Don't go there. The days when she knew not only every calorie, but also every Weight Watchers point of any food on the planet were over. She was comfortable with her body, comfortable with her life.

"Except for the fact that you never got to show Jackson Swann what he missed out on."

"Excuse me?" A voice with a decidedly Southern accent interrupted her frustrated thoughts.

Tess looked up to see the woman standing in the doorway. She'd taken time to use a curling iron or hot rollers on her shoulder-length blond hair and was wearing makeup, which Tess usually only ever bothered to put on when meeting with her publisher and editors in New York or getting her author photo updated. In sharp contrast to Tess's crinkled, Southwestern-patterned broomstick skirt topped by a T-shirt claiming *My favorite season is the fall of patriarchy*, and well-worn brown cowboy boots, her half sister was wearing a cream silk blouse, taupe linen slacks and a pair of sandals that revealed toenails painted in seashell pink. And pearl stud earrings. She could have been on her way to Sunday brunch at some chichi Charleston restaurant. She was also thin as a rail. But not in a good way, Tess, who knew a great deal about weight issues, considered. Her obvious gauntness suggested she'd either been ill or had some serious emotional problems.

"Hi. You must be Charlotte."

"I am." She paused. "And you're Tess."

"That's me. When did you get here?"

"Late last night."

"I thought Donovan said you were expected this afternoon."

"That was the original plan. But I had an—" she paused,

as if choosing her words carefully "—opportunity to change my flight. Mrs. White told me that breakfast was served in here. She seemed very nice when I woke her up last night."

"It is and she appears to be a gem," Tess agreed. "I got the impression from Donovan that she's more like a member of the family than a housekeeper." A family Tess realized she was, like it or not, now a part of.

As Charlotte sat down at the table, Tess noticed that her eyes were red-rimmed and her face puffy, as if she'd been crying. And at closer examination, blotches showing beneath the carefully applied foundation and shadows beneath her eyes suggested she hadn't gotten any sleep on the plane. Putting herself in her half sister's place, as she had when acting, and now writing, she tried to imagine what Charlotte must be feeling. Grief, certainly, as Tess herself would feel if she lost her mother. Or, even after such a short time, Rowdy. But wouldn't she also be resentful at her parents for keeping such a vital piece of information of two half sisters from her?

"I'm sorry for your loss," she said, sounding like a Hallmark sympathy card.

Charlotte paused while placing the creamy white linen napkin on her lap. For a moment something that appeared like confusion appeared in her eyes, but she recovered so quickly, it could have been Tess's imagination. "Thank you," she said. "This is all so strange."

"You're not going to get any disagreement from me." Tess had managed to create a quiet, uneventful life that suited her that unlike that emotional roller coaster she'd once been caught up in, never changed all that much from day to day. Which was just the way she liked it.

So yeah, she damn well found this entire situation strange as hell.

"In a way, once I was old enough to know what Daddy did

for a living, I worried about him dying." The voice, which sounded as if its owner should be sitting on a veranda sipping sweet tea, broke into Tess's thoughts. "But in another way, deep down, I always considered him invincible. So I'm still having trouble accepting that he's really gone. You know?"

"No." When her sister actually flinched at the sharp tone, Tess softened her voice. "Look, I realize you're hurting. And I'm truly sorry about that. But I never knew the guy. So to be honest, when Donovan told me the news, I didn't have any feelings one way or the other. It was like reading a stranger's obit in the paper."

Which she did nearly every day online. She'd told herself it was to look for names she could use in her books, but the truth was that she was drawn to the daily list of those left behind. Sometimes, she even made up little stories about the mothers, fathers, sisters, brothers and often, given that Arizona was heavily populated with retirees, long lists of grandchildren and great-grandchildren that read like all the begats of the Old Testament. Families had long fascinated her. And now, suddenly, like it or not, she'd landed in the middle of a complicated one.

"I'm sorry you never had the opportunity to know him." Charlotte looked about to say more when Rose bustled in with a table setting and a white cup and saucer.

"Here's your coffee, dear," the housekeeper said, putting a cup down on the table. "Black, no sugar, just as ordered." Her face revealed both concern and disapproval as it skimmed a look over her. "Are you sure I can't get you anything else?"

"No, thank you. I'm not a breakfast eater."

"It's the most important meal of the day," the housekeeper said in a way that had Tess holding back a smile. Donovan had obviously not been exaggerating when he said that the woman ran the house. "The pantry's well stocked. I'd be more than happy to make you anything you'd like."

"Really, I'm fine."

"All right, then. Well, I guess I'd best get back to work. But if you change your mind—"

"I'll be sure and let you know."

They both watched the housekeeper leave the room. Bustled, Tess would have described Rose White if she'd been a character. "The lemon-ricotta pancakes are out of this world," she said, happy to talk about anything rather than their situation. "Apparently, they're our grandmother's favorites."

"They look delicious. But coffee's fine." She took a sip as if to prove her words, but her hand trembled ever so slightly as she lifted the cup to lips perfectly lined in a mauve rose. Something more than grief at the loss of a father was going on here. Tess had a flashback to that day in her teens, when she'd been given a small orange pill to take that had seemed so harmless, but had ended up being a gateway to hell.

"Rose told me about our grandmother being in the hospital," Charlotte said. "I didn't even realize I had a grandmother. Did you?"

"Nope."

"Have you heard any news about her?"

"Apparently, it was just a little heart glitch Donavan said the doctor believes was probably due to all that's been going on. She's supposed to be discharged and back home later today."

"That's good to hear. I never knew anything about my father's family. My mother told me there was a rift, so it was better that I not ever bring it up." She sighed. "I should have pressed her. Or him."

"If there had been a serious rift, it'd be unlikely he'd have wanted to talk about it."

Charlotte sighed. "Which is why I never brought it up." Her

lips curved in a smile that held little humor. "The Southern side of my family doesn't believe in making waves."

"I may not be Southern, but I've certainly been there, done that." Tess had spent the first twenty years of her life allowing others to make all her decisions. At the time, when she'd been younger, it had seemed to make life easier to hand over control to others so she could concentrate on her work. Work that she'd decided long ago had started way too young. If she ever had any children, she was definitely going to try to ensure they'd have a normal childhood. Whatever that entailed.

One pill makes you larger. And one pill makes you small, the lyrics to Jefferson Airplane's "White Rabbit" rang in her mind. "It didn't work out all that well for me." She'd learned the hard way that the lyrics were true: when you chased rabbits, you were bound to fall.

"Me, neither." Those deeply shadowed sky-blue eyes glistened with tears that Tess suspected, yet again, were more than simple grief.

"Donovan told me that they met during the Second World War," Tess said. "Apparently, our grandfather's plane crashed not far from her family's French vineyard."

"Gracious. I wish I would've known. There's undoubtedly a wealth of wonderful stories there."

"I was thinking the same thing." She'd lain awake long into the night, playing with possibilities. And, although it was a terribly selfish thing to consider while an elderly woman's life could be hanging in the balance, Tess hoped Madeleine Swann stayed alive long enough to share her life story, which sounded as if it could offer some valuable grist for that much needed plot.

Charlotte's gaze had drifted back to Tess's breakfast, her expression reminding Tess of a starving Dickensian orphan, looking into the window of a bakery. Hell.

"Here." She removed the saucer from beneath her cup, took a fluffy pancake from the short stack, put it on the saucer and pushed it across the table. "At least try a bite. Believe me, you've never had any better."

Charlotte's wary gaze moved up to Tess's.

"It's okay," Tess said, knowing those tumultuous love-hate emotions regarding food all too well. "It's got blueberries, which have some of the highest antioxidants of all fruits and vegetables. And believe me, there's not a food I don't know all the values of. Including calories, which thankfully I gave up counting years ago, or I wouldn't be experiencing what have to be the best pancakes on the planet."

Recognition flashed in eyes that revealed her half sister's every feeling. Unlike Tess, who'd learned to repress her true emotions early, allowing them to be overlaid with those others had written for her. Then, dammit, despite her determination not to get involved with either of her two half sisters, a moment of shared understanding passed between them.

Charlotte picked up the heavy sterling fork, cut off a sliver of pancake and took a bite. Her expressive eyes closed as a soft sound escaped her lips. "Oh, my God," she murmured. "You're right. This may be the most amazing pancake ever."

"Didn't I tell you? You'd probably make Rose the happiest woman on the planet if you asked for one. Or two."

Bam. Shields up. So Ms. Moonlight and Magnolias could hide her feelings, after all. Tess was reluctantly intrigued. "Perhaps tomorrow," Charlotte said. "But thank you for sharing."

So much for any sisterly bonding. A thick silence settled over them. Tess continued eating, while Charlotte sipped her coffee. They were back to behaving like two strangers forced to share a table in a busy coffee shop.

Rowdy, who'd been in his usual place under the table waiting for a piece of people food to drop, sensed Tess was getting close to finishing and suddenly made an appearance, backing out to sit next to her chair to give her *The Look*.

"Oh!" The silence shattered. "You have a dog!"

"His name's Rowdy. And he's a mooch."

"He's beautiful. And you both have almost the same color hair."

"I guess we do." Her half sister had not been the first person to notice that. "But that's not why I rescued him."

"Of course not." Those shields lowered, revealing, yet again, a near childlike wistfulness. "I always wanted a dog."

"Here." Tess held out the piece of bacon she'd been saving. "Give the gluttonous beast this and he'll be yours for life."

Unlike the pause over the pancake, Charlotte didn't hesitate to take the bacon from Tess's hand. Rowdy, who'd been watching it carefully, immediately bounded the few steps to the other side of the table. And, as if sensing the same vulnerability Tess had felt, instead of the quick snatch and swallow that was his usual habit, he sat and delicately nibbled the bacon down to the last bit.

"He's so beautiful." Charlotte stroked the top of his head.

"He's a rescue, so the name came with him. But believe me, Rowdy fits."

"He seems perfectly behaved to me." She leaned closer and looked the setter in those expressive brown eyes.

"You're a good boy, aren't you, Rowdy?" Charlotte's voice had gone into the singsong tone Tess had seen parents using with their babies. "The very best dog."

Rowdy thumped his tail in agreement on the wooden plank floor. He was accustomed to being admired by strangers. It ranked right up there with bacon, fetching tennis balls and tummy rubs on his canine happiness scale.

"I always wanted a pet." Charlotte repeated her earlier words. "A dog, specifically, though I'd also have loved a cat, which wouldn't have been as much work. But my mother wouldn't allow it."

Because she appeared oddly fragile, perhaps due to losing her father or whatever else was going on, Tess resisted pointing out that it had been a while since she'd lived with her mother. So what was stopping her?

"The first dog I had wasn't really mine," she said instead. "It was rescued from the local shelter for the TV show I was on."

"Double Trouble," Charlotte said. "I watched that show every week for years. I always thought it was cool that we had the same last name. I envied you having a twin. I mean, I knew you were playing both parts, but the idea of having a sister to share clothes and secrets with seemed wonderful. My family was far from the stereotype of a typical TV family. But for an hour a day, I could pretend that your life was mine." Soft color flushed into her cheeks. "And that probably makes me sound terribly foolish."

"Not at all. I felt the same way and I certainly understood those other actors weren't my real family. But it felt like one for all those years... I just realized something. The three of us are only children."

"Not anymore," Charlotte pointed out as she bent down to give Rowdy, who'd collapsed onto his back beside her chair, a belly rub.

And wasn't that something to think about?

"What do you think she's like?" Charlotte asked. "Our other sister."

"All I know is the little bit Donovan told me and what I found online. She's a French photographer who was having a showing in New York when she found out about Jackson's death. She's scheduled to arrive today."

"I honestly had no idea about either one of you. My mother

knew. When I asked her why she'd never mentioned Dad had been married before, she told me that it had never come up."

Although there was nothing humorous about this situation, Tess laughed. "Like every kid asks her parents, 'Hey, Mom, does Dad have another family somewhere out there that you neglected to tell me about?'"

"That's the same thing I said when I called her about you and your mother! She said Daddy had already moved on when they met. As for Natalie and her mother, Mother said it didn't have anything to do with her, so there was no reason to bring them up, either."

"I've never been married, but I've witnessed enough break-ups to have decided that marriages are complicated."

"That's definitely true." Charlotte wondered why Tess had never married. It wasn't as if she wouldn't have had opportunities. Though the feminist message on her T-shirt was not something women in the properly stultifying Southern circle she'd grown up in would ever wear.

Although it wasn't easy to admit, during the drive down here from PDX, in the tiny car that had apparently been the only one available, with rain and the dark creating the sense that she was all alone in the world, Charlotte had realized she shouldn't be all that surprised by Mason's affair. Especially now that she'd learned that her father had had a mistress for nearly three decades. And she had friends whose husbands had strayed during their marriage. Most simply ignored it, seeming to take the "men will be men" idea that she'd actually heard used as an excuse for such behavior.

Others—like her mother—countered with their own affairs. Something, as she'd told Mason, Charlotte couldn't imagine doing, although there were times when she'd wondered if she was hopelessly old-fashioned, expecting wedding vows to be taken seriously.

In a way, the timing of her father's death could prove to be another gift he'd given her. If she'd stayed in Charleston, she might have been forced to watch Mason indulging in an affair with that woman. Perhaps even openly, now that she'd discovered his infidelity. And that was all it was. He couldn't really be in love. He'd come to his senses once he realized how much he risked losing. They were, after all, planning a family. A family he'd already stated was important for his political image. Her husband was too ambitious to risk having both a pregnant wife and a mistress. That sounded like something they might do in France. Which brought her mind back to her youngest sister.

"My mother used to take me to Paris Fashion Week."

"My mother went occasionally when I was growing up. I think most every year since she married into a Greek shipping fortune," Tess replied.

"The French intimidate me," Charlotte confessed.

"I always found them very friendly when I was touring during my pop days."

"You were superfamous, so everyone was undoubtedly thrilled to meet you."

Tess shrugged. "I suspect it had more to do with the music crowd being different, more open to various social behaviors, than the high-priced, high-fashion one."

"I just hope she's not snooty."

"Why would you care? It's not as if we're going to be cheerfully bonded together like *The Brady Bunch* after the will reading."

Charlotte tilted her head. "If you feel that way, why are you here?"

"Good question." Rowdy had moved back to Tess's chair, a pleading look seemingly meant to assure her that fluffy ricotta lemon pancakes were his new favorite thing. Tess placed her hand on his long, lean head. "I have no earthly idea."

Well, so far, this wasn't exactly going well. Despite the sharing of the pancake, which, under other circumstances, Charlotte wouldn't have let past her lips, her half sister certainly hadn't seemed open to a relationship.

What did you expect? she asked herself. *That you'd all immediately bond? Like Tess's sarcastic Brady Bunch remark?* Unfortunately, the pitiful truth was that was exactly what she'd been hoping.

She understood Tess's resentment, but the eldest of the sisters didn't seem to have an iota of regret about losing their father. Undoubtedly because she'd already lost him at such a young age. So she'd simply moved on with her life and never looked back. It occurred to Charlotte that possessing that ability might make Tess the most like their father of all of them. It'd be interesting to see once Natalie arrived how much she resembled him.

"Do you hate me?"

Tess, who'd risen to take her plate and cup into the kitchen, looked back over her shoulder in surprise. "Of course not. Why would I?"

"Because our father left your mother and married mine."

She shrugged. "Five years passed between when he left us and married your mother. It wasn't as if they'd been carrying on some torrid affair. So no, I don't hate you. At all. And I am sorry you're hurting."

She *was* hurting. Deeply. Because, as she'd flown here from Charleston, it had occurred to Charlotte that she'd lost the only person who'd ever unconditionally loved her. Her mother had always treated her as an inconvenience.

And Mason...well, after that first rush of courtship—an old-fashioned word, but it had felt more like that than mere dating—he'd taken her for granted. As if she were some 1950s housewife who'd do his every bidding. Which, she was forced to admit, dammit, she had.

She'd never been all that introspective, going along with the role set out for her by societal norms. Even when she'd been determined to have a career, she'd chosen one that didn't stray too far out of the box women in her circle were supposed to be happy to dwell in.

Despite Tess's words, Charlotte suspected her newly found half sister had to have been wounded by their father's desertion. How must it be to feel you'd been unwanted by a parent? In her younger years she'd wished for a closer connection with her mother. Even the loud, door-slamming fights Tara had described with her own mother during their teens would have been an improvement over the chilly distance she'd received. Fighting at least demonstrated emotion. Which her mother seemed to lack. The same way Mason had been so matter-of-fact about his affair.

It was at that moment an unpalatable idea struck. In an attempt to marry a man more steady, more dependable than her father, whom she'd always adored, but had known from an early age wasn't family material, she'd ended up marrying her mother.

In the cab on the way to the airport, she'd been certain that if Mason saw how life would be, even for a few days, without her, he'd come to his senses. Though she doubted he had it in him to grovel, the least he could do would be to assure her that she was the woman he loved. The only one he would ever love.

But what if he was incapable of loving anyone? Would she still want him back? Perhaps with some counseling...

"Are you sure you're all right?"

Tess's voice broke into Charlotte's tumultuous thoughts. She pasted an automatic smile on her face. "I'm as fine as anyone can be under these circumstances." If they *had* been the Brady Bunch, she might have told Tess everything. If only to have a sounding board. Given that the eldest Swann daughter didn't appear to want any type of sibling relationship, Charlotte was going to have to work things out herself.

After taking her cup into the kitchen, again turning down the full breakfast Rose White offered to make her, she went upstairs. From her bedroom window, she could see Tess, who'd left the house, walking the magnificent Rowdy through the vineyard.

12

Donovan was waiting for Natalie in the baggage claim area. Even in jeans, a blue-and-black-plaid flannel shirt over a black T-shirt and work boots, he still gave her the urge to muss him up. Just a little. Okay, she decided as she sighed inwardly at the knife crease pressed into those jeans, a lot.

Taking advantage of his greeting, rather than a brief, continental kiss on both cheeks, as she'd done in the gallery just days ago, she touched her lips to his. It was the first time they'd ever actually kissed, like a woman kissing a man she was attracted to, and it was as electric as she'd always imagined. Even more, she thought, her head spinning a bit as he lifted *his* head and stared down at her.

Oui, he'd felt those sparks, too. Although she'd planned the outwardly extemporaneous kiss all the way on the flight from New York to Portland, had imagined exactly how she'd surprise him and take what she'd been wanting for years, Natalie nevertheless felt shell-shocked. She had no idea how long they stood there, her looking up at him, drowning in the warmth of his eyes, him looking intently down at her as the crowd awaiting their luggage swirled around them.

"Well." He backed a few steps away. An adorable flush had risen in his cheeks as he seemed, for the first time that she'd known him, at a loss for words. He was always so serious, Natalie enjoyed being able to fluster him. And wasn't it about time?

"Welcome back to Oregon," he said.

"It's always lovely to be here," she said. "Although I'd prefer it be for a different reason." It occurred to her, for the first time, that her father would never walk her down the aisle. Raised by a mother who preferred the freedom of a committed yet unmarried life, Natalie nevertheless had always imagined herself being escorted up a flower petal–strewn aisle to her waiting groom. And in her fantasies, from the time she'd been a young teen, that groom of her dreams had always been Donovan Brees.

"How is *Grand-Mère*?" She'd received the call before her flight and had spent much of the time worrying.

"As I told you, it was a mild fibrillation. They did a chest X-ray, an EKG and an echocardiogram, along with blood tests for infections, none of which showed any heart problems. Nor did she have any risk factors, except age. So from what the doctor said, and what I could find online, it appears it was a case of what some refer to as 'lone afib.'"

"Is that dangerous?"

Donovan shrugged. "I suppose at ninety-six, anything can be dangerous, but the doctor said patients who experience it have a lower risk of stroke, which is a positive. Physical stress can cause it, but Jack hired a weekly crew to do the heavy work in her garden, so she mostly plans and putters. Emotional stress is another trigger."

"She's had a lot of that lately, what with Papa dying. And, I suppose, the arrival of the three of us. So if we can reduce her stress, she'll be okay?"

"Not entirely. I was told people with lone AF can still de-velop heart problems, so it's important to have regular check-ups. Meanwhile, they're sending her home with a smart watch that'll record any future episodes and push the results to her doctor."

"That's good news, but still scary. And, although I'm going to sound outrageously selfish, I just can't lose her. Not now, after both *Maman* and Papa."

"Life's always a crapshoot. But from what I was told, I don't think you have to worry about that. We'll be picking her up at the hospital on the way to the vineyard. When I called to check on her release, the nurse at the desk told me that she was already up, showered, dressed and impatiently waiting at six this morning."

Despite the seriousness of the topic, Natalie laughed. "That sounds so much like her. She's always been the heart and soul of Maison de Madeleine. Especially after *Grand-Père* died… Have the others arrived?"

"Yesterday. Charlotte's flight had originally been due to arrive about now, so I thought I'd be picking you both up together. But she called me last evening to say she was taking a night flight, got the directions to the vineyard and planned to get a rental car here at the airport."

"Honestly, that's a relief that we won't be stuck together on the ride. So what exactly am I walking into?"

"I told you. They'll like you. Everyone does."

As he stepped away to take the luggage she'd pointed out off the carousel, Natalie hoped he was right. But the doubts she'd felt about her two half sisters since he'd broken the news about her father's death continued to grow, like a wildfire on the horizon.

13

Most of the vineyard crews had arrived, and the rest were coming in today. As he watched the families moving back into their temporary housing, Gideon was grateful for the way both Jackson and Madeleine had given him carte blanche when it came to running their family wine business. One of the first things he'd done as vintner was hire Reynaldo Salvazar, a longtime seasonal crew chief at the winery Gideon had been working at in Napa, to relocate with his family to Oregon as a full-time foreman.

As Gideon approached the larger of the houses, which had been updated over the years, Reynaldo came out the door.

"So far, so good," he greeted Gideon. "We're going to have a great season." He glanced up at the morning blue sky and made a sign of the cross. "God willing. I hear you've got company."

"Yeah. Rose has been bustling around as if she's preparing for royalty."

The foreman's teeth flashed in a wide grin. "She's always bustled, anyway. But I can understand why this is a big deal.

It's only too bad it took Jackson's death to get all his girls home. Ana made a tres leches cake for the dinner tonight."

"That was kind of her."

"It was a gesture from the heart. Though I suspect the baking competition those two women have continued for years has her determined to top Rose's Italian cream Christmas cake."

"That's not a contest either you or I can lose," Gideon said on a laugh.

Then the conversation turned serious. "So," Reynaldo said, crossing his arms, "do you know any more about what's going to happen to the vineyard? Ana naturally worries."

Gideon guessed she wasn't the only one in the family concerned. "I won't know the specifics until tomorrow. But Jack assured me everything will be all right."

"I never knew Mr. Jack to lie," Reynaldo said. "Yet, you can't know a man's mind as he approaches that final door into the beyond."

"True enough," Gideon allowed. Wasn't Jack deciding to bring all his daughters here to Maison de Madeleine proof of that? Not to mention his claims to have been visited by Josette?

The short discussion ended abruptly as the door opened and John, Reynaldo and Ana's son came out.

"Good morning, Mr. Byrne," he said. He'd always been a polite boy and he and Aubrey had practically grown up together. But now, looking at the slight brush of hair above his top lip and hard biceps, Gideon realized that he was no longer a boy. Remembering himself at that age, he also realized the kid with his mother's soft brown Bambi eyes and his father's wide smile was nearly a man. Worse, he probably had the same raging teenage hormones as Aubrey.

"I'm going over to the court at the park," he told his dad. "We're going to shoot some hoops. I'm still working on my three pointer."

John was a smart kid, with a straight-A average at Aberdeen High, who wanted to follow in the bootsteps of José Moreno Hernández—who was, John had informed Gideon, the first Mexican American to go into space. Although only a junior, he had more than a few scouts from some powerhouse basketball programs looking at him for a scholarship.

He'd be the first in his family to go to college, so if that athletic ticket didn't come through, Gideon was going to make sure that somehow John Salvazar went to school. Once he got his education, becoming an astronaut wasn't going to be easy. But having watched his dedication to his studies, and his strong work ethic, as he'd worked in the summers in the vineyards, Gideon had the feeling John might actually have the right stuff.

Gideon returned to work, like Reynaldo, pleased with the progress of the vines thus far. They'd made it through bud break without a frost, and now the vineyard hillsides were a promising brilliant green color. A new season was beginning. One he had no way of knowing whether he'd be a part of. Jackson had assured him that he had no reason to worry about his future. And hadn't he said he'd come to think of him as his son? Which wasn't all that reassuring, given that Jack had sucked at being a parent.

He looked up from checking a vine and saw Tess Swann walking her Irish setter through the rows of vines. He'd noticed her doing the same thing last evening and first thing this morning. Her hair, in the glow of the sun rising in a boldly blue sky, gleamed a fiery bronze.

He waited as she turned the corner. The dog, who'd been prancing along, well behaved, but obviously not all that happy with the leash he was on, spotted him first. And stopped dead in his tracks, causing the redhead to look straight at Gideon. He watched her, seeming to make up her mind. Go back?

Or keep heading toward him? After a shrug, she continued forward.

"Good morning," she said in a voice he recognized immediately. She sounded like a grown-up version of that teenager from *Double Trouble* that Jack had streamed over and over again in his last weeks. But there was a sexy throatiness to it that the teen hadn't yet acquired. She was wearing a tiered skirt that hit at her ankles, a pair of cowboy boots and a T-shirt that let him know that she was a woman who spoke her mind.

"Morning," he said. "I'm Gideon Byrne. The vintner."

"Rose told me about you." She put her sunglasses up on her head, revealing eyes as blue as the sky. "She said you moved here from Napa to run the winery after my—" she paused for an instant "—grandfather died."

"Your grandmother didn't want to deal with the business end of the winery. Although she probably knows as much, if not more, about wine as I do, having grown up on her family vineyard in France. But she prefers her gardening and painting."

"Are those paintings in the house hers?"

While Madeleine might not have wanted to deal with the nuts and bolts, dollar and cents, day-to-day running of the eponymous named winery, her love for this land she'd married into had shown on every canvas. "They are. In earlier days, according to your father, her paintings were sold in a gallery and a couple restaurants in town."

"That's interesting, that she'd be artistic, too. It appears to run in both branches of my family. But it's odd enough having a late grandfather and a living grandmother I'd never heard of. I've spent most of my life not thinking about Jackson Swann as my father. I don't believe a switch is going to suddenly click on in my head and make me feel like part of an extended family."

He folded his arms. "Yet, here you are."

"Yet, here I am," she agreed on a sigh. "Rose says you have a daughter."

"Aubrey. She's fifteen going on thirty."

She laughed at that. "People used to say that about me. Although, having started working as a toddler, I certainly didn't have a typical American girl teenage life."

"You only played twin teens on TV." He cringed inwardly at the lame joke.

But instead of derision or annoyance, he saw humor in her gaze. "I think I like you, Gideon Byrne."

"Thanks. I like you, too." He'd felt a flash the moment she'd looked up at him. Not one that had come from having watched her play those crime-solving teenagers on TV back in middle school. No, whatever feelings had begun messing with his mind were definitely for an adult.

"You don't know me."

"You laughed at my bad joke. And you have a dog. That's a good start."

"I'm not sticking around."

"Okay."

"I'm just here out of curiosity. And to do a tour of wine country."

"Good plan." The dog tugged her closer, offering his head for a pat.

When Gideon obliged him, he moaned in canine pleasure. "You've definitely started your tour with a good winery."

"I know. I drink your Pinot Noir. It's excellent."

"Thank you. It's too bad you're not sticking around. This is when the vineyards really take off."

"As I told Donovan, I don't know anything about wine, except drinking it, and that the Pinot Noir from this house is excellent."

"I could give you a short course in the season, but I don't want to be accused of mansplaining."

She gave him a blank look, then, when he gestured toward her anti-patriarchy shirt, trying not to focus on her breasts, she laughed. "It was the first thing I grabbed when I got dressed this morning. You're safe. I didn't want to come here to Oregon. But now that I'm where the magic happens, I'd really like to know about it. Donovan already told me you're growing in volcanic soil."

"It's known as Jory, formed from ancient volcanic basalt that consists of silt, clay and loam, making it nutrient rich and able to hold water well." He bent down and scooped up a handful of the reddish-brown soil and smashed it between his fingers, where it stuck together. "All of which makes it perfect for Pinot grapes. Also for fruit, which is why Jeremiah Swann built his cherry orchard here before statehood, when Oregon Trail pioneers began flooding into the area in their covered wagons. Christmas trees flourish in it, too. In fact, Oregon represents ninety percent of all the live Christmas trees sold in this country."

"We passed some tree farms on the way here. I already know this area is part of the Ring of Fire, what with the Cascades being volcanic," she said. "So I suppose that explains the Jory?"

"In a way. It's also the state soil."

"You're kidding. Oregon has a state soil?"

"That may mean more when you realize that the state has 300,000 acres of the stuff in nine counties and produces a lot of crops, which, in turn, produces a great deal of state revenue."

"I stand corrected in my misguided comment."

He tilted his head. "How much do you want to know? I should probably warn you that you're talking to a soil nerd.

Which is a necessary thing when you start out your career in a region with more than a hundred soil varieties."

"Okay, now you've gotten my attention. I'm a serious trivia nerd. I collect little bits of information from everywhere because I never know when I'm going to need something. Since I've made the trip, I might go ahead and decide to set a book right here. So you'd be doing me a favor."

He liked her smile. The way it lit up her blue eyes and made little crinkles at the corners. "Okay. But don't say you didn't ask for it." He wiped his hands on his jeans, which already bore red stains.

"One of the first things I had to learn, coming up from Napa, is that dirt is all. And before you point out, as a card-carrying trivia nerd, that dirt is dead and soil is alive, for some reason, up here, people talk dirt."

"So when in Rome…"

He nodded. "Exactly. After a while, you get so you can taste a Pinot Noir and know exactly what vineyard it came from. In fact, it's so different from field to field, that a lot of houses, Maison de Madeleine being one of them, won't combine the grapes to preserve the taste of where, exactly, the grapes are grown. While we're not alone in that, other vintners believe that mingling the grapes from various fields gives you more variation. So it's six of one, half dozen of another."

"You could also be sabotaged," she said thoughtfully. "Perhaps a competitor could do something to the vines. Maybe introduce some sort of disease." She paused to look out over the rows of vines running up and down the hillsides. "Though that might take too long, even if there was a way to do it without it being spotted. I suppose burning would be the quickest solution."

"Don't even mention fire around here. What with climate change, we've been having more over the past few years. And even of those that escape losing their vines, some had to dump their entire season of grapes due to smoke taint."

"That doesn't sound like a good thing."

"Consider how it'd taste to lick a wet ashtray and you've pretty much got it. But I can't imagine any other wine grower burning a field."

Although he wasn't prepared to say it to this woman he'd just met, there was a certain reverence in what he'd chosen to do for a living. A reverence not just for the land, and the grapes and wine, but the history and tradition, as well. A reverence, he knew from the few stories about her family's burgundy vineyard during the war years that Madeleine had shared over the years, that others had risked death to preserve.

She shook her head. "I'm sorry. I've been living alone too long. We writers have a tendency of talking to ourselves, especially when we're working on a plot. And unlucky you, you've just been given an up close and personal look into a writer's brain. I've been writing a teen series for several years—"

"I know. Pleasant Meadows High. My daughter, Aubrey, has read them all. She's currently spending the weekend on the Oregon coast with a girlfriend's family, but prepare for her to ask you if Madison ends up with Ethan, the all-American high school quarterback, or bad-boy Brock. Needless to say, since she appears to take the stories as a guide to high school life, as her father, I'm rooting for Ethan."

This time her laugh was rich and throaty and pulled chords inside Gideon he hadn't experienced for a very long time. "That apparently seems to be the question of the day. Donovan already asked me so he could tell his niece, and the bulk of my reader email and Facebook posts ask the exact same thing." She lifted a hand. "As I've already told him, everyone will have to wait until the book comes out." She paused. Gazed out over the vineyards.

"When I started, I had no idea the series would go on so long, which you'd think would be every writer's dream. Those teenagers have definitely given me a very comfortable life and I've enjoyed my years with them. But I've been dealing with writer's block lately and I've been thinking that perhaps I should switch genres. Shake things up a bit for a fresh start. On the way here, passing the quiet, peaceful fields, it crossed my mind that this could be a good place for a thriller. You know...murder in a small town."

"You've just jumped from arson to murder."

"I have." She tilted her head and studied him. "I also have no idea why I told you that. Even my agent doesn't know I'm stuck. And, honestly, bored."

"Well, you don't have to worry about me telling her. Although it's good to know ahead of time that I might have to console Aubrey if you decide to end the series."

"Oh, I definitely will. I just haven't decided what to write in its place."

"Maybe getting away from your usual routine and place will help you sort it out."

"That's another reason I'm here. So you were going to tell me about the dirt. Jory," she said as if committing it to memory.

"It's specific to this part of the valley and the quick answer is that it's from the Missoula Floods back in the Ice Age between 15,000 and 13,000 years ago, having left behind all the fertile sediment. But our story actually begins around 200 million years ago when the Pacific Plate started sliding beneath the North American Plate. Over millions of years, it left behind shards, which, though it was once a seabed, began to build up and create Washington, western Oregon and the Willamette Valley. The movement creating new land still continues, causing about sixty volcanoes a year. Fortunately, although they register, we don't feel the earth moving unless it's a really strong one."

"I'm not certain if that's encouraging or not."

"Says the woman who grew up in Southern California."

"And lived to tell about a few," she said. "I'm never going to drink another glass of Pinot Noir again without thinking of the millions of years that went into making it."

"Stick around awhile, and I can have you being able to taste a glass of wine and you'll immediately know what dirt it was grown in."

"Now that's a line I've never heard before." She tilted her head and looked up at him. "Does it work that often?"

"I don't know. It's the first time I've tried it out."

"Ah." A red brow lifted. "So I'm a test run."

He thought about that and decided that yeah, it had been. "I suppose so. I'm admittedly a little rusty being a single widowed dad with a job that gives new meaning to the word *full-time*, so I don't get out that much."

"Same here. Except for the single dad part. I've got an idea."

"Oh?"

"Why don't we exchange numbers, in case you need more information for your research? Or just want to talk more to someone who won't share your problems?"

After taking a moment to consider that, she handed him her phone so he could type in his number and she did the same on his.

Afterwards, they stood there, looking at each other, as a topic about dirt—which had to be the worst ever pickup line in the history of guys trying to score with a woman—seemed to be segueing into something entirely different when the phone still in his hand chimed.

He looked down at the screen. "Sorry," he said, "but I have to take this. It's my daughter."

"No problem. Rowdy needs to walk off more energy, and I need to get more steps in against those amazing pancakes Rose made for breakfast. I suppose I'll be seeing you at the reading tomorrow?"

"I'll be there."

"Whatever he's left me, I'm not going to accept." When her dog gave another, more insistent tug, she surrendered, and with those parting words began walking away.

Gideon watched her and the dog disappear between rows of vines wearing their spring coats of bright green.

"Hi, Dad," Aubrey said as soon as he picked up the call. "How are things going? Did Jack's daughters show up?"

When they'd first arrived from California, Gideon had instructed Aubrey to address his employer as Mr. Swann. But Jack had vetoed that idea, claiming that his father had been Mr. Swann. He was just Jack.

Since Gideon hadn't felt right about a five-year-old using an adult's first name, they'd compromised on Uncle Jack. And he had been like that favorite uncle who shows up a few times a year bearing all sorts of cool gifts, with fun ideas that a child's stodgy old parent would never think of, then off he'd go again, disappearing without a word until the next time.

One thing that Gideon had noticed was that however drawn and tired and near burned out as he'd look whenever he'd arrived, Jack had always had the energy for Aubrey. During their first year in Aberdeen, he'd sit through tea parties, looking like a giant on a tiny chair next to various stuffed animals Aubrey would pour pretend tea for into tiny flowered cups. He'd push her on the swing he'd had installed in the backyard, and played hide-and-seek. Later on he'd taught her how to draw chalk boxes on the driveway stones so they could play hopscotch.

The penultimate time he'd come home, he'd taken her into

town for ice cream and warned her about boys who could break her adolescent heart, which Gideon found highly ironic.

She'd dropped the "uncle" when he came home to die, and although they'd spent a great deal of time in the sunroom together, sometimes engaged in long conversations, at other times just sitting quietly, looking out over the vineyards and flowering cherry trees, they seemed content with silence.

"Two of them," he answered her question. "Tess and Charlotte. Natalie's coming in today."

"I miss him so much." He could hear the tears welling up as her voice went weak and trembly.

"You're not alone there."

"It's not like he was around all that much. But it's knowing that he's never coming back again that's so hard to imagine."

"I know." Which was why he'd been relieved when she'd received that invitation to go to the coast with a friend and her family for the weekend.

She sniffled. "What are the other two like?"

"I've only met Tess. She seems nice enough."

"So she didn't act all stuck up?"

"Not at all. Why would you think she would?"

"She *was* a famous TV star. And now she's a famous writer. She's probably used to having people ask her for autographs and stuff."

"Well, she didn't seem to take offense when I didn't ask her for her autograph. She seemed like a normal person."

"Do you think she'd sign her books for me?"

"Now *that* I know she'd probably love to do. But she did tell me which boy Madison is going to end up with is top secret, so there's probably no point in asking."

"Darn. Okay. What time is Natalie coming in?"

"In the afternoon."

"I've always liked her. Remember how last year she took

me shopping in Portland? I'm going to need some new summer clothes. Maybe we can go again."

"She'd enjoy that."

"Oh! I caught a Dungeness crab yesterday. From the pier. Then the guy at the crab stand killed it, then steamed it in a big pot. Which was kind of gross, since I'd been responsible for it being murdered. But it was also dope because I got to eat something I caught myself."

"That's very dope." Would he sound ridiculous echoing her? Like some old guy trying to be cool? He never knew these days.

"Yeah. I wonder if that's how farmers feel when they eat fried chicken or steak?"

"I suspect it's like your crab. Part of the life cycle." He braced himself for the announcement that she was turning vegan.

"I guess so. I also decided that lobster is pretty much a butter delivery system."

He laughed. "It sounds as if you're having a good time."

"I am. I didn't think I would, what with Jack dying, and I feel a little guilty about that."

"Don't. You're fifteen, sweetie. You deserve to be having fun."

"Thanks. That's what Mrs. Ellis says, too. She says that she's sure Jack wouldn't want me to be sitting around and moping and crying."

"Mrs. Ellis is a wise woman."

"I do think about him. But everyone's keeping me so busy, it's hard to stay sad for too long. How come we never go here?"

"Because it's cold and stormy in winter."

"That's why we should go in the summer." They'd had this argument before, during the summers when all her friends would take off on vacation while he'd be deep into the season.

"We went to Seaside," he reminded her. "Twice."

"Which was a long time ago. I was just a kid and you were trying to distract me from missing Mom."

"I didn't know what else to do," he admitted. Before she'd died, Becky had warned him that when dealing with teenagers, the best thing was to tell the truth, no matter how difficult, whenever you could. "We used to go skiing every winter." They'd started their first winter here, spending five days at Mount Bachelor. They'd taken lessons together, and even at five-going-on-six, she'd shown more talent than he had. "You enjoyed it until you told me you wanted to stop."

"It was fun when I was a kid," she allowed. "But when you're thirteen, going on a ski trip with your dad is just lame and embarrassing."

She'd been firm about that. So they'd stayed here in Aberdeen where she'd spent most of her Christmas vacation either on her phone or staying over with whatever friends hadn't gone off to Hawaii, where so many in the Pacific Northwest tended to go to escape the unrelenting winter rain. While he'd worked pruning vines with seasonal workers in order to get ready for spring bud break.

Growing grapes for wine was a full-time job. Perhaps it looked as if nothing was happening when the vines were bare and gray, but the ultimate goal was to turn out a wine he could be proud of and that would uphold Maison de Madeleine's reputation.

"Well, I've got to get going," she said. "There's a surfing competition in ten minutes."

"You're surfing?"

"No. Well, I've been sort of learning. Brandon, he's Erin's cousin, is visiting from LA. He's a surfer and has been trying to teach me, but it's a lot harder than it looks."

A picture swirled in Gideon's head of his daughter in a bikini on a surfboard with some guy with a mop of California sun-streaked hair, his tanned hands on Aubrey's waist. And maybe other places. Hell.

"Isn't the water awfully cold this time of year?"

"It's cold all year up here, Daddy." Since she hadn't called him Daddy in months, he overlooked her huffy tone that he suspected came with the familiar eye roll. "That's why we wear wet suits."

"Of course." He'd known that and felt marginally better since it'd be harder for that California kid to cop a feel through an outside layer of neoprene.

At the advice of a woman he'd been dating at the time, he'd attempted an awkward safe sex conversation when Aubrey was eleven. He'd barely started when she'd breezily assured him that she knew all that because unlike back in the old days, when he was a student, she had sex education in school. Which had taken away the burden of getting into details.

Thinking back on nights parked beneath the stars with Becky, he could almost hear his wife laughing at him, telling him that worrying about what his daughter might be doing with boys was called payback.

Aubrey was an intelligent girl, Gideon reminded himself. Or had been, until aliens had taken over her teenage mind. And she'd never, not once, given him a reason not to trust her. "Have a good time," he said, trying to sound as if he was totally on board with the horny teen surfer dude. "And stay safe."

"I will, I promise. And Daddy... I really am sorry about Jack. I loved him, too."

She *was* a good girl, Gideon reminded himself as he began walking again. However, even though her mother had also been a good girl, the best girl, to Gideon's mind, a memory of those long, anxiety-ridden ten days of a pregnancy scare when they'd both been seventeen after spring break rose in his mind like a dark cloud of last year's smoke that had blanketed the West Coast.

14

While Tess was out walking her dog, Charlotte checked her phone for the umpteenth time. Her battery was at sixty percent, and she still had a signal. But there'd been no calls, not even a text, from Mason.

"Call Tara," she instructed Siri.

"Calling Tara," the Australian male voice said immediately. If only he were real, Siri would be the perfect man. Always there and ready to respond and help, and even if he did sometimes leap in to offer assistance when she was just talking to herself, at least he tried.

"Now you're officially crazy," she muttered as she realized that she had fallen so low she was anthropomorphizing her phone.

"I'm sorry," the voice responded on cue.

"It's not you. Oh, never mind." The phone stopped ringing.

"Hi," Tara's voice said. It was morning cheery, but she could hear the hesitation in it.

Charlotte decided to cut straight to the chase and blurted it out. "You were right. About Mason."

"Oh, hell. Honey, I'm so, so sorry."

"He told me last night. Over dinner."

"Your special dinner? After you'd gone to all that trouble to make his homecoming perfect?"

"That would be the one. The woman you saw him with is a lawyer in his firm."

"Is he at the house now?"

"He left last night. To go to her." She choked back a sob. "He thinks he loves her."

"I'll be right over," she said.

"You're going to Disney World today."

"The mouse can wait. You're my best friend."

"And you're mine. But I'm not at the house. I'm in Oregon."

"Oregon? Whatever are you doing there?"

"My father died."

"Oh. I'm so sorry. Damn. You've had a rotten twenty-four hours. But what does that have to do with you being in Oregon?"

"He owned a vineyard. Maison de Madeleine."

"No way! We served that wine at our Christmas party."

"I know."

"And Jackson Swann bought it? Without you knowing?"

"He didn't buy it. He grew up here. I have a grandmother in her nineties."

"Wow. Talk about family secrets. You had no idea?"

"None. Neither did Mother. But it gets even stranger. I have two half sisters."

"Seriously?"

"Seriously. One's older than me. She's Tess Swann."

"*The* Tess Swann? From my former favorite TV show?"

"That's her. She's older. From a previous marriage my parents failed to tell me about. The other one, Natalie, is from a decades-long affair with a French singer. Tess seemed nice enough. But I haven't met the French one."

"Wow. What a tangled web you've fallen into. Though, you did always wish for a sister."

"I did when I was younger. Then I realized I had you."

"That's sweet and I feel exactly the same. Although I already have two blood sisters, you're my favorite. And not just because I'm a middle, who pretty much always got overlooked being stuck between the beauty queen and the genius. Are you sure you don't want me to come there to be with you? As your support team?"

"No. I'll be fine." But she wasn't. Just thinking of her disintegrating marriage had tears flooding her eyes. "How could I not know?"

"Well, obviously your father was living a secret life."

"You think?" Charlotte was not typically sarcastic. But there was nothing typical about this situation. "I'm sorry. I didn't mean to snap. But I was talking about Mason. This mess has me all turned upside down and inside out."

"Honey, I'm amazed you're not cussing like a sailor. I wish you'd let me go over and cut his balls off with my butcher knife, the rusty one that Wyatt keeps putting in the dishwasher."

Charlotte laughed just a little at that. Not just because of her BFF's strong loyalty, but at the small domestic drama she'd give anything to watch right now.

"How could I not have known?" She repeated the thought that hadn't stopped spinning around and around in her head. "He was sleeping with her, sneaking around to Savannah, while I was home, trying like hell to have a baby I wasn't sure I wanted in the first place…

"Not that I don't want children," she tacked on quickly, not meaning to sound as if she was casting aspersions on Tara's life choice. "Someday. It was just that the timing was off."

"I never said anything, because you seemed to be all-in

on that program, but I did find the timing a little odd, given that your career was beginning to take off. I wasn't sure you realized how much time and work a newborn, and especially a toddler, was going to take."

"I did. Which is why I wanted to wait. But he had this political career plan all set out before we got married that he'd failed to tell me about."

"Fuck Mason's damn political ambitions. And fuck him."

"I'm not really in the mood right now."

Even as they both laughed together, as they had so many other times over the years, like when Tara and Wyatt had fought for a day over what had turned out to be an honest misunderstanding, tears began to flow again.

"I t-t-trusted him," Charlotte said. "Even when you were telling me about seeing him in Savannah, I was sure you were wrong... Well, at least eighty-five percent sure. But I still pushed doubts aside, because right after I got home, this lawyer showed up to tell me that Daddy had died of lung cancer he never told me he had."

"That sucks."

"I know. And the lawyer said that I was supposed to be here for the will reading. And to meet my sisters I had no idea existed."

"That is so weird. Like you've landed in a soap opera."

"I know! In twenty-four hours I discovered my father had two other families I knew nothing about, and my husband is not only sleeping around, but thinks he may be in love. How could I be so stupid?" she wailed as she paced the floor. "It's embarrassing."

"You are far from stupid and have nothing to be embarrassed about. That falls on Mason, and I don't see how he's going to get elected when that comes out."

"I don't think voters care about that anymore."

"Maybe not," Tara agreed reluctantly. "Yet, hey, they should, because having an affair shows character. Or, more accurately, a lack of. But here's the thing, honey. You're a good, loyal wife. And I don't want you to take this the wrong way, but I've watched you change since you got married. That girl who constantly redecorated Barbie's Dream House, with her eye already on the prize of doing big things, has gradually morphed into a trophy Stepford Wife."

"I have not!" Then, as the idea sank in, she sighed. Dragged her hand through her hair. "You're right. I have. I was thinking along those same lines yesterday. I should've just insisted on the cheese straws."

"Damn right you should've. But you didn't want to make a fuss and were afraid of being accused by bitch Melanie of behaving ugly."

Ugly, in Southern parlance, was the exact opposite of charming and the worst thing a woman of her social standing could be.

"You trusted that cheating, lying, snake-in-the-grass husband of yours because you believed in those words you said when exchanging your vows. You not only believed in them, you lived them every day. To extremes, in my view, but hey, you never criticized my choice to be building Wyatt's and my own basketball team. So I certainly wasn't going to question yours.

"But the thing is, Char, him cheating is totally on him. You have nothing to be embarrassed about. Though you should be pissed as hell. And, given the circumstances, relieved that your Sperm Meets Egg plan didn't work out."

"You have to have sex for it to work. And the last few months it wasn't me he was having that much sex with." Another thought occurred to her. "Oh, my God. I'm going to have to be checked for STDs, aren't I?"

"Yes. And again, that's nothing to be embarrassed about. You know you're not the first cheated-on wife to show up at the doctor requesting one. How long are you going to be in Oregon?"

"Probably just a couple days. Then I'm not sure what I'll do. I can't move back in with Mother."

"You'll stay with us."

"You're going to be in Orlando."

"Then you'll stay at the house and have some peace and quiet to yourself, to work out your next move, before we come back from Florida and my hordes descend on you. Unless you want to come with us?"

That drew a smile. Charlotte loved Tara's *hordes*, but they could be whirling dervishes on a good day, even when Tara was denying them sugar. She couldn't imagine the level of energy they'd crank up to at a theme park. "Thanks, but in a way, although I'm heartbroken about Daddy dying, at least this gives me time to plan my next move."

"The first move you should plan, right now, is to call a lawyer."

Charlotte's hesitation gave her away.

"Oh, God. Please tell me you're not considering giving him a second chance."

"I was. Maybe. If he'd called."

"But he didn't."

"Not yet."

The long pause suggested Tara was choosing her words carefully. "Call the lawyer, just in case," she suggested. She named a popular Charleston divorce attorney whom many women they both knew had used. "She's a dynamo at unearthing hidden money and other assets."

"Mason wouldn't—"

"Honey. Think. He's been fucking another woman while

insisting you procreate to advance his lofty political career plans while giving up your own. Not that I don't love my life as a stay-at-home mom, but you're meant for other things. What makes you think he's not going to hide income from you? Like Tiffany Grimes's bastard husband did."

Tiffany had been part of their crowd until her husband, a trust-fund baby who, from what Charlotte had been able to tell, mostly traveled the world on the yacht-racing circuit, had run off with his personal trainer to the Cayman Islands, where he'd hidden his billions in a network of offshore accounts scattered across the Caribbean.

While the others had essentially deserted her, Charlotte had tried to stay in touch, even secretly lending her money for the private investigator the lawyer hired, but after selling out her closets filled with designer clothes and all her jewelry, Tiffany had moved to Aspen, where she'd reinvented herself as a high-end real-estate agent. Charlotte had been glad she'd landed on her feet, but it had been a humiliating time for her friend and while she might sell seven-figure homes, she definitely no longer lived in one.

Neither had she paid Charlotte back, which had resulted in Mason's accountant discovering the withdrawals in their joint account, which, in turn, had earned a strong lecture from her husband about her apparent inability to handle money. At the time she'd pointed out that she had managed to build a successful career, and by the way, business management happened to have been one of her courses. Which she'd earned an A in. To which he'd responded that obviously "artsy" colleges and yes, he'd put that word in finger quotes, had lower business standards since how many graduates ever earned enough to live on anyway?

That memory served to strengthen her resolve to somehow manage to come out of this having regained the woman she'd once been. "When you put it that way... Okay. I'll call."

"Good. Oh, I just remembered something else Tiffany told me. Adultery is a crime in South Carolina."

"Seriously?"

"Seriously. And get this, the legal term is 'guilty of the crime of adultery or fornication.' Don't you love how old-fashioned Southern that is? Mason-the-bastard-fornicator could get fined between one and five hundred dollars and go to jail for six months to a year. I wonder how voters would take to that?"

"I can't believe any court would enforce it." Though the idea of Mason behind bars was definitely appealing.

"Probably not, unfortunately. But also according to Tiffany, South Carolina is an equitable apportionment state, which means that any property acquired during your marriage would be split between you and Mason in a way that's equable. Not necessarily fifty-fifty, like a community property state. Unfortunately, the house is his, unless he added you to the deed?"

"No. But I hate the house, anyway, so he can have it." And the scowling judge and fake Greek statues.

"Still, half the income from a forced sale would come in handy. But here's the thing. The court decides what's equitable, based on a set of factors, including income."

"I don't want his money."

"Well, unless you inherit the winery, which he can't have any part of because private inheritances during a marriage aren't considered marital property, unless you add his name to the deed, which you wouldn't do... Right?"

"Of course I wouldn't." But she might have two days ago.

"You may need those funds while you get your business back up and running. And here's another thing that Tiffany discovered. Bad behavior can factor into the settlement. So legally, Mason not only impacted your career by insisting you cut back on your business to concentrate on building up his, bad sexual fornication behavior can be factored into any settlement. Which you should, and will, take."

Charlotte pressed her fingers against her forehead where a tension headache felt like a steel band around her skull. "There's so much to consider."

"I know." Compassion and empathy had Tara softening her tone again. "Especially with your dad, and whatever your part of the inheritance may be, not to mention discovering those two sisters you'd never heard about. You must be angry at your parents for never telling you the truth."

Charlotte was not used to being angry and it felt like a sick, slimy ball in her stomach. "Although I'm very upset, I can't really be mad at my dad. Because he's dead. But I'm furious at my mother, who acted as if it was no big deal."

"That's good. It shows you've still got some of that spunk that had you bucking your mother not wanting you to go to SCAD and getting not one, but two degrees. Just try not to let all this overwhelm you because you're going to need a clear head. Especially if the other two show up with their own lawyers."

"I met Tess. She insists she doesn't really care one way or the other and has no intention of keeping any inheritance. So I doubt she'd have hired her own attorney. And I think Daddy's lawyer would've told me if Natalie was represented by anyone."

"Well, just keep your head and don't let anyone screw you out of anything. He might not have been around all that much, but your mother sure as hell didn't get pregnant by herself. If I were you, I'd take his estate for all I could get to at least get something out of his neglect."

"That's cold."

"It's reality. Promise me you'll try to keep emotions out of your decision. And keep in touch. And if you need me, I'll come there. Or, again, you can stay with us. Whatever, just know that I'm here. You can call anytime. Day or night."

After promising Tara she'd keep her filled in on unfolding developments, Charlotte disconnected the call. And the tears that had dried up during the lawyer talk began to flow again.

15

Tess was just returning to the house when Donovan Brees's SUV pulled into the circular stone driveway.

Always willing to give others the chance to admire him, Rowdy thumped his fringed tail just as the front passenger door of the SUV opened. Tess paused, watching as he got out, went around the car, opened the back door and held a helping hand out to the passenger.

Madeleine Swann was not the frail, elderly woman Tess had pictured in her mind. About five foot six, she was slender without being thin. She wore her silver hair in a tidy chignon tied with a jewel-toned burgundy silk scarf at the back of her neck, and even clad in dark jeans and a white cotton blouse with the sleeves rolled up halfway to her elbows, she looked every bit the lady of the manor. As if sensing she had an audience, she turned toward Tess, who felt every muscle in her body stiffen.

What if Madeleine, like her son, didn't want anything to do with her? What if she was only putting up with her first grandchild being here because of some legal matters that Donovan had only alluded to?

When the woman's eyes met hers, it was as if an unseen switch had turned on a light inside her. She was glowing, and while Tess had written that expression before, she'd never actually witnessed it in real life until now. She watched as Madeleine shook Donovan's hand off her elbow and hurried toward her. Although her stride was long and sure, not wanting to make a ninety-six-year-old woman walk to her, Tess met her halfway.

"Oh, my dear Tess." After decades in America, her voice still carried a soft, musical touch of France. Veined hands, the skin looking as thin as tissue paper, took hold of Tess's free one. Rowdy, having always proven intuitive, apparently recognized her possible fragility and sat down without a word of instruction. "Aren't you beautiful?" She swept a gaze over her. "You have your father's eyes. And height."

A smile curved lips tinted a deep rose that contrasted with her silver hair. The costumer for *Double Trouble* had been into dressing the cast in seasonal colors she'd explained suited them best and while Tess had been a fall, Madeleine Swann was definitely a winter.

"I wouldn't know." Tess could've bit off her tongue for the touch of bitterness in her tone. The woman was ancient and had just gotten out of the hospital. There was no reason to blame her for her son's lifelong absence. "I'm sorry. That was uncalled for."

"You were only speaking your truth. Which is all any of us can do. I told so many lies during the war that I swore I'd never tell another, so I'm not one to mince words now. You undoubtedly know your father had problems with relationships."

You think? Tess thought.

"Yes," she said instead.

"Your mother sent me a photo when you were born. You

were the most photogenic baby I'd ever seen. Given where
you lived, I wasn't at all surprised when you became a child
actress at such a young age. Although I couldn't know you in
person, I was, in a long-distance way, able to watch you grow
up from that adorable infant into a beautiful young woman.
But even then the camera couldn't do you justice."

"It didn't have to be long distance." If the elderly woman
was going to be outspoken, Tess decided to be equally open.
"Watching me grow up."

Gray eyes shadowed. "I'm afraid it did. After their divorce,
your mother wrote and asked that I remain out of your life.
She felt it was going to be difficult enough for you growing
up without a father and didn't want to confuse matters by
having your grandfather and me in the picture. She believed
it would make your loss that much sharper. She wanted you
to move on and forget Jackson."

"I hadn't realized that." Tess had moved on. And while
she couldn't remember Jackson Swann, Donovan Brees's arrival in Sedona had her realizing that she hadn't entirely forgotten the loss.

"I'm sorry. I'll admit to always being torn by that decision,
and it doesn't excuse my absence, but under the circumstances,
I believed, perhaps wrongly, that it would be best to respect
your mother's feelings."

Madeleine Swann had gone worrisomely pale and the earlier glow was gone, like a candle being snuffed out. The topic
was obviously not an easy one for her. Tess wondered if having
anticipated rejection and worry about what her reaction might
be had something to do with the elderly woman's hospitaliza-
tion. And wouldn't being responsible for killing off her grandmother be a dandy ending to this already surreal experience?

"It was probably for the best. Since I couldn't remember
him, I didn't really miss him." It was a lie. But a necessary

one, Tess decided. "I had a substitute father in the actor who played my dad on TV. And stepfathers. So I managed just fine without a birth father."

Her lack of any connection with her father's side of the family wasn't just her newly discovered grandmother's fault. There wouldn't have been anything to keep Tess from tracking Robert and Madeleine Swann down. At this moment she wished she had.

A bit of color had returned to Madeleine's cheeks. "Well, then, we'll just have to make up for lost time."

"I suppose we will." A slight tug on the leash had her aware of Rowdy. "I hope you don't mind that I brought my dog." Damn, despite what Donovan had told her, she really should have asked ahead of time. "He's very well behaved. He's gone through all the obedience classes and has passed the Canine Good Citizen test. In Arizona, he was a big hit on the nursing home visitation circuit." He'd always sensed, in some mysterious canine way, which of the residents were more wary, and needed him to remain calm and quiet, and those who were up for more show of doggie love.

"Of course not," the older woman said. "I'm French. We love dogs. What's this beauty's name?"

"Rowdy. But though he can live up to his name, he also knows his manners."

"So it seems." She leaned down and confirmed that not only did she love dogs, she knew them as well when, rather than pat the top of his head, she held her hand beneath Rowdy's chin, giving him the choice whether or not to interact.

He turned his head, inviting a pat, while rubbing the side of his face against her hand. "What a good dog you are, Rowdy, darling." Her still-strong voice was warm with the same emotion she'd shown Tess. "I'm so happy that you're here."

At that moment the back door of the SUV opened and a young woman a few years younger than Tess climbed out.

Her glossy, copper-hued hair was cut short, highlighting striking hazel eyes in a burnished gold face with cheekbones that could cut glass. A scattering of freckles added interest to that already exquisite face.

She was wearing a crisp white shirt beneath a cropped oatmeal hued jacket, a pair of taupe ankle pants and black ballet flats. The shirt appeared to have not a single wrinkle, not a hair was out of place, and if she was wearing makeup, except for a bold matte lipstick, it was so well done as to be invisible. She was stunning, without even having appeared to try, and so Central Casting French young beauty that Tess pitied poor Charlotte. She'd already seemed nervous about meeting Natalie. Now she'd have even more reason to be intimidated.

"Hello." She started to hold out a hand, then pulled it back. The slight show of nerves made her seem more accessible. Less perfect. "I'm Natalie, as you've undoubtedly already figured out, since I'm the last to arrive," she said in a quicker-paced Parisian accent than Madeleine's. "And you'd be Tess."

"And you'd be right. Hi."

Years of acting had taught Tess to not only learn to fake emotions, but how to read them well in others, too. Natalie Swann was definitely anxious. Perhaps even more so than Charlotte. *Thanks, Dad*, she thought with a spark of irritation. What had he thought would happen? That throwing them all together would make up for decades of neglect and have them all bonding with a group hug?

"How was your flight?" Tess asked.

"Uneventful. Which made it lovely. And yours?"

"It was fine. Not nearly as long as yours. Fortunately, my dog is a good flyer."

"He's gorgeous. I lost my dear Frenchie last year and my heart is still broken. May I pet him?"

"Sure." She loosened her hold on the leash, and when Rowdy glanced up at her she nodded, giving him permission to move.

He moved directly to Natalie, flopped down and offered his stomach for a rub.

The long, slender fingers massaging the fur were unadorned, save for a small topaz on the fourth finger of her right hand. Her unpainted nails had been buffed to a soft sheen. "You're a beauty, that's for sure. And such a very good boy."

Rowdy thumped his fringed tail in agreement, signaling his encouragement for continued rubs.

"He'd let you do that all day," Tess warned. "Unless he spots a rabbit or squirrel. Then all bets are off."

"It's good to have spirit." Natalie gave the furry stomach two more pats, then stood up.

Without the dog as a focus of attention, all conversation came to an abrupt, uncomfortable stop.

"Shall we go in?" Donovan offered his arm to Madeleine. At the same time the front door opened and Rose came bustling out, headed straight to the older woman.

"You're back. Thank God you're all right. I was worried sick all night."

"I told you I was fine. All of you worried needlessly."

"Perhaps. However, if we were right, and you wrong, you could have risked not ever meeting your granddaughters."

"Which was the only reason I caved in to all your pressure."

They did not behave like employer and employee. They reminded Tess of two sisters.

Rose turned to Natalie. "Hello, dear." The housekeeper's embrace confirmed Donovan's statement that Natalie, the daughter their father had kept, was familiar with the winery that Tess and Charlotte hadn't known about.

How was she supposed to plot a new idea that would get her agent off the idea of college for her overaged teens when so much personal drama was swirling around her? Before she'd decided to scale back her life, and not, as her mother accused, become a hermit, Tess had experienced enough drama to last a lifetime. She'd created a calm, peaceful existence that worked for her.

The thing to do, she decided, was to somehow get through tomorrow, then come up with a damn story idea, perhaps something to do with that intriguing idea of her elderly grandmother's former life as a French spy, that would let her move on with her life. As comfortable as she was with silence, the awkward one that had settled over them felt different. While she still didn't believe in the woo-woo of Sedona's vortexes, she could literally feel all the varied emotions swirling around her.

"You have a lovely home," she said to Madeleine, looking for a line of dialogue she might have one of her characters use in such an awkward situation.

"Thank you. Although I realize it's overdone for Oregon, my Robert—" she pronounced it the French way, *Robair* "—built it for me so I wouldn't feel so homesick."

"That's very sweet of him."

"He was a very sweet man. But strong. And brave. He put a lot of himself into the winery. But then, your grandfather never did anything halfway."

"He came home from the war with medals," Rose said. "But he wasn't the only one. You need to ask your grandmother about hers."

"Please." The elderly woman waved that enticing bit of information away. "It was a long time ago and I'm certain Tess isn't all that interested."

"Actually, I am," Tess said as her missing muse stirred again.

At the same time, Natalie said, "Oh, you must tell, *Grand-Mère*. Tess is a writer. She undoubtedly enjoys stories, and yours and *Grand-Père*'s is so exciting and romantic."

"With a teaser like that, I really want to hear it," Tess said.

"Perhaps later." Madeleine exchanged a look with Rose. "All that's happened, along with being in a strange bed, and excitement about your arrival, cost me sleep last night. I think I'd like to greet Charlotte, then take a short nap. Perhaps we could get together later in the day. For some pre-dinner wine and cheese?"

"That sounds lovely," Tess said, even though she wasn't certain what she was supposed to do in the meantime.

"I thought Donovan told me Charlotte had arrived," Natalie said.

"She's in her room," Rose responded.

"I'm so looking forward to meeting my middle granddaughter," Madeleine said. "Why don't you both go into the sunroom? It's lovely there this time of day and I'll send her down."

It had only been a suggestion. Not an order. But Tess realized that she was stuck. Making small talk with Natalie and Charlotte wasn't on her top ten list of ways to spend the day. It wasn't as if she was jealous. But she wasn't in the mood to hear their remembrances of lives spent with Jackson as a father.

One of whom must have been his favorite, having been fortunate enough, and loved enough to visit Maison de Madeleine every summer. To be part of the family. And yes, despite continuing to attempt to tell herself that she didn't give a damn about the man, that thought stung.

16

Charlotte paced the pretty bedroom, trying to burn off some of the turmoil that had kept her from sleeping last night. Maybe Mason and her mother were right. Maybe her beloved romances did cause her to expect too much from life. From marriage.

No, she decided, pausing at the window again as she viewed Donovan Brees's SUV pull into the driveway. There was nothing wrong with expecting her own happily-ever-after. The books had admittedly proven an escape during her teen years, showing a very different relationship than that of her parents'. Perhaps they'd also influenced her to decide that when she married, she was going to choose a man who openly loved her. Who put her first, like Wyatt always seemed to do with Tara.

Of all of them, Tara was the least wealthy, having chosen to marry a high school history teacher who'd worked his way up to school principal, instead of an attorney, doctor or any of the other high-earning occupations the rest of her social group had chosen. But having watched the couple from the outside, she'd always thought that Tara had won the marriage sweepstakes. Because it was obvious that her best friend was well loved.

Charlotte had gone into marriage believing that she'd chosen well. Wisely. Only to discover, that *she* hadn't been doing the choosing at all. She'd been played.

The idea that Mason had married her only to elevate his career was soul crushing. But she considered, still grasping at straws, perhaps he'd only said that because he was angry and upset, even embarrassed that she'd discovered his tawdry affair. Even the most perfect couples fought from time to time. There'd been times when even Tara had called or dropped by annoyed at some spat she and Wyatt had had over some seemingly, to his male mind, inconsequential thing.

Like that year he'd bought her a shiny new red Crock-Pot for Valentine's Day. Which, he'd defended himself by reminding her that she'd mentioned, when seeing it on display at Target while they'd been shopping for a new shower curtain for the boys' bathroom, how much prettier it was than the ancient beige one they'd gotten from his great-aunt for their wedding and, look, it was even programmable!

The night after that less than successful gift giving, he'd come home from work with a dozen roses, a gift-wrapped box of chocolate truffles and two tickets to *Giselle* performed by the Charleston Ballet Company, even though he was more into University of South Carolina football than watching dancers twirl and leap around a stage. The makeup sex, Tara had told Charlotte the next day, had hit twelve on a scale of ten.

Was the reason any disagreement with Mason had never turned into an actual fight because, from the beginning she'd caved into everything he'd wanted? By playing the role of a dutiful little wife he'd professed to want, she'd become diminished from that self-confident woman he'd taken to dinner that first night they'd met. The woman who, while allowing her heart to lead her head, had been swept away by the suddenness of what had felt like love at first sight, while somehow losing the creative, ambitious designer she'd worked so hard to become.

"No wonder he was bored." Just as Donovan helped an elderly woman—her grandmother!—out of the SUV, her phone chimed.

Perhaps it was Mason. Perhaps he'd returned home, found her gone and realized the mistake he'd made. Perhaps he was calling to grovel. Beg her forgiveness and assure her that she was the one he loved. The one he wanted by his side as he entered the political arena.

But no. It was her mother. Tempted to ignore the call but knowing that Blanche Lillington Swann was not going to give up until she had her say, Charlotte hit the green accept button.

"What do you think you're doing?" that all-too-familiar judgmental voice snapped without so much as a hello.

"I told you that I was going to Oregon. My father died."

"So you said. You did, however, fail to tell me that you were leaving your husband."

That news had traveled fast, even for Charleston. "You have it backward. He left me. And who told you?"

"Anne Cunningham. Apparently, he called and told her that he wouldn't be needing her to come in for a few weeks. Because you were leaving town and he was moving into The Spectator."

Having always maintained tight control on her emotions, Charlotte had never realized that anger—no, fury—could run hotly through her veins. "And she thought to run to you with this news flash why?"

"Because, naturally, she's concerned about how appearances might affect any future senatorial race."

"She's a housekeeper!" Remembering that the window was open, Charlotte lowered her voice. "Not his mother."

"She's been with the family since he was a child." Her mother reminded her what Mason always pointed out when Charlotte complained about the hatchet-faced woman who'd felt like an interloper in her marriage from day one. "She's like family."

Another thing Mason always said. There were times, and this was one of them, that Charlotte considered that for some, the antebellum period had never ended. She wondered how many other places there were in the country where house staff was handed down to grown children like all the heavy furniture and oil paintings cluttering up her overdecorated house. Or where an adulterous husband could move into a hotel where every guest was given his or her own butler.

Anne Cunningham had been an annoyance since the beginning of her relationship with Mason. Charlotte had been looking forward to newlywed privacy, fantasized about him wildly taking her on the dining room table, up against the wall, or in the pool beneath a full summer moon. He hadn't been happy when she'd first presented him with the idea of them having their home to themselves, but when she'd shared those sexual fantasies, he'd appeared to find them appealing enough to agree to a compromise. Mrs. Cunningham would come in twice a week to tidy up and prepare a week's worth of meals that they could heat up. Given that Charlotte worked from home, even that intrusion wasn't ideal, but knowing that marriage required compromise, she'd agreed to his counter-offer. As she'd gone along with so much.

"He's been having an affair."

"Men stray. Your father never stayed on that pedestal you put him on."

"I know he had his faults. But I also understood by the

time that I was in middle school that you and he had an open marriage, although I didn't know the term at the time. You certainly haven't stayed celibate."

Silence. Charlotte had known that moment she'd heard the words leave her mouth that she'd broken a lifelong taboo by bringing up her parents' unspoken arrangement that had existed for seemingly all of her life.

"How I choose to live is none of your business." Frost dripped from every word. There was a time Charlotte would've backpedaled because she was supposed to be a "good girl" who never challenged anything. Even her career had been a sore point between her mother and her.

"Just as my life is no longer yours," she pointed out.

Another longer, deadlier silence.

Then, finally, her mother found her voice. "You will take care of whatever business Jackson left behind for you to deal with, then you will return home and do whatever it takes to fix your marriage."

"And I'd be the one forced to do the heavy lifting, why?" It was what Charlotte had first intended to do. What she'd always done when the slightest disagreement would cause her husband to punish her by trivializing her feelings, shutting down communication, withholding affection and, as he'd done again last night, walking out. Now that she'd put some distance between them, Charlotte was no longer sure what she was going to do about her marriage. What she wanted to do.

"Because even you wouldn't be so selfish as to ruin your husband's career and throw a comfortable life as a senator's wife away because you have a juvenile, overly romanticized view of marriage." Her mother's sharp tone returned her mind to their conversation.

There it was again. That accusation that expecting her husband to abide by his marriage vows was a childishly idealistic viewpoint. But once again she thought of Tara who had the marriage Charlotte had always dreamed of. Maybe she hadn't fantasized all those kids and dogs, but it was obvious that Tara adored Wyatt and he loved her unconditionally right back.

"I have to go," she said as she saw the group walking toward the house. And before her mother could say another negative, cutting word, she broke the connection.

Deciding that she couldn't hide up here forever, she took a few deep breaths to calm the anxiety when there was a knock at her bedroom door. She opened it to find Rose and the grandmother who'd been kept from her all these years, standing in the hallway lined with watercolor landscapes.

"Oh, my darling Charlotte," the older woman said. "I'm so grateful to finally meet you!" Eyes brighter than her age drank Charlotte in. The only other person who'd ever looked at her with so much affection, and seemingly love, had been her father. "You're even more lovely than your photos."

"You've seen photos?"

"Of course. Online and in all those glossy decorating magazines in the market. Although, as you can undoubtedly tell from this house, I don't have a decorating gene."

"I think your home is beautiful." The decor might be a bit dated, but the bones were good, and unlike the one she'd been residing in the past two years, it felt like a home. All it was missing, she thought, was a family, which was a shame.

"Aren't you sweet? Robert never cared about such things, and to be honest, as I said, I lack any French home style gene, which is undoubtedly why my mother felt it necessary to ship some pieces of furniture over with me after Robert and I married. Although Rose keeps excellent care of it, once your grandfather died, the house was so large that I felt I was rattling around in it, so I moved into the guesthouse.

"My husband," she confided, "always hoped for a large

family, which partly explains its size. I'm sure he imagined all the rooms overrun with children and grandchildren. Unfortunately, pregnancy proved difficult for me, so I ended up with a single son."

Her eyes shone, which could have been a trick of the sun shining through the tall windows, but Charlotte didn't think so. Whatever thought had gone through Madeleine's mind, she shook it off. "But although Robert didn't live to meet you, at least I now have all three of my granddaughters under my roof. And as heartbroken as I admittedly am about losing my son, having you girls here soothes my soul."

Charlotte didn't know what to say to that. Then, taking a page from Tara's playbook about speaking out, even when the topic was difficult, she steeled her nerves and told the truth. At least as she knew it.

"I wanted you at my wedding. But I was told there was a family rift that I shouldn't bring up because it'd only hurt my father."

"Ah." A silver brow lifted. "I suspected it might be something along those lines. But I did see the photos in *Town and Country* magazine and *Charleston Living*, both of which I subscribe to. And I honestly haven't been stalking you, but I also follow your Instagram page, which Aubrey, Gideon's daughter, showed me how to access. You were a stunning bride."

In a dress her mother had chosen for her. Charlotte's favorite of the dozen plus she'd tried on at the bridal boutique had been a simple, long silk slip dress. Instead, her mother had gone all out, insisting on something more suited to an antebellum plantation wedding. All that had been missing was the hoop skirt and parasol.

"Thank you." She wasn't about to share the argument over the dress and the formal, stiffly sprayed upsweep hairstyle woven with pearls. "I'm sorry you weren't there."

"Bygones. I wouldn't have wanted my presence to cause any discomfort. I myself had two weddings."

"You did?"

"The first one in France, at a church dating back to the thirteenth century. It took a lot of paperwork for the wedding to be approved so Robert could receive the proper permission from the army. Then, after he returned home, it took another six months before he was officially out of the service and could return to take me back to America as a war bride."

"That's so romantic," Charlotte said.

"Wait until you hear the rest," Rose murmured. "Their courtship was anything but typical."

"That's a story for another time," Madeleine responded. "At any rate, the second wedding was held right here so Robert's family and friends could celebrate the occasion." A reminiscent smile crossed her lips and warmed her eyes. "It seemed as if everyone in the valley came. Rose was a child then—her mother had worked for the family for quite some time—and she looked like a little angel as a flower girl, scattering her rose petals on the white runner laid down on the grass. "It was a very special day." She turned to the housekeeper. "Rose, we'll have to get out the album."

"That's a great idea," Rose agreed. "Right now I think it's time for your nap."

"Rose was in the military," Madeleine revealed. "A nurse who rose to major, and there are times that I believe, while well-meaning, her inner commanding officer comes out."

Rather than an insult, the look the two women exchanged showed fondness and what sounded like a lifelong friendship. Almost like a mother and daughter. At least the type Charlotte had always wished for.

"But I'll admit I'm a little tired from all that's been going on and heaven knows you can't get any sleep at the hospital with all the people coming in and out of your room to check on you," Madeleine allowed. "I hope you won't mind if I go over to my little cottage to take a rest, then we'll meet up with your sisters for some wine and cheese before dinner."

"Of course I don't mind." Despite her problems with Mason and her mother, Charlotte felt a warmth toward this elderly woman that had her impulsively bending to brush her lips against the powdered cheek. "I'm heartbroken to have lost my father. But it eases the pain a bit to be here. In his house. With his mother."

"I feel the same way, darling." Madeleine kissed both of Charlotte's cheeks. Then said *"Je te verrai plus tard,"* which, thanks to Charlotte's high school French, she knew was telling her that she'd see her later.

"Bien," she responded. "I look forward to it."

"She reverts to her native language when she's tired or overly emotional," Rose explained under her breath as she paused before following Madeleine out the door.

"I'd guess this occasion would be a great deal of both," Charlotte said.

"You'd be right," Rose agreed. "Your sisters are in the sunroom. You'll find it past the front parlor at the right of the foyer."

Charlotte went over to the window again and watched as the two women walked arm in arm to the small cottage. Then, unable to put it off any longer, she went downstairs, headed to the sunroom to meet her French sister who had stolen time that Charlotte could have been having with their father.

Then again, she admitted, as she heard the murmur of voices, despite her denial and insistence that Tess didn't feel anything for their father, she wondered if Tess might well feel that same way toward her. And wasn't that a less than encouraging thought to an already depressing two days?

17

"Are you certain that you're all right?" Rose asked once they were alone in the cottage's bedroom.

Madeleine sank onto a rocker, the same one she'd rocked Jackson in after bringing him home from the hospital, while Rose unpacked the overnight bag she'd thrown together while waiting for the ambulance to arrive. "I'm as fine as any mother could be after losing her only son."

"I've never heard you admit to being tired like you just did."

"Getting old has disturbed my internal body clock. It's very frustrating."

"It's better than the alternative."

"There are days I could argue that. But for now, although I am, in fact, tired after my unplanned trip to the hospital, where, by the way, it's impossible to sleep, the pitiful truth is that I'm a coward."

Rose barked a laugh. "You've never been afraid of anything in your life."

"Of course I have. I simply learned that showing fear was a good way of getting you killed."

"This isn't Nazi-occupied France."

"I know that," Madeleine snapped. "I'm merely ancient. Not suffering from dementia. I loved my son with my entire heart, but I'll have to admit that I dread having to attempt to get through this evening dodging questions about the real reason Jackson had Donovan bring my granddaughters here."

"You could always lie and say you have no idea."

"May I remind you that I don't have that many years left and I don't want to waste them being untruthful with my last remaining family. So I'm taking the coward's way out and hiding out in the cottage for a few more hours." She rubbed her eyes. "There were so many times over the years that I wished that Jackson had chosen any other career. I do understand why he wasn't enthralled with the business of growing grapes."

"His mother's son there," Rose murmured.

"True enough. I love the product, but you need more patience than I have to be a vintner. And although he had a true talent for capturing moments, why did he have to spend his life chasing wars? Couldn't he have settled down with a wife and family here?"

"Would you rather have had him being a wedding photographer like wife number two supposedly wanted him to do? Spending his life catering to bridezillas?"

Madeleine laughed at that. "He wouldn't have lasted a week!" She sighed. "It's not easy being a mother. We raise our children, give them wings to leave the nest, but we have no control where they will fly off to."

"I imagine your parents had the same thoughts when you decided to join the Resistance."

"Papa was furious. When I insisted on becoming a courier, *Maman* took to her bed for a week."

"Yet, you persisted."

"I had no choice. The same way I had no choice but to bring Robert home with me to protect him when I found him hiding in the woods after his plane crashed. And at the end of the war, when I left France with Robert, I knew going off to America was not the life my parents had hoped for me. But the heart wants what the heart wants. I would have loved to have been the cookie-baking, sweater-knitting grandmother, like the ones always portrayed as the norm," Madeleine said regretfully. "Which could be some sort of karma for me having deprived my parents of the same opportunity."

"You and Robert went back to France once a year after harvest."

"True. But once a year is hardly enough. Yet, we have been blessed with Aubrey."

"Who's driving poor Gideon crazy."

"She'll grow out of her teen years and as good a father as he's been, I have no doubt that she'll go on to live a fine and fulfilling life. She's determined to be a physician, and I'm convinced that she's not going to let some boy lead her off that path. I'll always be grateful to Jackson for bringing both Gideon and her into our lives. Speaking of my granddaughters, what's your impression? Do you think they'll stay?"

Rose considered that as she opened a dresser drawer and took out a pair of sapphire-blue silk pajamas. "Tess is a wild card. Being a writer, she can live anywhere, so it's certainly a possibility. Yet, of the three, she doesn't have any happy memories of her father to give her a reason to want to connect with him now. From what I overheard while she and Charlotte were having breakfast, she had no interest in being here in the first place. I got the impression Donovan had to pull out all his charm to even get her to show up for the reading."

"That's what I was worried about," Madeleine admitted as she began to change out of the clothes she'd worn home from the hospital. "But that young man's charm is considerable. And, of course, Charlotte appears to have a very active social life back in South Carolina. Her husband's a prominent, politically connected man who undoubtedly wouldn't want to begin again here in rural Oregon even if she wanted to give it a try. So I'm afraid that takes her off the board."

"Probably. Yet, she surprised me by showing up at two this morning instead of this afternoon, which seemed odd. And while she's lovely, though very thin, she seemed terribly stressed and looked as if she'd been crying."

"Well, that's not unexpected. Given that her father did just pass," Madeleine said as she changed into the pajamas Rose had handed her.

"True," Rose said. "But I thought I sensed something else, although it may have just been shock that she hadn't known Jackson had a secret life and a thriving business down here in Oregon. She does seem very sweet to Tess's tart, so she might decide to come visit from time to time, as Natalie will undoubtedly do. But stay?" Rose shrugged. "I doubt it."

Madeleine sighed. "Unfortunately, our Natalie seems to have inherited Jackson's wanderlust. Always jetting off to take photos all over the world."

"It's true that her work, like Jackson's, takes her to different cities. Yet, we have people to photograph here."

"Rural people. She's building a reputation for more urban scenes. I wonder what the other girls will think when they see that photo of her parents dancing in the streets at the *Fête de la Musique*." The photo was framed and currently hanging in the sunroom.

"I thought about calling from the hospital and having you take it down," Madeleine admitted. "But decided that it wouldn't be fair to Natalie. It shows such joy, which she deserves to remember."

"You had to weigh your options, and, in my opinion, that was a good choice. In any event, it shows a side of their father the other two girls never saw." Rose took the comforter off the bed and turned down the light blanket and top sheet.

"True. And I've been thinking. We're not that far from Portland or Seattle. Both cities have an active street life."

"San Francisco is only a few hours south. And Los Angeles might be thought of as one huge urban sprawl. But it's made up of so many different neighborhoods with their own color and vibrancy if you know where to look," Rose suggested.

"She could use Aberdeen as a home base," Madeleine mused as she slipped between the sheets that Rose, even after all these years, continued to insist on ironing. "It's not as if she has any family ties to France, with her poor mother now gone."

"Losing Josette was a tragedy."

"True, but perhaps now that she's alone, and I'm willing to admit to being selfish, she'll decide that we're her last remaining family."

"*You're* her last remaining family. Along with her sisters. I'm not family."

"Of course you are. Don't be foolish. You've grown up here. You're definitely family. And together we have to figure out a way to make Jackson's plan work."

18

September, 1939

It was fall when the air began to turn crisp and the afternoon light took on a golden glow over the vineyards when Madeleine and her *maman* took the train to Dijon to go shopping because harvest was approaching, and her mother, known to be a grand fashionista, needed a new wardrobe to wear to the celebratory parties.

A sign, written in a lovely calligraphed hand, had been placed in the window next to mannequins showing off the latest fashions from Paris, telling the women of Dijon that they must remain elegant during this time to aid the war effort.

"I don't understand," Madeleine asked. "How will buying new clothes help us defeat the Germans?" She didn't want to admit it, but she'd been having nightmares ever since the French had declared war on Germany two weeks ago. Yet, strangely, everyone else around her seemed to be taking the matter in stride. Passing the sidewalk cafés, she saw people eating and drinking and laughing together, as always. As if they weren't in danger of German tanks filling their streets, and goose-stepping soldiers bound on retaliation.

"Because it will lift the spirits of our fighting men who do not want us looking as if we've surrendered before the fighting even begins," her *maman* explained. "We women may not carry guns or drive tanks, but we have our own weapons. Living well, looking attractive and remaining sophisticated is our patriotic duty."

"So when the Germans invade Dijon, they will realize that we French women don't fear them?" Her mother knew a great many things about entertaining and fashion, but about this, Madeleine feared she might be mistaken.

She'd grown up hearing tales of the last war, and seeing the old men with missing limbs, and wheezing from the gases they'd inhaled while in the trenches. Wasn't her papa's own uncle in a special home for soldiers with what the doctors had diagnosed as an incurable case of shell shock? While she didn't want to argue, she seriously doubted that shoes, no matter how pretty or fashionable, would save her country.

"They will never get here," her mother assured her with absolute confidence. "The wall will stop them." She lifted a gloved hand and patted Madeleine's cheek. "Don't worry, my darling." She ran a fingertip along Madeleine's furrowed forehead. "And you mustn't frown. It will give you wrinkles." She turned, pointing to a pair of burgundy-and-white square-toed shoes with cutouts lined on a cloth set up on a display table.

"Those Spanish high heels made them impractical for every day," she said. "But they'll be perfect for dancing at harvest celebrations." Her mother was stunning, her father dashingly handsome, and last year, at the chateau's Christmas ball, Madeleine had watched other couples stand back, granting them the spotlight in the center of the parquet dance floor. The shoes *were* beautiful, and Madeleine couldn't wait to be old enough to wear higher heeled shoes than the more practical Cuban ones her mother had presented her in a gilt paper–wrapped box for her fifteenth birthday this past April.

"Let's go inside and we'll buy them, and both get fabulous new wardrobes. After all, we must hold up the Bourgogne royal house's reputation." It had long been a matter of pride that their family was descended from Louis, Duke of Bourgogne, grandson of Louis XIV and father of Louis XV.

In a flurry of shopping, they managed to buy so many things that the shopkeeper, proud to have the honor of dressing the region's wealthiest and most celebrated family, had to arrange for them to be delivered to their chateau. But they'd each kept out one new afternoon dress to wear for a special afternoon tea before returning home.

The harvest festival held at the vineyard was declared a grand success by one and all, with no sense of impending war dampening the mood of the participants. *Maman* looked especially glamorous in her new shoes and a form-fitting asymmetrical Schiaparelli gown in a deep burgundy that reflected the Pinot Noir grapes that had made the house wealthy; and Madeleine danced on air with Bernard Deschamps, a boy from the vineyard next door she'd had a secret crush on for the past year.

In a rite of feminine passage, this was the first festival that she'd been allowed to wear a long dress. It was white chiffon sprigged with lavender flowers, and had puffed sleeves, a ruffled sweetheart neckline and a matching ruffle at the bottom of the full skirt that flared when she turned. She felt like a fairy-tale princess and later, upstairs in her bedroom, she wrote in her journal that it had been the best night of her life and she was sure that Bernard would someday kiss her.

The following May the Germans invaded Belgium, the Netherlands and France. While tanks, artillery and dive-bombers attacked the Maginot Line, the main assault went through Luxembourg, bypassing those fortifications the French had been assured would protect them, and changing Madeleine's life forever.

19

"You missed Madeleine," Tess said after Charlotte arrived in the plant-filled sunroom boasting glass walls, a domed glass ceiling and a provincial hexagon terra-cotta floor. As she and Natalie introduced themselves, surprisingly, for someone seemingly so perfectly put together, her French sister appeared a little on edge. Charlotte, on the other hand, looked as if she'd awakened and found herself having fallen down the hole into Wonderland. *Join the club, sis.*

"I just met her." She sat down on a white woven wicker chair, its cushion covered in a cotton fabric printed with an explosion of colorful flowers. "She seems very nice. And welcoming."

"Why wouldn't she be?" Natalie, who was seated on the other side of a glass-topped matching wicker table, asked.

Charlotte shrugged. "I wasn't expecting that. I was told that our father's family didn't come to my wedding because there was some terrible rift I wasn't supposed to talk about."

"I've never heard of any rift," Natalie said. "Nor seen any signs of it."

"Natalie spent summers here," Tess revealed as she studied

the Meyer lemons growing on a tree in a tall pot. This room was like walking into a terrarium.

"Here? On the winery?"

"Not entire summers," Natalie said quickly. Too quickly. Yes, she was definitely uncomfortable. Again, Tess felt a stab of anger at Jackson Swann. What the hell had he been thinking, tossing them all together like this? "Merely two or three weeks in August, which is when we French take our holiday."

Tess hoped yet again that Charlotte didn't play poker. Because her face gave away her every thought. Like now, when she was obviously hurt that this sister that she hadn't known existed had been a yearly visitor to a home she hadn't been aware of.

Personally, Tess didn't give two damns about not having ever been invited to this place, as stunning as it was. She'd made her own life for herself and had never expected, nor wanted, anything from her birth father. But Charlotte appeared to have had her pretty little fantasy of her father blown to pieces.

"I'm sorry," Natalie said. Her accent became stronger, giving away her own stress.

Yeah, this was turning out to be a great idea, Tess thought, throwing herself down on a white wicker love seat that matched the chairs and crossing her legs. *Thanks, Pops.*

"I always just assumed that, despite Papa's vagabond lifestyle, his real home was with you in South Carolina," Natalie said. "That I was just, well, to be perfectly honest, the illegitimate daughter he kept a secret to protect you and your mother."

Charlotte's expression hardened. "As it turns out, my mother always knew about you. And Charleston was never his true home. Even on the rare occasion he'd show up, it was obvious that he didn't fit into my mother's lifestyle."

"Like he never fit into Hollywood," Tess said. To give her

mother credit, she'd never blamed Jackson for their breakup. Or his desertion. She'd merely said that it wasn't in the man's nature to settle down anywhere. Except, perhaps, Tess thought as she looked out the window at the rolling hills covered with green, occasionally here.

Having the least emotional connection with their father, and having spent years first playing different characters, and now writing them, Tess was able to study their situation more dispassionately. Natalie appeared concerned that she'd be viewed as an interloper. Jackson Swann's bastard daughter. But the fact that their father had preferred Natalie's mother, enough to have maintained such a long relationship with the woman, certainly wasn't her fault.

Charlotte, on the other hand, was obviously shattered. Yet, again, there seemed to be something more going on than just Jackson's death. Because you couldn't get as painfully thin as she was overnight. Her life had apparently been going off the rails before their father's death. And she kept not so surreptitiously checking her phone.

"I wonder what's going to happen to the winery?" Natalie finally broke the silence that had settled over the room.

"Logically, it should go to Madeleine," Tess said. "Yet, I was told that she'd signed the place over to our father, who wasn't interested in the business, so he hired Gideon Byrne away from Napa to run things for him."

"That's true," Natalie said.

"And although Donovan was purposely vague, each of us had to be here in person to either accept or sign off on our inheritance," Tess continued. "Which sounds to me as if it includes the vineyards and house. Though undoubtedly with some arrangement for his mother to remain living here." If even half of what she'd been told about Jackson Swann was true, he would have made some provision to protect his mother from being evicted from the home his father had built specifically for her.

"I was told much the same thing," Charlotte said. "Although I'll admit Mr. Brees's words were sort of a buzz and all the details didn't sink in. Partly because I was already distracted by another recent issue I've been dealing with. Just learning about this property was yet another surprise because I didn't even know Daddy owned a winery. Was Gideon the man I saw you talking with earlier?" Charlotte asked Tess.

"That's him. He lives here on the property with his teenage daughter."

"Is he divorced?"

"Widowed. Apparently, he lost his wife about the same time our grandfather died."

"I'm worried about Aubrey," Natalie said. "Gideon's daughter. She was very young when they moved here. She probably can't remember any other home. If they're forced to leave—"

"Why would they have to leave?" Charlotte asked. "If we actually did inherit this place, which I still have trouble believing—"

"More likely a part interest," Tess interrupted. "Donovan was clear that each of us had to be here together in person. And if we all signed off on it, it could be sold off to charity."

"That doesn't sound right. Surely, Madeleine would get the controlling share." She repeated what Tess had stated. "She did establish it with Robert, after all. And it wouldn't make any sense to let Gideon go," Natalie said.

"She's ninety-six," Tess pointed out. "With an apparent heart condition. Maybe she just wants to give up the responsibility of the place and move out of the rain to Arizona. Or Florida."

"The doctor said that her afib was hopefully just stress," Natalie argued. "Her mother lived to a hundred and four. Her father was widowed for four years after that and passed at a hundred and eight."

"I suppose you knew them, too?" The edge in Charlotte's voice had Tess thinking yet again that of the three of them, she appeared the most hurt.

"No, they were already gone when Papa took *Maman* and me to visit their winery in Burgundy. The one Madeleine had grown up on. They'd already sold it to another house: Maison Louis Latour, who'd let them continue to live there. Monsieur Latour resisted the Germans during both of the World Wars, so being like-minded rebels of sorts, my grandfather knew that his grapes would be in good hands. If you buy Pinot Noir from their house to this day, you could well be buying wine from our family's grapes."

"We're not a family," Tess pointed out.

"Perhaps not in the conventional sense," Natalie agreed. "But like it or not, we're connected by blood."

Because Natalie seemed like a nice person, and the mess Jackson had made of his personal life certainly wasn't her fault, Tess decided against pointing out that it took a lot more than shared DNA to make a family.

"From that history, I'm surprised that since she had no interest in running the business, Madeleine didn't sell this place after her husband died."

"His death was unexpected," Natalie explained. "Everyone was quite shocked because he'd always been so strong and healthy. I was here the summer it happened and she seemed very lost. They'd been through so much together and married so long, it had to have been difficult for her. There's a possibility that our father put in a contingency that if Maison de Madeleine is sold to some other local winery—like *Grand-Mère's* mother's family did back home in France—that his mother would remain on the property and be taken care of."

"If that were the case, I don't know why we have to be here."

"Perhaps it was his way of arranging a way for us to meet."

"Without him having to face the consequences."

"He was a very good man," Charlotte and Natalie said in unison. In the time it took for the two of them to exchange a long look, Tess opted not to be the dissenting voice. Soon she'd be on her way out of here so there was no point in making waves.

"I've been worrying that the land may be bought by some developer, because that would be the most practical thing to do," Natalie confessed. "Papa was definitely a romantic, in the original meaning of adventurous, so he left business details to Donovan, who isn't talking."

"Lawyers," Charlotte and Tess said together.

Apparently, a distaste for the profession was something she and Jackson's middle daughter shared. Yet, Charlotte was married to an attorney. Which brought up more questions that were none of Tess's business because once they got through the damn reading of the will, they'd all be going their separate ways.

"Donovan's not your stereotypical attorney," Natalie insisted. "He's very sweet and caring. Which was partly why he sold his more lucrative Portland practice to his partner/brother and opened an office here. To ensure that *Grand-Mère* was well taken care of."

"For which he was undoubtedly well paid."

Natalie shook her head. "Are you always so cynical?"

"I'm a writer. Therefore, I'm an optimist, because it's not the most stable way to earn a living. But writing isn't only about sitting down at a keyboard and spinning stories. It's an often difficult business. So I've learned to look for the fine print, which has me seriously doubting that Donovan Brees handles all of the estate's business out of the goodness of his heart."

"Well, I guess we'll find out tomorrow," Charlotte said, jumping in as peacemaker. "When the will is read."

"I don't want anything." Tess repeated what she'd been saying all along. "I'm only here because Donovan said I needed to be at a time I happened to be between books and I thought perhaps a new location might give me a new story idea."

"I seriously doubt that Papa left me that much," Natalie said. "As I already told Donovan, I'm the illegitimate daughter."

"No one uses those terms or thinks that way any longer," Tess said.

"I know. It's just that…" She shrugged. "Okay, I'll admit it. I'd love it if he left me a photo or two of his. Or three."

"Really? But they're so violent."

"You've seen them?" Charlotte seemed surprised. "I thought you'd had nothing to do with him."

"I hadn't. But there's this new-fangled thing called a Google Machine. After Donovan left my house, I looked him up." Tess's gaze turned to Natalie. "He had talent. I'll give him that. While I was online I donated to Doctors Without Borders in his name. Then last night I had the first nightmare I can remember in years."

"They weren't all crisis photos," Natalie responded. "There's this one of the three of us in Deauville, which is considered Paris's Riviera. It was a special family trip because usually Papa would stay close to home when he visited. *Maman* would say it was to decompress."

"I can understand that," Charlotte said.

"Yes. That's why the trip was so memorable. Coco Chanel set up her first atelier there. Your mother would probably enjoy it," she told Charlotte. "Although it's a lovely family resort, it caters to the rich and famous." She smiled. "There's a story, mostly true, that wealthy Frenchmen would keep their wives in Deauville, where they would shop and lunch, and their mistresses in nearby working-class Trouville."

Tess noticed Charlotte tense at that and wondered if part of those morning red-rimmed eyes had to do with anything going on in her marriage. Deciding it was time to change the subject, she said, "I was there once. For the American Film Festival. A small budget film a friend directed was being featured, so I went for emotional support. It's a lovely little town. Very different from the beaches of California I was used to. Although the streets that week were crowded with paparazzi because George Clooney attended."

"That's definitely a week to avoid if you're there for relaxation," Natalie agreed.

"I'd like one he took of us together on one of his visits to SCAD," Charlotte said. "It somehow got lost when I moved into Mason's home."

"You moved into your husband's house?"

"It made the most sense. Since I was living in an apartment, and he already had the house."

"Probably designed to his own personal guy taste. So I suppose you made it your own?"

Charlotte colored a bit at that. "He'd already spent a fortune with another designer whose reputation far exceeds mine." It was her turn to shrug. "I added a few touches, but it was basically already done."

Once again, her face gave everything away.

One of Tess's Pleasant Meadows High's cheerleaders, who, on the outside, appeared to have the perfect life, came from a home with a father who emotionally abused her mother. Unconsciously repeating the example learned from her parents, she'd been dating the school quarterback who controlled her every move the same way he called plays in the huddle on Friday nights.

Her character arc had continued for several books, but she'd finally break free and demand her life back in the upcoming and final book that was currently in the production stage. Because despite what Gideon had suggested when they'd been talking about the series in the vineyard, in this case, "bad-boy Brock" was actually a misunderstood kid from a broken family who, underneath his tattoos and cynical attitude, had a heart of gold and had been secretly in love with the cheerleader since arriving in Pleasant Meadows his sophomore year.

"Well, like I said, I don't want anything."

"Then why are you here?" Charlotte asked.

"Donovan suggested you might not come," Natalie added.

She shrugged. "I was due for a vacation after finishing a manuscript, and wine country sounded like a nice change from Sedona." Then, what the hell, why not tell the truth? "Plus, although I'm loath to admit it, I was curious. About both of you."

"I think that's what he intended." Natalie's voice choked up a bit. "For us to get to know each other."

"That makes sense," Charlotte agreed. "He really was a very kind person," she assured Tess. "Flawed, but kind. And generous and supportive."

Tess's expression didn't hide her skepticism.

"He was," Charlotte insisted. "My mother never wanted me to have a career. Women in our family were far more traditional."

Natalie laughed at that. "While women in my family were just the opposite. My great-grandmother was not only a *Folies Bergère* dancer at the Moulin Rouge, she modeled for some sexy Jazz Age French postcards."

"Seriously?" Charlotte sounded more fascinated than scandalized.

"It was a part-time job. She didn't pose totally nude, like some of the girls did. And they weren't at all like today's porn. They were more artistic, using a lot of feathers and fans. But she was, so the stories go, quite the tease and certainly had many, how do you say it in English—" she snapped her fingers "—stage door Johnnies." She took out her phone and opened to an album of photos.

"You're right. She's not totally nude. But it's the suggestion," Tess said, "of what she appears to be promising." She glanced from the sepia photos to Natalie. "I don't want you to take this the wrong way. But you look quite a bit like her."

"You have her cheekbones and her eyes," Charlotte said. "Gracious, she surely must have turned some heads."

"As I said, she's rumored to have been very popular. Though she certainly didn't dress like this when she went out. And I'm going to take you both seeing a resemblance as a compliment."

She closed the photo album. "She caused a bit of a scandal, even among some of her liberated set, by marrying a hot Black drummer ten years younger than her, who'd escaped Jamaica during the sugar rebellion."

"That's quite a biography," Tess said. "Did you ever think of writing it down?"

"*Non*, I'm a photographer, not a writer, but stories about her escapades did appear regularly in *La Vie Parisienne* and other risqué gossip magazines at the time."

Tess glanced up at a photo on the wall and walked over to it to look closer. "Did you take that?" The photo focused on a couple dancing with a crowd in the street. Since she recognized Jackson, the woman must have been Natalie's mother.

"I did. It was during the *Fête de la Musique*, a Summer Solstice music festival that takes place all over Paris. It's one of the city's most popular and largest celebrations."

"They look very happy," Charlotte said. A bit wistfully, Tess thought.

"They were."

"And your mother was very beautiful."

Moisture glistened in Natalie's eyes. "She was. Both inside and out."

"What about your grandmother?" Charlotte asked. "What did she do?"

"She *was* a showgirl. Which makes sense since she literally grew up backstage at the Moulin Rouge. All the adult showgirls and guys would watch out for her when *Grand-Mère* was on stage. Or at a photo shoot.

"Then *Maman* turned out to be left-footed, which she always complained kept her from being one of the dancers because she couldn't stay in line and do the routines, which is how she ended up a singer, which she enjoyed, but I always had the impression that she would have loved parading around in all those feathers and headdresses in front of a theater full of admirers." Natalie went over to the photo to stand next to Tess, looking at the photo, as if remembering that day.

Her gaze turned reminiscent, and a smile brightened her eyes. "When I was twelve, she held a Roaring Twenties party, and had a seamstress make her an outfit from a photo of one of my great-grandmother's outfits. It was skin-tight ivory lace, which showed off her skin, which was lighter than my grandmother's, but darker than mine, given that she was second generation French Jamaican. Those artfully placed lace flowers probably kept the party from being raided." She ran her fingers through her short, bright hair, which fluttered back perfectly into place. "I thought she was the most glamorous woman in the world."

"It sounds as if we have more in common than it would first appear," Tess said, surprised by the revelation. "Because I felt the same about my mother. There were certainly women more beautiful—it was Hollywood, after all—but the way she lit up a stage, or a room…"

She shook her head. "I spent a lot of time last year watching her old TV series and movies, and I realized that I was a better actress. But I was never born for the spotlight. Which is why the anonymity of writing suits me."

"And photography, me," Natalie said. "I've recently realized that I use the camera lens to put a distance between myself and others. And, considering the more colorful side of my family, you'll probably have trouble believing it, but I'm usually more of an introvert with people I don't know."

"Perhaps it's a natural bond that we're feeling," Charlotte offered hesitantly, causing Tess to think, yet again, that for someone so accomplished, she certainly seemed less secure in stating an opinion. And less willing to share any aspects of her life.

"Donovan told me our father met your mother when she was a cabaret singer in a Paris nightclub," Tess said to Natalie.

"They did." Natalie nodded. Her eyes grew a bit shiny. "It's been a year since I lost her, and there's not a day that goes by that I don't miss her. When Donovan came to New York to tell me the news, my first thought was to call *Maman*."

"That was what I did," Tess admitted.

"And?"

"My mother wasn't all that surprised, given his line of work, which is what she first thought was the cause. I've always gotten the impression that their marriage never clicked. Which made sense given that they eloped to Las Vegas after knowing each other just a few days. And, according to my mother, who's been known to overshare, alcohol was involved."

"I've always suggested that was the same with my mother," Charlotte said. "Neither of them would ever share any details, the way most people do, except to say that they met in New York. My mother was there shopping, and he was visiting the Magnum office—that's a photographic cooperative owned by member photographers. There must have been some immediate attraction, because less than a year later, at their huge social plantation wedding at Boone Hall, she was already pregnant with me."

"I wonder how many more of us there are," Tess pondered. "Given that the guy seemed to be into pretty casual sex with women he'd just met."

"Don't even say that," Charlotte said with a visible shudder. "I may have always wanted a sister, but I don't want to think of a crowd of them."

"We'll probably find out once the obituary comes out." Tess had already wondered the same thing when she'd heard about Natalie. "If there are any more siblings out there, we'll probably be hearing from them."

"Fortunately, we have Donovan to handle that possibility, if it does arise," Natalie said. "Although I never had any reason to think about it before, with its reputation, this winery is undoubtedly worth a great deal. The only thing Papa ever seemed to own were his photos, and not all of them, since he worked for different publications over the years. *Maman* had already owned her own apartment, and while it's small, as Paris apartments tend to be, neither of them ever appeared to want anything more."

"Mother owns the house I grew up in," Charlotte said. "She inherited it from *her* mother. Which is why it didn't feel strange to move into Mason's house. It's not that uncommon where I come from."

"As far as I know, besides your mother's house, and mine, the rest of the time he lived in hotels," Natalie said.

"If he lived in both your mothers' houses, and I assume his living expenses were covered by whoever he was working for, he must have some money stashed away," Tess suggested. "Because from what I read, he definitely wasn't into the high life."

"That was one of the contentions between him and my mother," Charlotte said. "She always seemed just as happy when he was gone, because he definitely wasn't into the Charleston social scene."

"He mostly enjoyed being alone with my mother and me," Natalie said. "Though he did enjoy hanging out with her friends from time to time. But as I said, they were all musicians and theater people. I suppose you'd call them bohemians. He took some wonderful candids."

"Like a modern-day Toulouse-Lautrec."

Tess couldn't help thinking that their father seemed to live on two very disparate ends of the human spectrum and considered that this place might have been where he came to find balance. After having seen the horrors he'd lived with, she was glad that there had been a part of his life when he'd laughed and loved and been happy.

"Exactly," Natalie said. "Everyone always teased him about it. Once, at an after-party for a final performance about the artist's life at the Odeon, *Maman* surprised him by showing up in a bright red cancan dress." Her smile lit up her eyes, making gold flecks sparkle. "After a couple glasses of champagne, she danced on the table! Everyone applauded and shouted, and as always, she was the hit of the evening."

"Too bad we couldn't have traded moms," Charlotte said. "Your life sounds far more exciting."

"It could be colorful," Natalie said. "Though to me, it seemed normal. Although it was usually just *Maman* and me, I was fortunate because I had so many surrogate uncles, including a magician who cut me in half for my tenth birthday and a psychic who did readings at dinner parties. *Maman* collected a colorful cast of characters as friends, but even with so many eccentric people filling our apartment, she was the brightest light in the room. Like a human Eiffel tower."

"My mother was the same way," Tess volunteered. "The film clips of her USO tours are amazing. Even in some very bad movies, which, as much as I love her, I have to admit she didn't rise to the performance level of the B actors, she definitely lit up the screen. If she'd had real talent, she could have been a superstar. There are a handful of clips in the military public domain of some of the tours and after Donovan left, and I went online looking, I found one that shows our father with his camera around his neck, looking at mom at what appears to be the moment he fell. Hard."

Just saying that out loud had Tess thinking of what her mother had said about never forgetting your first love. The look on her father's face had been more than lust. It had, Tess realized now, been love. They'd just been too young, and their circumstances too different for it to have ever worked. And wasn't that a different take on the situation than she'd considered her entire life?

"It's funny," Charlotte mused. "Thinking about it, my mother's the same way. But not glamorous like both of yours. It's more a power thing. She's always the most important person in the room. I always thought that because she's one of the First Families of South Carolina, which I realize sounds really trivial these days, but it's sort of like I imagine it must be if you live in Massachusetts and are one of the Mayflower families. Roots are an important thing where I grew up."

Tess laughed. "Where, in contrast, where I grew up, except for the movie families, which have formed a sort of dynasty of their own, finding a Los Angeles native is akin to running across a unicorn. It's a place where people chase their dreams of getting discovered and becoming famous. And usually fail."

"You didn't," Charlotte pointed out.

"I just happened to be in the right place at the right time while my mother was chasing *her* dream. Fortunately, she was never a stereotypical stage mother, though she was my manager. But then, after those early years of success, I failed in spectacular fashion."

"Failing spectacularly is still probably better than failing because you're mediocre," Natalie suggested.

"Or were afraid to try. Or gave up entirely," Charlotte added quietly.

As Charlotte appeared to have done. This was all getting too personal, Tess decided. More than personal. Intimate.

She was pondering how to escape both this situation and the conversation, when, with a low groan, Rowdy rolled over from having been on his back, and after a long stretch, rose to his feet, came over and put his red head on her knee.

"I need to walk Rowdy."

"You already walked him this morning," Charlotte said.

"And now I'm going to walk him again. Irish Setters have very high energy that needs to be worked off."

"He seemed pretty mellow a minute ago."

"That's on the outside. Inside he's wound up like a spring. And believe me, none of us wants him suddenly taking off and knocking everything over. Or peeing on the rug."

Her sisters looked skeptical, but apparently, neither wanted to rock what had been a fairly even keel boat by arguing.

"I have to unpack," Natalie announced. "And call my agent. I was having a show in New York when Donovan told me the news about Papa. I never got the final sales count."

"I'd like to see more of your work," Charlotte said. "Donovan said you photograph street scenes."

"I do, mostly as a rule. I also took some of this place."

Charlotte glanced around at the landscapes, many of which included workers in the field. And one of Madeleine in her garden, wearing a broad-brimmed straw hat, and an apron with pockets for pruning shears over a white shirt and jeans. "You took these?"

"While growing up. Our father was my first teacher."

Silence descended.

Tess didn't envy either of her two sisters. *Half* sisters, she reminded herself. And wasn't that a lie? While Jackson Swann might not have been a model of monogamy, they'd both known and loved him, and had received whatever little pieces of himself he was willing to share. And what had she received? A damn check every month like she was nothing but a car payment. Which was when she realized what he was probably doing. He may have wanted his daughters to meet each other, but her inheritance was undoubtedly whatever amount he would have paid had she not insisted her mother stop accepting those child support checks.

She stood up. "Well, like I said, I have a dog to walk. And some writing to do."

"I thought you were between books," Charlotte remarked.

"I am. But I've gotten a few ideas I'm going to play with. So I guess I'll see you both tonight at dinner." With that, she escaped before Charlotte could invite herself along in another attempt at some sisterly bonding.

20

The fields spread out over softly rolling hills, so unlike the bold thrusts of Sedona's red rocks. The fog was lying low in the valleys, trailing along the ground. Having headed in a different direction than she had this morning, Tess turned a corner of the house and viewed a building that was a smaller version of the mansion. It was built with the same gray stone and had the same tile roof, but instead of a grand entry, it boasted a covered front porch with a wooden swing along with a table and two chairs made from the same wood. The porch looked out over the vineyard, and she imagined herself sitting there at the end of the day, sipping a glass of wine, perhaps having some cheese and crackers. As they'd driven through the town on the way from the airport, they'd passed a dairy farm with a blue sign featuring a black-and-white cow that advertised organic cheese.

The burgundy F-350 parked in front with the Maison de Madeleine logo on the side suggested this was Gideon Byrne's house. Continuing on, she came across a row of small, bungalow-style houses with front porches. A family, whom she took to be seasonal workers, was moving into one of the larger ones. The woman, who was carrying a baby in one of those kangaroo pouch things, waved to Tess, who waved back.

Two little girls who appeared to be around four and six had run to the swing set at the small park behind the cabins and began to pump their way into the gray sky that had parted to reveal a patch of bright blue.

Watching the children had Tess thinking about her own sisters. If things had been different, and they'd grown up together, she thought she could have been close with Natalie. On the other hand, Charlotte, while sweet, could have come from a different planet. Nature or nurture, she wondered the age-old question. Depending how things went tomorrow— she'd known seemingly strong families splintered to pieces over inheritance battles—she supposed they could keep in touch. Maybe even have the occasional get-together.

She'd love an excuse to visit Paris and thought that Natalie would probably get a kick out of Sedona's New Age scene. Granted, she'd said her photos were usually urban, but the area had its own personality that might call out to Natalie's photographer muse.

Having never been to Charleston, she'd certainly be interested in visiting. She'd seen postcards of the historic district and the harbor, and Low Country cuisine was supposed to be fabulous. But her father's second wife didn't exactly sound as if she'd be nearly as welcoming as Madeleine had been.

"Imagine lying to your own daughter to keep her father's family away from the wedding," she murmured to herself. Then again, wouldn't Jackson have had to go along with that? Or, if he was even half as kind as both sisters claimed, might he have kept silent in order to spare his parents Charlotte's mother's snobbery?

So much to think about. Hopefully, her mind would clear after tomorrow. Because with all these other thoughts bouncing around in her head like pinballs, she wasn't any closer to coming up with a workable story idea.

As she was returning to the house, Tess ran across Gideon again, who was back in the vineyard, plucking off leaves from the vines. "Hello again."

"Hi."

"What are you doing?"

"Getting rid of some of the shoots before they flower out. Growing grapes too close together shades them and uses up nutrients."

She glanced down at the discarded leaves scattered on the ground. Having been in such a negative mindset the first time she'd walked Rowdy past the vines, she had missed what had been right in front of her eyes. "I just realized that the vine-yard doesn't look like all the photos on tourist booklets and postcards."

"The floor looks messy to you," Gideon guessed.

"Actually, I was going to say it's pretty." What he'd called the floor was covered in various grasses. Queen Anne's lace and dandelions and other things she couldn't recognize bloomed. Bumblebees buzzed, birds chirped in the trees at the ends of the rows and not a spot of bare earth was visible.

"Studies are finding that the more native plants you have as ground cover, the better and more balanced biological control you'll get. Milkweed and yarrow do very well here, and milkweed is especially good because it feeds Monarch butter-flies. We're on their migration path and they've been disap-pearing in large numbers. This could help bring them back.

"The past few years we've gotten totally into permaculture—never plowing, but letting the vegetation grow naturally be-tween and under the rows. Here, dandelions and other plants with deep roots break up the clay in the soil and allow it to breathe and manage water better. We also don't use any irrigation, which requires the roots to grow stronger and deeper, which has been helping during these hotter summers.

"And we discovered, by total accident about six years ago, that Madeleine's rosebushes provide an overwintering for a tiny wasp called anagrus that, once we stopped chemicals, took care of most of our control of grape leaf hoppers."

"So essentially, instead of fighting nature, you're working with it."

"That's the plan, but it's going to take time for every vineyard to make the commitment to change methods, which takes a leap of faith. When I first came to Aberdeen, all I really knew was that the valley is one of five places on earth that provides an ideal environment for Pinot Noir, which is what I mostly worked with when I was in Burgundy. It's my personal favorite wine to grow. Winters here are typically cool, wet and mild. Spring is usually rainy, and summers are warm with cool evenings. That was its reputation. But real life turned out to be far more challenging.

"By my second year here, I realized there's only so much I can control. Most people tend to think of wine growing as a slow, tedious endeavor. Your father certainly did, which was one reason why he had no interest in sticking around. The job takes a lot of patience, but you still have to have a gambler's blood, because always, in the back of your mind, you know that you've chosen a high-risk business over which, despite all you know, and all you do, you can lose an entire season to Mother Nature."

He resumed thinning the leaves as he talked. "It's definitely a crazy way to make a living. Some years I think I'd be better off going to Vegas and taking up poker for a living. Which probably wouldn't be all that successful, since Aubrey could beat me at Go Fish when she was eight. But I can't imagine doing anything else. Like I told Jack, sometimes we just find where we fit."

"That's nice. I felt the same way about writing. Until lately."

He'd been crouched down, ridding the vine of some lower leaves, and looked up at her. "You'll figure it out. Get back on track."

"I wish I were as sure of that as you are. Especially considering you've just met me and have no idea who I am."

"We're about the same age," he said. "Granted, our lives were very different, but we grew up during the same era, which has to have given us something in common. Also, like just about everyone else, I sat with my parents in the living room watching your show."

"That wasn't me. The characters I was playing were fictional."

"I get that. I got it back then, too. Though I will admit to having a slight crush on Emma."

"She was the nerd. Most of the fan mail from adolescent boys came to Ella, the cute one who always wore the latest fashion."

"They were wrong. Emma had it all over Ella, especially with those glasses."

"They were supposed to make her look smart," Tess laughed.

"I thought they made you look great. Ella was cute, but kind of clueless. Pun intended."

"But she was better at flirting, so boys would all go dead in the brain and slip up and give away the answer to the crime."

"Like whose idea it was to TP the football coach's house," he remembered.

"She could go over-the-top. But I'm not going to lie and say that it wasn't fun to get to wear all those cute clothes from the teen fashion magazines and act like someone so different than the twin who was more like me."

"Showing my good taste at a young age," he said. "Anyway, when I wasn't fanboying, I thought about how hard it must be to even learn all those lines and do all that acting every week. And you were essentially doing double duty as two very different girls. While I was playing sandlot baseball and video games without any thought to what I was going to do with my life. My father had always intended for me to follow in his footsteps, so when adulthood seemed like a gazillion years away, I just went along with the plan."

"Your father's a vintner?"

"No. He's a surgeon."

"Oh. Well… That must have been some conversation when you told him that you weren't going to med school."

"It was…interesting. Because to say he wasn't pleased would be an understatement. But I knew, after a summer working on a winery instead of shadowing him at the hospital as he'd intended, I'd found what I wanted to spend the rest of my life doing. And even during the most difficult times, worst times, when I picture myself in an operating room, I know I chose the right path."

"I thought acting was my right path. Until it wasn't. When our series ended abruptly, my agent couldn't get me the roles my mother and I wanted that would allow me to stretch. And, unlike you and your father, we were always a team and pretty much agreed on everything. In fact, now that I think about it, the only two times we argued were about me going the pop star route. Which I didn't have a lot of choice in, because the company that produced the series had a habit of rolling its stars out on the pop tour circuit once they got too old to play kids, and I was still under contract for two more years.

"Mom thought we ought to fight those conditions. But at

sixteen, I thought it'd be fun to wear sparkly costumes and be a pop star on stage in front of an entire coliseum of screaming fans instead of performing to a small studio audience. Having been on all those USO tours, Mom pointed out that it was a lot harder than it looked. She also pointed out former child actors who, once they were out on the road without a lot of supervision, got into all sorts of trouble. What she hadn't known was that I'd been taking drugs for a few years. I was just a good enough actress to hide it." This time her laugh held no humor.

"I guess drugs are pretty easy to come by in that environment."

"It's not like you're probably thinking." She looked out over the fields again. "Ella and Emma weren't supposed to age. Because once they got past middle school, there'd have to be more complicated storylines, more characters to hire and pay for, and subplots about boyfriends and more mature subjects that would take away from the initial high concept of two very clever little girls solving crimes. It was wholesome television the entire family could watch after dinner.

"The problems came when I started maturing. I grew taller. And started getting hips and breasts." She held out her arms. "As you can see, unlike my mother, who never had to watch her weight and stayed model thin, I'm genetically tall and, well, curvy.

"Wardrobe started putting me in really tight body shapers, and the catering people and my mother were instructed to put me on a low-calorie, no-carb diet. But those *damn breasts* as William Moore kept referring to them, kept growing."

"Since you brought the subject up, am I allowed to say that, in my opinion, they turned out quite nicely?"

That earned a half smile. "Yes, that's allowed and thank you. But eventually, even binding them didn't work, so one day William gave me this pill. He told me not to tell anyone. Not even my mother.

"I argued with him about that, because we always shared everything. She was my best friend. Hell, I went to school at the studio and never long enough at Beverly Hills High to bond with anyone. She was my *only* friend. But he warned me that if I didn't take them, and if I kept growing, that the show would be canceled, and we'd all be out of work. Then he went into a bunch of stuff about how badly it would affect his family, which was so hypocritical, considering he was having that torrid affair that shut us down. But I was thirteen. And I believed him. So I took the pills. Then another for sleeping, since the first made me so wired, I had insomnia."

"You took amphetamines and sleeping pills, starting at thirteen, for three years until the show ended?"

"Longer than that. By then I was hooked. Both physically and psychologically. Mom knew that something was wrong, but the studio doctor William sent us to to examine me found nothing—"

"Surprise, surprise." She could hear the scorn and repressed anger for her sake in his voice. "Given that the studio had an asset to protect."

"Yeah. Well. Anyway, it got worse on the road because that life really is crazy and I don't know how anyone should be expected to be rocking at the top of your lungs and dancing your ass off around a stage late at night, then falling right to sleep before waking up in the bus the next morning and doing the same thing again and again.

"During that time my mother was having her own romantic problems with marriages and divorces, so she wasn't around the way she had been when I was on the show. Then one night I was on the stage in Hamburg and things were rocking along really well, although I felt sort of out of myself, as if I were floating up above the stage and watching myself, the way some people say they feel when they die, before coming back to life.

"Then I had a hallucination, which can be a side effect of amphetamines, and imagined that big, hairy, black spiders were crawling over me. Which is when I made all the tabloid headlines for tearing off my clothes. On stage in front of forty thousand people." Fortunately, her band and crew had dragged her offstage before she'd dispensed with her underwear.

"That all must have been unimaginably terrible," he said.

"Luckily, there wasn't social media back then. So at least I was saved that." She rubbed her forehead where a headache threatened. "You know, if you had given in to your father's pressure to go into medicine, you could have been a shrink. Given the way you get people to talk. Or maybe I've just been alone too long, hermiting, as my mother insists, so the first time I get out in public, I just get all talkative."

"You've been under stress. Even if you gave up thinking about Jackson, hearing that he's gone had to have some effect on you. Meeting your sisters—"

"Half sisters," she corrected with less strength than she had been.

"Meeting them. Then there's the problem with your plot. I don't know squat about writing, but I do know about the need to make it through a season and end up with a wine people are going to buy. About not knowing what tomorrow's going to bring. That uncertainty is one more problem you don't need right now."

"My mind's been going around and around in circles. Correction, it's more trying to find my way through a maze. In the dark. Plus, I still have to get through a family dinner where everyone's going to bring their own stress, and since none of the three of us have any idea what's going to happen tomorrow, it could end up a hot mess."

"It could. But since we seem to be getting along pretty

well, does it help knowing Madeleine told me that she expected me there, too?"

"I think it does. It also shows she considers you family."

"Families don't just come from blood. Some we make of our own. Jack, Rose and Madeleine are every bit as much family as the one I was born into."

"You're lucky. To find that place you fit." She repeated what he'd said. Rowdy, deciding the conversation had lasted long enough, took the loose part of the leash in his mouth and began walking away.

"I think that's a sign that we're supposed to continue his walk," she said on that laugh he was really beginning to like. "I'll see you later."

"Later," he said, enjoying watching the sway of her hips in that tiered cotton skirt.

Jack hadn't told Gideon exactly what he was going to do with Maison de Madeleine. And Gideon hadn't asked. But having come to know him as well as anyone could know Jackson Swann, he suspected that he'd left the business to his three daughters. With the caveat that his mother could remain in her home.

Until his last few months, Jack had lived his life on the edge, never knowing what the next day, hell, the next minute, might bring. Despite his problems with PTSD, it was obvious that part of what had kept Jack going was the adrenaline bursts that came with things literally and figuratively blowing up around him.

While explosions weren't involved, Gideon, too, lived with the risks of each growing season. Risks he'd learned to accept. Wine making did require a great deal of patience. But with his and Aubrey's livelihoods hanging in the balance, he was more than ready for tomorrow to arrive.

21

Tess stood in the doorway of her closet, looking for something to wear. She had brought her single, all-purpose little black dress but had to save that for tomorrow. Maybe her mother was right. She'd been alone so long, she'd stopped thinking about dressing for occasions. And surely, your first dinner with a grandmother and two new sisters and a winemaker who had a knack for getting you to unload personal stuff that you usually kept to yourself, seemed like an occasion.

After nearly everything she'd packed was lying on the mattress of the sleigh bed, she opted for a sleeveless royal blue dress that deepened the blue of her eyes and fell to midthigh. And although she was loath to admit it, she wanted Gideon to see that unlike the character he'd claimed to have a middle school crush on, she wasn't always the nerd sister. She'd thought there'd been a moment earlier, just before his phone had rung...

Or maybe she'd just been in the sexual Sahara too long, and who couldn't want to jump a hot winemaker with a great butt? Maybe she'd imagined his interest. But just in case, the blue dress was definitely it.

Along with the cowboy boots she'd worn on the plane, she'd packed a pair of sneakers, heels for the will reading, and bronze, flat-heeled sandals. Since she decided the sneakers were too casual, the heels too formal and the cowboy boots would make her look as if she were auditioning for a country music video, she opted for the sandals.

The pre-dinner wine and cheese chat in the great room with Madeleine, Rose and her sisters had been...she supposed the word was *cordial*. A light mellow jazz played softly from hidden speakers and the delicious aromas coming from the kitchen added to the cozy atmosphere. It was obvious that everyone had been feeling each other out, stepping carefully, not wanting to enter into any sensitive territories. Tess had shared some of the more humorous outtakes from the TV show, which all of them seemed familiar with, which she supposed wasn't that big a surprise, given the show's weekly ratings during its run.

Charlotte complimented Madeleine on her garden, not just the herbs, but the profusion of flowers that were beginning to burst into bloom, which led to a discussion of plants with actual botanical names, which allowed Tess to stay out of that conversation since they might as well have been speaking Klingon.

Natalie talked about her travels, and how she loved capturing spontaneous moments. To which everyone agreed that spontaneity was a good thing and they all could probably use more of it in their own lives.

When they moved into the dining room for dinner, Tess realized just how big a deal either Rose or Madeleine, or both, considered this occasion—polished sterling candlesticks with tall cream candles sat atop a cream linen tablecloth. Irises she'd seen in the garden had been arranged in a cut-crystal vase between them. Gold-rimmed plates, the porcelain nearly translucent, sat on burgundy chargers. The linen napkins had been folded into fans, held with a ring that matched the plates, and the sterling flatware was heavy, but well worn, showing not just age, but that it had been used regularly over the years, not stuck away in some chest.

Which had her wondering if Madeleine and Robert had eaten at such a table every night. Had her father grown up surrounded by such luxury? She was accustomed to occasionally dining in high style during her Hollywood days, although the past few years she'd taken to eating in front of the TV, or more likely, while watching the sun set over the towering red rocks from her patio. She imagined that this all could be normal for Charlotte coming from Charleston's high society and being married to a jet-setting lawyer who dealt in high-end real-estate deals, but it seemed as if it would have been a jolt to Jackson to adapt from whatever war zone he'd been in to such graceful elegance. Hand-written name cards sat at each place setting, and Tess was not displeased to find herself sitting next to Gideon.

The dinner, a delicious coq au vin that Tess suspected even Julia Child or Ina Garten would have not been able to find fault with, was served family style. "As it was meant to be," Madeleine said. The chicken and mushrooms were served atop boiled new potatoes. The bread was a homemade sourdough. The butter, Rose said, was from a local dairy that used a higher percentage of butterfat, which gave it its smooth, rich taste. And dessert was a tres leches cake, topped with whipped cream, sprinkles of cinnamon and a fat red strawberry.

She watched Charlotte take the tiniest bite of the chicken that had been cooked in the house wine and looked as if she might cry. It couldn't have been because she didn't like it because it was, hands down, the best thing Tess had ever tasted.

"This is amazing," she told Rose.

"Don't thank me. Madeleine, who doesn't let me use her old family recipes, made it. This one is how many generations old?" she asked the elderly woman.

"At least ten," Madeleine said. "For the longest time it was passed down orally, so it's changed since the mid-eighteenth century, even during my lifetime. My papa, who came from an area that borders Germany, grew up eating it with egg noodles, so that's how *Maman* would make it. I took it back to an earlier potato recipe, because making pasta is not something I do all that well."

"I like the new potatoes," Tess said, taking another bite. "It makes it a lighter dish."

"Thank you, dear." Madeleine's eyes lit with pride. The idea of a woman her age going to so much trouble to welcome her granddaughters to her home had Tess feeling guilty for all the negative reasons she'd had for not coming here in the first place.

"I can't take credit for the cake. It was made by Ana Salvazar, the wife of the crew foreman. She and Rose have been having their own version of that *Great British Bake Off* show for the past ten years."

"Everyone keeps saying that," Rose complained. "It's not a competition. We just both happen to enjoy baking."

"Which is what you both keep insisting," Madeleine countered. "No one really believes that, but since we're the benefactors of such good desserts, we're not going to complain."

Rose harrumphed. "It's not a competition," she insisted again. "But wait until you taste the Pinot Noir chocolate Ganache on my cupcakes tomorrow."

"As I said," Madeleine responded, "no one's complaining."

After a round of laughter, Tess changed the topic to Madeleine having been a war bride as a roundabout way of asking the elderly woman to tell the story she promised earlier.

"It must have been difficult, leaving your family to come to America."

"It wasn't easy. After VE day, we still had to fill out papers and wait months for permission to marry. But even then I couldn't get documents to travel to America because the war had officially ended in August and the soldiers had expected to be home for Christmas. Which was logistically impossible given that it had taken four years to get all those millions of troops overseas and there weren't enough ships to get them home that fast. There were riots at base towns all over Europe and even in America. But the delay allowed Robert and me to get married in Burgundy, along with what was left of my family there to witness it."

"You lost family?"

"The better question would be who didn't lose family? I lost two brothers who'd been in the French Army, and a cousin was pulled out of a ration line and shot after making it almost to the end of the war. He hadn't done anything wrong. But the *Maquis* were causing enough chaos that the Germans said that they were going to kill a thousand French for every German killed by the Resistance, and he was simply unlucky that day.

"Also, an elderly great-uncle died of a heart attack when the Gestapo invaded and confiscated their house on Christmas Eve. They were thrown out into the snow. Neighbors took him to the hospital, but it was too late. His wife, Esa, died three hours later. The doctors said, literally, of a broken heart. They'd been married seventy years. The only small comfort was knowing that they were together and free of the monsters who'd killed him."

"I can't imagine," Charlotte murmured, tears swimming in her eyes. She was not the only one. Tess felt her own eyes fill, and risking a glance at Gideon, noticed that although he'd undoubtedly heard the story before, both his jaw and eyes had hardened.

"It all seemed horrific, but oddly surreal, as well. As if we were suddenly living in another dimension. Nearly everyone in our community had already lost family members in the Great War. That war had been so terrible, that in the beginning days, even after the Germans invaded Poland, even after France and Britain declared war on Germany, everyone continued to live in denial. Because surely, there could never be anything as horrible as what they'd been through... You've heard of the Maginot Line?"

"The concrete barrier the French built from the Swiss to the Luxenberg and Belgium borders." Which the Germans simply went around, Tess remembered learning in a high school history class.

"It was more than just a wall. The bunkers had recreation areas, spaces for living and dining, with trains running between sections. They were even air-conditioned, which none of our houses were in those days. Our soldiers were living in comfort, eating well, with wine from all the best vineyards in the country. Including from ours, of course. Letters from men stationed there claimed that they were bored to tears. This great planning, but little doing, became known as the *drôle de guerre*. Or as it was known in English, The Phoney War.

"We civilians continued to live life as usual. In fact, two weeks after France declared war on Germany, *Maman* and I went shopping in Dijon for clothes for school and the harvest festival. No one believed the Germans would ever invade France, let alone reach our part of the country."

"Dijon is a lovely city," Tess said. "I did a concert there once."

"Did you? After the liberation of Paris and the German surrender, Robert and I were going to be married at the civil office, like most marriages those days, but my parents insisted on a church wedding, so we were married at Notre Dame. Not the one in Paris that tragically burned a few years ago. But in Dijon. It dates back to the thirteenth century and thankfully, the Allies hadn't bombed it.

"Although he'd been stationed in England at the end of the war, Robert had been granted a three-day leave to return to France for our marriage. We couldn't go anywhere and the Allied troops had taken all the hotel rooms, so we ended up staying at a hunter's cabin my papa had in the woods. I was admittedly glad about the forced delay in Robert's return home that gave us those days together, but never would have asked him to give up his place in the wait line because I realized how homesick he must have been. And although he never showed any resentment, at least to me, he must have felt cheated because the return to America was based on a points system, with those having served in the theater the longest being the first to be sent back home.

"But his situation was very different, which caused his paperwork to be mishandled. The fact was, he'd been one of the very first Americans to fight, because he'd volunteered to join the RAF when Great Britain started accepting American pilots.

"The US hadn't entered the war yet, but Robert always had a very strong sense of right and wrong, and insisted he had to help save lives. His mother later told me that they weren't at all happy about his decision. Since he'd flown crop dusters for his family's farm and orchard, he knew the basics of flying, which saved training, and to hear him tell it, they quickly put him in a Spitfire, which was a British plane, and sent him off to gun down German fighter planes. The American volunteers had a high loss rate, but Robert always returned to base. He even achieved Ace rating."

"That's amazingly impressive," Natalie said. "He never told me that."

"Oh, you know your *grand-père*," Madeleine said. "Once he got home, he was very closemouthed about the war."

"Like someone else we know," Rose commented beneath her breath from across the table.

"I heard that," Madeleine said.

"Of course you did. Like Jack always said, you have ears like a bat. Which was probably one of the things that made you such a good spy."

"Which we're still waiting to hear about," Tess reminded her.

"And you will," Madeleine promised. "But Robert was also a spy. Which is how I met him. So I have to tell you about him first, for our stories to connect."

"He was a spy?" Gideon asked. "I thought he was a fighter pilot."

"He was both. Once the Americans got into the war, the volunteers were switched over to the army air corps, but they were still allowed to wear their RAF wings on their uniforms. He told me later that there'd been a great deal of negotiation between the two countries over money and ranks, which frustrated him because he just wanted to get back to flying. As far as we could figure out, it was during all that confusion when his papers got mishandled. Especially since the Americans moved him from shooting down enemy planes to taking spy photos from his plane."

"There were spy planes in World War II?" Tess's muse suddenly reappeared to take notice.

"There certainly were. Some of the American Photo Group flew various American-built reconnaissance planes, but Robert and others stuck with a retrofitting of their beloved Spitfires. Speaking of which, here's a little bit of trivia you might enjoy. Do you know why they were called Spitfires?"

"No," Tess said, shaking her head. "I suppose because their firing capability was like spitting bullets."

Madeleine nodded. "That's what many people thought. But the more prosaic reason was that it was the pet name for the manufacturer's young daughter, who he called his little spitfire."

"Oh, I like that," Charlotte said.

"Me, too," Natalie and Tess said together.

"Jinx, you owe me a Coke," Natalie said.

Tess arched a bright brow. "You say that in France?"

"Our father taught me."

An awkward silence settled over the table at yet another indication that of the three of them, Natalie knew Jackson Swann the best.

"How did they retrofit them?" Gideon asked, deftly leading the conversation back on track.

Madeleine sent him a grateful look and continued. "Robert told me they took out the guns to allow extra fuel tanks in the fuselage and leading edges of the wings. They installed two large thirty-six-inch focal cameras in the back. Then they took out the bulletproof glass in the canopy."

"They removed the bulletproof glass?" Gideon asked. "Why?"

"Supposedly, to maximize speed and range, but Robert always believed that if the enemy got close enough for that to matter, you were already dead."

"But surely, he had a fighter escort," Tess said.

"No, because that way he'd be more likely to be seen. He always flew unarmed. And alone. Their planes were painted a special blue they created called PRB blue, Photo Reconnaissance Blue, to better blend into the sky and make them less visible."

"Gracious," Charlotte said, pressing her fingers against her temples. "Now I know where Daddy got his crazy death-defying risk-taking from."

"Wait until you hear about your grandmother," Rose murmured again, earning a sharp look from Madeleine.

"As I said, that's for another day," she said firmly. "Getting back to Robert, part of his squad's job was to provide photographs of bomb damage assessment for the strategic bombing campaign of the German Army's transportation infrastructure in advance of the D-Day landings in Normandy. He completed forty-nine flights, a dozen of them over Berlin. All in all, his small squad took fifty million photos. He'd never owned a camera before that, but he told me that studying all those photos he'd shot, many taken while he was in active combat, is when he caught the photography bug."

"More like an adrenaline rush," Gideon suggested.

"But he must have stuck with it once he got Stateside and passed it on to his son," Tess said.

"And from his son to me." Natalie shook her head. "Papa never said a word about any of that."

"I'm not sure Jackson knew. As I said, Robert didn't talk about the war. Neither do I, as a rule. It was a dreadful time and the only reason we should remember it at all is to honor the fallen and those whose injuries affected their lives postwar, and work to ensure such evil never happens again.

"However, your grandfather had a powerful sense of wanting to make the world better that he passed down to Jackson, whether in their conversations, or perhaps it was just genetic." Another shrug. "Who knows? But I always did suspect that they talked about the things they'd seen, because whenever they'd come back from fishing together, Jack always seemed

less tightly wound. Robert would spend those evenings looking off into space and brooding. I assumed he was reliving his
war experiences."

"I'm still trying to imagine him flying all the way from
England to Berlin in a Spitfire," Gideon said. "How far was
that?"

"He flew from a base outside Oxford, which made it six-
hundred and twenty-four miles one way. He said he'd take
about three runs of each target. Which added up to more
than twelve hundred and forty-eight miles, often under fire.
When I saw his plane, the day we met, it was badly pocked
with round marks from all the times it had been hit.

"Robert was annoyed that many people, even other pilots,
didn't always believe that you could fly that many miles in a
Spitfire. Most didn't even know the Allies had photo reconnaissance. He said that when they first told him what he'd
be doing, *he* hadn't even known what it was. He once got in
a fight in an Oxford pub with an RAF flight crew about it.
And got thrown out."

"Sweet, quiet *Grand-Père* was thrown out of a pub for fighting?" Natalie asked, her eyes wide.

"I believe the word used was *brawling*," Madeleine said.
"He seemed very proud of that because it was one of the rare
stories he'd tell." A smile brought the light back to her eyes.
"But it was definitely true."

She placed her linen napkin from her lap onto the table.
"And that's enough for tonight." Her tone was firm. And
final. And while Madeleine might not have any interest in the
running of the business, it was obvious that her word ruled
the house.

"Tomorrow will be a difficult enough day, and legal details
are tedious. If I don't see you all in the morning for breakfast,
Donovan has been kind enough to move the reading from

his office to the library here." She turned toward the lawyer who had been seated next to Natalie. "At ten sharp, correct?" she asked him.

"Whatever time you wish," he said.

"Then ten it is." She blew a kiss to them all *"Bonne nuit,"* she said. "My granddaughters, once again, it's a blessing to have you all here together. As the years went by, I grew more concerned that I'd never meet you, Tess. And you, Charlotte. My only regret is that I had to lose my only son for it to happen."

As she turned to leave the room, Rose reached for her arm to steady her, but Gideon was faster, putting his arm around her waist and letting her lean against him as they departed. Rose followed, but not before letting the others know that their grandmother would be taking breakfast in her cottage.

"Well," Tess said, letting out a long breath. "That was quite the evening."

"It all sounded like a novel. Or a movie," Charlotte said.

"I could picture it. Picture them," Tess mused.

"You're thinking of writing their story," Natalie guessed.

"It's only a kernel of an idea. Many never turn into anything useful."

"I imagine it's a lot like photography," Natalie said. "Every day I thank God for digital because I never could've afforded the film to take as many photos as the ones I reject."

After saying goodbye to Donovan, each went upstairs to their own bedrooms. Tess was getting ready for bed where she intended to spend some time researching details about the flying photo group when her phone rang.

"Hi," the deep, already familiar voice said. "I'm sorry to have to take off like that, but I got a text from Aubrey during dinner that she's back from the coast, and I thought I'd better get home."

"Of course. Are you there now?"

"No. Look out your window."

Gideon was standing in the moonlight below, looking good enough to have her thinking that if she'd been back in her teens, or that if he didn't have a teenage daughter waiting for him, she'd invite him to climb that tree right beside the window ledge.

"So Madeleine got to bed all right?" she asked, still holding the phone to her ear.

"Yes, but that's not what I was calling about."

"Oh?" She paused, waiting for him to say that whatever happened tomorrow morning, he hoped that she'd stay. So they could explore whether or not that moment between them might turn into something more.

"Whatever happens in the morning," he began, "I hope it works out the way you want."

"Oh. Thanks." If only she knew what she wanted. Gideon Byrne was a distraction she just couldn't deal with right now. The attraction was surely there, but the timing was all wrong.

That was what her head was telling her. Even her heart had the feeling that any man so good-looking who hadn't remarried after ten years of being widowed must have left a trail of broken hearts in his wake. The part of her body whose sex life had been dryer than the Arizona desert for longer than she wanted to take a calendar and figure out, was definitely hoping for something else.

"I'll see you in the morning," he said.

"I'll be there." She gave a wave, then ended the call and shut the curtains. But only after watching him disappear into the night.

22

After a restless night, tossing and turning, and a strained, nearly silent breakfast with her sisters, who seemed to have had no more appetite than she did, wearing a simple black long-sleeved sheath dress she'd packed specifically for this purpose, Tess went to the library. Photos of what she guessed were various Swann family ancestors took up one wall, while the others were lined with shelves of books. There was a mix of heavy, leather-covered tomes that looked like antiques, to hardcovers with well-worn paper jackets, to mass-market paperbacks. Although she didn't seem to see at first glance any order to them, she couldn't wait to delve in and check out the titles. To her mind, what a person read revealed a great deal about them.

As the others filed into the room and sat down, she spotted Gideon, who'd chosen a chair at the very back, along with other people she didn't know, whom she assumed to be vineyard employees. Exactly at ten o'clock, Donovan entered, looking even more like an attorney than the day that he'd trespassed onto Tess's Sedona property. He was accompanied by Madeleine, Rose and a woman who appeared to be in her fifties. She was wearing a pair of slim, dark dress pants, a grape-hued tweed jacket over a jewel-toned purple silk blouse and a double set of pearls at her throat. The heels of her black ankle boots clicking on the parquet wood floor broke the silence that had settled over the low hum of conversation that had come to an abrupt halt as they'd entered the room.

"Good morning, everyone," Donovan said, glancing around. Madeleine, also dressed in black, sat on a maroon leather sofa, Rose beside her, holding her hand. The others were seated in hard-backed chairs that appeared to have been brought in from another room for the occasion. "I'd like to introduce Barbara Williams. Those of you who haven't met her personally will have probably seen her photo on real-estate signs around the Valley. She's here to discuss property prices."

"Hello, everyone." Unlike the perky Realtor who'd sold Tess her Sedona home, Barbara's expression was appropriately sober. "I'm so sorry for your loss. Jackson Swann meant a great deal to our close-knit community, and please know that many others of us share your sorrow."

Donovan waited until the appreciative murmur humming through the room died down before sitting at a large mahogany desk with an inlaid black leather top that looked to be an antique. He took a thick binder out of his briefcase. "You'll probably be glad to know that Jack was as typically succinct in the division of his assets as he was in everything else he did," Donovan said. "So let's get started."

He read off a list of bequests. One was an amount intended to cover college and medical school costs for Gideon's daughter, Aubrey, a pretty brunette teenager seated beside her father, whose hand flew to her pink-tinted mouth in surprise. A second was to cover college and graduate school through the doctoral level, for a young man called John sitting next to Aubrey. Tess assumed the pretty Hispanic woman seated next to him who began openly weeping, was his mother. Next, John's family was granted full ownership of their house and ten acres of grapes on one of the sun-facing fields for their own production. That second part of the bequest appeared to stun John's father, who made the sign of the cross and looked upward. As if thanking the man who'd employed him for obviously some time.

After other requests were handed out to workers, the amounts seeming to have been chosen according to years spent at the winery, they left the room and Donovan turned to what Tess had been waiting for.

"Jackson did not make this decision lightly," he began. "In fact, he and I had been talking about it long before his diagnosis. Since Madeleine already signed over the vineyard to him when Robert passed, she will continue to own the cottage she prefers, as well as receive an income to cover all her expenses for as long as she lives. Enough for, as Jack added in his words, 'one hell of a bash for her hundredth birthday,' which he had not a single doubt she'll celebrate in grand style."

Even as Madeleine smiled, her eyes misted.

"As to the business itself, equal shares of the main estate, which includes the acreage, most buildings and income, go to Tess Swann, Charlotte Swann Aldredge, Natalie Seurat Swann, and Gideon Byrne. All will be part of a privately held foundation Jackson set up that will be headed by Gideon, given that, again, in Jack's own words, he's 'the best kickass vintner in the wine business.'

"He will also be given ownership of his house. In the matters of decision making, while each member of the foundation has a vote, Gideon, as head, will have the ability to overrule the others."

"Even if all three others agree?" Tess asked, even as she reminded herself that she hadn't wanted any of this and would prefer to sell her share to whichever of the others wanted it. Or better yet, have Donovan figure out how to give it away to the local foodbank. The foundation was a twist she hadn't seen coming. "Unless I missed a chapter in math, three against one would top the one."

"In math," Donovan agreed. "However, because he's the only one of you who knows how to run the place and Jack trusted him implicitly, that decision seemed logical."

"If any of us intend to sell, then knowing how to make wine isn't really necessary," Tess pointed out.

"That's what Barbara is here for," Donovan said. "To give you a market value price of the property. I also have the ac- counting records for the last ten years of production income. The production and sales are in a separate company than the houses and land. For reasons I can explain more in detail later. All you need to know now is that it's been set up this way since Robert returned from World War II, and tax wise, it's worked very well. So neither Jack nor Gideon ever saw any reason to change it after Robert's death. As for selling it, there's a caveat to that."

"What's that?" Tess realized that she was the only one ques- tioning Donovan. Which she realized sounded impolite, but this was business, and despite what his other two daughters had said about him yesterday, Jackson Swann never gave her any reason to trust him.

"Although he didn't spend that much time here once he'd left home, he'd worked these same fields with Robert from the time he was a boy. He appreciated the process and the product. And he wanted each of his daughters to appreciate it, or at least understand it, as well."

Tess could feel this coming. "So?"

"So before any of the three of you can inherit your share, you must go through a season until after harvest when this year's wine is bottled. When he updated the will last month, bud break had already occurred—"

"Bud break?" Tess suspected Donovan and the others were getting annoyed by her questions and interruptions, but she didn't give a damn. She was accustomed to handling her own life and that wasn't going to change just because her birth father was going to try to now dictate it from beyond the grave.

Donovan looked toward the back of the room to where Gideon was seated. "I can give an overview of the season when you and Barbara are finished." Gideon answered the unspoken call for help.

"Fine." Donovan blew out a breath and avoided Tess's steady stare. A bit like Rowdy did when he acted as if, if he couldn't see her, she couldn't see him. "Moving on, at the end of the harvest, any one of you is free to sell, but only to Gideon. A line of credit has been set up for Gideon to buy out any or all of you at market value."

"Which is?" Charlotte finally joined the conversation.

"It varies. The area's been growing as more and more people are choosing to move to a more rural setting, away from city crowds."

"They haven't seen Main Street during the height of tourist season," Natalie snorted.

"That's true," Barbara allowed. "Which is why it's best to keep as much of the land agricultural as we can. People come from all over the world to see how Oregon wine is made. The wineries bring in far more income than any housing development would. And," she tacked on with a smile, "I say that as the wife of a contractor/developer."

"You were about to tell us the value," Charlotte reminded her.

"Well, give or take a few hundred thousand given the season…" When she named an amount in the mid-seven figures,

Tess nearly spit out the sip of the coffee she'd brought with her. Then jumped to her feet.

"Are you telling me that our father is bribing us to stay here?"

Donovan cleared his throat. Fiddled with the knot of his tie. "That's a bit hyperbolic and not at all as he meant it."

"Maybe not." She folded her arms. "But that's certainly the upshot. Can it be challenged in court?"

"Anything can be challenged in court. However, inheritance issues are always problematic."

"I've read *Bleak House*, Mr. Brees. I understand how lawyers can drag things out while lining their own pockets. How was the length of that case described in that story? *Innumerable children have been born into the cause; innumerable old people have died out of it?*"

"Dickens did have a very bleak view of family inheritance issues," Donovan allowed easily, not biting on what Tess belatedly realized had been an inadvertently personal insult. His knowledge of the story had Tess wondering if it was required reading in law school. If not, it certainly should have been. "But there's no reason why that need be a problem in this case."

"Given that not all the equal benefactors might have the same view of the bequest, what I want to know, with you speaking in a professional capacity, not as Jackson Swann's personal friend, is can that particular clause be challenged?"

"As I said, any clause in any will can be challenged. Including this one, as I informed Mr. Swann at the time we drew up the document." Tess could tell that he hadn't appreciated that Dickens comparison when he referred to his client in such a formal tone for the first time. *Tough.*

"Even discounting the expense involved, this is not like on TV, where you receive a judgment in under an hour, leaving time for commercials. This situation, since you pointed out each benefactor's circumstances are different, would undoubtedly require each of you to have a separate attorney, and individual cases to be heard."

"I'm well aware that this is not television. Having *been* on television." Tess's tone mirrored his.

"My point is, Ms. Swann, that even if you were to get a court date immediately, which, trust me, you wouldn't, you undoubtedly wouldn't receive a judgment until harvest time. Which would make challenging the clause moot."

He glanced down at his watch. "Unfortunately, I have another appointment." Tess bet that was a lie. "Why don't you let Gideon fill you in about the logistics? If Barbara can stay, she can answer any real-estate questions you or your sisters might have—"

"Oh, I'm free as a bird," she said as if she'd missed the battle of wills occurring right in front of her. "I had my assistant clear my calendar for the day in case anyone would want to drive around and look at other property listings for comps."

"Well, then. There's just one more item we need to deal with before you make your final decision." He opened the laptop computer he'd carried in with him and hit a few keys. "Jack left you each a private message I'm sure you'll want to hear. He had hoped to speak to each of you in person, but unfortunately, time caught up with him."

Tess wasn't certain she believed that part, but decided that she'd already caused enough tension and there was nothing that could be changed about that now, so she kept her thoughts to herself that while he might have risked his life several times on any given day, Jackson Swann was undoubtedly afraid of having this conversation he'd avoided for over three decades.

Looking relieved that she'd remained silent, Donovan gathered his laptop and file and stood up. "I'd suggest you listen to them before Gideon does his presentation. Then I'll call tomorrow morning for your decisions."

"I can give you mine right now," Tess said.

"Your sisters may want to take more time," he suggested. "It is, admittedly, at least a short-term life-altering situation." He glanced down at his watch. "In any case, I need to be back in town in twenty minutes, so why don't you three discuss the situation, sleep on it and, as I said, I'll call tomorrow morning to hear your decisions and we can go from there."

"That's certainly fine with me," Charlotte said, her magnolia tone a contrast to Tess's brisk one.

"As it is with me, too," Natalie said, her Parisian accent adding a musicality that Tess guessed she'd picked up from her singer mother. "I can use the soft evening light to take some photos."

"I'm in," Gideon agreed.

"Great. Again, I'm sorry for your loss." His gaze swept over them. Lingering, Tess noticed, a bit longer on Natalie. Whose cheeks colored a bit. Interesting. Then, making his escape, Donovan left the room.

23

"Well," Charlotte commented to Tess as they walked upstairs after agreeing to meet with Gideon later in the library. "You and Mr. Brees don't seem to care for each other very much."

"I like him fine."

"You *were* a little hard on him," Charlotte said.

"He was only doing his job," Natalie pointed out. "I thought it was very sweet that Papa left something to all his workers. Especially Aubrey and John. Who, I sensed, have young romantic feelings for one another."

"The French see romance in everything." They'd reached Tess's room. "I'm going to listen to my recording. I'll see you downstairs after." She swept into the room, shutting the door firmly behind her.

"Don't mind her," Natalie assured Charlotte. "Donovan's really very kind. He'd have never let our father do anything to hurt any one of us."

"But he did, didn't he? Oh, I don't mean Donovan. But Daddy."

"He's the same person you knew. I'm sorry if this insults you, but your mother does not sound like a very nice woman.

From the little bit of your life you shared, I suspect that she's very cold and distant. And could well have been jealous of how much he loved you."

"He did love me." Charlotte could feel the waterworks about to start up again. "Thank you for reminding me." She paused. Then touched her lips to Natalie's cheek. "I'm glad that you're my sister."

Natalie exchanged the embrace. "As I am about you."

After entering her room with the pretty flower-sprigged wallpaper, the wood and wrought-iron sleigh bed and the view of the mountain, she threw herself down on the pretty white embroidered quilt and hoped that whatever their father had to say to Tess might soften her some. The woman who'd shared the world's best pancake yesterday and obviously loved her dog, had seemed, if not overly friendly, at least somewhat caring. But the way she jousted with Donovan showed a very different side. A negative, divisive side that could definitely cause problems for all of them. And right now, if there was one thing Charlotte didn't need, it was another problem.

She'd shut off her phone during the meeting in the library, and after turning it back on, noticed that, along with a video file from Donovan, she had three missed calls. All from Mason. She wondered if he was calling to beg her to come home, then noticed the text message demanding her to call him. ASAP. She could imagine his cold tone and decided that there was nothing he had to say to her that couldn't wait.

So she sat up, leaned against the headboard and downloaded the video. Despite how shockingly frail he appeared, her father's voice coming over the speakerphone was like a soothing cashmere blanket wrapped around her.

He began by apologizing for not having told her about his illness. He hadn't wanted her to suffer any more than he feared she might soon be in her marriage, if she weren't already. And yes, he answered the question he hadn't allowed her to challenge him with face-to-face; he had hired a private detective to watch her husband from the day they'd met at her wedding.

All his Spidey senses had gone off that moment he'd shaken hands with Mason, and felt the ice within the handsome, suave exterior and imagined he heard the rattle of a Northern Pacific rattlesnake.

"I stayed alive as long as I did by learning to trust my instincts," he told her. "And I knew that Mason Aldredge is going to hurt you. Perhaps he already has, but knowing you, your first instinct would be to try to make things work, which would take even more sacrifice on your part. However, since you were a grown woman, with a life and career of your own, there was nothing I could do but be there for you when your heart was shattered. Unfortunately, my old nemesis, death, had other plans for me."

"You were right, Daddy," she said. "But if you'd told me, I wouldn't have listened, so in the end, it doesn't matter."

"Not that I was there often enough," he continued, "but on those rare times I'd be back in Charleston, I grew more and more concerned that you'd become too acquiescent."

He went on to say that while he knew her sweet disposition was her nature, he feared that his having missed so much of her life was to blame for her willingness to cave into other people's expectations. To having spent her entire life trying to live up to her mother's impossible demands, she'd forced herself into tidy boxes others had created for her.

He'd watched her struggling to earn her mother's love when, in truth, her failure to do so wasn't Charlotte's fault. Blanche was merely incapable of that emotion.

"I never knew whether something had happened to her early in life to have her close herself off from her emotions," he continued. "But her heart was an iceberg that no amount of effort would ever melt. So my fatherly advice is to simply stop trying to please. Forget about winning your mother's and husband's approval, or anyone else's for that matter, and live a life that you feel passionate about, honey. Not one that you merely *want* to do. But that you're driven to do. A life that's as necessary to you as breathing…

"And I guess that's about all I can say, except, and you've no idea how I've debated whether or not to tell you, but I've decided, that even though you don't smoke, at least not that I know about, I don't want you worrying that you're carrying some genetic cancer thing. I need to tell you that your mother was already pregnant with you when we got married."

"I realized that long ago, Daddy," Charlotte said to the deathly gray face on the video.

Then, suddenly, that comment about genetics sank in. "Are you telling me that you're not my birth father?" she asked the voice on her phone.

As if he could hear her, Jackson continued. "Since this is truth time, I want you to know and believe that you were always a daughter of my heart. I couldn't love you or be any more proud of you if you had been. But it turns out that your mother had something going with her sister's husband before she and I met."

"Uncle *Frank*?" Her blood went as cold as a rare Southern ice storm.

"Blanche was in New York City to get an abortion, then changed her mind. She was staying at The Plaza and we met at the bar in The Oak Room, where I'd stopped in to have a drink after a meeting."

Her mother always stayed at The Plaza during New York Fashion Week. But needless to say, the planned abortion had never been mentioned.

"Well, although this is hard to admit, when we hit it off,

instead of it being my magnetic personality or good looks, which I arrogantly attributed her attention to, it had occurred to her that I could possibly be the solution to her problem.

"Two months later her out-of-the-blue call about her being pregnant came as one helluva surprise. Tess's mother got pregnant because we didn't use a condom, so I was always careful about never having unprotected sex. She'd told me at the time that she was on the pill, but admitted that she'd forgotten one while traveling. And since condoms aren't a hundred percent effective, I figured mistakes happen and proposed. We both agreed it would be a marriage of convenience to protect her reputation, which meant a great deal to her."

That part of the story was the only thing that was no surprise.

"I didn't know you weren't mine until she told me the truth during a blazing argument after you were born. But by then it didn't matter, because the moment I saw the sonogram, you were my baby girl. As it worked out, my lifestyle suited Blanche just fine, and it wasn't until I started visiting you at SCAD that I realized how much I'd cheated you out of a father."

"You were a hell of a lot more of a father than Uncle Frank," Charlotte murmured, finally understanding why her aunt had always chillingly ignored her at family gatherings.

"But that thing I said about your work being like breathing? That's how mine was. You're a smart woman. I know you can figure out how to juggle a career and a family better than I did. And just maybe, this time here at Maison de Madeleine might give you the time to sort things out.

"Meanwhile, I hope you'll forgive me telling you all this, and for neglecting you. It wasn't because I wasn't your birth dad, but because I've belatedly come to realize that I was too driven. Too selfish. Despite my lack of a relationship with your mother, I should have worked things out. Believe me when I say that I could never have loved you more, and don't ever forget that you'll always be my sugar pie."

So many things made sense now. Despite the revelation that the larger-than-life man she'd always thought had been her daddy wasn't the man who'd gotten her mother pregnant, she'd never had a moment's doubt that he'd loved her. It also explained the tension and often outright hostility between her parents.

So deciding that he was right, that it hadn't mattered that he wasn't her birth father, that he was, and always would be, the only father she'd ever had, she was going to concentrate on the part of his message about having a passion that was as important as breathing.

Which wasn't all that easy itself right now. Not when her already messed-up life had just turned even more upside down. She'd come to realize that over her marriage, she'd been losing more and more of who she was. Now the fact that she wasn't who she'd always thought she was had her head spinning.

After allowing herself to surrender to the tears that had been burning her eyes, she took a few deep breaths, then hit Play, and listened to the recording a second time.

That he'd known about Mason's infidelity stung, but she admitted that he'd honestly believed that he was doing the right thing, trusting her to make her own decisions. As he'd always told her she should do.

That her uncle Frank was her birth father had nothing to do with who she was. She was, and always would be, Jackson Swann's daughter. And she'd had a life she'd felt passionate about, she considered as she sat alone in the bedroom, listening to the music of the birdsong outside her window. While at SCAD, every morning she'd risen with so many ideas tumbling in her head. Classes had been a joy, and yes, she knew she was too needy for approval, but fortunately, when God had been handing out talent, He'd been particularly generous with her. She was good. Better than good. She had the touch; all her professors had told her.

Turning down offers from prestigious firms that wanted her to start as a draftsman, or a decorator, until she gained more experience, she'd gone solo on a shoestring right out of school, doing work that she was proud of, even knowing that she could do better. And more. And she *had* grown. Enough to start building a reputation for herself, she'd ended up in that ritzy conference room where she'd met the man she'd allowed to sweep her away.

She was still pondering her father's words when her phone chimed. Mason again. This time, her decision made, she picked up the phone.

"So?" the curt voice that had once seemed so charming asked. "What did you get?"

No apology. No begging, or even asking that she consider trying to repair the marriage he'd fractured. She wondered if she told him the entire truth about her wealth, whether he might reconsider. "A quarter share in a winery that's in the red," she said. Which was mostly true. Like so many other businesses, especially those in food service, Donovan had said, Maison de Madeleine hadn't turned a profit last year during a down economy. "Is that all you called for?"

"No, I called to tell you that I've hired an attorney. I'm divorcing you."

"Shouldn't it be the other way around?"

"Well, you did leave me."

"Because my father died!" It dawned on Charlotte that as terribly sad as she was, and would undoubtedly be for some time about losing her father, she was suddenly feeling more emotion than she had during her entire marriage to Mason.

The decision to rebuild her life included divorcing her lying, cheating husband. She was annoyed, however, that he was accusing her of being in the wrong. "Did your lawyer happen to mention that adultery is a crime in South Carolina?"

"You're going to play that card?"

"Well, as I understand it, the legal term is guilty of the crime of adultery or fornication. I wonder how voters would take to that?"

"As it happens, Olivia's father is a federal judge with a great deal of pull in the party, so I'm not overly concerned." He brushed off that potential problem. "If you're trying to blackmail me into giving you half the house, it's not going to work. South Carolina is an equitable apportionment state. I acquired it before we married and you were never added to the deed."

"I hate that house. It's atrocious and whoever decorated it is guilty of design malpractice." Although there could be lawsuits against architects and contractors for breaking code or zoning regulations, she'd never heard of anyone being sued for an ugly house. But in the case of Mason's, it should be possible. "Still, I'm told that the court decides what's equable, based on a set of factors, including income. Which I don't currently happen to have due to your insistence I cut back on my business to procreate and help yours.

"Plus," she tacked on, while she heard him starting to sputter on his end of the phone, "apparently, sexual fornication behavior can be factored into any alimony settlement."

He cursed. More roughly than a proper Southern attorney about to run for public office in a politically conservative state should. "How much?"

"Nothing."

"What?"

"I don't want a thing from you. Except my personal belongings, which you can have packed up and sent here to Oregon." She gave him the address.

"You didn't tell me the winery was Maison de Madeleine. That's got to be worth a fortune."

"Oh…well, as it turns out, despite a down year, it is. Which really doesn't concern you, because although we're still technically married, as a hot-shot attorney, you're obviously aware that any inheritance isn't considered a shared marital asset. So if you'll just send my things, my lawyer will be in touch. Goodbye, Mason.

"Oh, and one more thing. I know you're proud of your monstrous fake antebellum mansion, but don't be surprised if your next wife rips all those dreadful paintings and tacky gilt the fuck out of there."

She ended the call. Then, as sad as she felt about losing her father, she felt a sense of empowerment that was a far better inheritance than a quarter interest in a winery her mind was already spinning plans to help turn around. And just in case he was actually looking down on her, as she'd been taught in Sunday school, Charlotte looked up and smiled. "Thanks, Daddy. You might not have always been around. But you always came through when I needed you." And that, she decided, as she felt her broken heart begin to stitch itself back together, was what a good father did.

24

She wasn't avoiding the tape, Tess assured herself as she changed out of the black dress into jeans and a T-shirt with a scene of Cathedral Rock silk-screened on it by an artist she'd met at a Sedona animal rescue fundraiser. She checked her phone, finding three emails and three texts from her agent and another from her editor, saying how much they were looking forward to more Pleasant Meadows High stories. All of which she decided could wait.

Finally, she opened the video file. The face frozen on the screen was nothing like the world adventurer she'd seen on the various news clips on YouTube and internet photos. And a far cry from the outrageously handsome man in the wedding photo she'd come across when she'd been eight, while poking around in her mother's closet. It had been hidden away in a box with a marriage license and a plain gold wedding band.

The cancer had obviously ravaged his body, leaving him mostly skin and bones. But even close to death his eyes still burned with a fiery passion for life. "Where the hell should I start?" he asked.

"How about at the beginning?" an off-camera voice she recognized as Gideon's said.

"Okay." He dragged a large, scarred hand down his face. "If you're watching this, Tess, you've already gone further than I thought you would. If you're watching it at Maison de Madeleine, well, Donovan is more of a miracle worker than I'd have ever guessed possible…

"So. Though I've been known to lie from time to time—hell, in my job it was a necessity in order to stay alive—what I'm going to tell you is the God's honest truth. And if there's one thing even I'm not foolhardy enough to do, it's tell any lies when I might finally be standing at heaven's gate. To be honest, even though your grandmother would drag me to Mass when I was younger, I never really believed in any afterlife. When you witness as much death as I have, you can't allow yourself to think about what happens after. And you definitely stop believing in any God who'd allow such atrocities to happen… Though I'll admit that my thoughts about that might be changing lately. Which is not what this is supposed to be about, so let's move on to the important parts.

"I loved your mother," he said. "From the moment I saw her." He paused. Took a deep, rattling breath that sounded so painful Tess placed her hand on her own chest. "Okay, that's not true, and this video, which was all Gideon's damn idea, by the way, is supposed to be about truth. The whole truth, and nothing but the truth, as they say.

"At first I was pissed. I was young and cocky in those days and considered myself far too important to be stuck following some bimbo starlet around. I was a war photo-correspondent. Not some damn Hollywood studio flack. I should've been out in the jungle. Bringing the truth about the ravages of war into viewers' living rooms.

"But over those days we were together, I realized that your

mom was a better person than I was. Because at the time, I was just there for the action. The adrenaline rush of being out in the jungle along with my byline on photos that might tell stories long after I was gone. While your mother was there for the troops.

"As you already know, Amy wasn't much of a dancer. And, since we're being honest, she sang even worse. But she knew that. She also knew, by her first tour, that the only reason she'd been booked was because she was so sexy. And, maybe it's the wrong thing to say to a daughter about her mother, but she was the hottest woman I'd ever seen.

"She'd insisted on landing in Saigon under gunfire because, she told me, she wasn't about to disappoint those men and women who were so very far away from home, risking their lives for a cause no one really understood. They'd taken an oath to defend America, and they'd do their job. Just as she would do hers by bringing them a couple hours of home, distraction and reminders of the happier times that would be waiting for them when their tours were over and they returned home.

"I had a big ego back then—hell, I still have one now—but Amy honestly humbled me. And that's why I loved her. Unfortunately, except for getting her pregnant with you, I'm probably the worst guy she ever could've met at that time in her life."

He went on to describe how much energy she'd poured into her performance. How exhausted she'd be afterward as she'd gamely climbed back into the helicopter to take off for the next stop on the tour. And when he described her reading mail call at some distant outpost that wasn't usually on the entertainment list, how she'd kissed each recipient on the cheek, a kiss from home, she'd called it, then how, after they were back in the copter, she'd break down and weep, Tess's eyes teared up, as well.

"Yeah, we were admittedly drunk when we got married, but all that alcohol did was take away my common sense. I knew I wasn't good enough for her. Knew that I couldn't be anywhere near the kind of man she deserved. But during those few days together, I wanted to be."

When he took another of those deep, painful breaths, Tess realized how hard this must have been for him. Not just physically, but emotionally. It also crossed her mind that Gideon Byrne had understood how important these last words would be for his daughters who had such different relationships with their father. She didn't know what Charlotte and Natalie were experiencing. But until this moment, she hadn't realized how much she'd needed to hear these words straight from the man she'd spent much of her life resenting, and the rest trying to forget his existence.

"When I returned home from China for your birth, there was nothing I wanted more than to be your father. You stole my heart the first moment I looked into your big blue eyes. And when you took hold of my finger..."

He choked up. He closed his eyes and took another one of those rattling breaths. Then opened them, revealing the pain, both physical and emotional, he was feeling.

"I wanted to be the same kind of father that mine had been for me. Always there. Whether it was when I broke my arm falling off my bike while standing up on the handlebars, or when Walter Wallace dared me to steal a six-pack of Coors off the back of the mini market delivery truck just as Sheriff Ferguson happened to be pulling into the gas station to fill up his squad car.

"But the truth of the matter was that I couldn't be that stand-up guy like Dad. Even for your mother. Even for you. And there was no way on God's green earth I could fit into Amy's Hollywood lifestyle."

Okay. Tess got that. If she hadn't grown up in it, she

would've found those years really weird. As it was, they'd been, for her, normal. Until they weren't.

"Despite the clause in the will, you're free to leave. What Donovan didn't tell you was that there's no way anyone's going to enforce it and you can sell today, if you want. I'm not asking you to stay. That's up to you. But you're fortunate to be able to do your work, which is damn good, by the way—and yes, I've read all your books, and watched the TV series—anywhere.

"What I'm hoping is that you'll use this time to get to know your sisters. And your grandmother, who, although she has a core of pure steel and is the gutsiest woman I've ever known, can't live forever. She never got to know you and Charlotte, and depriving her of being able to be the type of grandmother she wanted to be, *deserved* to be, is on me. I can never make that loss up to her or to either one of you and have no right to ask you to stay at least long enough to get to know her, and her to know you. But I hope you'll consider it.

"I realize you're known for writing about teenagers. But in reality, we both know that you're writing about families and it doesn't take a therapist to see that you've spent all these past years creating fictional families rather than the one you ended up with.

"So…" Another ragged breath. And a painful, rattling cough that pulled Tess's heartstrings, even as she tried to tell herself that she'd feel compassion for any human in such pain. That her own pain watching him struggle to breathe didn't have anything to do with a father-daughter connection. "I hope you'll at least give it a shot. For all your sakes…

"Well, I guess that's about it. I'll have to admit that I wasn't wild about the idea of making this video, but Gideon can be relentless. And once again he was right because I'm feeling better having gotten all that off my chest. And yes, again, I just made this all about me. So I better fucking quit while I'm ahead. Have a wonderful life, my darling Tess. You deserve it."

Fade to black.

Tess wasn't aware of how long she sat there, taking it all in, trying to sort out her feelings, which were as wild as the darkening clouds she could see storming toward the valley over the mountaintops from the coast. Except for her current frustration over her writing career, and that breakdown, which she'd totally recovered from once she'd gotten off the pills, she'd been living a good life. Better than most. Okay, maybe her mother was right about her having become a bit of a hermit in Sedona, but what was wrong with that? She'd had plenty of peace and quiet to think about her characters, and their very differing families—and how perceptive had Jackson Swann been to have understood something she hadn't figured out until book three?—that she had been creating fictional families. Just as she had on *Double Trouble*. Also, she had Rowdy, who was currently lying on the rug beside her, and provided all the company she needed.

Yet…she couldn't deny that she was intrigued by the idea of a grandmother who was a member of the French Resistance. And it wasn't as if she had any pressing need to be in Arizona, which was approaching summer. Perhaps Sedona didn't get anywhere near as hot as Phoenix or Tucson, but the past few years had the temperatures rising into triple digits. Plus, the days were unrelentingly sunny. Which most would think was a good thing, but in truth, it could get tediously boring.

Unlike this Oregon valley, where Mother Nature appeared to change her mood nearly hourly.

"Okay, Dad," she said to the darkening sky. "I'll give it a shot. But I'm not in the market for being in the wine business. So if you're somewhere up there watching me watch this video, don't expect me to stay beyond this harvest. Because that isn't happening."

25

Natalie was conflicted. On one hand, she was heartbroken about her dear papa. Her only comfort was that if her years of Catholic school taught her anything, at least he and her *maman* were united again. Because she'd known how hard it had been on him losing her. He'd grown so withdrawn, even more than usual whenever he'd come home from his wars. She'd thought what she took for depression was his sadness over her *maman*'s death. But now she knew the change had been because he'd been dying.

Which made her angry at him for keeping her away, not allowing her to be with him at the end. Then, her Catholic guilt kicked in, and she felt guilty for being angry at her dead papa. His work had kept him away for years, depriving her of having a father to talk to. Oh, she could talk to *Maman* about such things, but to have had some window into the male mind certainly would have been helpful. Especially when it came to Donovan.

Was it possible, she would have asked her father, that a man might be attracted to a woman, but didn't want to risk damaging their long friendship? Or was that just hopeful thinking and should she give up waiting for him and move on with her life? It wasn't that she hadn't had opportunities. And she wasn't a virgin. But those times she'd had sex with any man, no matter how attractive he might be, or how caring, or skillful in bed, something vital had been missing. Her heart just hadn't been in it. Unless she fantasized about being with Donovan. Which, despite this terribly sad time, made her laugh. Perhaps she, not Tess, should have been the actress. She'd certainly had enough practice faking orgasms. Not that any of the men she'd had sex with would have noticed.

Sighing, she clicked on the link she'd downloaded and heard the oh so familiar voice.

"My darling Natalie," he began. "Gideon has told me time and time again that I'm being unfair to you. That you shouldn't have to learn of my death this way. That I should have given you the chance to be with me at the end, especially after you lost your mother so recently. But that's why I chose to keep my condition to myself. Because I knew you'd feel that it was your duty to be with me. To nurse me. To provide care and comfort as you did with your mother.

"Her death cost you not only a great deal of emotional pain, but a year of work, just when your career was beginning to take off. There was no way I was going to be responsible for slowing the momentum you've begun to build, thanks to your talent, yes, but just as much due to how hard you work. You'll never know how intensely pleased and proud I am that you chose photography. Although I'm all too aware that for reasons I'll never understand, I chose to make public the dark side of the world. The horrific events people don't want to look at until you shove it in their faces.

"While you, on the other hand, were always a bright, optimistic girl. Even during the darkest, grayest, rainiest winters, returning to Paris to you and your mother was like being bathed in sunshine. You're definitely your mother's child, and if I believed in God, I'd be thanking Him or Her for blessing you with the innate talent for always finding the good in any situation. As I hope you will do now, with this rather difficult one I've selfishly left you with.

"It undoubtedly hasn't been easy for you, being thrown together at this time, for this reason, with Tess and Charlotte. But they *are* your sisters. And if there's one thing Gideon, your *maman* and your *grand-mère* have insisted over the years, it's that the three of you should have had an opportunity to know one another long ago. Each of you is an exceptional woman in your own right and I'm hoping that you'll find common ground, only if it's to be angry at your father for all the lies of omission I've told over the years.

"I also realize that you may have to work the hardest to create your family of sisters, because Tess and Charlotte could well resent you for having been the one I shared the most time with. The one whose mother I stayed with for so many years. Until death do us part, as the vows go, the vows your mother was never willing to take. Which was ironic because of the three women I fathered daughters with, yours was the one I believe I could have been a good husband to. Not because I was able to change, but because Josette never needed nor wanted me to. From the first night we met, she knew who and what I was and accepted me fully, entirely, as I was. But I'm getting off track… These damn drugs have my mind wandering and leaping topics.

"Do you remember that book I'd read you at bedtime when you were young?" he asked.

"Bonsoir Lune," she murmured, pausing the recording to respond as if her father was still there in the room with her. "A mean boy at school told me that his parents called you a crazy American who was going to get yourself killed someday."

She'd been so worried that she hadn't slept well for nights. Until her papa, whom she'd only later learned her mama had contacted about the problem, had returned home with a book wrapped in blue tissue paper with shiny gold stars.

At the time she just knew that being with her father, listening to his deep voice reading about the little rabbit saying good-night to the stars, the air and the noises everywhere, had calmed her into sleep. She'd continued to enjoy it even when she was old enough to read it to herself partly because, in her mind, she could hear her father's voice along with hers and it was only later when she bought the English version, *Goodnight Moon*, for a friend's new baby, that she'd understood that the book she'd so loved was a lesson in not worrying about problems that had happened during the day or what tomorrow might bring. He had been, she considered now, teaching her to live in the moment.

Was that why, she wondered as she hit Play again, she'd been drawn to take those photos of people frozen in time? At moments when they were carefree and happy?

"I know that if you choose to put your mind to it," he continued, "you'll forge a strong bond. I've left you all a challenge. And I've no doubt that each of you will find your own way to turn this negative into a positive situation. And create a family not just of the blood, but of your hearts. *Au revoir, ma chère fille.*"

"Until we meet again, Papa," she echoed. Then she buried her face in her hands and wept.

26

"Thanks for the warning, Jack," Gideon muttered as he prepared for the meeting with the three women who were now his partners. But not equal partners.

He hadn't been surprised about the clause keeping the vineyard intact. He'd wondered if Jack might not do like Madeleine's parents and many in the Valley had done, and sell off fields to other vineyards. There was, after all, only so much land to be developed, and acquiring established fields was the best way to grow your business. He'd also hoped that a recommendation that he stay on would have been put into the will. Not that any new owner would necessarily want to fire him. A great many competitive vineyards had approached him over the years, trying to lure him away from Maison de Madeleine. But he'd never been tempted. Not even when the salary offers got to nearly double what he was making now. With his salary, the house, the truck, the freedom to hire and fire as he pleased and one of the best crews any vintner could wish for, he'd been more than satisfied. He'd been content. And always grateful to the man who'd come along at a time when he was just trying to make it through each day.

Gideon understood why Jack had wanted his daughters to get to know one another. Hadn't he, Madeleine and Rose, been attempting to convince him to do that very same thing for years? He'd thought there was a possibility that he'd leave the business to the three daughters equally. He'd never expected to get a piece of the pie. Maybe that was what Jack was telling him, that last day, when he said he'd thought of him as the son he'd never had.

Tess, Charlotte and Natalie had already professed to know little or nothing about wine, except drinking it. Putting him in charge was logical. But the question of the day was whether they would understand that in this decision, at least, Jackson Swann had done the right thing.

In the event Jack left the vineyard to his daughters, Gideon had prepared a presentation to give them an idea what they'd be getting into. Now, as he set up the presentation with both slides and video on his computer, he thought about what he would face when they came downstairs.

Tess was the toughest of the trio. Now that he'd heard her backstory, he knew she'd had to be strong or she would've ended up just one of those tragic died-too-young Hollywood stories. She was also the most outspoken, and although she hadn't held back on the snark during the reading of Jack's will, call him perverse, but that made her even more appealing.

Becky had never held back her opinion, either, although she usually spent more time leading up to a topic, preparing him for her argument instead of barreling forward, full steam ahead, as Tess had done. Along with teaching art history at the local community college, she'd been a whiz at multitasking, keeping the house together and teaching Aubrey her numbers and how to read even before their daughter started preschool. She'd even made cookies for church and school fundraising bake sales.

As her cancer had progressed, it had fallen on him to do so many of the things he'd always taken for granted. He'd learned how to cook basic meals, although the chemo and radiation had done such a job destroying Becky's taste buds, she hadn't had enough of an appetite. He'd started making Aubrey's lunch the night before because mornings had turned out to be more rushed than he'd ever noticed.

After Becky had lost her valiant battle far too young, he'd resorted to feeding their daughter the sugary, fluorescent-colored cereal that her mother had never allowed for breakfast before waving her off to kindergarten on the bright yellow school bus. Then, already exhausted, he'd head out into the fields, or the testing room, and feel guilty for never having any idea about all his wife had been doing to keep their lives running smoothly and seemingly effortlessly.

Not that Aubrey would have let him, but he never missed a fundraiser bake sale, although he'd cheated with macaroons from a local bakery. There were times he thought of his daughter as a little Napoleon, but without the oversize ego. She had, he realized, a great deal put on her young shoulders.

Feeling that dull hum of remaining grief, he dragged his mind back to his presentation, preparing for questions the women might ask him and thinking about how each of them would respond.

Which took him back to the sister he hadn't been able to get out of his mind for the past two days. His attraction to Jack's eldest daughter had nothing to do with the fact that she looked like an actor Central Casting would choose for a superheroine movie. Nor was it the fact that he'd had a crush on her, or at least on her character, back in middle school. What he found compelling was the way she'd opened up to him; giving him an inside look at what her life behind the camera and tabloids had been like. She'd probably gone through the worst of the three, but had survived. Having a teenage girl of his own, he could only imagine how much inner strength that had taken. It also, he guessed, was why she was the least likely of the three to trust anyone.

She wasn't the only one wondering why she'd chosen him to share what had to be her deepest, darkest secret with. He'd been wondering, too. Perhaps because she had every intention of leaving as soon as possible, and he'd been safe, since they'd never see each other again after tomorrow.

Or perhaps she'd felt the same, out-of-the-blue connection he'd experienced. A pull that had him wanting more.

The three returned, followed by Barbara, who would be answering the real-estate questions. Aware of what Jack had said in each of his videos to his daughters, Gideon wasn't surprised by Natalie's red-rimmed eyes. He was, however, surprised that Charlotte wasn't still weeping. Of the three of them, she had to have been the hardest hit with that revelation about her paternity.

"Okay," he said, once they were all seated. "I thought I'd start with terms around you staying for the season so you'll understand what time frame you'd be looking at. Then I'll try to answer any questions you have so you'll better understand what you're seeing."

He paused, half expecting Tess's hand to shoot up. But she seemed more subdued than she had at the reading, and remained silent, crossing her long legs, clad in a pair of ripped jeans and folding her arms over the front of a graphic T-shirt.

He showed the first slide, which was a photo of the bare vines in winter. "The first thing you need to know is that a winery is a full-time, year-round business. In the winter, when the vines are dormant, they're pruned to get ready for the next cycle. Since we're a sustainable vineyard, the clippings are put through a chipper and ground into mulch and recycled back beneath the plants." He saw Tess's concentrated expression and, from their earlier conversation about her search for a plot, suspected she was back to imagining mulching a body after having a character commit a murder.

"You need an expert crew to do the pruning because the proper placement of cuts will determine where the growth will come when the vines awaken. Early in the spring that same crew will tie the vine canes to the trellis fencing to support the growth of the grapes that will become that year's vintage."

"Once the ground temperature reaches fifty degrees—and that depends on the weather that season and the location of the vines—the starch in the vine turns to sugar, creating sap, which moves through the vine and escapes through those earlier pruning cuts. The sap escapes, or weeps, through those cuts, creating drops of sap all along the vines. This is the start of the actual growing season.

"After that, small fuzzy brown buds begin to form. As the temperature continues to warm, they'll break open, revealing a bright green shoot. That's always an exciting time because the vineyards turn that dark gray-and-black landscape into a bright green color. The more leaves on the vine, the more photosynthesis from the growing warmth of the sun will occur, allowing those shoots to develop faster. Leaves unfold as the shoot grows taller.

"That's where we are now. The crews out in the fields are doing a first grooming, trimming canes to regulate growth. Too many leaves cause nutrients from the vine to be more thinly distributed, which makes more grapes. You'd think that would be a good thing, but those grapes would lack the complexity and flavor concentration."

"Quality over quantity," Tess said.

"Exactly. Pruning began, according to what was recorded by monks, in 345 AD, when Saint Martin rode out on his donkey to check on the monastery's vines in the Loire Valley. He was a great lover of wine and was always teaching younger monks the proper procedure. The vineyards were not just important to have wine for Mass, but they provided a key source of income for the Order. He tied his donkey to some vines and was gone for several hours, tending to business, but when he returned, he discovered that the donkey had eaten many of the leaves right down to the stalk.

"Yet, the next year the monks saw that the vines that had been damaged grew back more abundantly and produced the best grapes. Ever since then winegrowers do early pruning."

"I grew up in France and never heard that story," Natalie said.

"Ah, but you grew up in Paris. Parisians know a great deal about what wine they enjoy. But like Americans, I doubt if they give all that much thought to what goes into the making of it before it ends up in a bottle on their table."

"Guilty as charged, Monsieur Vigneron," she admitted.

"If you look closely at the vines, you'll see small clusters among the leaves. As the days warm, and we get more sun, tiny flowers will appear on those clusters. After the flowers bloom, they self-pollinate, which is when the grape clusters begin to form. The berries are tiny, bright green, hard and dense because they're made up of mostly acid and short tannins."

"Which means nothing to me," Tess said. "Which, I suppose, is why Jack was wise to leave the wine-making part of this business to you."

"Thanks. I'll try to make this quick. Not because I think you won't understand it, but I want to keep this introductory. As the season progresses, we'll get into more detail. But basically, tannins are a compound that occur naturally inside the grape skins, seeds and stems that when they soak in the juice after the grapes are pressed, gives wines characteristic dryness or astringency.

"What makes wine have a strong or weak tannin depends on how long the juice sits with those skins, seeds and stems after pressing. The longer they soak in the juice, the more tannin you'll have. When we make red wine, like our Pinot Noir, I want the skins to impart more color, which adds more tannin, and a deeper complexity to the wine."

"So white wines have less tannin?" Charlotte asked.

"Right. Tannins also are a natural antioxidant that protects the wine. Which is why certain wines can age so long."

"And why red wine supposedly keeps people healthy," Natalie said.

"Madeleine insists that she's lived as long as she has because she drinks our Pinot Noir every day." Gideon shrugged. "While there's no hard science behind it, I'm sure as hell not about to argue with her. At this stage, almost all grape varietals look the same. The clusters will continue to grow and develop for the next month or two, then the varietals are harvested at different times, depending on the type of grapes, the elevation and type of wine.

"Chardonnay comes from burgundy grapes, which is why we grow it with our Pinot Noir. Again, when you taste it, it's a dry, full-body white wine with primary fruit flavors of apple, yellow melon and starfruit. It's one of the few white wines commonly aged in oak. At Maison de Madeleine, we always used French oak, which added a richer flavor and aroma of cream, vanilla, or butter.

"But now, since tastes are changing, we've moved to aging most of our Chardonnay in steel drums, which gives the wine a lighter, zestier acidity, more along the lines of Pinot Gris, which is also harvested earlier, when the acid level in the grapes is still high. Statewide, Pinot Gris now outsells Chardonnay two to one."

"So that's your reason for moving most of your Chardonnay into the steel barrels?" Tess asked. "For that lighter taste?"

"That and the fact that it's less expensive. French oak barrels have to be changed out every couple years because the oak degrades, which can let air in. Also, at a cost that can go as high as a thousand dollars each, the expense adds up. Steel just needs to be washed out between using, so once you've made the investment, that's pretty much it."

Charlotte had been looking at the papers in the folder they'd all been given. "That's how you plan to bring the bottom line back up."

"It's one of the ways I have in mind."

"That makes a great deal of sense," she said. "Especially since, as you said, tastes are changing. In that respect, wine making sounds a lot like designing. Finding a balance between what people like, keeping on top of trends and making sure you stay within the budget."

"That's the plan in a nutshell." He realized that he shouldn't have been surprised that the Southern belle sister would've been the first to zero in on the economics and changing tastes since the business she'd established required a knowledge of both. "Maybe I should've just let *you* do the presentation."

"Oh, no." She surprised him by laughing. "It's very interesting, though. I especially love the story about the donkey. You should find a way to add that to your advertising and social media. It's a fun fact."

"I'm glad you enjoyed it." He wondered if she'd done her homework and discovered that Jack, wanting to keep the winery private, had, against Gideon's advice, ignored creating any social media accounts. "And now, since you've gotten a take on the way things work, Rose has set up a buffet lunch outside. Afterward, feel free to wander the grounds. If you have any questions, please bring them to me rather than interrupt a worker."

After his presentation, they went out onto a back deck where Rose had set up their noon meal. A long table held a silver tray of fancy finger sandwiches with the crusts cut off that reminded Gideon of a fancy tea he'd had with Becky at the San Francisco Fairmont on a weekend anniversary trip. A single-cup coffeemaker sat alongside a variety of coffee pods and tea bags, lemonade, water, as well as opened bottles of the house estate bottled Pinot Noir, Chardonnay and Pinot Gris.

There was a tray of red wine chocolate cupcakes drizzled with Pinot Noir chocolate Ganache that Gideon knew from previous experience were delicious, along with red wine truffles with dried cherries from the orchard. Rose had always used food as a way to show love. And for a woman with a heart as big as this valley, any gathering required food. And a lot of it.

Although he really should get back to work and a loaded Italian sub was more his idea of lunch than those girly sandwiches, Gideon decided he wasn't going to pass up a chance to spend more time with Tess.

"I understand Papa not wanting a big funeral," Natalie said. "But all those workers showed up this morning, not expecting anything. Only because they respected him and this family. So it seems we should do something for the family's closest friends and the workers, at least."

"In the evening," Charlotte, who had yet to put anything on her plate, suggested. "It's a lovely time of day and there's plenty of room out here. We can set things up on the deck, and tables on the lawn and maybe get a caterer."

"Excuse me?" Rose said, looking horrified. "I do the cooking around here. And I've also pitched in to help neighboring wineries during the harvest time celebration."

"There's a celebration at harvest?" Charlotte asked.

"Of course. Most of the vineyards have their own, open to visitors. And the town has a big open-air concert. We never have because Robert was as private as Jack. Something to do with the war, I suspect. But Madeleine has told me about the ones she attended growing up in Burgundy, and I know she'd love one. And off topic, since you only had a banana for breakfast, you must be hungry."

"I'm fine," Charlotte responded. Almost automatically, Gideon considered.

"Of course you are," Rose agreed. "As the bard would say, you're as fine as a summer's day. But you need to eat." She snatched up Charlotte's empty plate. "Are you allergic to shellfish?"

"No, but—"

"Good, because I got some lovely fresh Dungeness crab from DeRito's Seafood Market just this morning. Kira, the fishmonger, who you'll be meeting if you stay, is from a family of fishermen. Her brothers caught some beauties just yesterday." She put a round crab salad sandwich on the white plate, then added another with a slice of smoked chicken, sliced avocado, diced tomatoes and sprouts served on a triangle of whole wheat bread that had been lightly spread with green goddess dressing.

"That's quite enough," Charlotte murmured. Gideon, whose attention had turned back to Tess, noticed that she was watching her sister carefully.

"You can't have lunch without dessert." Rose plunked down one of the cupcakes, along with two lemon cookies. "You can save the cookies for later," she suggested.

"Thank you." Charlotte studied the plate for a moment.

Then shrugged, and bit into the crab salad. And although he wasn't certain, because Rowdy had chosen that moment to thump his tail to suggest that crab salad might just be his favorite new food, Gideon thought he'd heard a soft moan come from those perfectly outlined lips. "This is delicious!"

"Better than your East Coast crab?"

Charlotte took time to consider that. "Different," she decided, proving loyal to her roots. "It's more meaty, and a bit briny, while ours is softer and milder. More like a scallop. But this is amazingly scrumptious."

"We West Coasters think so," Rose said. "I tasted your blue crab when I was stationed at Fort Bragg before I returned to civilian life. It's very tasty, as well. My motto is to love the crab where you are."

"That's a good motto," Charlotte agreed as she poured a bit of the lemonade into a glass.

Natalie, who'd gone with smoked salmon with crème fraîche and dill, truffles and a glass of Pinot Noir, entered the conversation. "I'm sure we all agree whatever Rose makes is delicious, but we still need to consider what to do as a remembrance of Papa."

"We could do a small, quiet celebration of Daddy's life now," Charlotte suggested as she plucked a truffle from the plate. "Then throw a big bash in the fall after the harvest."

"It hasn't been determined we'll all be here in the fall," Tess said.

"True. But what about the smaller remembrance this week? Saturday evening, perhaps. You mentioned something about driving around the other wineries. Surely, you could stay here that long?"

Tess, who'd also chosen the crab, since fresh off the boat shellfish wasn't something easily found in Arizona, could feel Gideon looking at her from where he was seated at the end of the table. There'd been a connection between them, but she had enough on her plate right now and definitely wasn't about to complicate her life further with a man. Even one who somehow had her opening up to him.

"Sure." She shrugged. "I could do that. As for the harvest celebration deal, while I found Gideon's presentation very interesting, I'd prefer to consider my options before making any long-term decisions. Also, I'd like to talk more with Madeleine." She glanced around. "Where is she?"

"This is her day for Tai Chi class at the Aberdeen senior center," Gideon said. "She always has lunch there afterward. Donovan dropped her off on his way back to the office. Then there's a van that'll bring her home later."

"That was his appointment? I figured it was a lawyer thing."

"No," Gideon said, "it was a friend thing."

"Should she be doing exercise with her heart problem?"

"It's very gentle, designed for seniors, and the doctor told her it should be okay since it's calming. Though if she felt any fibrillation, or got an alert from that watch, she should stop and get to the hospital right away."

"Well, as long as she'd be up for it, I like the idea of having a reception to celebrate Papa's extraordinary life," Natalie said. "I told Donovan when I first heard about Papa's death that we needed to do something, so having a small, private gathering now, and then, perhaps a grand fete in the fall during the harvest festival sounds fabulous." She glanced at Charlotte. "But it may be more difficult for you to stay, having a husband back home."

"I don't have a home at the moment since the house in Charleston belongs to my husband and he called this morning to tell me he's kicked me out and is filing for divorce."

"Oh, wow. I'm sorry," Tess said.

"Me, too. But only because since I don't like to fail, I tried

everything I could to make our marriage work, and I'm furious that I didn't get to divorce him first. Do you know what
I've been doing for over a year?"

"Blogging," Barbara answered. "I've always followed your
posts like an internet stalker. My husband's a developer—
Williams & Son, you may have seen his signs driving down
from Portland—who mostly builds luxury custom homes,
but he's starting a new project—not taking up any vineyard
land," she quickly assured them all. "Just outside Portland.
Close enough to commute, but far enough out of the city
that the land is less expensive. He's planning a much-needed
community of starter homes and I've been studying all your
designs, trying to find ways to make them special. And not
just your average cookie-cutter ones." And speaking of cookies, she plucked one from the plate and bit into it. Then took
a drink from the coffee she'd stuck with, having said she had
an appointment to write up a contract later that afternoon.
"These are delicious." She finished the small, crispy cookie
off in three bites before returning to her discussion of Charlotte's designs.

"I've been missing your posts on Houzz and Pinterest. I
realize that you're a designer, not a decorator, but your ideas
of how to use space in a new way have helped me so much
when I'm staging my husband's spec houses, or for some of
my listings that need some special touch to appeal to buyers."

"I haven't been on social media all that much because
Mason—my cheating, soon-to-be ex-husband—has been
dragging me around to all these social events," Charlotte,
who surprised Gideon, and, he suspected, everyone else, said.
"And when I'm not standing around having to charm people
I'd never in a million years be friends with to raise support
and money for my husband's political career, for months I've
been struggling to get pregnant, giving up my work, my *pas-*

sion, because he insisted that having a child would help him with the family value voter. While in the meantime, the bastard's been sleeping with a colleague at his firm. A woman he's planning to marry and move into his house. Which, speaking professionally, is a design nightmare."

"I was wondering what had happened to your career," Tess admitted.

"My *former* career, you mean. I'll bet Madeleine wouldn't have allowed a husband to stop her from rescuing people from the Gestapo," Charlotte said. "Not that designing a house is anywhere near all her accomplishments. But she remained driven. Never giving up. Like our father."

"Since we seem to be speaking the truth, I'll admit to having had moments of resentment," Tess offered. "Not remembering the man who fathered each of us, I created a fictional father, who wasn't really my father, but only played one on TV. But he was the closest thing to a dad I'd ever known, so I allowed myself to believe that I truly was part of his family. Especially since we'd often have barbecues, swim parties and Christmas dinner at his house.

"But he turned out to be flawed, and, like your husband, Charlotte, unfaithful. Which not only blew up his real-life family, but left me feeling as if I'd been deserted a second time when his affair caused our show—a program that I'd literally grown up on—to be canceled in what seemed, at the time, overnight. After some messed up years, I got my act together and moved on and told myself that not knowing my birth father didn't matter. But I'll admit that the thought of you getting to live the good life, a life that I'd been cheated out of, irked me from time to time. On the rare occasion I'd let myself think about it."

"Wow," Charlotte laughed scornfully, "you couldn't be more wrong about my family life. Just to add to my suckfest of a week, I learned from my video that Daddy—or maybe I should call him Jackson—wasn't even my birth father."

"What?" both Natalie and Tess asked at the same time.

"It seems my mother had an affair that resulted in a child. Who would be me." She polished off her lemonade as if wishing it were something stronger. "The night she met our dad, she saw him as an answer to her problem and seduced him, which didn't sound as if it took much effort. When she later informed him that she was pregnant, he did what he thought was the right thing and married her. Not that you could call it a marriage because he was hardly ever home. And when he was, it was like living in a war zone. A cold war," she clarified. "I was a disappointment to my mother from the day I was born. No. From the day I was conceived by a man she couldn't ever be with because of the family scandal it'd cause. Her sister's husband."

"Wow," Tess said again. "That sounds like a soap opera."

"That's the same thing my best friend said when I told her. She's a big fan, by the way."

"That's always nice to hear. Did your uncle know? And did he and your mother continue to see each other?"

"I'm not sure what he knew. They did run into each other at family affairs from time to time, but I always thought of him as my uncle, so it never occurred to me he might have slept with my mother. It does explain why my aunt always acted so coolly to me, so maybe it was one of those family secrets no one talked about.

"Mother did have other men in her life. I hate to say this, but she's a coldhearted snob who sets standards for others that she could never meet herself. The only time I felt that I was allowed to be myself was with my father. And I'm truly sorry you never experienced that because he was, in his way, a wonderful, loving man."

"The last thing I want to do is cause you any more pain, Tess," Natalie broke in. "But I have to agree with Charlotte about Papa. And I, too, am very sorry that you never had an opportunity to know him the way she and I did."

"It's neither of your faults. And I survived."

The reputation recovery team her agency and record label had brought in to clean up the all-too-public disaster had written off her strange on-stage behavior as flu and dehydration. Unfortunately, that false cover story had blown up after photos of Tess Swann entering the rehab clinic showed up on the cover page of the *National Enquirer.*

"And for the record," Tess told Charlotte, "it's obvious that as failed at parenthood as he was, Jackson thought of all three of us as his daughters. So you're every bit as much a Swann as Natalie and me."

"Absolument." Natalie raised her glass. "To sisters of the heart. I'm at a pivotal point in my career, so I may bounce over to Portland and up to Seattle from time to time to take some photos, but I'm in," Natalie said.

"As I stated, I'm homeless at the moment, so I'm staying," Charlotte said.

Tess could feel Gideon looking at her again. "Oh, hell. Count me in," she said, lifting her glass to join in the toast. "At least until after the harvest fete."

27

June, 1940

Madeleine had been in the house with her *maman* and Yvette, their kitchen helper, cooking a meal for the workers who were busy pruning the leaves off the flowering vines to ensure that only the best grapes would ripen for this year's harvest when she glanced out the window and noticed cars coming down the road in front of the chateau. Out here in the country, there wasn't much traffic, but as she watched, more and more began coming.

"*Maman,*" she said, "look outside."

Her mother glanced up from the bread dough she'd been kneading. "It's beginning," she said in a voice far calmer than the expression on her face, which had gone as pale as the egg whites they'd whisked earlier for meringues. "Madeleine," she said, "I want you to run and tell your papa about the cars." Cars, Madeleine noticed, which were piled high with suitcases, bags and boxes.

Not quite understanding what was happening, she raced out into the vineyard and did as she was told. Her papa's face, unlike her mother's, hardened to stone. As soon as she'd given him her message, he called a group of workers—young, large and very strong men—to stop their pruning and come with him. And then they raced toward the house. Lifting her skirts and running behind them, Madeleine, still unsure what was going on, only knew that this was not a good thing.

By the time her *maman* was pulling the bread out of the oven, the road in front of their chateau was thick with not only cars, but bicycles, carts piled high with what she later learned was whatever people could grab in their rush to get out of Paris before the Germans, whose tanks had gone around the French's heralded Maginot Line, invaded the city.

"Madeleine," *Maman* said. "I want you and Yvette to gather up all the baskets and bottles you can find. Then start filling them with bread and water you and I can take out to give to those poor, desperate people, while Yvette, you keep baking."

"But *Maman*, won't they hurt us?"

"Papa already has men there."

"Not enough," Yvette, whom Madeleine had never heard argue with her employer, pointed out. It was true. It would have taken an army to hold back all those people if they decided to storm the gate. An army willing to shoot desperate women and children.

"God will provide," *Maman* said with her unshakable calm as she made the sign of the cross. "Did our Lord not tell us to feed the needy? We may not be able to duplicate the loaves and fishes parable, but along with our prayers for those travelers, we will share whatever we have."

Although Madeleine was terrified they'd be overtaken by the teeming crowd, she did as her mother instructed, and together they stood on the inside of the gate, putting loaves of bread and bottles of water into outstretched hands. Yet, as panicked as they were, the people did nothing to harm, but only offered appreciation and prayers for whatever they received.

Meanwhile, Madeleine's papa walked among them, offering those who looked ready to drop in their tracks the opportunity to sleep on the property.

Madeleine, Yvette and *Maman* baked long into the night. When she awoke, after finally falling asleep for a scant two hours, to begin baking again, Madeleine, who'd forgotten to close the curtains before falling into bed, looked out the window to see people gleaning her mother's formerly tidy kitchen garden. Greens had been pulled up by the roots, and apparently, the hungry were eating or hoarding everything they could harvest because even the soil around the root vegetables—carrots, beets, turnips, which were months from maturity—had been kicked up, revealing that the tops were being eaten.

Meanwhile, the road was even more crowded than it had been last night, the cars bumper to bumper, along with people on bicycles and on foot. She saw one young girl carrying a cage with a yellow canary inside, and old people huddled in carts usually used for farmwork being pulled by what she guessed were members of their family or friends.

Her pulse leaped when she viewed the trucks of soldiers, some crowding people, even those carrying children on their backs and babies in their arms, off the road. At first, she thought the Germans had arrived, but at closer look, she saw they were her own country's soldiers, retreating. Which was when her heart sank.

Not bothering to change the dress she'd worn yesterday, then slept in, she ran a brush through her tangled auburn hair, then ran back down the stairs to find her mother still at the stove, the kitchen as hot as Madeleine imagined hell might be.

Her papa, looking less robust than he had only a day before, was pouring boiling water into a jug of freshly ground coffee beans while her mother and Yvette had moved on to mass producing meat tarts.

"We are lost," he said bleakly. "Our troops are retreating, our government has deserted us, fleeing from Paris to the safety of their country estates, and the Germans are expected to arrive to an empty city any day."

"Will they be coming here?" Madeleine asked. This was not what she'd been taught at school. The nuns had assured the students that although the Germans may have invaded Belgium and Austria, France's brave soldiers would send them running back to their dreadful motherland.

He ran a hand through his hair. "The question, my darling daughter, is not *will*. But *when*."

He glanced out the window just as a German plane, marked with yellow on its engine, wingtips and tail, roared low overhead. Even before the *rat-a-tat* of machine gun bullets that rattled her chateau's windows, people dove into the ditch alongside the road, landing on top of each other. Amazingly, which Madeleine's *maman* attributed to God's protection, there were only slight injuries, taken care of by doctors, and a veterinarian who'd slept on bags of grain in their barn last night.

The crowds began to thin out by the third day and just as the women began putting the usually tidy kitchen back to some semblance of order, and the men returned to the vineyard, still determined to produce a harvest, the first German military convoy rumbled by. It was led by two sidecar motorcycles, followed by jeeps, then tanks.

Madeleine let out a breath as it headed toward Paris without stopping at the chateau.

"Perhaps they will leave us alone," she suggested. "We don't present any danger."

"Perhaps," her *maman* said, running a comforting hand over Madeleine's head.

Her father said nothing. But she viewed his less-than-reassuring answer in dark eyes that had so handsomely flashed during that harvest tango.

28

"I do have some more questions," Tess said after agreeing to go along with the terms of the will. Not because she was all that interested in the money, but she wasn't so coldhearted that she was going to cause the breakup of something the family had worked so hard to build. And then there was Madeleine to consider. And, of course, Gideon and his daughter.

"Now, there's a surprise," Gideon said drily.

"Why don't you have any tastings?"

"Because neither Robert nor Jack wanted them."

"I understand that. But they're not here anymore."

"I picked up a tourist guide at the car rental place," Charlotte said. "There were a lot of wineries listed. I think it'd be a good idea."

"I agree, having suggested that same idea to Jack many times," Gideon said. "But as large as the house is, we don't have any space that could serve as a tasting room."

"My Joel could build you one." Barbara spoke up. "He's the son half of Williams & Son and works on some of the smaller jobs on his own. He could build it with folding glass doors so it could be an outside space in nice weather, and cozy, with a fireplace during the wet winter."

"Ooh, I like that idea," Natalie said.

Tess and Charlotte immediately agreed.

"There's something else," Tess said.

"Yes?" Gideon looked as if he was clenching his jaw. She could tell he was beginning to lose patience with her. Which was a good thing. That way they'd be less likely to do anything she'd end up regretting later.

"Why do you only list wine on your website?"

"Because that's what we sell."

"But that's what everyone around here sells. You need to make yourself stand out. Tell the story of the origin of the winery. Put up more photos. Including ones of the workers at various stages during the season." She glanced over at Natalie. "You could take some, right?"

"Of course."

"And I could write the copy. We definitely need to include the vineyard's history. About the original Swann Family Farm, and how Robert came home from the war with his lovely French bride and began experimenting with how to change some of the acreage to vineyards. And, of course, we need to tell their war love story. The details of which we still need to hear from her, by the way."

"He didn't like to talk about that. Neither does she," Gideon said.

"Do you have any idea how many retired veterans would visit Maison de Madeleine because of how they both helped save the world?"

"No," Gideon admitted. "But I do suspect not that many who served in the Second World War are traveling around visiting vineyards. Given that they're at least in their nineties."

"True. But wine tourists have a lot of choices here."

"Bunches, according to the booklet I read," Charlotte agreed. "Most vineyards offer tastings. Some even give tours and have a clubhouse for special members."

"Well, I'd bet veterans of all ages would love to come here, if for no other reason than to honor one of their own." Tess stuck with her argument. "Especially a hero."

"And see the museum," Charlotte said.

Gideon frowned. "What museum?"

"Not a full-size museum," Charlotte assured him. "Perhaps a small area in the tasting room. With old newspaper clippings, photos of Robert in his Spitfire if we can find them and a story about how he flew his spy plane. Along with all their framed medals."

"I have some old newspapers from that time," Natalie said. "*Maman* found them in a trunk after *Grand-Mère* passed. But they're all yellowed."

"All the better," Charlotte exclaimed. "That makes them so much more authentic. And historical. Surely, Madeleine has photos of their weddings. Perhaps we can even find one of him in his plane."

"She has photos of both weddings. And you might be able to find one of him in the plane he sent her, though I doubt that because the military censorship was obviously very careful about what details they allowed to be sent back home." Gideon swiped a hand through his hair.

"Look, I know Jack gave me the final vote, and I'm not saying I'm against all these ideas, although I've worked at wineries with tasting rooms and it's not as simple as you're making it out. But there's no way I'm going to go along with the idea unless Madeleine agrees. Because despite her signing over her rights to the business, this is still her home."

"That's only right," Tess, who appreciated her own privacy, said.

"We'll broach it over dinner," Charlotte suggested. "When she's back and rested."

When Gideon had folded his arms, Tess couldn't help noticing the biceps stretching out the sleeves of his shirt. She skimmed a glance over him, wondering if the rest of him was as ripped, when she realized he'd caught her looking and felt the color—the bane of all fair-skinned redheads—rise in her cheeks. All he did was lift an ebony brow. But it spoke volumes and suggested she wasn't alone in her attraction. Oh, yes, she thought. Gideon Byrne could well be trouble.

"Remember, she's emotionally vulnerable right now, what with her only son's death and getting to finally have you all together," Gideon warned. "She'd probably give you anything you asked for. So be careful."

"We're not going to pressure her," Tess said. "Believe it or not, even I'm more sensitive than to do anything like that. But if she does think it's a workable, or even better, a good idea, I'll throw in a new website. Because, wow, do you need one."

"You design websites?"

"No, but I have an excellent website team who works out of Austin. I'll simply have Dawn and Crystal create a new template and help us come up with something that'll bring a lot of attention our way."

"You did understand, from my presentation, that this is a working vineyard," Gideon reminded her. "This time of year especially, I don't have time to give tours and neither does anyone else on the crew."

"No tours," Charlotte, who seemed to have taken over as social director, agreed. "At least until perhaps the harvest party. Oh! Maybe the party should include a silent auction for charity." She chewed on a persimmon-tinted thumbnail while considering. "I don't suppose you know what Daddy's favorite charity was?"

"Sure," Gideon responded. "Doctors Without Borders."

"Terrific. We'll see if they have any promotional items for the table and meanwhile, I'm sure local businesses will be willing to donate items and services. And, of course, there will have to be gift baskets of wine. And some of these delicious truffles and crackers with local cheese."

Tess watched Gideon rub his temple as if he was getting a killer headache picturing a circus taking over his vineyard. And yes, it might belong to all of them, but it was only natural that he'd feel protective of what he'd been part of creating.

"Why don't we work out all those details later," she suggested, taking pity on him. "After we talk with Madeleine?"

"Good idea," the others said with enthusiastic nods while Gideon's relief was obvious.

"I need to go test some wine that's been aging," he said, picking up his laptop. "I'll see you all at dinner."

"Won't your daughter be home?" Tess asked.

"Later this afternoon. But she's supposed to be working on a paper about Oregon's Indigenous tribes for her state history class. Then she and a friend are going to stream the latest episode of your *Pleasant Meadows High* show with pizza for dinner. The downside of her weekend was her friend's parents don't have Wi-Fi, so she missed it… Later," he repeated.

Tess watched him leave the room. Apparently, she wasn't alone. "Mercy, that man has a very fine butt," Charlotte, who was sitting beside her, murmured.

That was one thing Tess couldn't argue about.

29

Tess spent most of the afternoon online, researching to expand more on what Gideon had already told her about wineries. Particularly ones in Burgundy. She had the scenery in mind from her long-ago pop star tour, but she wanted to know how life would have been back when Madeleine was growing up on one of the country's premier wineries. She was still hoping the woman she was beginning to think of as her grandmother would be willing to share her stories with her, but even so, it would help to have a head start.

Later, after changing into another tiered skirt and a fringed-edge tunic, she saved the research information she'd found and followed the delicious aroma coming from downstairs.

The dinner tonight was a rack of spring lamb, fresh peas from the garden and asparagus risotto that could have held its own against any three-star Michelin restaurant. The conversation flowed easily, almost as if they were a family beginning to blend together. Or at least good friends, Tess considered.

Madeleine shared stories about her classes at the senior center, which included the Tai Chi, along with dancing and painting. Despite her background in watercolors, she'd never tried oils before now, and although she was still at the stage where painting a pear was a problem, she made everyone laugh when she said that she hoped they'd eventually get to painting nudes. Specifically, some young, buff stud.

"That's a very busy schedule," Charlotte remarked.

"Not nearly as busy as I once was. When I first arrived, trying to fit in and make friends, I began teaching French to people who just wanted to be able to converse a bit while visiting France. Eventually, I finally decided I'd gotten a little old to stay up late grading papers."

"How long ago was that?" Charlotte asked.

"Oh, quite some time ago," she responded with a casual wave of her hand.

"Ten years," Rose clarified, which caused everyone to laugh again. Tess was starting to understand how Madeleine had survived during her years in the Resistance. The elderly woman appeared indefatigable.

Natalie, who knew their grandmother best, gently broached their idea about the small reception for the workers and close friends, which Madeleine found to be a lovely idea, and all agreed it could take place on Saturday evening. Charlotte, who'd taken a calligraphy class at SCAD, volunteered to do the invitations.

Madeleine was also pleased with the suggestion to open a tasting room and for the charitable silent auction. "Although the winery has always supported various causes, both Robert and Jack felt very strongly against having strangers on the property. Having been through war myself, I understood, so I never pushed, but I always wished we could open our beautiful property to visitors and let them taste our fine wines as my family had done during the harvest festival and our annual Christmas ball."

As for Charlotte's idea of the grand fete and a community

celebration of her son's life during the harvest celebration, in a tear-choked voice, Madeleine said that although it might cause some grumbling from Jackson in heaven, she couldn't think of a better way to remember her son.

After dinner, when the plates were cleared away by a young woman from town whom Rose had hired to help out, everyone moved to another part of the deck, where a grouping of comfortable padded chairs surrounded a gas fire pit. As if it was the most natural thing to do, Gideon sat next to Tess on the two-cushioned love seat.

"You've asked me to tell you about my time in France under the occupation," Madeleine said to Tess.

"Not if it's too private. Or uncomfortable," Tess responded quickly. As much as she wanted to hear everything, both for herself and the story that was stirring in the far recesses of her mind, she didn't want to cause this elderly woman, who'd already been through so much, any additional emotional pain. Especially since the talk about the harvest celebration had nearly brought her to tears.

"Perhaps, since you'll be staying, at least until the harvest, we can do it in stages. It was such a long time ago," Madeleine suggested.

"I can understand how some things might be difficult to remember," Tess said gently.

"Oh, no." The misty eyes cleared. Hardened. "I recall every detail of those years. Every face, every event. Which is why I'm willing to follow the advice from my doctor, who believes my silly old heart is averse to stress these days, and take things more slowly."

"We don't have to discuss it at all, if it proves too uncomfortable."

For a woman of her advanced years, that grandmother in

question's eyes were remarkably clear as they met Tess's. "Are you planning to write my story?"

"I don't know," Tess said honestly. "I'm very intrigued and it sounds compelling, but even if you're not comfortable having it out in the public, I'd still like to hear it. Again, only if you're willing to share."

"Gideon and Rose worry talking about it will be hard on me. But sometimes keeping things in is even more difficult. I never, ever discussed it with anyone but Rose, who's always been like family, because of Robert. It was his story, too, of course, and he deserved his privacy. But now…"

"But now?" Tess prompted after Madeleine's voice drifted off and she gazed out over this beautiful place she and her husband had created.

"And now I believe it's time for the story to be told. So yes. Let's arrange for me to share a bit each evening and you can determine if you believe anyone would be interested in reading it. Is that a deal?"

"Deal." Tess stood to shake her grandmother's outstretched hand. Then, on impulse, bent down and kissed her cheek. Beckoning her down lower, Madeleine returned the light touch of lips on each cheek with a continental kiss of her own. Then Tess sat back down next to Gideon and after being given permission to record it for accuracy, and to keep her from having to interrupt, turned on the record app on her phone.

"My family had been famous for making wine in Burgundy for generations," Madeleine began, "so there was a great deal of very fine, valuable vintages. Still, during the First World War, many of us in the region had suffered when the vineyards became battlefields, so much so that all the chemicals from the shells killed the vines, some of them more than two hundred years old.

"Although we'd been assured that the Germans would never

be able to invade us, Papa was a cautious man and believed we should be prepared for that eventuality. We'd also heard that Hitler was a great wine aficionado. And everyone knew that once the invasion began, the Germans would begin raiding all our wine cellars, not only to give to occupying soldiers and those on the front, but also to send back to Germany. Not just for Hitler and his evil henchmen to enjoy, but to sell to raise money to help pay for their war.

"Although it might sound prideful, even arrogant, most of us believed that our exquisite, aged, high-dollar wine would be far too superior for an enemy with such plebian, unsophisticated palates."

"It's not arrogant if it's true," Gideon interjected. "Especially since the Germans didn't have the terroir to grow decent Pinot Noir."

"Not that they'd have known how if they had," Madeleine scoffed. "Papa always said they should have stuck to their beer. At any rate, since our wine was stored in labyrinths of stone-walled caves to keep it cool, with the help of friends we moved all of our best bottles to the very back of the caves. Then sealed them off with bricks and even stones dug from the ground."

"That must have been incredibly hard work," Tess said.

"*Oui*. Very hard. One of my fingers broke when my brother, Jean Luc, dropped a sharp stone on it. It's always been a bit stiff ever since."

She held out her right hand, displaying a pinky that was, indeed, a bit kinked.

"Yet, it was worth doing, you see. Not just to stop the Nazis from enjoying the fruits of our hard labor. We knew that we'd need to have wine to sell after the war."

"How many bottles did you hide?"

"Two thousand."

"That many?"

"Other houses hid more than that. There was one that hid theirs in tunnels under a hospital run by the nuns, who bravely risked their own lives cooperating. After it was done, we dirtied the wall up and even rubbed soot on it to make it look older. Then, my eldest brother, Phillipe, got the idea to collect spiders."

"Spiders?" When the very idea made Tess shiver, Gideon, who didn't miss a thing, guessing correctly that she was remembering her hallucination meltdown that she'd told him about, put a comforting hand on her thigh.

"To make webs," Madeleine explained. "I, myself, had a strong dislike of spiders, so I'll admit I didn't help collect them, but my brothers seemed to enjoy their task. And it worked. Soon the entire wall was covered with webs. When it was completed, my brothers, who could have been excused because they would have been considered essential workers, volunteered to go fight for France.

"It all happened so fast. On May third Paris was bombed for the first time. On May tenth the Germans not only invaded Belgium, the Netherlands and Luxembourg, but had managed to move forward to thirty kilometers from Paris.

"Phillipe was in the infantry, and part of the Allied forces. He was killed during the Battle of Belgium. That same week my other brother, Jean Luc, was one of forty thousand French and another forty thousand British troops left behind after the evacuation of three hundred thousand Allied troops from Dunkirk. For years, we had no idea where he was. Or even if he was alive.

"After the war ended, a kind British soldier who'd been at Dunkirk looked my parents up. He had become friends with Jean Luc during their imprisonment, and told them that they were first taken to Poland where he was worked nearly to death under Nazi guards. Later, ill, weak and starving, Jean

Luc collapsed and died on a nearly thousand-mile march to Berlin in the depths of a frigid winter. His body was never found."

Even as her eyes glistened, Madeleine's voice turned distant and flat, almost as if reporting a news story, giving Tess the impression that somewhat emotionally distancing herself from the deaths of her beloved brothers was the only way to live with such a horrific truth.

"Hearing that the enemy was on its way to the capital, the government packed up and left." She shared the story of that time, of the bread baking and the people, so desperate, sleeping on the ground and in the barn and eating the tops from the carrots not yet fully formed. Of the jeeps and the tanks rumbling by, shaking the ground.

"Two million people ran from the capital, joining another eight million already on the road in a chaotic mass movement called '*l'exode de Paris.*'"

"The exodus of Paris," Natalie translated.

"*Oui.* Later, we learned that ninety thousand children became displaced during the exodus. Reunification was made difficult because many were too young to say who their parents were, or babies, who couldn't speak at all."

Tess, who'd never heard the story, was too horrified to speak. A silence, like a dark cloud, settled over the group as she knew everyone was imagining the scene.

"Papa decided we were safer where we were. He also refused to surrender the vineyards to the Germans, who he knew would be coming next. So we stayed." Madeleine's voice drifted off and her eyes took on a faraway look. Going back to those days? Tess wondered.

Ten days after the horrific exodus that Madeleine knew would be burned into her memory for life, her family had just sat down to her sixteenth birthday dinner when the wooden front door burst open and jackbooted German soldiers marched in.

Her father jumped to his feet. "What are you doing here?" he demanded. "This is my home. You have no right to enter."

Madeleine's papa was the head of a group of regional vineyards that negotiated wine prices with other countries, and had taught her and her brothers both English and German while they were growing up. So she understood, when the oldest of the group put his hands on his hips, and said, "Perhaps you have not been informed. We have taken your country. We own everything." He swept a hand around the room. "Including this house. And your vineyards. And animals. Victory has its rewards. Your army fell like tin soldiers. And now, all that was once yours, is ours."

With that claim declared, they sat down at the table, and acting as if Madeleine and her parents weren't even there, started tearing apart the golden brown, plump roasted chicken *Maman* usually saved for Father Guyot's monthly after-Mass dinner visit. They also devoured the roasted potatoes and carrots.

After the platters were empty, the youngest one, who'd been leering at her from across the table, reached for the beautiful mixed fruit tart *Maman* had made for the celebration.

"Bitte," *Maman* said in the German she'd learned in order to accompany Madeleine's papa to wine trade events in Berlin. "The tart is for my daughter's birthday."

Instead of appealing to whatever humanity they might possess, her request only made things worse. As all their attention immediately turned toward Madeleine, her skin turned cold as they seemed to be undressing her with their eyes.

"How old is she?" asked the one who seemed to be in

charge. The one who'd claimed to own everything they possessed.

Her parents exchanged a look.

"Only fourteen," her mother said, shaving two years off her age. "A mere girl."

The young one took a long drink from the bottle of Pinot Noir. Then wiped his mouth with the back of his hand while lust rose in his eyes as they crawled over her. "Old enough," he said. Then looking her straight in the face, he thrust his wine-reddened tongue in and out of his mouth, in a demeaning pantomime of sex.

"That's enough," the older man said, pushing himself up from the wooden chair. "We're here for the wine. Although," he said conversationally, as he casually pulled a pistol from the holster he wore, walked over and pressed the barrel against her papa's temple, "if you make one move to stop anything we have every right to do, I will allow my men to rape not only this lovely little birthday girl, but your wife. Do you understand?"

It was the first time Madeleine had ever seen fear in her papa's eyes. He nodded, his mouth pulled into a hard, tight line.

"Say it," the man demanded.

"I understand," her papa said in a voice far from his usual strong, self-assured one. While Madeleine sat frozen, helpless, and silent tears slid like silver rain down her *maman*'s chalk-white face, they began filling bags with the silverware and sterling candlesticks, which had been a wedding present to her parents. Then finally, after one of the men had grabbed her birthday tart, they left the house.

Silence descended like a stone.

Madeleine's papa put his arms around both her and her *maman*, holding them tight. As they watched from the window, the soldiers marched out to the cave and loaded up two truckloads of wine.

"At least they didn't find the valuable vintages," her papa said as the men drove off into the darkening night. "Because of the wall."

And, Madeleine thought, Jean Luc and Phillipe's spiders. Which had her sending up a silent prayer that this time next year, after the war that the people had been assured would never happen was over, her brothers would be with her at this table with their parents, singing *Joyeux anniversaire* to her.

"Of course I had no way of knowing at the time," Madeleine said as she shook herself out of the still-vivid memory of that horrific night, "that we'd never see either of them again." She choked up at that and her eyes welled. Her hands, folded in her lap, were visibly trembling.

"I think that's enough," Rose said.

"No. Just this one more part tonight," Madeleine insisted. "If for no other reason, I've never said it aloud to anyone but Robert, Rose and you. Sharing it after all these years may help dull the pain." She paused and took a calming drink of the Pinot Noir carrying her name.

"Three months after that terrible night, while Dijon was fully occupied so the Germans could use the airfield, just a few kilometers from our home, my mother's great-uncle, Henri, was dragged out of Gestapo headquarters and hanged in the Ducal Palace square. His crime was gluing his famed house label on bottles of *vin ordinaire* after being ordered to send several cases of his best wine to Germany.

"He was a stubborn man, and tended to speak his mind, which was a dangerous thing to do in those days. He loudly declared, to all who'd listen, that his wine was too good for the enemy who didn't possess the palates to tell the difference in quality. He'd gotten away with the ruse until one of our own countrymen, in an effort to curry favor with the Germans, turned him in to the Gestapo.

"As the story goes, instead of begging for mercy during his beatings, he told them that he should have filled the bottles with piss, which resulted in worse torture. Making their evil worse, the Germans forced everyone to come into town, to gather in the square and witness, firsthand, the final cost of resisting. They wouldn't let us retrieve his battered body for forty-eight hours."

She took a handkerchief from her pocket, dabbed at her damp eyes, then straightened her shoulders. "None of us said a word on the way back to the chateau after the hanging. I remember *Maman* didn't cry. Not one single tear. I can still see her face to this day. She was as white as a ghost, and all the light had gone out of her eyes. It was as if those Nazis hadn't just killed an ill-tempered old man, even she had complained about from time to time. They'd killed something inside her.

"Somehow, she'd survived losing her two sons and now, knowing how badly it hurts, I can't imagine the pain of losing Philippe and Jean Luc at such young ages. Before their lives had really gotten started. I imagine it must have been difficult for her to even get out of bed in the morning. But she did. She carried on, although she'd lost the joy and optimism that I, who was more serious, had always both admired and envied.

"But the brutality of Henri's murder and the shameful disrespect shown a fellow human being seemed to be, as the saying goes, the straw that broke *Maman*'s back. She was never the same.

"Once we were home, I went upstairs into my bedroom, locked the door and took a flyer a young man in the crowd had surreptitiously slipped into my coat pocket during the execution. And that was the day I decided to join *Maquis. La Résistance.*"

30

After hearing the first part of Madeleine's story, there was no way Tess was going to require the elderly woman to relive what had to be horrific times. But having made her decision, Madeleine proved determined to see the project through.

"How would you write it?" she asked Tess the next day as they walked Rowdy together through the vines. Natalie was busy taking photos for the new website, and Charlotte was working with Rose on plans for Saturday's reception. "As fiction? Or nonfiction?"

"I'm not sure. Do you have a preference?"

"You're the writer. That should be your call. What works for you. I did a little freelance writing when I first came to America, a column in a newsletter for war brides. It caught on and ran in *Ladies' Home Journal* for two years, until the powers that be assumed we'd all assimilated. Which does happen over time. As much as I love France, I now feel far more American than I do French. And it's true we war brides had an advantage by marrying into our husbands' families, so we started living an American life as soon as we arrived. I was more fortunate than some because Robert's parents welcomed me with open arms, while many other women were treated more poorly, because families had lost sons, fathers and husbands fighting what some felt was *our* war. We banded together, had weekly meetings, the more established ones helping the newer arrivals learn the ropes, so to speak." She sighed. "I seem to be one of the few remaining from those days."

"You've lived an amazing life."

"It's been interesting," Madeleine allowed. "And I do like to keep busy. I tried to remind myself of that whenever, during your father's younger years, there were times I seemed to have given birth to a whirling dervish. Of course, his father had an adventurous spirit, as well, so I suppose Jackson could never have lived a quiet life." She glanced over at Tess. "I'm sorry you missed knowing him. You have every reason to disbelieve me, but as flawed a man as he was, he did have many good traits."

"I've come to figure that out for myself. And I can understand how his work must have impacted his life. Though," Tess said, thinking out loud, "living in such dangerous times and witnessing such dark events hasn't seemed to affect you."

"It was different for me," she said. "Unlike Jackson, who chose to be a witness to evil, I was an active participant in fighting it. As terrible as things were, and they were especially horrific during years of rationing when people were starving, I was kept so busy that I didn't have time to dwell on the possibility that we'd fail. I was not naive enough to believe that we could cause the Germans to surrender. But we were determined to hold out until the Americans arrived. They say that the more emotional events get etched into your brain, which makes sense to me. For instance, I can remember so many details of those days as clearly as if they happened last night but I couldn't tell you what I had for breakfast three days ago."

"Given that you were in the hospital, that's probably just as well."

"That's a very good point," Madeleine said with a laugh.

"Did you keep journals?" Tess asked hopefully.

"Oh, no. That would have been far too dangerous. We always burned our papers. In fact, the orders I had that day Robert and I met were so sensitive that they'd been written on cigarette paper so I could quickly eat it if I were stopped by the Gestapo, the SS, or the soldiers who'd set up guard points everywhere around Dijon, because it was the capital of Burgundy and where the train station and transportation hubs were. And still are."

"I'm going to call my agent this afternoon," Tess said. "My initial thought was, if you agreed, to write a biography. But after what you've shared so far, I'm leaning toward using your story as inspiration and background for a novel."

"I don't know anything about the publishing business, but that sounds like a very good compromise," Madeleine said.

Although Tess normally disliked talking about a work in progress, personally believing it took some of the energy out of the story, this case was different. Because it wasn't *her* story. But it *could* be, she considered. It would be a collaboration between her and her grandmother. Now she just had to convince her agent, whose job it would be to convince Danielle Carpenter, the publishing house's "new eyes."

They were passing the workers' houses. She suspected that the larger one set away from the others belonged to the foreman. All had a profusion of mixed annuals in front, but the larger one also boasted hanging baskets of fuchsia on the porch.

"Is this where the boy who received the scholarship lives?" she asked.

"Yes." Madeleine smiled. "Gideon stole his father, Reynaldo, away from a crew he'd worked with in Napa. They're a lovely family. His wife, Ana, made that tres leches cake you enjoyed. John intends to be an astronaut. He's so dedicated we're sure he's going to achieve his goal. He's also the forward on the school basketball team and I have the feeling he'd like to be Aubrey's beau, but Gideon has a strict no-dating rule until she's sixteen. Her birthday's right around the corner. I'm looking forward to watching a young romance bloom. My teenage years under occupation didn't allow for one, but I believe that's because I was meant to meet my Robert."

"My work also didn't allow much time for dating," Tess said. "The studio sent me out on dates to premieres and things like that, but it was merely for publicity. Not the real thing. And the boys from high school were too shy to ask or seemed to only want to date me because I was famous."

"Which would give them bragging rights." Madeleine nodded. "But surely, there were those who liked you for the special girl you were."

"Perhaps," Tess allowed. "Let's just say I had trust issues." And still did, which was why sex, when she did make time for it, remained strictly recreational.

"Because of my son." Madeleine's tone revealed regrets.

Tess wasn't going to lie. "Partly. But also my mom, who really is a wonderful person, was a serial marrier while I was growing up, so I've never viewed marriage as a permanent situation."

"How sad."

"It's never really bothered me. But I have to admit, your and Robert's story has me thinking that happily-ever-afters might actually exist."

They'd reached the door of Madeleine's cottage. "Believe me, *ma chère*," she said, touching Tess's sun-warmed cheek. "They truly do. I'll see you tonight for dinner."

31

September, 1940

The flyer that had been slipped into Madeleine's pocket bore a copy of General de Gaulle's stirring speech from London, where he'd formed a French government in exile. She was told to memorize it as a way of identifying herself to other resistors, since their country was not only occupied by soldiers, the Gestapo and SS, but by spies and collaborators, too, like the one who'd turned in her *maman*'s great-uncle. Written in a corner of the flyer was a meeting time at the Dijon train station for two days away.

The next day seemed to crawl at a snail's pace as she was called out by Sister Jeanne-Marie for a lack of attention in class.

Finally, after an anxious night spent tossing and turning, and then telling her *maman* that she was going to be working on a school project with a girlfriend, she rode her bicycle to the station and took the train into Dijon. After arriving, she leaned her bicycle against the wall of the building and sat on a green bench outside. Nerves jangling, she waited for whatever would happen next. She hadn't been there five minutes when a young woman, perhaps three or four years older than herself, came up to her, kissed her on both cheeks and suggested they go have coffee.

Having assumed she'd be meeting the man who'd given her the flyer, she was concerned it could be a trap, but because of the memory of that old man hanging from the rope, and her *maman*'s obvious devastation at his brutal death, Madeleine was not about to turn back now.

As they walked together to a small café on Place François Rude, Madeleine was asked to repeat the speech. Then, being seated at an outdoor table and ordering their coffee, the young woman took a gift-wrapped package out of her purse. "I'm so sorry I missed your birthday," she said. "But with all our farm help now in the prison work camps, I was needed to help harvest beets."

"Of course you had to help your family," Madeleine assured her as she opened the package and found it to be a slim book of poetry. "How special! Thank you."

"I know how much you love poetry, so I hoped you might enjoy it," this stranger said easily as if they were old friends. It was Madeleine's first realization that resistance would require lying. Something that had never been easy for her. Her stomach was still aching from telling that falsehood to her *maman*. But she would learn to do it. For her family. For France.

Over coffee, they chatted briefly, supposedly catching up with the innocent things girls talk about—clothes, school and boys, which had Madeleine thinking how much had changed since she'd danced with Bernard last fall. There was a group of German soldiers seated nearby, drinking wine, talking and laughing too loudly. With the memory of her birthday still so vivid in her mind, often keeping her awake nights, hatred ran hot through Madeleine's veins, though with effort, she managed to keep a smile on her face.

After finishing their coffee, they got up to leave, and, while once again giving her kisses on both cheeks, the woman quietly told her to look for the dots above letters on various pages of the book. Then she left, disappearing past a line of people waiting, ration papers in hand, for whatever scant bit of food they might be fortunate to acquire.

Feigning calm, carrying the book rewrapped in the paper, Madeleine walked on trembling legs past the raucous soldiers and back to the train to Dijon. When she reached home, her *maman* needed her to feed the chickens the Germans hadn't yet taken, so it wasn't until later, after dinner, that she was able to examine the book. It took some close scrutiny, but she found the tiniest little pencil dots above some of the letters. Which, when all spelled out, gave her an address on Rue Monde where she was instructed to go next Saturday. Now she just needed to think like a spy and come up with another excuse to tell her *maman*.

Madeleine jerked awake from her afternoon nap, the memory of those days, as she'd told Tess earlier, as fresh as if they had happened yesterday. Or even today. It was becoming more and more painful to relive those years, but her granddaughters, being part of a new generation, needed to hear her experiences with war and living under fascism. Because, as the saying so wisely stated, "Those who don't remember the past are condemned to repeat it."

So as difficult as it was, she'd continue her story, comforted by the fact that she'd soon be getting to the part where God had sent her the love of her life.

32

Taking advantage of the spring sunshine, Tess called Phyllis from the love seat where she'd sat with Gideon, listening to Madeleine spin her tale. Although she'd braced for an argument, her agent jumped right on board with the plan.

"How lucky are you?" Phyllis enthused. "Falling into a fully formed story just when you're telling me you want to change direction?"

"I'm not writing a biography," Tess clarified.

"Thank God. The market's already flooded with nonfiction. Who wants to compete with that? This is wonderful! I love it." Tess could hear the excitement in her agent's voice. "This vineyard you're on. Is it beautiful?"

"Stunning. And the house looks like a French Downton Abbey."

"Even better. Do you think they'd allow filming?"

Tess thought of that bottom line Gideon was working to raise and wondered how much filming rights could possibly earn. "Perhaps. So long as it didn't interfere with work."

"Terrific. Send photos. And a story outline. Then I'm calling my film agent. This is going to be so much fun!" Then she must have realized how that might sound, because she added, "Though I am so very sorry about the death of your father."

"Thank you. But I never knew him. And he's not in the story, either. Unless I end with him being born."

"I love it. Go listen to more dinner tales. Then write like the wind."

"That's what I plan to do." Seeing Gideon walking toward her, Tess ended the call.

"Hi," she said. "I was just out walking with Madeleine."

"I know. I saw you." He bent to pet Rowdy, who'd roused from a sunbeam to greet him. "I've been thinking about something," he said.

"If it's about me upsetting Madeleine—"

"No. But I don't want to talk about it out here. Can you spare a few minutes?"

"Sure."

She walked with him back past the vineyards to where a pair of huge double-rounded arched doors seemed to have been erected against a hillside. Taking a heavy iron key from his pocket, he unlocked and opened them. Inside what turned out to be the cave he'd told her about, the air was perfumed with the scent of oak barrels and aging wine.

"This is amazing!" Tess looked around, realizing she was standing in a place made by a millions-of-years-old volcanic flow. She glanced up at the rough ceiling. "No crystal chandelier."

"No. Robert put those iron sconces into the wall himself. In the beginning, it was lighted by beeswax candles Madeleine made from the orchard's hives. It was electrified in the late '50s, and updated twice, the last time being five years ago to be more energy efficient."

"You do realize that Charlotte will absolutely want to use this space. And she'll be right."

"I do. I also realize that we're one of the few naturally made caves, which adds to the appeal, but my feet are set in concrete, or should I say cooled lava, when it comes to fussifying it."

"She's a brilliant designer. I've seen her work online. She'll definitely honor its history, both geographically and the family's... So is this what you brought me here for?"

"Only partly." He framed her face with his hands. "It's up to you," he said, his voice roughened with the same hunger she felt coursing like red-hot lava through her veins. "Yes?" His blue eyes, a darker blue than her own, turned nearly black. Of course, that could be his pupils expanding due to the dim light, but Tess didn't think so. "Or no?"

As she looked up at him, although she knew that it could only complicate their relationship, she had to go for it. To find out for herself. "Yes."

As Tess held her breath, she could've sworn he was moving in slow motion. Frame by frame, like when she'd be looking at videos to edit on her phone.

And then, finally, his lips touched hers. They were warm and firm and soft at the same time. In other words, perfect. As his long fingers slid into her hair, she went up on her toes, pressed her mouth against his and opened her lips, inviting more.

His tongue slid in, sweeping, tangling with hers, and his hands moved from her head to her butt, pressing her against him so closely she could feel every rock-hard ridge of his chest against her body. Just when the last remaining rational cell in her brain ceased to function, thinking that having sex against a lava wall, or floor, probably wasn't the best idea, she felt a buzz against her hip.

With her brain so fogged, Tess wondered if it was possible for her ovaries to vibrate with lust, when he cursed, pulled away and yanked his phone out of the front pocket of his Wranglers.

"What is it?" he snapped, which effectively broke the mood. "Oh, hell. Did you take him to the ER?" She could hear the voice on the other end of the phone, but couldn't make out the words. "Okay. I'll be there in ten minutes. Fifteen, tops."

He ended the call, took two long steps back and shoved his hands through his hair. "That was Reynaldo. One of the guys cut himself with a pruning saw."

"Oh, no! How bad is it?"

"It went to the bone. Reynaldo couldn't tell if he'd cut a tendon or not, so they're taking him to the hospital for an X-ray."

"And if he cut a tendon?"

"Then he may need surgery. And lose this part of the season. Bad news for us, but fortunately for him, his medical costs and time off work will be taken care of. But I need to go to the hospital and see how he is and talk to the doctor."

"Of course you do." She pressed her fingers to her lips, which were still tingling. "Will I see you at dinner?"

"I hope so. It depends. But I'll let you know."

As they left the cave, about to turn in separate directions, she grabbed hold of his shirt and pulled him to her so she could kiss him again. This kiss was hard, hot and definitely deeper.

"Good luck," she said when she could breathe again.

"Thanks." He looked nearly as shell-shocked as she felt. Then he trailed those roughened fingertips from her lips over her chin and down her throat, where she knew he could feel her pulse crazily hammering. "To be continued..."

"Thank heavens," she said. But she was talking to his back as he headed toward his truck.

33

"Fortunately," Madeleine assured everyone that evening as they sat down to dinner, "Gideon assured me that no tendons were cut, so he's bringing Carlos back home tonight. But he had stitches and won't be able to work for a week to ten days."

"That's a relief," Tess said. She'd already received the call from Gideon, while he was still at the hospital, but had felt it was Madeleine's place to share the news.

And speaking of the best kisser she'd ever met, which had her toes curling at the thought of what other parts of her body he would hopefully soon set tingling, Gideon arrived just as Rose was delivering the meal. It was a simple but delicious flat-iron steak with a peppercorn sauce, served with ratatouille and a crunchy French baguette and that creamy butter that Tess was becoming addicted to.

Gideon confirmed Madeleine's update. "He's back home now and playing the patient for all he's worth. His wife, who'd planned on just getting a pizza for the kids, is, as I left, rolling out dough to make him his favorite fish tacos with guac. He *was* grumpy when she refused to let him have a beer because the doctor had given him some pain meds."

The conversation turned to the upcoming Saturday night reception. To support local business, Charlotte had found a nearby event rental store that would supply the tables and chairs, plus tablecloths and napkins in the same color as Maison de Madeleine's signature burgundy. Also plates, glasses and flatware as well as a centerpiece for the buffet table and small round vases for bouquets, which the store would source from a florist she did business with.

"That's pretty impressive," Tess said. "To take care of all that with just one call."

"Well, I got lucky. Madeleine taught the event supplier's parents French for a dream thirtieth anniversary trip to Paris, so she was eager to help. And gave us setup and takeaway all at a very good price."

"You're not only a great designer, you're a magician." Tess was feeling both very grateful to and proud of her sister. "There was no way I could've pulled that off. Left to me, I'd probably lose all track of dates and time while writing and we would've ended up with crepe paper in dreadful colors no one wanted in the sale bin at Party City and helium balloons. Which I think you can get something to blow them up with. But that's moot now because we have you."

"Thank you." A soft pink blush rose in her cheeks. "I fell into event planning by accident when a couple of clients asked me for help with an open house to show off their remodels, and deciding that it could win me some new clients from among the guests, which it did, I agreed and discovered it's a lot of fun."

She looked as happy as a woman holding up a huge multimillion-dollar lottery check for the news cameras. Tess had come to realize Charlotte wasn't playing some Southern-blonde-Reese Witherspoon movie role; she truly was the sweetest of the three of them. And definitely the most entrepreneurial, which would be helpful, not only with the reception and the harvest festival, but also with helping turn Maison de Madeleine into a wine tourism destination.

They were back outside on the deck, sitting in their same places as the previous evening. Aubrey was over at the Salazars', playing Minecraft with John. It wasn't a date, Aubrey had insisted. Because his parents were going to be there. Personally, Gideon thought she was skating a very thin line with that argument, but he trusted the Salazars. Plus, wanting to be able to sit on the love seat by the fire and hold Tess's hand without having to face the third degree from his daughter, he'd let her win him over.

"The flyer the young man had given me copied a speech Charles de Gaulle gave over the BBC to people in France, while his government was exiled in London." Madeleine began tonight's chapter. "Every resistance faction of the *Maquis* had different rules, but ours was very strict because the Germans had taken over our capital city and surrounding homes, so each member was required to memorize the speech as a way to prove that you weren't a German plant pretending to be a member. Or, later in the war, they often pretended to be downed British or American pilots needing help. It was one of the only ways we could recognize each other in such dangerous situations. I could probably still recite it today."

"I've seen that poster in school textbooks and museums," Natalie said. "But I know the others would love to hear it, if you think you could."

"Let me try." As if the words were too important to speak sitting down, Madeleine stood. "It began, To All Frenchmen— and we'll forgive him for leaving out the women, given those times—France has lost a battle! But France has not lost the war!

"A makeshift government may have capitulated, giving

way to panic, forgetting honor, delivering their country into slavery. Yet, nothing is lost!

"Nothing is lost because this is a world war. In a free universe, immense forces have not yet been brought into play. Someday these forces will crush the enemy. On that day France must be present at the victory. She will then regain her liberty and her greatness.

"That is my goal, my only goal! That is why I invite all Frenchmen, wherever they may be, to unite with me in action, in sacrifice and in hope.

"Our country is in danger of death. Let us fight to save it! *"Vive La France!"*

Her voice had grown stronger, louder, and at the end, she'd raised her fist and in that moment, Gideon knew that he wasn't the only person sitting around that circle who could see the determined teenager, only slightly older than his own Aubrey, declaring that she would do whatever it took to save her country. Even risk torture and death.

A silence had settled over them. From respect and awe, he considered as she sat back down.

"I'm a writer, and even I have no words," Tess said finally.

"De Gaulle was a little-known general when he fled to London," Madeleine said. "But his broadcasts gave us courage and hope during those dark days of deprivation and death. They certainly stirred my young soul. Written in a corner of the flyer was an address in Dijon, and a meeting time for two days away. Of course I could not resist."

"I'm understanding my father more and more," Tess murmured to Gideon as Madeleine shared the story of first meeting her resistance contact right under the noses of a group of German soldiers.

"She can't stop now!" Charlotte protested when, once again, Rose tried to shut down story time.

"I'm beginning to feel like Scheherazade," Madeleine complained to Rose.

"The doctor says you're supposed to get rest and avoid stress," Rose countered.

"Just a bit longer," Madeleine insisted. Then stubbornly continued on. "I was always going off hiking in the mountains. I belonged to a regional ski club and my dream was to represent France in the Olympics, so my parents were used to me doing a great deal of walking and biking to keep in shape. But once the Germans arrived, they became much more concerned, so I placated them a bit by wearing my hair in braids as I'd done as a child. Although I was sixteen, I looked young for my age—"

"As you still do," Gideon said.

Which drew a laugh. "You're a liar, Gideon Byrne. But a chivalrous one, so I'll gladly accept the compliment. At any rate, the braids made me look more like a young girl than a teenager, so the Germans were much less likely to perceive me as a threat. Or, what my parents most worried about, especially after that night the soldiers had invaded our house, sexual prey.

"Not telling *Maman* or Papa where I was headed, I went to the address spelled out in the book pages, which I'd made sure to erase, for caution, after reading, and when the door opened a huge man frowned down at me.

"He roared a name back over his shoulder and a moment later the young man who'd put the flyer in my pocket appeared. They argued, as if I wasn't standing there, about me. The older man insisted I was just a baby. Too young to be trusted. The other man, who appeared to be in his early twenties, and whose name, I'd learned, was Julien, insisted that I was older than I looked. Then he brought up my skiing, which didn't seem to have anything to do with what I was there for, but I was smart enough to keep my mouth shut and wait things out.

"After much back and forth, I was asked if I could type.

"I assured him that I was a very competent typist, having helped keep records for our winery. Julien argued that I could help with the newsletter. But the older man still had his doubts and warned me that even that small task, as important as it was, could be dangerous. That I could tell no one what I was doing.

"His expression was as sober as a priest serving Mass. He asked if I was prepared to risk my life for my country. And to crush the Germans.

"It sounded so exciting. Was I frightened? Honestly, yes. Was I tempted to say no? Only for a moment, when I thought of what it would do to Papa and *Maman* to lose their only remaining child.

"Then I remembered de Gaulle's stirring words, and how my mother's great-uncle had been left to hang like the poor stags Papa would hunt every winter. And the Nazi thugs I'd seen from the train window, beating Jews in the streets of Dijon with no one making a move to stop them. One was an old man who appeared to be nearly the age that I am now.

"And there was no other possible answer, but *absolument!*"

34

Deciding that it was time that she have her own wheels, Tess called Barbara Williams the next morning to ask if her agency ever dealt with shipping cars from a former home to a new one. Luckily, not only did the Realtor know of a place, she also called them and set up the pickup and delivery of Tess's car from Sedona to Aberdeen. All they'd need was the car fob to open the garage door and start the car, a problem that was easily solved, since Tess had already given her housekeeper the combination to her front door. One call to tell her where the extra fob was, and the housekeeper agreed to not only be there when the transport truck arrived, but also would continue to clean every other week until Tess decided what to do about the house.

It crossed her mind that if she stayed in Aberdeen beyond the harvest, having a second home in sunny Arizona might be a good idea. Last night's kiss from Gideon would definitely enter into her decision. If it looked as if it might be going anywhere, despite her telling her grandmother that all her relationships were recreational, and to be truthful, often didn't make it past the first date, this felt different. At least to her.

She would be the first to admit that she came with baggage. But so did Gideon, having lost his first wife. Along with being a single dad of a fifteen-year old girl who might not be willing to share her father or have someone replace her mother.

Remembering a time when she had her therapist on speed dial, Tess decided just to let things play out. That certainly had worked for Madeleine. What were the odds of a young French woman and an American pilot from a family on the other side of the world who owned a cherry orchard ever getting together? Yet, Madeleine was convinced that Robert had been her destiny.

"What do you think," she asked Natalie and Charlotte over breakfast, "since Donovan is coming by with papers for us to sign, that we ask him to drive us into town so we can rent a car until mine arrives? Charlotte's rental is way too small for all of us."

"It was the only one available, so I took it," Charlotte said. "I was lucky to get it, but it's admittedly more of a clown car."

"Cars that size in Paris are quite common," Natalie said reassuringly. "We don't have much room for parking and do possess a good transportation system."

"I called and checked, and every additional driver has to be there in person with a license, and, in your case, Natalie, also your passport," Tess said.

"Sounds fine to me," Natalie agreed. "As long as I get to ride copilot next to Donovan on the way into town."

"Is there a thing going on between you two?" Charlotte asked. "Because that would be fantastic."

"There's been a *thing* for a decade," Natalie said. "Unfortunately, it's always been one-sided."

"But anyone can tell how much he likes you," Tess said.

"He does. Like a friend. I know couples who've gone from friends to lovers. But I'm afraid that even if he feels a bit of interest in any romantic way, he's not willing to risk our years-long friendship."

"You'll never know if you don't ask," Charlotte said. "I went into my marriage thinking I knew everything about Mason. But I've come to realize the hard way that I only knew the slick-surface gloss. I never dug deeper."

"Donovan has much more depth than slick-surface gloss." Natalie quickly defended the man who'd recently changed their lives.

"Of course he does," Tess jumped in. "But I think what Charlotte is saying is that she never asked the hard questions. The important ones we always want to know but are afraid to ask."

"Because I was afraid of offending him. Or learning something that I couldn't live with," Charlotte admitted. "Donovan may be feeling exactly the same way as you do. But as your bossy elder sister, I do have one suggestion, since you two have been playing what seems a game of cat and mouse."

"And that is?"

"Have the sex first. Then, just in case the answers to those hard questions aren't what you're looking for, at least you'll get something out of it."

Natalie laughed. "What questions should I ask? I've known him most of my life."

"I suppose the most common differences that could cause conflict would be does he want children? How many? And who will care for them when they're babies, and after school once they get older?" She was ticking the questions off on her fingernails that today were painted a bright spring turquoise that matched her sandals and the flowers on her spaghetti-strapped sundress.

"Another thing you should ask is now that Jack, who must have been his biggest client, is gone, is he planning to stay in Aberdeen, or is he going to return to rejoin his brother in

Portland?" Charlotte continued. "And if so, how do you feel about that? Would you be more comfortable living the country life here, or with the buzz of a progressive city?"

"You're very thorough," Natalie said. "I've always believed that we French are practical, but I never would have thought of doing that."

"Which is probably one reason about half the marriages end in divorce."

"There's one more question you might want to add," Tess suggested to Natalie. "Does he have a red room? Which would be fine if you're into that sort of thing, but if you're not, or don't feel like experimenting with the kind of sex that needs a safe word, that'd probably be a deal breaker."

Natalie blushed to the roots of her hair. "Oh, I'm sure he isn't into such things. He's always been very sweet and tender."

"It was always the outwardly sweet and tender guys who ended up being the serial killer in those *Lifetime* movies I made," Tess countered. "Just saying."

After salads at Cork, a very chic but unpretentious wine restaurant, Tess noted that the servers helped customers pronounce the wines without a hint of the superior snark she'd experienced in other restaurants and made a mental note that once the wine-tasting room asked for recommendations for lunch or dinner, she would definitely send them there. Wine should be fun. Not a pop quiz.

They walked the streets of the small town, doing a little shopping. Tess bought a big glossy coffee table book featuring photos of Willamette Valley wineries and was pleased to see that Maison de Madeleine was nicely featured. She also picked up two others—one on cooking with wine and another claiming to be easy French dishes.

Except for Julia Child's beef bourguignon, she'd never cooked French food. Since both Rose and Madeleine were

competitive, and a little bossy—okay, *very* bossy—they'd probably be willing to help her learn. After all, she couldn't spend
all her time writing her novel and kissing Gideon Byrne. The
second of which she hoped to be doing a lot more of.

Natalie found a book of black-and-white photos showing
Aberdeen and the Dundee Hills area in the 1940s. All three
agreed that it would be cool if she took photos in those same
places, then they could be framed and hung together in the
tasting room.

When they returned to Maison de Madeleine in the SUV
Tess had rented, they decided that given that the planned reception was only days away, they should deliver their invitations to the crews by hand. Since Rowdy, who greeted them
with the glee that suggested they'd been gone years, not a
couple hours, was due for a walk, they decided to take him
along. "Who doesn't like dogs?" Natalie said. "They'll be
more likely to open the door to us."

As it turned out, the Irish setter worked like a charm. Since
Tess and Natalie both spoke Spanish, they explained about
the party, and to a person, all the workers seemed excited and
pleased by the idea. Mr. Jack, as he appeared to be known, was
described as a kind man, and nearly at every stop they heard
a story about his generosity and kindness. Which wasn't, one
more outspoken woman said, all that typical as they worked
their way across the country, supplying Americans' tables.

Since Rose knew they'd be having a late lunch in town,
she'd prepared a light dinner, an asparagus two-cheese quiche
with tomato soup on the side.

"Rose, you should really try out for *Master Chef*," Tess told
her. "You'd sweep all the challenges for a win."

"Oh, go on with you." Rose waved away the compliment,
but it was obvious that she was pleased.

35

October, 1940

Although Madeleine was impatient being stuck with typing, when her notions about being a spy had involved much more exciting adventures, she didn't complain because, as Julien explained to her, with the Gestapo, SS and German soldiers all breathing down their necks, they had to use extreme caution.

By the end of the second week, because she was the fastest typist of the group and had written winery records for her papa, she'd been assigned to write some of the tracts telling the truth about the war that the radio operators would receive from London. She'd also been elevated to riding her bicycle around the town and through the countryside, scattering the newsletters. Always in different places, so the enemy wouldn't be waiting for a drop.

After her first month at that job, Julien came to her, his expression as serious as she'd ever seen it. "You've impressed Albert, who's been watching you. And investigating you."

"Investigating me?" She supposed she shouldn't be surprised that the giant who'd wanted to reject her that first day would have done such a thing. After all, lives and eventually, the restitution of her country's freedom, was at stake. Nothing and no one could be taken at face value. Even she had been on edge when a new typist arrived last week from a nearby city. Which was common, since members were moved around often, so as not to be noticed.

"He talked to some of your teachers. They all assured him that you were extremely responsible for your age, and that they believed you could handle more responsibility than you have now."

"Some of my teachers are members of the *Maquis*?"

He arched a brow. "Of course. Why should you be surprised? Who would expect *you* to be working with us? If you'd known about your teachers, they wouldn't have been very good at their work, now, would they?"

Of course he had a point. These days no one knew whose side anyone was on. Hadn't a Dijon collaborator turned in her mother's great-uncle, which was what had brought her to join the Resistance in the first place?

"What do you want me to do?" she asked.

"We're going to elevate you to a courier." As he explained the task, Madeleine could barely conceal her excitement. Yes! A courier was more what she'd been hoping for when she'd first decided to join the movement. They were go-betweens for the various members. And often different groups. They'd help move downed pilots and crews, escaped prisoners, or Jews, homosexuals and any of the other targeted groups from house to house until hopefully they could escape the country. Another of their jobs was to transport weapons and explosives to members involved in more violent measures than she'd be doing.

Her initial assignments had gone exactly according to plan. So smoothly, in fact, although she always remained vigilant, she'd actually begun to feel a bit overly prideful. Until the day a few months later, during a trip to Paris on the train, when a young, handsome blond soldier, who could have appeared on a German recruiting poster, sat in the seat facing her.

She was wearing a blond wig that day, and a simple but feminine white blouse, navy blue-and-white-gingham skirt, a blue cardigan and plain black short-heeled shoes. Because it would have seemed out of place for a young girl to be traveling alone, rather than the braids she so often wore to take years off her age, the wig had been styled to fall in waves to her shoulders. She'd already looked up from the book she'd pretended to be reading when he'd sat down, so now, when he smiled at her, fighting off nerves, she shyly smiled back.

"What's your reason for going to Paris?" he asked conversationally.

She told him her cover story, that she was visiting an older sister who'd recently had a baby. "I'm very excited about being an aunt." She managed another smile.

"What a coincidence," he said. "My sister recently gave birth back home in Berlin. I'm very eager for this war to be over so I can return home to my wife and children and meet my new nephew."

"I can imagine it's difficult," she said, feigning sympathy. She could not start thinking of this nice-mannered young man with a wife and children and apparently close family as anything but the enemy. One who'd turn her in to be tortured and murdered without blinking an Aryan blue eye if he'd known what was in that suitcase on the rack overhead. "I imagine your family misses you, as well."

That said, not wanting to continue a conversation that might risk her making a fatal mistake, Madeleine returned to pretending to read her book while nerves had the words blurring on the pages, while he contented himself with watching the scenery.

When they reached Paris, although she assured him that she could handle her own luggage, proving himself to be more gentlemanly than those soldiers who'd stormed into her home, he insisted on lifting the suitcase down from the rack. Although there'd been a moment she'd thought she'd surely pass out due to lack of oxygen from holding her breath, he retrieved it and handed it to her without incident.

Yet, her concerns weren't over when she saw that the Gestapo was at the station, checking papers as the passengers disembarked. Some SS members entered the cars, walking down the aisle, looking at each face as if searching for someone specific. It didn't matter how good she believed her papers and cover story to be, or how many times she'd slid through checkpoints, or how many times she'd achieved her mission without incident, Madeleine never forgot that this could be the day everything could come crashing down, putting her life and those of others, including her *maman* and papa at risk, so her heart was beating against her ribs.

Yet, as she walked off the train with the uniformed soldier, resuming their casual chat about babies, possibly due to her companion, the grim-faced Gestapo agents waved her through without giving a second glance to her suitcase carrying the deadly explosives.

It was only after she and the German soldier had said their farewells and parted that she was finally able to fully breathe again.

36

Gideon had stayed home and grilled burgers with Aubrey, then come over for Madeleine's story time while his daughter did her homework. When he showed up and sat down next to Tess, taking her hand as naturally as if they were a couple, she realized that during dinner, when she'd been missing him, he'd still been with her because that kiss had kept swirling around and around in her mind. Especially when the chirpy car rental clerk in town was listing the features on the SUV and told her that the passenger seat reclined all the way back. Hadn't that caused her neglected lady parts to jump up and say, "Get this one!"

"So continuing on." Madeleine picked up her story as if it hadn't been twenty-four hours since she'd told of accepting the life of a Resistance fighter. "Since all the fighting-age men were away at war, the groups were mainly made up of women and old men. Naturally, misogyny tended to be a given, and when meetings were held to put out a new underground newspaper, the men talked, argued, then wrote, while any new girls were resigned to being typists.

"Julien, my recruiter, was the only young man there because he was working for the Gestapo."

"How could he do such a thing?" Natalie, sounding outraged, asked.

"He'd already been a civil servant, translating papers for the French government. And, because he spoke several languages, the Germans kept him on. Which was a good thing, because not only did he pick up news, such as who they might be targeting for arrest, he had access to all the filing cabinets. Some of which held blank ID cards and travel passes."

"Oh," Natalie said. "That was a good job for him to have, then. But it must have been quite a moral dilemma, working with the enemy."

"It was. It was also very unnerving. Especially since he was gay, which made him a target because, as you undoubtedly know, as part of their mission to *purify* Germans, the Nazis arrested thousands of LGBTQ individuals, mostly men. The United States Holocaust Memorial Museum *estimates* a hundred thousand gay men were arrested and between five to fifteen thousand sent to concentration camps. Yet, there he was, risking his life every working minute of his day.

"He almost got caught once, stealing one of the new ID cards. The style would change every so often, in order to prevent so much counterfeiting. At any rate, he'd been truthful when he'd told me to stay, and soon I was distributing the newspapers. Carrying them in a rucksack as I rode around the city and countryside."

"Wasn't that a dangerous job for a young girl?" Gideon asked, thinking, Tess guessed, of his daughter.

"In truth, it was safer for us because the foolish, sexist Germans didn't believe women were smart enough to be part of the *Maquis*. And, as I said, I looked a great deal younger than my age. Often I'd wear my school uniform. Who'd think a

young Catholic schoolgirl could be part of the group determined to crush you?

"I did that job for a month, when Julien decided it was time
to make me a liaison agent, although the large, angry man,
whose name I would come to learn was Albert, or at least that's
the name he went by, argued that I'd get caught and cause
their entire group to be arrested and killed."

"Obviously, he underestimated you," Tess said.

"He certainly did," Madeleine said with a smile. "I was not
only a very smart girl, fire burned in my veins. I shot a man
to death once and still have never felt a moment's regret."

There was a long silence as everyone took in that amazing
statement. Then, Charlotte asked the inevitable question everyone was wondering, "Why?"

"We'll get to that when the time comes," she assured them.

"What, exactly, did a liaison do?" Tess asked.

Madeleine went on to explain, sharing the story of the day
when she'd managed to dodge discovery not just by a soldier
on the train, but also the Gestapo.

"You could have been killed," Charlotte said, looking ap-
palled.

"So could anyone at any time. Those actively fighting the
war, those of us resisting and, as history has taught us, millions more during the occupation.

"We also worked with spies that Britain would drop into
the country. Winston Churchill was running a group of secret
agents called the Special Operations Executive. They were
ordinary citizens—housewives, university students, bakers—
people you'd never imagine would be doing such dangerous
work. They were put through weeks of vigorous training and
it was very difficult to make the cut.

"One was a darling young Englishman who'd been a co-
median in his civilian life. He was our main radio operator

and no matter how terrible things would seem, he'd always find a way to make us laugh at the absurdity of the war we were living through."

Her expression sobered, and her eyes misted. "He was captured and killed after being exposed by a member of the group who'd been caught in a weapons drop zone and, under torture, gave the Gestapo the names of some of the members of our group. It was a terrible loss. Not just because we became scattered, but because he was a sincerely wonderful person with a huge heart. Some days he was the only thing that kept us all going."

"How did you not all get captured?" Charlotte asked.

"As I said, we all worked underground, with aliases and disguises. Only a very few knew individuals' true names. I certainly wasn't at a level to possess that information. Nor would I have wanted to. Plus, it's not that hard to change your appearance. A pair of glasses, a different way of dressing or walking, or styling your hair, and I found myself becoming those characters."

"Perhaps you should have been an actress," Natalie suggested.

"Oh, but I was, my dear. Every day for years. It was only with Robert that I ever felt I could be myself."

"Are we getting to when you met?" Tess asked.

"We are. But I'm afraid you'll have to wait a while longer. Because reliving those dark times is something I've avoided doing for decades, and I'm honestly finding it tiring."

"Of course you are," Charlotte said quickly, rising to kiss her grandmother on the cheek. "You must take your time to tell whatever you can as you feel up to it. I know that we all appreciate that you're willing to share what had to be harrowing memories at all."

"Thank you, dear. And while I'm admitting leaving you

in suspense, I can assure you that Robert's and my love story had a happy ending for many decades."

After Natalie and Tess followed Charlotte in kissing their grandmother good-night, while the other two went upstairs to their rooms, Gideon accompanied Tess as she took Rowdy on his nightly walk.

37

Although she knew it was selfish, Tess was frustrated when it was decided they would forego tomorrow night's story hour due to all the baking and preparations going on for the reception.

"Then, of course, Saturday night's out, too," she complained to Gideon. They'd walked the dog to a field on a higher hill, which gave an even better view of the house, cottages and vineyards below.

"At least we know it turned out okay," he said.

"True." She blew out a breath. "Though patience has never exactly been my strong suit."

"Wow." He tucked some curls that had blown across her face by the evening breeze behind her ear. "I never would've guessed. I do have one question."

"Oh?" Just that slight touch caused the air to seem to heat between them.

"If I let go of this leash, your dog's going to take off, isn't he?"

"He's extremely well trained. Unless he sees something to chase. Then he takes off like a rocket." She didn't want his hand on Rowdy's leash. She wanted both his hands on her. All over.

"Well, then, we'll just have to risk it." When he dropped the leash and pulled her against him, she wanted to do what she'd done in her dreams last night. Rip off his shirt and lick him, all the way down that six-pack. Then continue lower.

When Rowdy, thinking that they were playing a new game, tried to shove his way in between them, Gideon simply said, "Sit." And amazingly, the dog backed up, dropped down to his haunches and stayed there.

"You never told me you were a dog whisperer."

"I didn't know I was. Having never kissed a woman with a dog trying to worm his way into the action."

"Well, then." Refusing to wonder how many women he had kissed, she gazed at his mouth and said, "I guess there's nothing stopping you now."

A slow smile curved his lips in a way that had every nerve in her body on full alert. Waiting. Wanting. "I guess not," he said.

She parted her lips, bracing for the kiss she'd been waiting for, when, instead, he brushed his mouth against her neck. Who knew that the little place behind her ear was an erogenous zone? Apparently, he did, because he was causing her bones to weaken.

"Gideon." His name came out on a ragged sigh.

"So impatient," he scolded lightly. He skimmed those wicked lips down her throat, and across the scooped neckline of the T-shirt she'd bought in town screen-printed with a glass of red wine and the words, in glittery red script, reading I Am Woman. Hear Me Pour.

Sure, it was tacky and touristy. But Gideon had smiled when he'd seen it, and hadn't that given her heart a little flip? He tugged the neckline down, then kissed his way from one shoulder—lingering at that sensitive spot at her throat where her pulse beat wildly—to the other shoulder.

And when she was about to scream, "Just do it!" his mouth finally took hers. There was no more teasing. This kiss was deep, hot, fierce, primal, and as he ravished her mouth, she twined her arms around his neck and kissed him back, their tongues tangling.

As heat coursed through her and a sound like thunder echoed in her ears, she was thinking that the next time they were together, it wasn't going to be a threesome with her dog, because she wanted to rip open his belt, undo those five metal buttons and take him in her hands, and…damn!

Just when she was about to risk it, because Rowdy undoubtedly knew his way back to the house by now if he got away, the sky opened up and she realized that actually *had* been thunder, and not the wild, out-of-control pounding of her heart she'd been hearing.

"It's raining."

"Spring rains are good for the grapes," he said against her mouth. "Not so good for making out." He didn't seem overly bothered, just lightened the kiss she'd felt all the way to her toes and brushed his lips back and forth across hers. "I guess we'd better get back."

"I guess so," she said regretfully as Rowdy, who'd only ever been a Texas and Arizona dog, began whining about getting wet.

38

July, 1944

Although she knew it was dangerous, Madeleine was breaking curfew for the second night in a row. Last night she'd escorted a Jewish violinist to a safe house, where he could stay until they managed to find a courier to get him out of the country.

On the way home she'd heard what sounded like muffled cries coming from a leafy park. Following the sound, she found a young woman lying on the ground, a soldier kneeling between her legs, the skirt of a black-and-red, off-the-shoulder frilly cancan dress the owner of a nearby music hall required his waitresses to wear to attract free-spending German soldiers pushed up nearly over her head. As drunk as he was, he was struggling to unbutton his trousers, when, without a moment's hesitation, she pulled out a pistol she always kept strapped to her thigh on her more dangerous missions and called out to him.

When he half turned, cursing at her to mind her own business and get on her way, having been well trained, she shot him point-blank in the heart. Fortunately, because she'd gotten the silenced pistol from a British SOE—Special Operations Executive—agent who'd worked behind enemy lines, the loud music and singing from the music hall drowned out what sound there was. Then, when he fell over onto his back, she shot him again.

"Well," she said calmly, extending a hand to the woman to help her to her feet, "if the bastard does survive, at least he won't have the equipment to rape any other women."

Having been schoolgirls together, she recognized the woman as Yvonne Laurent, a daughter of a journalist whose newspaper had been shut down by the Gestapo. Madeleine knew she'd been working at the tavern to help put food on the table.

Yvonne scrambled to her feet, her eyes wide with shock. "Thank you. But I can't believe you did that!"

"We all do what we must these days," Madeleine said, realizing how much she'd changed from that young girl who twirled in her first long skirt at a harvest festival dance.

"He must have been watching me. I always take this short cut from work to my parents' house."

"That music hall is no place for you." She knew women who enjoyed the extra money slipped into the top of their corsets or their ruffled garters. Women who'd done a great deal more to survive during these times. Including turning to prostitution, or worse, to her mind, becoming well-kept mistresses for Gestapo agents.

"I know a hatmaker who lost her helper last week." She didn't say how. People disappeared on a daily basis, and it was safer not to discuss the situation. She wrote the address on a piece of paper. "Tell her I sent you. But you must never, *ever* tell a single soul what happened here tonight. Now hurry home before someone finds him and sees you leaving here.

Believe me when I tell you that you do not want to be connected with this."

Promising to remain silent, Yvonne gave her a hug, then lifted her torn skirt and raced into the park, toward the street where her parents lived. The hatmaker was a member of another group, so it was possible that Yvonne might also be recruited to join the Resistance. Life, Madeleine had learned, took its own twists and turns.

Tonight she was riding her bicycle away from the chateau to meet with others at a weapons drop site when the night sky exploded with flack, which wasn't all that unusual these days. The sound had replaced the *rossignol*, or as she'd later learn was called a nightingale in America. The Yanks had finally joined the war in December of 1941, after the bombing of Pearl Harbor, a day, their president had declared, that would "live in infamy." As tragic as she found that attack, and as grateful as she was for the Americans, Madeleine would have liked to tell their president that the people of France had been suffering many personal days of infamy.

Still, it had taken until last year for American planes to appear. At first they sent hundreds, then thousands of bombers; as many as half the huge, lumbering planes had been shot down by the more technically advanced German fighter planes, keeping the *Maquis* busy rescuing downed crews. Which was when her hiking and skiing skills that Julien had mentioned started coming into play as, along with her courier job, she'd been assigned to escort downed airmen over the Pyrenees, where they'd cross over the dangerous border into supposedly neutral Spain.

Once the United States sent fighter planes to accompany the bombers, the odds had begun to change, which was fortunate because the casualties lessened, but Madeleine's work became even more dangerous because there were so many people involved in the exfiltrations; leaks became more likely, allowing the Germans to infiltrate the groups, capturing hundreds. The leaders were executed while others were sent to concentration camps.

And yet, Madeleine persisted, convinced that victory would soon be at hand. Suddenly, she saw a flash in the sky. It was too far from the drop site to be the expected delivery of food and weapons. Seconds later a plane was spinning down, crashing through a small copse at the far edge of the vineyard. Then a white canopy of a parachute floated down.

Knowing that the Germans would be looking for the pilot, she pedaled madly to the scene, where she found him caught in the branches of the tree. Before she could call out to him, he'd cut his harness and came crashing through the tree limbs, only to land on her, knocking her down.

His head was bleeding profusely, and after she'd scrambled out from beneath him, she realized that he'd passed out. She was trying to rouse him, knowing that the Germans would be searching for him and that his parachute was still stuck in the tree like a huge white arrow, signaling his location. Making matters worse, the blue plane, a model of a Spitfire that hadn't appeared on her identification charts, exploded.

Feeling as if she'd been granted superhero strength, like the heroes in those colorful comic books so many GIs carried with them, she managed to drag him away from the flames and out of the trees, which were in danger of catching fire, into a row of vines, then raced to the chateau for her papa, who with her *maman*, had also joined the *Maquis*. While they didn't take an active role, they sheltered those needing a temporary hiding place.

He hitched their last remaining goat to a cart, lifted the pilot onto it, then together they ran through the vineyard. Attempting to hide those in danger of discovery was too risky because the chateau was only a few kilometers from the airfield, and pilots or Luftwaffe officials often moved into the house, even sitting at the table with Madeleine and her parents, which was very uncomfortable.

But as her *maman* reminded her, they should consider themselves fortunate that they hadn't been forced out of their home entirely, as so many had been, because their vineyard was important to the enemy who needed to ensure a steady quantity of wine. Both for the Germans in France, and to sell back home to help fund their war.

Since none had ever shown any interest in how the wine was made, there was no reason for them to go into the pressing room. So Madeleine's papa had dug out a deep room beneath the floorboards, made a hinged door and rolled empty barrels over it to conceal it.

Fortunately, for this newest pilot, who'd roused slightly during his bumpy ride through the rows of wine, a British tail gunner had moved on two days earlier, so the room was empty. After assuring her papa that she'd come fetch him if anything went wrong, he returned to the house, leaving her alone with the pilot whose jacket, for some reason, bore both the RAF and USAAF pilot wings.

She sat down on the floor and after wrapping his head in the bandages kept in the room, put it on her lap. She'd lit a candle when they first entered, and spent most of the night looking down into his face, which was American movie-star handsome, with his black hair, square jaw and striking blue eyes, which would flutter open from time to time.

Once, toward morning, he'd opened those flame-blue eyes, looked up at her and asked if he'd died.

"Non," she'd assured him, brushing soothing fingers over his brow. "You're alive. And safe."

"I figured I was a goner," he'd told her, his deep voice

strumming chords she'd never felt deep inside her. Not even that long ago innocent night when she'd danced with Bernard Deschamps at the harvest festival. "Because you're so beautiful, I was sure you were an angel."

Before she could think of a proper response to that, he'd passed out again. "God sent you to me, Captain Swann," she whispered, reading the patch with his name and rank. "You don't know it yet." When she bent her head and touched her lips to his, he stirred, but didn't awaken. "But you're mine." And for that reason, as treacherous a journey as he had ahead of him, she knew that the God whom her mother had always trusted implicitly, would keep him safe.

Because she hadn't shown up at the drop site, the member in charge of that mission, Raul, came to the house the following day to ensure that she hadn't been caught and arrested. He checked Madeleine's pilot, who was now in pain from a concussion and broken ribs, and told him that he'd be back to get him tomorrow because they couldn't put the vineyard at risk with anything but short-term stays.

"Don't worry, *mon capitaine*," she assured him, taking one of his much larger hands in both of hers and lifting it over her heart. Which, during the night, she'd given to him. Forever. "We'll take good care of you. You have my promise."

39

The special-events coordinator Charlotte had hired to plan the reception had outdone herself, even bringing portable heaters to warm the spring night air. Although the sky was clear, Barbara had sent her son, Joel, to install a temporary awning, strung with white fairy lights, over the expansive deck, just in case of rain. The buffet table looked beautiful and what Tess had tasted so far was delicious, and everyone seemed to appreciate the opportunity to tell their stories about Jackson Swann's life. Pieces of conversations filtered through as she moved past various groups. "He paid for my daughter's braces… He brought me a mobile with jungle animals for my son's crib after I brought him home from the hospital… He taught my Jessie how to do plane geometry, when I couldn't figure it out… He pulled some strings and got my aunt and uncle and nieces from El Salvador immigration papers."

And there were so many more. So she realized her father hadn't just hidden away here as she'd imagined. He'd engaged with the people, helping so many. Perhaps, she considered, because here at Maison de Madeleine he was able to help, unlike in those war- and plague-torn places he'd spent most of his life. Perhaps these people reminded him that not all the world was a flaming dumpster fire.

She saw Charlotte at the buffet table and wove her way over to her.

"You've been eating," she said, eyeing the platter of loaded nachos.

"Doesn't everyone?" Charlotte scooped up guacamole with a chip.

"You weren't when you first got here. Were you taking pills?"

"No. Of course not!" Then, appearing to realize she could have insulted her sister for having had a well-publicized pill problem years earlier, quickly tried to recover. "I'm sorry. I didn't mean—"

"It's okay. It's certainly not any secret. I was worried about you."

"Really? I thought you disliked me."

"I didn't know if you were genuine. I admittedly thought you were just all Southern big blond hair, perfect makeup and manners, and dangerously too damn skinny."

"My husband liked me thin. I was never heavy, but he had very specific ideas about what he wanted in a wife."

"You definitely married a piece of work."

"Tell me about it. I realized that I was getting too thin, but he'd been so controlling about everything else, after a while losing weight by not eating was the one thing in my life I *could* control."

"I get it. But you're okay now?"

"I am." Charlotte nodded. "Funny, as soon as I shed Mason, I got my appetite back."

Tess laughed. "I'm glad. I'm also glad you're my sister."

Charlotte dimpled. "Me, too. Glad I'm your sister and glad that you're mine. And Natalie's, too."

"Together we're a force," they said together. Then laughed again. Together.

Then Tess noticed a teenager standing nearby, looking as if she was trying to get up the nerve to approach. Charlotte, following her gaze, noticed her, too. "I'll see you later," she said and drifted back into the crowd.

"Hi," Tess said to the girl she realized had to be Gideon's daughter. "I'm Tess Swann."

"I know. I recognized you from your book covers. I've read your entire series," she said earnestly. "Every one of the books at least three times. Maybe more. I'm Aubrey Byrne. And don't worry, Dad already warned me not to ask you who Madison ends up with."

"It wouldn't be any fun to read the book if you knew ahead of time," Tess said. "Unless you're one of those people who reads the end of the book first."

The girl's eyes, so like her father's, widened. "Of course not! Why would I want to do that? The entire point of reading is the discovery and trying to guess what's going to happen."

"Oh, I do like you," Tess said warmly. "You're my favorite type of reader. Though many tell me that they like making certain that they'll get a happy ending before they put the time in."

"Well, duh, that's just silly." She shook her head, causing silky, shiny brunette hair to swing over her shoulders. "Anyone who reads your books knows that they're going to get a happy ending." She furrowed her brow. "I just don't know whether Ethan or Brock will be right for Madison in the end."

"Well, you'll be finding out soon."

"That's what Dad said. I'm sorry about your father. I liked Jack. He was always nice to me."

"I've been hearing that a lot lately. Your father told me about your mom," Tess said. "I'm so sorry."

"She died of cancer."

"So he said."

"I'm going to cure ovarian cancer." She raised her chin as if expecting Tess to scoff at the idea of a teenager taking on such a herculean task that had escaped so many older and more educated people.

"That's a very admirable goal."

"I started studying the disease when I was eight and intend to be the person who cracks the code."

"I was posing for sugary cereal boxes when I was eight. You're making me feel like a super underachiever."

"I didn't mean that!" Aubrey looked horrified.

"I was kidding. I think that's very impressive. Your dad must be proud of you."

"Yeah. He is. Though I think I've been driving him crazy."

"Isn't that what teenagers are supposed to do?"

"I guess. But Jack dying, just like my mom, then Madeleine having that heart thing, even though she is really old, made me realize that you never know what's going to happen."

"You're very wise," Tess said.

"I'm writing a paper on ovarian cancer for school. About possible environmental links."

"Oh, that's an interesting idea." Tess put her hand on Aubrey's back. "Let's go talk somewhere more quiet," she said, leading her away from the crowd. "I think I may be able to help you with that."

Gideon wasn't big on parties. He was standing at the edge of the deck, watching everyone else having a good time, wishing he could just be alone with Tess, like they had been in the cave, when Aubrey appeared in front of him.

"I met Tess," she announced.

"Did you?"

"Yes, and before you say I should call her Ms. Swann, she told me to call her Tess, and I told her about how I'm going to cure cancer. So other kids won't lose their moms. And guess what?"

"What?"

"She told me that was *a very admirable goal*, instead of acting like I was just a kid with big ideas I'd never pull off. I told her about the paper I'm writing for biology class. About how environmental causes may be a link to cancer, and she said her agent doesn't just handle fiction. Which was embarrassing at first because I thought maybe she thought I'd want her to help me write the paper. Which wasn't at all why I brought it up, Dad. Really."

"I believe that. And I'm sure she did, too."

"Good. Because it's true. But here's the thing. She—the agent, not Tess—has Dr. Martin Jacobson for a client."

"Okay."

"Dad! He literally wrote the book that gave me the idea for my paper in the first place. I've cited him in a bunch of footnotes."

"That's quite a coincidence."

"Right? And listen to this! It gets better. Tess said that she'd have to talk with her agent, but she's sure that he'd be willing to let me interview him and answer any questions I have. For my paper."

"That would be pretty dope."

"Dad." She rolled her expressive eyes. "I know you're trying to be cool and connect with my generation, but that sounds really lame when you say it. But thank you for trying."

"You're welcome. I think."

"You need to ask her out."

"Ask Tess out? Like on a date?" One of his concerns about

getting in any deeper with Jack's eldest daughter had been how Aubrey would take it.

"No, like to show her the auto wrecking yard outside of town, in case she ever wants to set a book there and kill someone in one of those crushing machines because she said she'd been thinking of writing suspense... Yes, a *date*, Dad. Soon. Because she said she's probably only staying until the harvest."

"That's the same thing she told me. And I got the impression she meant it."

"That's why you need to take her out. Nowhere too fancy, because that might seem too big a deal and you could scare her away. But not a place with paper plates and ketchup bottles on the table, either. You need to go somewhere middle-nice, you know, be casual about it. Then you can talk her into staying."

"According to the will, she has to stay the season."

"But you need to stake your claim right away. Before anyone else does."

"I thought you were a feminist."

She put her hands on hips that had him realizing she was growing up on him. So fast, he thought. "I am."

"Then you should know that guys don't stake claims on women anymore."

"Not literally. Like you want to own her or anything. But you can claim her heart. Like John has mine." She crossed her hands over that heart.

Gideon was grateful for the change in topic, even though it wasn't his favorite one, either. It had been one thing when they'd been young and had been deep in puppy love. But now the kid was sixteen. With a car.

"You're both still young."

"Duh. I know that. But I know my heart. I also know my mind. I'm not going to mess up and get pregnant, Dad. I'm going to find a cure for cancer and John's going to be an astronaut, and maybe someday I'll be a doctor doing experiments in space and we might even end up on the space station together.

"But being a medical scientist doesn't mean that I have to go all my life without someone. Someday I want to be married. And have a family. Like you had with Mom."

"Then that's what I want for you." Much, much later.

"So see? I've got my life all planned out. You don't have to worry about me screwing up and ending up on *Teen Mom*."

"Point taken," he agreed. "But although you didn't come with a manual, I think it's part of my job description as a dad to worry about my daughter. And, so as not to insult your gender, I'd be just as concerned if you were my son."

"I know." She went up on her toes and kissed his cheek.

Their conversation ended immediately when she saw the Salazar family come in. Ana, Reynaldo and John, looking all too grown up in a suit and tie. "See you later at home." She put her hand on his arm. "Ask her out, Dad. Now."

With that, she was gone. Gideon watched John's eyes light up as she wove her way through the crowd to him, taking both his hands in hers. He remembered when his heart had shone in his eyes like that for Becky. And felt a tug of something bittersweet stir deep inside him.

Tess was talking to the waiter hired for the occasion and had just accepted a glass of estate-bottled Pinot Noir when she turned and noticed Gideon coming toward her. Then, despite the initial gravity of the reason for this gathering, she smiled. A warm, intimate smile that crinkled the corners of her eyes. And it was at that moment Gideon realized he wanted her. Not just for a hot date night. Or a season. But forever.

Donovan was watching seemingly every man in the room watching Natalie and knew exactly what they were thinking. And worse yet, feeling. Comfortable in this now-familiar setting, she'd let her inner extrovert out, and the energy radiating from her drew you into her orbit. That long-ago summer that they'd first met, he'd thought she was a cute kid, but was careful not to encourage her crush. Then every year when she'd show up in Oregon, *she'd* have gotten older, until that one unforgettable summer when he'd realized that while he hadn't been paying attention, he'd fallen. Hard.

But what to do? Because each year, while she was always fun to be with, she'd never given him a sign that she wanted to be anything but friends and the thing was, that as much as he wanted to drag her off to the nearest bed, her friendship was important to him. And if he hit on her, only to discover that her youthful crush was long past, she might always feel uncomfortable around him. So he'd spent these past years following her lead and kept it to that. Even as much as it hurt.

He watched her walking toward him, slender hips swaying, a teasing smile on her face. That stunning, beautiful face. But he knew that the woman inside was equally beautiful. Which was why, sometime over the years, he'd fallen from like to lust into love.

"What are you being so Mister Frowny Face about?" she asked.

"I wasn't frowning."

"Yes, you were. Which is impolite after everyone has gone to so much trouble to make this a nice remembrance." Her expression turned serious. "Come inside with me. There's something I need to tell you and I don't want to share it with an audience."

"Okay." He prepared himself for complaints of some sister drama, although they'd seemed to be getting along far better than he'd expected, but nevertheless followed her into the house. As good as her hips had looked coming toward him, they looked even better walking away.

As soon as they were alone, she grabbed his tie.

"What are you doing?"

"Isn't it obvious?" She started walking toward the stairs. With her literally leading him by his tie, he had no choice but to follow. "I'm taking you to court, Counselor." They began to climb the stairs to the bedrooms. She paused for a moment, and instead of the Gallic cheek kisses he'd grown used to, or that quick, maybe not-so-accidental one in the airport, she kissed him quick, hard and deep, in a way that left his head spinning. "Where you can properly make your case."

Which, he did.

Twice.

And not once did she object.

"So," he said, much, much later, as they lay in the tangled sheets, her head on his shoulder, long, slender leg over his, their hastily strewn clothes all over the floor, "what's the verdict?"

"Well, there's not any doubt that you won your case." She laughed and rolled over on top of him. "And to tell the truth, the whole truth, and nothing but the truth, I'd say we both finally did."

40

"What took you so long?" Tess teased when Gideon suggested going out for dinner. "When?"

"Since Madeleine promised to continue the war part of her story tomorrow night, how about Monday?"

"How about tonight?"

"Tonight?"

"I told you that patience isn't my strong suit. Besides, I keep getting stopped by people who want to share stories about my father, which is fine, because that's what the evening's about. But it's kept me from having any more than a bite of smoked salmon mousse on a toast round. Which, while very tasty, isn't very filling, and I worked through lunch, so I'm starving.

"Meanwhile, I've already turned down invitations from three seemingly very nice men tonight. One was even a doctor. I've been told by single friends that doctors and lawyers are considered to be real catches. And Natalie has already claimed dibs on the town lawyer."

"Aubrey warned me about that," he said.

"About Natalie?"

"No. That there'd be guys standing in line to claim you."

She raised an auburn brow. "Claim?"

"We agreed that she hadn't meant it as in, you know, a guy taking over your life or anything. Just claiming your heart."

"Ah." She lifted the glass to her lips, took a sip, then eyed him over the rim. "The romance of youth. Madeleine and I were talking about that the other evening. That neither of us had ever experienced that heady, first young love. She believed that in her case, it was because Robert was her destiny. And that it just took a little longer for their stars to align. But to answer your question, I'd love to go out with you. And I'm especially happy that your daughter approves. I wouldn't want to cause any problems."

"At this point, you could do no wrong. Do you like Italian?"

"Is the Pope Catholic?"

"There's a place in town, Bella Italia—"

"Oh, we passed it today while we were downtown. It wasn't open for lunch, but the menu in the window looked delicious."

"Not wanting to be responsible for you fainting from hunger, we should leave. Now."

"Ooh. I like that commanding tone. Here's a little bit of advice for you, Gideon. Even a feminist, especially a hungry one, can appreciate a take-charge man from time to time." She patted his cheek. "Let me just tell the others I'm leaving, while you tell Aubrey, and I'll meet you at the front door in five minutes."

"I *knew* it!" Charlotte crowed when Tess told her she and Gideon were leaving. "The first time I saw you two in the vineyard, after you'd shared that world's best pancake, I thought I saw some chemistry."

"What you saw was two people talking about dirt."

"Maybe that's what you were saying, but I could sense an

energy between the two of you. And don't think we haven't noticed him holding your hand at the fireside stories. So you're a couple?"

"I don't know. I guess for now. It's all happening so fast." She glanced around the room. "Where's Natalie?"

"Upstairs." Charlotte paused a beat to allow the suspense to draw out. "With Donovan."

"She went for it?" Tess gasped. "Right here during the reception?"

"She literally dragged him away by his conservative rep tie. He looked a little stunned. But I didn't see him complaining."

Tess laughed. Then something occurred to her. "I don't want to leave you alone."

"Don't be foolish. Go." She waved Tess away. "It's amazing that Gideon has stayed single this long. And don't worry about me. I have a blog to write and a new life to plan."

"Are you sure?"

"Positive. Have a wonderful time. Do you have protection?"

"Yes." Given her parents' drunken marriage experience, Tess always kept some condoms in her purse. Just in case. "I think they're still good. How long do they last?"

"Years," a woman standing next to them volunteered. "Three to five on average, so unless you've been through a really long dry spell, you should be fine."

"Uh. Thanks. And, I'm sorry. I don't think we've met."

"Kendra Mackenzie. And you're Tess, Jack's famous first-born. I was Aubrey's fifth-grade teacher. Good luck. Many other women in this town have tried to snare that man. And failed. So go for it and score a win for all of us who'll be rooting for you from the sidelines."

With that, she excused herself, making a beeline over to a woman who was talking to the bartender hired for the evening. When her friend's blond head immediately spun toward them, Tess knew that she'd landed back in the spotlight.

"Small towns," Charlotte said, laughing.

"It's not that funny."

"Yes, it is. Admit it. If you end up sending those fictional high school kids to college, you can use it in a book."

Tess had shared her writing dilemma over lunch at Cork. "I'm not sending them to college. But," she admitted, "if it had happened to anyone else but me, like you, for instance, I'd be laughing, too."

"I've given up men," Charlotte said. "I've decided they're not worth the trouble."

"Yeah, I could see you thinking exactly that while you were drooling over Joel Williams setting up that awning."

Charlotte shrugged. "What can I say? There's just something hot about a guy in a tool belt."

"Especially when it's a guy who already looks like sex on a stick without it." After meeting the son this morning, then Barbara's husband, the developer, tonight, Tess had decided good-looking genes definitely ran in the family.

"That, I cannot deny. But I was just window-shopping because you and Natalie seemed to have nabbed the last two good men on the planet."

"I haven't *nabbed* him."

"Well, what are you waiting for? Go forth and nab before some other woman does."

Unsurprisingly, Madeleine had already heard the news by the time Tess found her. Life might seem slower than in the city, but gossip, it appeared, moved at supersonic speed.

"I heard you and Gideon are going out to dinner! Have a fabulous time. And by the way, Rose just changed the sheets in all the bedrooms today. Including the master in the separate south wing of the house. It hasn't been slept in since I moved into my cozy little home."

"You couldn't have known—"

"Oh, darling, of course I did. I've spent the past decade watching the women of Aberdeen try to catch the newly widowed vintner who'd just hit town. I swear, so many took casseroles and desserts over to his house, Rose had to order an extra freezer. But as soon as I saw the two of you together, I could sense the click. Why did you think I kept dragging out Robert's and my story a bit at a time?"

"Because Rose kept dragging you off to bed?"

"Ha! Didn't we make a good tag team?"

"I'm suddenly understanding how you made such a good spy. You completely fooled me. Is everything you told us true?"

"Of course. As was the stupid anxiety afib. As I said to Rose the other day, I told so many lies in the war, I vowed not to tell any more. And I have been trying to relax more to keep that in check. But I wasn't certain how long it would take for Gideon to make his move. When I heard you girls were finally coming to visit after all these years, I had no idea how much you three were going to enliven things around here."

41

August, 1944

Madeleine's group was shaken when the main escape route through the mountains was closed down due to several *Maquis* forces being exposed by an informant pretending to be a priest. Several members were arrested, along with two hundred American Army Air Corps, French and other Allied airmen who'd been waiting in various safe houses to evacuate Paris for the Pyrenees.

Fortunately, because of all her time in the mountains, she was very familiar with another route, one so infrequently mentioned that the Germans did not yet know of it. Because of the devastating raid, on this trip she'd be escorting ten travelers, a much smaller group than usual, all who had to pretend to be total strangers as they rode the train out into the country. After their time together in the pressing room hideaway, she and Robert could not even look at each other because having fallen in love during that time together the strength of their emotions would have endangered the mission.

When they reached the end of the line, they were taken by

truck to a farmhouse where, while enjoying a meal of warm milk and potato soup, served to them by a kind and friendly woman, a Basque burst through the door. His name was Basajaun and having worked with him before, Madeleine trusted him implicitly and knew they'd be safe, not just because he was the best guide in the mountains, but because surely God wouldn't drop a man out of the sky for her only to let him die. Without a word of greeting, which she'd learned was his way, he told everyone that they would be walking at night and sleeping during the day, then instructed them to get moving, stay in a single line and no talking.

He set a fast and steady pace and although Robert's broken ribs had been taped, making it painful for him to breathe at this altitude, he never once uttered a word of complaint. As morning approached, the Basque led them to an old barn, where they collapsed onto the straw. Lying beside Robert, Madeleine fell like a stone into sleep.

The second night they'd been walking about three hours through the brush, a sliver crescent of moon peeking through the dark clouds moving across the night sky, when suddenly, they heard the sound of dogs barking.

Hissing at everyone to hide in the tall brush, the Basque dove off the roadway. The rest followed, keeping their heads down as a spotlight swept across where they were making themselves as small and quiet as possible. When a deep voice instructed them, in both German and French to come out, they remained as silent as mimes.

Madeleine heard a discussion, but couldn't make out the words. Finally, quieting the barking dogs, the German soldiers turned off the light and returned the way they'd come. After twenty minutes Basajaun decided that it would be safer to abandon the trail and head up the snowy mountainside. It was not easy, the ascent so steep it seemed that for every three steps up, they'd slide down another.

Finally, after two more hours, when Basajaun allowed them to stop for a rest, Robert asked him why he thought the patrol had given up. The Basque shrugged his huge shoulders and responded that the men could have believed that they'd come across a troop of armed resistors hiding in the high brush and had decided that it was better to leave and stay alive.

The trek grew more and more difficult, enough that even Madeleine, who'd spent her life hiking in these mountains, could feel the burn in her legs. Every time someone would ask Basajaun how much farther, he'd simply tell them, "One more mountain."

Finally, as the shimmer of dawn cast a rosy glow on the mountains, he led them to a clearing in the trees and told them that was where they'd be spending the day. But beforehand, he had something for them. He dug into a hole at the roots of the tree, pulled out two cans of evaporated milk, handing one to Madeleine, and another to an RAF pilot, telling them to share with the others.

She took a drink, the sugar content giving her entire body a wakeup call, and from the look Robert gave her after drinking, she could tell it affected him the same way.

"We're going to make this," he assured her.

"Bien sûr." She smiled, and not caring what the others might think, kissed him. It wasn't a proper romantic kiss, like the stolen ones they'd shared before the group's conveyers had arrived at the pressing room hideaway and begun to move him from house to house. But it was a promise. A vow for the future.

They spent four long, dark, cold, snowy nights climbing up and down those mountains she'd once loved. Four days sleeping in each other's arms on hay in a barn, or on the hard ground, waking up with their clothing wringing wet.

At times, while trudging up a mountain, they could see the sparkling lights of Spain in the distance. Other times, in the valleys, the lights would shine a soft glow against the bottoms of the clouds. Together they crossed icy rivers, sometimes with the churning water nearly up to their waists, but as they got closer and closer to their destination, she could hear Robert murmur "Freedom" to himself.

From time to time as they neared the border, spotter planes would fly overhead. Circling, circling, looking for escapees. But they'd dive into the trees, and dressed all in black, were never seen.

Then, just as they were about to cross the last river that created a border between the two countries, a big truck came rumbling up on the Spanish side.

Madeleine felt Robert freeze behind her. Heard curses from the men behind him. "It is all good," Basajaun said in French. Then saluted, turned and walked away, disappearing into the night mist.

"What the hell?" Robert asked.

"It is all good," Madeleine echoed in English, taking Robert's hand as they crossed that last barrier to freedom together.

42

Although the restaurant was charming, Tess and Gideon chose to eat outside. The back patio was lined with trees draped with white lights. Just as the event company Charlotte had hired had used at Maison de Madeleine, outdoor heaters provided warmth.

"I feel as if I'm in Tuscany," Tess said over a plate of fresh ribbon pasta, lemon, thyme and a touch of cream. Gideon had gone with the slow braised wild boar ragù over pappardelle—which turned out to be wide, flat pasta, similar to fettuccine, with ruffled edges—with parmigiano reggiano. "Back when *Double Trouble* was swimming in profits, William talked the network into sending the crime-solving twins to Italy on a school trip."

"When Emma discovered a forged painting in one of the museums."

"Yes. I have to admit that sometimes I could understand why she wasn't the favorite twin." She took a bite of crescentine, an amazing, puffed fried bread. "She was, after all, impossibly and conveniently clever, which could make her rather annoying. Nancy Drew would've probably been jealous."

They shared a laugh.

"Paolo started out with a food truck," Gideon told her, referring to the restaurant's owner, "and that became so popular that when this space opened up, he grabbed it. He grew up on an olive farm outside Florence, where he learned to cook in his grandmother's kitchen. When he decided to bring his talent to America, we were lucky to be the place he chose."

"You *are* lucky." She took a sip of the wine he'd suggested. "This is so good. I never have sparkling wine with dinner. I've been missing out."

"It doesn't work with all meals, but in this case, your dish does because the acidity in the lemon contrasts with the aged cheese and cream. A sparkling wine enhances that acidity due to the bubbles. Paolo offers our wine on the menu because we're friends. But to be honest, his Italian wines are better suited to his dishes."

"So to be a vintner, you also know about food."

"Remember when you said that all you knew about wine was drinking it?"

"Of course."

"Well, I don't know how to cook. I'm lucky that despite Madeleine and Rose trying to convince her that orange mac and cheese is not food, Aubrey still likes the blue box. But learning pairings is an important part of becoming a vintner. Wine can be drunk alone, but it's important to know what food pairs best with it. I spent a couple weeks during my Burgundy internship up in Tuscany, studying their wines, learning how to compare them to the French."

"Which won?"

"Both are made to suit their terroir, their grapes and their food. As a good wine always has."

She twirled some pasta around her fork. "And don't forget the dirt."

"Exactly. Which is part of the terroir."

She realized that if it hadn't been for Jackson Swann, she wouldn't be here, enjoying herself. Sitting under trees strung with lights, sharing a *Lady and the Tramp* romantic pasta dinner with this man.

"I wish I'd known him." Tess hadn't realized she'd said her thoughts out loud until he reached across the table and linked their fingers together.

"I do, too. Of the three of you, you're the most like him."

"Since this is a date, I'm assuming you mean that as a compliment."

"I do. You're independent, tough. Smart. And let's not forget, a survivor. As was he for a very long time. I suspect, when he started out, he thought he could make the world a better place. Then little by little more and more of him died inside. It was only when he was physically dying, that he had time to look back over his life and realize that by trying to help the world, he'd fucked up what was really important. His family."

"Or in his case, families."

Life, Tess decided, was more complicated than it was in TV shows or books. Everyone—even her, she admitted—tended to skim the surface, never really digging deep. She'd thought she'd worked out her feelings toward the man she was coming to accept as her father, but she hadn't come close because she'd only had her imagination to create what kind of man he'd been.

"He wanted his daughters to meet each other. Hopefully, even forge a bond."

"Well, dropping us into this situation didn't really give us any choice," Tess said. "You may be surprised, but I'm glad he gave you control of Maison de Madeleine, whatever happens. None of us knows about making wine. Of all his decisions, that was obviously one of his better ones."

"Thanks. I had no idea he was going to do that."

"That was obvious. I'm surprised he didn't tell you ahead of time."

"I've thought about that and decided that he was afraid I might not agree."

"That's possible, considering some of us might have objected."

"I seem to remember you mentioning something about challenging the clause," Gideon said.

"To avoid having to stay there for so many months."

"And now?"

"I told you, I'm in."

"For the season."

The way he said it, like it wasn't a question, but not exactly putting a full stop on it, more like ellipses, had her thinking that there was more he wasn't saying.

"Maybe longer," she said. "It depends."

"On?"

"You know Madeleine's belief about Robert being her destiny."

"Of course."

She almost wept when he took his hand away and sat back in his chair, looking at her. Not like he had right before kissing her. Well, sort of like that, but sweeter. Gentler.

"I grew up with Becky," he said.

"Okay." She didn't know where he was going with this, but could tell from the gravity of his expression that this might be one of the most important conversations they were ever going to have. Fortunately, they were all alone on the patio. She was vaguely aware of the waiter keeping an eye on them as he passed the glass doors. But he was giving them privacy.

"I honestly couldn't tell you when we fell in love. Our moms were best friends, and we literally spent a lot of time in the same playpen. Somewhere along the way, we became boyfriend and girlfriend and not a single person was surprised. Her parents were both elementary school teachers, which is, of course, an essential profession, but they don't get paid nearly what they're worth. So they hoped Becky would go into something more lucrative. Like finance, or tech. But she stuck to her guns, getting a degree in art history. I told you my dad wanted me to be a surgeon."

"You did. And that it didn't go well."

"Which was putting it mildly. But I transferred from pre-med to UC Davis's viticulture and enology program, then did an internship in France and stayed for another year after graduation, working basically for room and board.

"After coming back to the States, I got a job in Napa, and Becky taught art history at a community college, not making much more than her parents, but we couldn't have been happier."

"That's nice." She thought about Aubrey's comment about happy endings and felt an ache in her heart that theirs hadn't ended that way.

"We couldn't afford the time or money on a big wedding, what with college loans and work pressure, but I'd promised someday I'd take her to France so she could see where I'd worked, and we'd visit all the galleries where she could see the originals of the paintings and statutes she so loved to teach about.

"But we never made it. Never took the time and, cutting a long story short, I lost her two days before our seventh anniversary. Then eventually ended up here. Thanks to your dad, who rescued a guy drowning in a sea of grief who didn't have a clue how to take care of a five-year-old girl who didn't understand why her mommy couldn't just come back home from heaven."

This was not the turn she'd expected the conversation to take. Tess linked her fingers with his.

"I'm so, so sorry. I can't imagine how terrible that must've been."

"It was a tough two years while she was sick. Jack stuck around two weeks after I got up here. He'd already had Barbara's husband build the house in record time, and Rose and Madeleine stepped in as surrogate grandmothers. They're both very wise and were wonderful helping Aubrey through her grief without letting her forget her mother. They're as responsible, maybe more than me, for her being such a great kid.

"Hell." He dragged his hand through his dark hair. "I'm as bad as Madeleine at drawing a story out. Okay." He drew in a deep breath. Blew it out. "I'm a scientist, not a poet. But here's what I'm trying to say. I loved my wife. But although I wasn't anywhere near as bad a husband and father as Jack was, I let my work take precedence over what was really important. There was no reason why I couldn't have taken a couple weeks off to take Becky to France. She never complained, but it always seemed as if tomorrow would be out there. Same as taking Aubrey to the coast, which she complained about again that day you and I met. But you don't need to know that chapter in this story. At least not right now."

"Okay."

"The thing is, when I saw you standing at the end of the vineyard that first day, I felt as if a bolt of lightning had come out of a clear blue sky and hit the ground right at my feet. And when you laughed at my bad joke, ice I didn't even know was left inside my heart all these years began to melt. By the time I kissed you in the cave, I felt that something serious was happening. Then tonight, watching you from across the room, I just knew."

"Knew?"

"That you're my destiny, Tess Swann. Just like Robert was Madeleine's. I don't know why. Hell, Jack thought he was seeing Josette at the end, so maybe he's somewhere pulling the strings, and yeah, I know that sounds crazy. I also realize it's a lot to take in because a week ago you didn't even know you had sisters, or a grandmother, or were going to inherit a winery, and I get why you'd have trust issues, so I'm going to take this thing between us slow—"

"Why?"

"Which of all those things that probably sound crazy are you asking about?"

He was more than a little flustered. Since she'd come to the assumption that he was typically calm and measured, Tess enjoyed knowing she could affect him like this.

"Could we save the slow for later? Because if that waiter doesn't bring the check in the next sixty seconds, I may just jump you right here."

He blew out a relieved breath and waved over the waiter, who was hovering in the doorway, holding the cannoli they'd ordered for dessert in a takeout box. Glancing at her watch, Tess realized that they'd stayed past closing time.

Not only had Bella Italia worked its way to the top of her planned Maison de Madeleine restaurant recommendation list, she was also awarding it five gold stars.

43

The house was quiet, with some soft lights having been left on. After climbing the stairs, they turned in the direction away from the rooms where she'd been staying, where Natalie and Donovan were undoubtedly working off years of frustration, and where Charlotte had decided to reclaim her life.

Inside the double doors to the master bedroom suite, a beautiful tall, high, four-poster bed, covered in a quilted white comforter and a mountain of accent pillows in shades of white, cream and ivory was waiting for them.

"What is it with women and pillows?" he asked.

"They're pretty. And dress a bed."

"They're in the way."

He sent them flying onto the floor with a long sweep of his arm. Then pulled her close, slid his fingers through her hair and kissed her, his lips warm and silky, tasting of the Chianti that he'd drunk with dinner.

Proving that he was a man who could, indeed, multitask, while Gideon's tongue was teasing hers, he threw back the coverlet and unzipped the back of her dress. Then, as he scattered kisses like a string of stars down her neck, he pushed the straps of her dress off her shoulders, causing it to slide down her body and join the pillows on the floor.

Beneath the dress she was wearing some new lingerie she'd bought while shopping in town. The saleswoman had assured her that the lacey black demi bra and matching black panties were a perfect foil for her fair skin and auburn hair and would cause any man to swallow his tongue.

Gideon didn't swallow his tongue. But he did back up enough to allow those dark indigo eyes to sweep a long, hot look over her. "Thank you." His voice had gone all rough and deep again, in that way she knew would still be able to thrill her when she was Madeleine's age.

"I'm glad you like them. Because I bought them especially for you."

"I'm flattered. And since you went to all that trouble, I'm going to restrain myself from ripping them off you."

"Perhaps I ought to take them off, just in case you lose control. They were quite pricey, and as memorable as this night is turning out to be, I'd hate for it to be the one and only time I got to wear them." She reached around, undid the back hook and eye, then, holding the front to her chest, as she imagined Natalie's great-grandmother must have done in the *Folies Bergère*, smiled slowly, letting him wait a moment before she let it drop. Next, she shimmied out of the panties, in her best French showgirl moves, stepping out of them to stand in front of him wearing only a pair of black high heels.

He stood there for what seemed like forever, drinking in the sight of her, causing first her cheeks, then her entire body to flush. Then he put his arms around her and moved her so the backs of her trembling knees were up against the edge of the mattress and finally, his warm, perfect mouth was on hers again she felt herself falling. Falling. Falling…

★ ★ ★

Not wanting to have Aubrey wake up to an empty house, Gideon finally left the bed sometime before dawn, but not before he'd touched, tasted and loved every bit of Tess's body. As she had his. They'd eventually gotten around to eating the dessert the waiter had packed up, and if a bit of the creamy cannoli filling had—oops—fallen onto Tess's breasts, Gideon had been right there to lick it off.

"I hate to go," he said, bending to give her another lingering kiss.

"I hate to have you go." She sighed. "But the reason you are, is only one of the reasons I love you."

It didn't make any sense. Liking her single life just fine, Tess hadn't even been looking for a man. She'd come here to Aberdeen's wine country to find a story. And had, amazingly, found both.

She listened to his footfalls fade down the stairs as she leaned back on the pillows and stretched like a cat, feeling a lovely, not unpleasant ache all over her well-loved body. Then she looked up at the ceiling that had been painted French blue and finally said the words she'd never had a reason to say during Jackson Swann's life. "Thank you, Dad."

44

The next night they were back around the fire, in their usual places. With Gideon sitting next to Tess, his arm openly around her shoulder, Rowdy sprawled in front of the fire over his feet. One difference was that Aubrey, who'd listened to Tess's recordings, had joined them for the final chapter of the adventures that had brought Robert and Madeleine together.

She'd told how his plane had been hit by flack and crashed, how he'd landed on her after cutting his chute and how she and her papa had hidden him from the Germans.

"Robert was moved around a twenty-kilometer area three times over two weeks. There was a lot of pressure on the Germans to find the missing American pilot because he wasn't just an Allied pilot, but an American spy, so I didn't dare visit him. We had to move him out of the country.

Although it had taken some haggling, the *Maquis* had been able to convince the British and American embassies that it was worth paying the Basques who led the groups through the mountains well, because they were the best chance of getting Allied pilots back into the air rather than wasting away and dying in POW camps.

There was also money needed for bribing Spanish police once the men got across the border. The Spanish people loved Americans and were willing to house them during transfers. The police didn't care, as long as they got their bribes. But the Spanish army, while technically neutral, didn't like Americans and preferred the Germans who'd supplied them with tanks, air cover and other equipment during their own civil war. The Germans weren't fond of the Spanish or Franco, but that civil war had given them an opportunity to test their new weapons before they put their plan in place to take over the world.

Everyone listened, spellbound, as she told the story of the treacherous escape and how confident she'd been that she and Robert would spend the rest of their lives together.

"After safely crossing the border, we were driven to a farmhouse not far away, where we were able to bathe, change clothes and were fed a Spanish *albondigas* soup made with beef and rice meatballs simmered in a tomato broth with potatoes, carrots and zucchini, which everyone agreed was the best meal we'd ever had. Every year after we were married, I'd make it for our anniversary dinner. That night, with the stars shining in the window, in a high wooden bed with clean sheets, Robert and I made love and swore that once the war was over, and we settled down on his family vineyard here in Oregon, we'd never, ever be apart again. Although the American embassy sent him first to Gibraltar, and then back to Great Britain, once the war was over, we never were. Until ten years ago."

There was a catch in her voice, her eyes misted. "But every night, when I say my prayers, I thank God for sending me my dear Robert, and I know that someday we will be together again. This time for all eternity."

Epilogue

Eighteen months later

"How are you feeling?" Charlotte asked.

"A lot like an elephant." Tess ran her hands over the baby bump prominently displayed by the purple dress beneath a red tuxedo jacket. Despite her complaint, she loved stroking her belly, feeling what the sonogram had shown to be a daughter, respond to her touch.

"You look beautiful," Madeleine said, sipping on a glass of the Maison de Madeleine Pinot Noir that she swore was going to keep her living long enough to help send her soon-to-be-born namesake off to kindergarten. Given that she was ninety-seven and still going strong, no one had reason to doubt her.

"It helps when you've got a Parisian fashionista shopping for you," she said. Between Natalie and her mother, who was loving spending her Greek billionaire husband's money on maternity clothes and infant outfits for her upcoming grand-daughter, Tess was going to have to have Barbara's son, Joel—now Charlotte's fiancé—expand her and the baby's closets. The two of them had fallen in love while Charlotte had been working with him on those starter homes he and his father were developing. Tess had never seen her happier than she was using her talents to make life better for people, and couldn't imagine how she must have felt during the years when that joy had been taken away from her by that horrid ex-husband.

Last year's harvest celebration had been a community-wide celebration of her father's life. Other winemakers, not just from Dundee Hills, but the rest of the Valley, had shown up, as had winemakers from the southeastern part of the state, and even Washington. Restaurants had supplied the food and the official Jackson Swann send-off party had extended long into the night.

The next evening, as sunset approached, Madeleine, Tess and her sisters, Gideon and Aubrey had rented a boat at the harbor at Shelter Bay and driven a mile out onto the water. Then Gideon had turned off the engine and lowered an environmentally friendly paper urn shaped like a peace lily— chosen by unanimous agreement because peace was what Jack had risked his life for all those years—into the water. The instructions had said that they could expect the urn to last between thirty seconds to three minutes. For some reason it had taken much longer, which gave everyone time to think about the complex man who'd brought them all together. It had still been floating on the surface when the lowering sun went down, turning both sky and water a brilliant gold.

"Well," Gideon had said as they watched the sun-gilded white lily finally sink beneath the water. "Jack always had a knack for choosing the perfect moment." Which had made them all laugh and eased still-aching hearts.

What a lot had happened since Donovan Brees had first shown up at Tess's door in Sedona and literally changed her life. Her recent book, inspired by her grandmother's adventures as a French Resistance member, had sold to a major studio before the book had even hit the bookstores, creating a buzz. And she was working on a new book about sisters, which she definitely knew something about.

Which was all good news, but after coming here to Maison de Madeleine, becoming part of a now-growing family, she'd come to realize what her father had discovered too late. That there were more important things than work, and maintaining a balance was what made life worth living.

"As much as I'm looking forward to being a mother—which, to be honest, I never thought I'd hear myself saying—there were some times during those first morning sickness months when I wondered what in the world I was thinking, getting pregnant at thirty-five." Gideon had been wonderful, bringing her tea and dry toast so she could have something in her stomach before getting up, and rubbing her back when it was aching.

"My mother had me when she was thirty-seven," Natalie, who'd returned from her Hawaiian honeymoon with Aberdeen's hottest lawyer just last week, offered.

"Just think," Charlotte said, "in the next week or so, you're going to be a mom. And Natalie and I are going to be aunts."

"And I'm going to be a big sister," Aubrey said.

She was holding hands with John, who'd gotten a basketball scholarship to Oregon State, which made everyone happy since he'd only be about fifty miles away. Far enough to enjoy his independence, but close enough to come home and visit family. And the teenage girl who'd stolen his heart had already enrolled in an OSU accelerated program that would allow her to earn credits for college courses while still in high school.

Tess glanced up as she felt Gideon watching them. Waited and watched as he walked toward her, with that smile that would always make her feel as if she were about to melt into

a puddle of lust, which she wasn't certain was even appropri-
ate in her ninth month of pregnancy, but didn't care.

A hush gradually came over the tasting room that Joel had
built to be expanded to the outdoors with glass walls that
folded out.

Gideon turned to face the group. "Eighteen months ago
we gathered to celebrate the life of a colorful, talented man
who'd added so much to our community with his commitment to this land we've all been blessed with. Tonight I'd like
to announce a new estate-bottled wine, made from grapes
from three different fields, which will be labeled as *Maison de
Madeleine Three Sisters Pinot Gris*. And, of course, you've come
to know the three sisters who are owners of the winery." He
waved them forward. As she stood there among friends, in
this beautiful place, holding hands with Charlotte, who was
in turn, holding hands with Natalie, while her grandmother
smiled up at them from her chair at the center table, and her
baby kicked hard against her free hand, as if eager to join the
party, Tess didn't think life could get any better.

Until Gideon bent down, placed his large, but oh so gentle
hand on her stomach, connecting with his daughter as he so
often did, then kissed Tess, proving her wrong.

★ ★ ★ ★ ★

Acknowledgments

The saying about it taking a village to publish a book has never been more true than during the writing of this one and I'll always be thankful to a number of people during a difficult time: Dianne Moggy, who first reached out to invite me home to HQN, and encouraged me to write this story; Craig Swinwood, who (at least that I know of), never asked if this book was ever going to be finished; my remarkably patient editor Susan Swinwood, who remained excited about the story, never asked me when it would be finished, and whose insightful suggestions made it so much stronger.

Denise Marcil and Anne Marie O'Farrell—the wisest, most supportive agents in the business—remained steadfastly in my corner rooting for me, both professionally and personally, and never told me when they were being asked those above questions.

A huge thank-you to Quinn Banting and her fabulous art team for such a stunningly beautiful cover that captures the essence of the story I've lived with for the past two years, even when I couldn't be writing. Thanks also to friends and first readers, Amy Knupp of Blue Otter Editing and Donna Cromeans, for jumping in to proofread the manuscript on short notice, and HQN copyeditor Kathleen Mancini, who provided the final polish.

I'll always be profoundly grateful for the exceptional care I received from the nurses at Providence Saint Peter's Hospital, who lifted my spirits while keeping me alive so I could finish *The Inheritance*. The world has come to realize what I already knew: you're all superheroes.

Huge thanks to all my fellow writers and readers who reached out with encouragement, positive vibes, and kept me in their prayers. There were so many times when your emails and social media posts kept me feeling not so alone. And special smooches to all the readers who've allowed me to live my dream all these years. In the end, it's all about you.

Finally, last, but definitely not least, much love to my husband, Jay, who brought skinny mocha lattes to the hospital every day for months, and who, once I was finally home, got up in the middle of the night for an additional fourteen weeks to administer IV medications. I knew, that long-ago summer day we met when I'd just turned fifteen, that you were The One. You still are and always will be.